Greed Kills

Sunny Collins

For Casey Erin Groves

And

In Memory of
John Roger Collins

Book design by Todd E. Groves
Back Cover Photograph by Frank A. Simonetti

chapter 1

THEY FOUND SONNY Bob Bonnaire somehow and made their move. He knew it was inevitable. It could have happened in New York, even Nashville or Mobile. If he had made the sentimental journey his heart yearned for, it could have happened in Rome. He'd stepped outside of the large Victorian- style house for a quick smoke, and it was happening here, on this elegant street in New Orleans and now, a little past one in the morning.

He lit up, then looked up. He saw that the street lamp usually shining bright at this hour was out, the only illumination provided by lights from the upstairs windows of the home. Otherwise, the entire area was black as coal. And soundless. It was then that panic set in, even as he continued to smoke and did not move, did not try to run or calmly go back inside. He could not panic forever, the fear had to end some time and the time was *now*.

Sonny reviewed mental images of his last tour—standing outside in the Tennessee sunshine and watching the stage preparations, the stadium crowd at night. They were a blur, but he already knew the most relevant fact about them—they were far fewer in number than the tour two years ago. Being a country western star turned out to be a far more fleeting proposition than he'd anticipated. He took a long drag on his cigarette, shook off the reverie, and looked up at the low-limbed, moss-hung oak tree in front of him. Between its higher branches, a few July stars shone yellow. To his left, the long wrought-iron fence fronting the house was overgrown with lavender wisteria. He silently cursed the suffocating humidity but the weather was not the source of his discomfort. He knew the signs. The shortness of breath, the trembling, as if he were going crazy or having a heart attack and, worse, the sense of dying. He'd felt this way many times, but under more benign circumstances. The signs could differ—a burning sensation in his neck, a feeling of choking or cold flashes. A shrink once told him it was anticipatory anxiety and what he anticipated at this moment was the ultimate: *death*.

The hum of a car penetrated the soft, damp night air, then the sound of heavy footsteps behind him. He was immediately in what martial arts experts call "condition black"—fight or flight. There was no time to do either. There were others who felt the time was *now* also.

Within seconds, he felt the heavy metal business end of a Colt 1911 against his chest. It was Alex's gun, or one like it. Gun shops wouldn't mention it was ideal for concealed carry, but this gun was not obtained via the normal route in any event. It was used widely in World Wars I and II, in the Korean and Vietnam wars. Alex had recited this history once, as if it gave his own use of the weapon a gravitas that somehow rendered justification for his acts.

Sonny knew the slide stop pin of the 1911 could be depressed with firing if the index finger is placed along the side of the pistol to assist in aiming it. He prayed that was not to be the next move of the large man holding it, as the stiffness of his cheap raincoat rubbed against Sonny's bare arm. Ludicrous, wearing a raincoat in this heat but that's how these people were.

Then the old woman suddenly appeared at the open door and began screaming. Her sickeningly sweet perfume commingled with the stench of sweat and bad breath of his assailants. The oppressive humidity of the night air made it even harder for him to breathe, he felt nauseous.

Escape was impossible. He was unarmed, there were two of them. He looked into their mean, dull eyes.

A Mercedes-Benz, circa 2007, was idling at the curb. He was pushed inside. He knew what the route would be: I-10 to I-65 to I-85 to I-95. They would pass through Mississippi, Alabama, Georgia, the Carolinas, Virginia, Washington, D.C. and beyond. He knew the final destination.

Once there, it would take a miracle to obtain his freedom. It would take resolve, money and time but he didn't know where he'd find any of those things. He'd lost his resolve two years ago, his money six months ago and now the last necessity—time— was running out.

chapter 2

HE LOOKED THE way he always did. And moved, and walked the same. The lazy, insolent swagger, the almost spastic arm movements. And the eyes. The eyes were a contradiction to the rest of the image. A cold, icy pale green, they belied an intensity, an almost controlling fierceness. In other words, they could look menacing. Also seductive.

I'd taken the red eye to New Orleans, and I was dead tired. Tired enough to sit still for a silly, sentimental video my grandmother's current gentleman friend had taken days ago of my ex-husband, Sonny Bob Bonnaire.

The three of us sat quietly watching the film of Sonny strolling around my grandmother's garden in the golden daylight, pretending to study the roses and azaleas, standing still for several beats, then sitting on a white wrought-iron bench and offering a slight giggle and a grin. The usual self-conscious behavior we all adopt for home movies.

"I smell death."

Gram was not usually given to melodramatic statements, but today—this entire past week—had been an exception for her in many ways.

"Why'd you let him stay here, Gram?"

"Sugar, he was wanting to see you. And he looked exhausted and sad, but he also seemed sincere. He said just the nicest things about you and I said to myself, that boy loves my girl, he loves her still. Lord knows, lately you don't seem to be taking up with any distinguished men that I've heard tell about and . . ."

"Gram." I spoke sternly in a tone meant to change the subject.

"Oh well, forgive me for rambling on, darlin'. . . Roland, turn off that projector, dear. I think Frédérique's seen quite enough."

Roland Figgins, a tall, lanky eighty-three year old retired banker, obeyed.

"I think I'll mosey on now, Hermione. You and this lovely young lady have some catching up to do."

"Quite so, Roland. You've been just so sweet to…"

I heard her voice trail off as she walked her elderly beau to the door.

Slouching into the comfort of the large velvet couch, I nursed my glass of sherry. Paris, France had been my birth-place but I'd lived in New Orleans during a period of my childhood, and I'd grown up very near this stately home in the Garden District.

Nightfall arrived hours ago but we were still up, my grandmother and I. I loved this old house but being here this particular day at this particular time no longer felt like home. I don't know what it felt like…prison?…a command performance?…pending doom? All of the above.

I gazed around the large, musty living room and indulged in a bit of nostalgia. I'd already achieved a very successful modeling career in New York when I married Sonny Bob Bonnaire, a lusting-for-life country-western singer. We'd honeymooned for over six weeks in Italy, but four short years later, I divorced my crazy country-western singer. I'd retained two good friends from that period—Jeannette Sullivan, a plus-size model, and Buck Lemoyne, once a cop, now a private investigator. I'd completely lost touch in the last two years with Sonny.

The sound of the front door closing interrupted my reminiscing, and seconds later the heavy, sweet scent of Gram's powder again filled the room.

"I think something's happened to that boy." My little grandmother's voice sounded like a low growl. "I smell death."

I got that the first time around, but if you're eighty-two you're allowed to repeat yourself.

"Why do you think he came to visit you? Did he ever really say?"

I received no answer, just several beats of silence and then a question. "Can I get you some more sherry, honey?"

"I'm good, Gram."

I sat up straight and placed my glass on the small antique coffee table. The time for entertaining and reminiscing was over.

"Why do you think Sonny Bob's dead, Gram? He came, he stayed here with you for three days, fed you a lot of bull… baloney…about his undying love for me and then left. How does this suggest he's dead?"

"Well, I just have this feeling. You know the kind you get when…"

"Sonny Bob gambled away a lot of money. Often *my* money. He was an indifferent husband, thoughtless, downright self centered … he wanted to live so . . . so high on the hog, as you would say . . . he craved excitement way too much and . . ."bondedShe shook her head as she spoke, "Now who's rambling?"

Hermione Toussaint then smiled sweetly at me and crossed the room to get the bottle of sherry. She re-filled my glass, placed the bottle on the coffee table and sat down primly on a straight-back chair facing me.

"I want to tell you about my visit with Robert Arthur— let's call him by his given name, dear—but I don't want anything I say to taint your opinion of him."

I closed my eyes, took a gulp of sherry, opened my eyes.

"Gram, I've just recited a laundry list of that man's faults. Could my opinion get more tainted?"

"Oh pish tosh, he broke your heart. I understand that. We're always hard on our men folk when they do that. Why, once your grandfather...." She frowned. "No, I'm not going to ramble so don't give me that look. I'll get to the point. I just want you to be in a receptive mood."

"I have what feels like jet leg, I'm exhausted from visiting with a stranger for the past hour...not that Roland isn't charming...and I'm slowly getting inebriated on sherry so I'd say my defenses are down and I'm ultra receptive."

"Oh dear, I've made you angry, haven't I?"

I reached over and took her fragile, veined hand in mine.

"Oh, Gram, you could never make me angry. I adore you and always have, you know that. I'm sorry to be grouchy, but you called me out of the blue and said that Sonny Bob's life was in danger. You can't blame me if I'm anxious to..."

"I just thought you'd want to know . . ." she began.

"I do. In our marriage, Sonny wasn't perfect but neither was I. I was too absorbed in my own career at the time...I couldn't always go with him on tour...and . . . I do still have feelings for him. The truth is I'll always love him. To this day, I think about him . . . oh, so many times. He had a core of goodness in him that I'll always cherish . . . I know, I know," I smiled. "I'm rambling. To get to the point, I just want to know why you're so worried and . . ."

"Not just worried, honey. Downright scared." She turned away and looked toward a nearby window even though it was pitch black outside and no view was possible.

My grandmother, my father's mother, had helped raise me and my brother during our early years here in New Orleans until my parents moved our little family to Manhattan when I was seventeen. She was so very dear to me but right now aggravation trumped devotion. I'd been here only a matter of hours and already I missed Pierre, my red haired Persian cat, and even the irascible Joseph Buckley Lemoyne. He'd be calling my cell phone any minute and, when he did, I needed some plausible explanation for my sudden flight to Louisiana. Buck and I had met when he was a moonlighting cop and provided security at some of my fashion shows. Now he was a private eye and divided his time between California and New York, delving into insurance fraud, chasing cheating spouses and mostly providing security for movie stars and Broadway types.

Seconds ago, Gram seemed inclined to pout, but my own silence provoked her curiosity. She looked back at me and did the head cocking, sad-eyed number again.

"What are you thinking about, sugar?"

"Buck, at the moment. He'll probably call… he just may fly out here."

"Well, you told me your private eye friend was born and bred here. Maybe he misses it. Maybe it would be a good thing if he *did* come."

Now Gram surprised *me*. She'd long been dubious about Buck, declaring he wasn't "proper company" for me. Now she was eager for his arrival? Between this new liaison with Monsieur Roland and welcoming Sonny Bob as a houseguest, she seemed to be branching out into new worlds.

"You know, Gram, I told you Buck may entertain romantic ideas about me but I also told you that…"

"Oh, don't get your knickers in a knot, sweet girl, I'm not sitting here cogitating about match making. I just thought this Buck person could be of some help for poor Robert Arthur…oh, all right, Sonny Bob."

"Why, Gram, *why*?"

I pumped the air with my outstretched palms, nearly upsetting my sherry glass.

It was Gram's turn to look startled. The poor lady was probably bone tired herself at this hour of the night and here I was being a rude, impatient ninny.

I sat back, took a couple of sips of the sherry and waited.

She looked into my eyes with a confused expression. Perhaps she didn't know where to begin.

"What was the last thing Sonny Bob said when he left, Gram?"

My grandmother picked up my glass and drank the rest of my sherry.

"He said, 'Help me, Mrs. Touissant, get help.'"

"Did he say what kind of help? Was he sick? Was he out of work? Was he…"

"I think it was those two awful men who took him away at gun point."

Well now, that just might explain the smelling death part.

Needless to say, I was shocked big time. Gram calmly described the men as crude and "like absolute thugs," adding expletives they used and their general demeanor. As she warmed to her subject and elaborated further on her uninvited gangster-type guests, I recalled a college acquaintance of mine, Alex DeCicco, who—if rumors over recent years were true—was of a similar ilk as the offensive visitors and who, further, was said to have mob connections.

"I'll find out about them, Gram," is what I then promised her and so I decided to remain in New Orleans until I'd tracked down mysterious friend Alex on the hunch that he might know how to locate my ex-husband.

chapter 3

In a small, airless room behind an aging clapboard restaurant sat two slightly overweight men, sporting five-o'clock shadows beneath heads thick with black hair. The shorter man had chalky white skin, a thin moustache and a nervous tick. The taller man had a thicker moustache, a light tan and looked as if his muscles would burst forth from an ill-fitting beige suit jacket. He poured small amounts of Jack Daniel whiskey into a glass, gulped the contents and poured again. A narrow window, which was never open, provided a view of a clump of bushes and a large, rusted Dumpster. Even through the grimy glass, the hot, moist atmosphere outside appeared almost palpable.

The establishment, called Sylvester's Sports Bar, was situated in Metairie, Louisiana, located on the shore of Lake Pontchartrain between the cities of New Orleans and Kenner. The latter city was mainly distinguished as the site of the New Orleans airport. Sylvester's was surrounded by an acre of gravel where the patrons didn't so much park their cars as abandoned them at all angles.

The shorter man suddenly grabbed the whiskey bottle and took a quick swig, slammed it down on the scarred wooden table and lit a fresh cigarette.

"Damn it, Beppe, get your own booze."

"Effing no, Gio. I'm tryin' to give it up. But yah got it sittin' right here in front of me."

"You shittin' me, right? *You* giving up drinking? That'll be the day."

"My girlfriend says it makes me ugly mean and she can't take it no more."

"Yeah? And what's the missus say?"

"Gloria? My wife knocks 'em back as good as me."

"Fine woman Gloria is. What you getting her for her birthday?"

Ambrogio Lombardino extinguished his cigar in a large red ceramic ashtray as Beppe Vitale ignored the question posed to him.

They were very different men but bound together by virtue of employment. What camaraderie they did possess sprang from the fact that both their families originated in Monte Cassino, a southern Italian town between Rome and Naples, best known by the sixth century Catholic monastery it boasted and the strategic location it represented to the Americans, and especially its allies the Poles, in World War II.

Beppe once more grabbed the bottle of liquor.

"Hey, lay off that. It's almost empty anyways. What's up with you? You're shakin' like a leaf. That'll teach you to give up booze."

"It ain't the booze, it's the girl."

"What girl?"

"The one comin' here today, asshole. I don't like the looks of this."

"The looks of this? *Her* looks? I hear she's a real looker. The babe's a model. From New York, high fashion, the whole nine yards. Long legs, about five feet ten, Alex says."

"Don't be an idiot, yah know what I'm talkin' about. I mean what's she really want? It's too damn fishy."

"She wants what Alex say she wants. The name of the guy in New York who does business with Sonny Bob Bonnaire."

"Jeeze, Sonny Bob's such a loser. What she want with him? You tole me he's her ex-husband? What kind of broad with all that goin' for her goes lookin' for an ex-husband like that has-been?"

"It ain't that long he was a big time country singer with a lotta gigs, tours, the whole bit. Anyways, she wants to help him, that's the story," Gio said, drawing a second cigar from his shirt pocket.

Beppe said, "Great, but what's in it for us?" He went on to mouth a string of expletives in relation to their boss, Alex DeCicco, and the menial jobs he sometimes gave them. Gio puffed on his cigar and largely ignored the commentary.

"Alex talked to her over the phone. He ain't actually seen her in years. Wants to keep it that way. Don't want her to see what he looks like now. He used to know her when they went to some college."

"Alex went to college? You shittin' me?"

"Some place back east. She and him were just friends but he. . ."

"I don't give a damn, Like I said, what's in it for us?"

"You gotta ask? Doing what DeCicco wants is what's in it for us. You know Alex, you handle the small stuff for him right, he gives you the big jobs. There's a deal coming up in Florida and he. . .'

"Cool it," Beppe said, "Somebody's knockin'."

The door creaked open and a tall, slim blonde stepped inside. She wore fitted black jeans, a long, loose gray tank top and silver flats. Over one shoulder she carried a large gray purse with a long dangle of crystals, silver circles and pearls hanging from one end. Her cheeks were flushed, but her expression was unreadable as she slowly took off her sunglasses and looped them over the center of her jersey top. Behind her rose the sound of black men's voices and pool cues hitting balls along with the smell of cigarettes and beer fumes.

"Shut the damn door," Beppe mumbled.

Gio stood up. "He means please close the door, Frédérique. Do I got your name right?"

"Yes, you do," she said, quickly closing the door. "But please call me Freddy."

Gio crossed the room and pulled an extra chair up to the table.

"Have a seat, Freddy. Beppe don't mean no harm, it's just so damn noisy out there. Them niggers talk louder than my wife, and that's loud." He gave her a slight smile.

Frédérique Bonnaire managed a small smile of her own as she sat down and placed her bag on the table.

"Can I get you a drink?" Gio asked.

"No. . . well, a coke would be fine."

"One coke comin' up," Gio said, "And Beppe, bring it in a glass."

"On second thought, do you think they'd have iced tea?" Freddy turned in her chair to face Beppe who was now standing at the door.

"They better have one, right Beppe?" Gio grinned, revealing large yellow teeth.

"Sure." Beppe suppressed the scowl he felt inwardly and matched Gio's cheerful tone, adding a forced smile for good measure.

He quickly returned and placed the drink in front of Freddy. As he did so, she moved the bag and set it on the floor, eyeing the drink as if it were a foreign object.

"Good job, Bep," Gio said. "Ice, lemon, the whole bit. Drink up, Freddy, and relax. You look tense."

"Just tired from travel I guess," Freddy offered. She took a couple of tentative sips of the tea, then two longer swallows. "I appreciate your time, gentlemen," she said, putting the glass down and pulling a spiral notebook from the huge purse. She placed it next to the glass and reached down again, this time producing a black, felt-tip pen. "If you can give me. . ."

"Here's the deal. . .," Gio interrupted. He gave her a name, and she spelled it aloud as she wrote on the pad.

Gio continued, adding the man's first name and the phone number of his home. "But you're better off contacting him at work, yah know what I mean?" he added and supplied a second number. "I don't know New York area codes so who knows where the fu . . . heck . . . it is. Could be Chinatown for all I know. Could be Little Italy. Could be Brooklyn. Yeah, I think that's it, Brooklyn. Alex D. told me, but yah know how fast he talks. Who can follow? Anyways, there's the number. You call, he's gonna be nice to you when you tell him you know Alex DeCicco."

"I really appreciate this," she said, then looked at her notes and repeated everything that she'd written on the small pad.

Freddy advised her burly companions that she owned a house in Brooklyn, a brownstone. She elaborated that she was currently renting it to tenants and added a general description of the surrounding neighborhood. She was babbling but at the same time, she seemed more relaxed than when she first entered the room.

As she talked, Beppe looked her over. She was very tall, like Alex D. had said. Really thin, but not too skinny, with shoulder-length blonde hair that had some kinda streaks in it. Not big in the tits department, but when she'd walked toward the table he'd noticed she had a nice butt; and now he noticed the vivid blue eyes and white, even teeth. She had a slight southern accent that seemed to come and go. Alex had said she had a rich grandmother who lived on St. Charles Avenue in New Orleans and that Freddy had been born in Paris.

"I gotta say, yah don't sound French," Beppe said.

"Hey, the lady's talkin', pal. You got no manners?" Gio scowled at his cohort.

"That's quite all right," Freddy said, "I have to go. I've taken up enough of your time and. . ."

"Yah got a ride home?" Gio asked.

"Yes, thanks. I've got a rental car. I'll be fine."

She picked up her bag from the floor, tucked the note-book and pen inside and rose from her chair.

At the door, she turned and favored the men with a warm smile. "See you guys," she said, closing the door carefully behind her.

"Some chick," Beppe said.

"Nice girl," Gio said.

"So what's DeCicco's interest? He bangin' her?"

"No, you crazy Italian prick, I told you he never even seen her since she got here. Alex's no fool. Her ex, Sonny Bob owes the New York guy money, which is really owing Alex money if you catch my drift."

"So what's the problem here? Alex has the guy put the squeeze on Sonny and he gets the dough, you know what I'm sayin'?"

"The problem here, Beppe, is the New York guy don't have no idea where Sonny Bob is. Alex don't know where Sonny Bob is. He had two jokers—his cousin what's got your name and that fat slob what's-his-name pick Sonny up here. Then Sonny gives 'em the slip. Dumb wops. Now nobody they know got no idea where Sonny Bob is."

"So this girl, Freddy, she's. . ."

"The bait," Gio answered.

chapter 4

IT WAS SURPRISINGLY satisfying to be back in Manhattan. Even though I was on the frustrating and seemingly impossible mission to locate my ex-husband in this city of over eight million souls. After more relentless interrogation from me, my poor Gram was able to recall that the two men who spirited Sonny Bob away had New York accents. She also remembered that, as she watched from her front door, they dragged him into the night toward a waiting car, with its motor running. She heard Sonny say the words "double cross" and one of the thugs respond, "cross country is the only cross you gotta worry about, buddy." This had further buttressed my theory that Sonny was in trouble with a person or persons in New York.

My ex-husband had been away from New Orleans for years, so it made sense that Sonny had acquired these obvious enemies back in New York and that was to be his captors' destination. Thus I'd booked a flight and a room at the ancient St. James Hotel on 45th, near the theater district, on the presumption that I somehow had the ability to find Sonny and execute a rescue. I checked into the hotel and decided some breakfast might alter my current anxiety and enable me to think clearly, so I headed next door to the Dunhill Cafe. The atmosphere and clientele of the Dunhill were quintessential New York: fast-talking counter guys taking orders with great impatience but not without courtesy, customers who ranged from executives in expensive suits to secretaries in dresses and walking sneakers to blue-collar types in flannel and leather and denim. I made swift work of a scrambled egg sandwich and two glasses of iced coffee, returned to my hotel and rode one of the two tiny elevators back to my room. Making some phone calls was next on the agenda.

The first was to reach Buck and get his advice as to precisely what I needed to do *vis-à-vis* my current project. He wasn't home and I felt panicked and impatient so I left a voicemail as to what I had just done: flown from New Orleans to New York City with plans to commence a hunt for my ex. I gave him the name and location of at my current hotel and advised I'd be there until I "decided what my next step would be." *Next step* was an understated phrase which encompassed where I'd live, where I'd look for Sonny Bob, whether what this supposed Mafia contact Alex DeCicco had provided would prove helpful and just exactly how I thought I was qualified to play CIA operative or FBI agent or whatever the heck I thought I was.

My next call was to the family who were renting the brownstone I still owned in Park Slope, Brooklyn. After a couple of rings, a recorded voice advised this was not a working number. Even in my state of anxiety at Gram's, I'd consulted my address book and made sure I had their phone number before rushing to catch a red-eye flight at the airport, so I was certain of its correctness. The phone gods were not cooperating with my goals, but I decided against trying to solve the mystery of why my tenants apparently hadn't paid their phone bill for the moment.

I then called my accountant, Howie Goldstein. Howie was a wonderful guy, recommended to me by my booking agent, and he'd taken marvelous care of my taxes during the years I lived in New York. He'd formerly worked for the IRS and knew which deductions to claim that, as he said, "would not set off bells and whistles." As Sonny Bob was going through my funds with breakneck speed at the time, I adjusted my moral compass to allow any creative tax deductions Howie wished to make. He also handled my real estate matters and the rental and maintenance of my Brownstone.

"Howie, it's Freddy. I'm here in New York. How are you?"

"I'm great, sweetheart. Good to hear your voice. Come on out to Great Neck, the missus will cook dinner. You moving back into Park Slope place?"

"Yes and no, Howie. My living arrangements have been up in the air for some time. I wasn't sure the Bishops had renewed their lease of my brownstone. If they hadn't, I just might bunk there. I called the house and no answer. I guess you're telling me they moved. I assumed you'd tell me if I needed to find new tenants."

"Listen, doll, I was in the hospital for awhile for a knee replacement, then a long recuperation. Got a little backed up. Was just about to email you. Tom Bishop hasn't paid the rent in three months. I drove out there last week and the place was vacated. Outside doesn't look too bad but inside is a disaster. Hate to tell you this way, you now wanting to move back in and all. I'm so sorry about this, Freddy. I'm afraid I let you down."

I opted for a deep sigh as opposed to my first reaction of choice, that of leaping through the telephone lines and strangling one Howard J. Goldstein.

"Define disaster."

"Well, there are some tears in the living room couch and the seats of the dining room chairs. There's some stains on the upstairs walls and some scratches on the dining room table. Most of the patio furniture is pretty banged up. I don't know, maybe they were on drugs."

"Drugs? Howie, they do have five children but neither parent drinks or smokes. Mrs. Bishop once told me she even stays away from coffee. I have a hard time equating their lifestyle with drugs."

"I'm just telling you what I saw, Freddy. I planned to get good prices from local vendors for the cleanup and tell you when the place had been restored, rather than give you something to worry about."

"I'm going over this afternoon to see the place. Then we'll decide what to do. But we *will* have to keep closer tabs on the next tenants, Howie."

"You have my word, honey. My life just got a little hectic there. It won't happen again. But maybe we can sue the Bishops."

"I hate to think of it coming to that. They're friends of Buck's and . . ."

"That police officer pal of yours?"

"Yes, and when I met them, their kids did seem a little wild but otherwise they seemed like a nice couple. I'll call you tomorrow when I've seen the damage for myself."

"Okay, doll, but you know the saying."

"Saying? What saying, Howie?"

"Beware of cops bearing tenants."

chapter 5

It was an unusually pleasant day for late August in New York which often boasted the same summer weather as New Orleans, that of heat and oppressive humidity. There was a slight breeze and I wanted to get some air and just enjoy being outdoors so I got off two subway stops prior to the one nearest my address in order to walk for the exercise and to take in the view.

I crossed the street to Prospect Park. Unlike most areas of Brooklyn, it is rarely overcrowded. Tourists seem to have not yet discovered it even though the Botanic Garden and the Brooklyn Museum are nearby. In the summer, there are some wonderful free concerts in the band shell and on any given day you'll see Frisbee, football and soccer games, even horseback riding on occasion.

It was a weekday so there was little traffic on the sidewalks and I walked the leafy, shaded streets swiftly, reaching my Brownstone in record time. Howie was right, the exterior appeared presentable. The black wrought-iron fence appeared freshly painted. The grass in the tiny front yard looked recently trimmed. I climbed the ten steps to the front door and fished a key from my purse.

Whoa! And double whoa! A horrible, unfamiliar smell hit my nostrils the moment I opened the door. Good grief, what have those Bishop children done? Or maybe their dog? Or dogs plural? I wanted to retreat outside, but curiosity trumped comfort. I pulled some Kleenex tissues from my purse and clasped them over my nose. A layer of dust covered most of the furniture and in a corner I spied some frequent guests of New York homes, cockroaches.

Howie was right about the couch, except that it also boasted stains in addition to fabric tears. The glass coffee table was intact but the dining room table was scarred, as reported, and the poor condition of its chairs exceeded Howie's description. The beautiful drapes I'd had in both rooms had disappeared but, strangely, the black and red Oriental rugs appeared free of damage and the oak flooring was intact. Perhaps the Bishop family pets were a discriminating lot.

I made mental notes about the cost of repairing or replacing, but the truth is I love to redecorate and didn't this state of affairs provide a perfect excuse? This more cheerful thought did not last long, obliterated by the reality of the foul smell of the place. I'd noticed it seemed more pungent in the front hallway when I first entered, so perhaps it emanated from upstairs. I would have preferred to inspect the kitchen first and dreaded the thought of what the putrid aroma ordained the Bishop kids had done to the bedrooms and bathrooms but curiosity prevailed. I'd bypass the garden level for now. I remembered their designated playroom was there so perhaps it was in even worse shape. As I mounted the stairs, the smell grew in intensity. I put one hand on the banister and covered my nose and mouth with the other. Had the Bishops left a dead dog on the premises?

I peered quickly into the two smaller rooms at the top of the stairs and, seeing nothing unusual, headed toward the master bedroom. My God! I took one step backward, and then another. My purse dropped to the floor as I grabbed the doorjamb, feeling suddenly dizzy.

There was a body on the floor!

chapter 6

EVERYTHING HAD GONE purple. That's the last thing I remembered. Now conscious and alert, I looked around me to see a semi-darkened house. It was apparently almost evening and also apparently I had fainted because I was flat on the floor outside the master bedroom and experiencing a dull headache. I rolled over to one side in order to raise myself to a sitting position. At first it felt like way too monumental an effort and I lay back down, curled in a fetal position and bemoaned the fact that I was doing all this resting on a less than clean floor. Despite this condition, I remembered I had a small water bottle in my purse and needing to assuage my thirst was just the motivation necessary to make a second attempt at becoming upright.

Somewhere nearby a neighbor's dog began barking furiously and in my altered state I wondered if his purpose was to summon help for me and my current dilemma. In the movies, doesn't someone always arrive and find a person who's passed out, question them, call the police, summon their relatives? This scenario was definitely not going according to script. I wondered if I'd sustained some kind of injury that was not readily apparent. Should I use my cell phone to call an ambulance? I used the hand that was not pressed against the floor to feel around my body in order to detect any strange bumps or bruises. I felt my head, and it suddenly occurred to me that perhaps I had not fainted but rather someone had hit me over the head. Feeling no bump that wasn't already there, I concluded my mind was drifting off to movie scenarios again, and I should stop with the drama already.

I raised myself up on one elbow and, this time, achieved the sitting up goal. Unzipping my purse and feeling around, I located the water bottle, now warm, and took several swigs until it was drained. With this refreshment accomplished, I focused upon what had occasioned my case of the vapors in the first place. My immediate instinct was to stand up and turn on the wall switch to bring light into the master bedroom, but that meant confirming my worse fears.

I was on a rescue mission. My ex husband, Sonny Bob, had been kidnapped or at least initially spirited away against his will and was in trouble. Usually Sonny Bob *caused* trouble. I could not recall a time in our four years of marriage when he was actually *in* trouble. Even as I boarded the New York-bound plane in New Orleans, I wondered if the scene Gram had observed at her home was some boyish prank initiated by Sonny Bob's cronies. He was, after all, a musician, a country-western singer, and harmless pranks of one kind or another were common on the road and especially in hotel rooms or at the end of tours. Had we been over-reacting I'd asked myself then. I didn't really know the answer and it didn't deter me from flying into JFK, doubts and all.

The first two years of our marriage had been bliss, or nearly so. Sonny's career was going well and so was mine. I'd scored two *Vogue* covers and bookings were always available. I loved what I did: the clothes, the designers, the photographers. I especially loved runway shows: the lights and music and excitement, the camaraderie with the other models, hair and makeup people, the show producers and staff. I'd yet to have an unpleasant experience nor had to deal with difficult, temperamental people. I missed my husband when he was on the road, but my life had been full when I'd met him and remained so. I had my girlfriends and colleagues in the business, and I absolutely adored living in New York City. I could go places alone and entertain myself for hours or days, if need be, by visiting museums, relaxing at home with good books, browsing at Bloomingdales or Saks, eating a take-out lunch in Central Park or just strolling around the city.

Sonny Bob was not so easily amused. When he was in town, he preferred going out to eat almost every night. Since I am a fairly good cook, but am far from being a passionate chef, I usually found this particular extravagance too tempting to resist. He loved Broadway shows as much as I did and only seats in the first two rows were acceptable. We'd go to Greenwich Village on Sunday mornings. He'd find a coffee shop where he would patiently sit and smoke and wait for me until I got out of church. I went to nine o'clock mass at the Church of St. Joseph on Sixth Street, between Waverly and Washington Place. I got Sonny to go with me once when he learned it was the oldest Catholic Church building in Manhattan, but after this one touristy turn attendance lost its appeal.

We'd then hit our favorite place for brunch, enjoy the jazz and afterward head somewhere else to drink Bloody Marys until noon or so. Lunchtime involved another spot that featured jazz—Dixieland if we could find it—and a round of beers or wine. We'd then, thankfully, take a breather from all this pub hopping and walk around until dinner time presented itself as an excuse for a meal and more jazz and later an after-hours club. I followed Sonny's lead with this kind of schedule until I experienced too many days showing up for modeling gigs sporting bags under my eyes together with a feeling of exhaustion.

Sonny felt angry and abandoned if I too often begged off nights on the town. He also resented the fact that I would not always accompany him on trips, feeling my zest for my modeling career often exceeded the desire to be with him on his latest road tour. I have to admit it often did exactly that. I loved him with all my heart, but I felt more comfortable with us occasionally being apart than he did. I considered such absences to be par for the course for two people with vital professions. Sonny felt my independence indicated I was less than a dedicated wife, less than a loyal spouse and, worse, less than a real woman and he let me know this in no uncertain terms. I'd stress out over his accusations, even repair to the bathroom for crying jags, but my grief did not extend to giving in and going on tour with him except on two occasions. I did not have the excuse that doing so would seriously impair my modeling career, I simply did not want to risk it. Our marriage eventually became like the nursery rhyme of the little girl with the curl in the middle of her forehead: when it was good, it was very, very good and when it was bad, it was horrid.

In time Sonny Bob apparently became resigned to my independence and the schedule that I preferred. But only *apparently*. Unbeknownst to me, he began draining our joint money market and mutual fund accounts and gambling to fill his leisure time on the road. When he hit our joint checking account, I began to notice. The time came when I'd find fewer bills in my wallet than I knew had been there the day before, and then I became truly alarmed. When I confronted him on this, he would turn on his considerable charm and take me out to dinner the next night complete with a diamond bracelet or a sapphire ring, which ultimately showed up on our joint credit card. He'd apologize profusely but also extract a promise from me to go on his next tour. I truly wanted to heal my marriage so I would agree but then something would come up and I'd find some reason to renege. Sonny's assertion that my career was all-important was apparently not off base. Part of me regretted it then, and I've regretted it often to this day.

Despite the fact that my girlfriends and even my booker began urging me to leave my husband, I could not find it in my heart to do so. I didn't believe in divorce, and I still loved him. I just wished he'd change. I'm sure he thought exactly the same about me. Ultimately, it was Sonny Bob who insisted we legally end our marriage.

For performers, especially charismatic and hand-some and ostensibly wealthy ones like Sonny, women were always available on the road. I'd heard rumors since we'd begun dating that he succumbed to several of them, but I didn't believe it then and I still don't. It wasn't quite his style. He wanted a true and lasting and exclusive love, he just wanted that and also all the good things in life that wealth could provide. I was not entirely adverse to material advan-tages myself but they meant less to me. What I loved about my modeling career was not simply the money but the whole Big Apple lifestyle, as did Sonny. The conflict was that I preferred a more casual, low-key version, and the mode Sonny favored was not only far from casual but *plus cher*. Neither of us was about to alter our preferences.

All these memories and feelings of remorse and guilt churned in my brain, worsening my headache and delay-ing the inevitable task of standing up and facing the night-marish reality in front of me. For when I first laid eyes on the lifeless body of a man on the floor next to the large four-poster bed, my mind registered a grim recognition. One I dreaded and one I feared to confirm.

I set the empty water bottle down and struggled to my feet, placing my hands on each side of the door and bracing myself for a few seconds before moving forward. I could hear the neighboring dog howling mournfully now, for some strange reason. I hit the wall light switch. I looked, and then turned off the light. I didn't really require the extra illumination to determine what I already knew: *the body was Sonny Bob Bonnaire.*

chapter 7

MY 911 CALL provoked an explosion of activity. On the street were several cop cars, their red and white lights punctuating the darkness. Numerous uniform police milled about. The medical examiner, who turned out to be a dwarf, arrived. A local ABC television van joined the scene and their reporter, an attractive and petite woman with a bouffant confection of pale hair, held a mike and advised New York of the crime of the moment. Radio traffic from the cop cars penetrated the night air along with the sound of murmuring neighbors. And the saddest sight of all—Sonny Bob Bonnaire, once upon a time my husband and the love of my life, being carried out the front door, down the steps, to a waiting ambulance, in a body bag. My memory of that night was that I viewed all of this dispassionately, but a week later one of the detectives told me I was sobbing constantly.

I wanted to accompany Sonny in the ambulance, as if I could somehow provide aid or comfort to him but the police asked that I go with them to the stationhouse to reiterate my discovery of the body and supply information about Sonny Bob and his life. I indulged one bitter moment when I silently considered that I had not known everything about Sonny Bob's life when married to him and thus it was dubious I was exactly well versed on the subject now; but once at the precinct, seated in an interrogation room with a hot cup of coffee in front of me and seemingly kind, sympathetic detectives, one female and one male, I was eager to help.

We'd no sooner begun our interview than the detectives had to excuse themselves, "for a few minutes." I asked them to take their time as I had some calls to make. Nervy of me I know, but inwardly I congratulated myself on my practicality and presence of mind.

I dialed Gram's number. My first thought was that Sonny's funeral must be held in New Orleans where his roots and his family existed. My sweet grandmother answered on the second ring. Some increased mindfulness kicked in and I asked if her beau was there. I could tell Gram loved that term and, almost gleefully, she put Roland on the line. I explained the events and learned Gram had picked a gem in Roland Figgins as he rose to the occasion in spades, declaring he'd give Gram this devastating news in the morning, when she'd had a good night's sleep, and also advising that he would take care of the transportation of the body, notifying Sonny's family and friends, and all the funeral arrangements.

My sense was that I breathed a huge sigh of relief and thanked him profusely. Roland later told me I *did* express sincere appreciation but, again, I learned I'd been sobbing uncontrollably at the time. I then recalled that, in life, Sonny had often complained I did not really care about him. Thus, again somewhat cynically, I mused that I hoped he had looked down and viewed my profound grief.

My next call was to my accountant. Mrs. Howie answered and was none too pleased at the lateness of the hour. Howie, on the other hand, reacted with shock and then, still feeling remorseful over what he deemed as his neglect of my rental situation, eager to do whatever he could and whatever I asked. I told him I'd be flying back to New Orleans for Sonny's funeral and to proceed immediately, or as soon as the police would allow, to restore my Brownstone to a pristine condition. Howie assured me he'd take care of everything and would find new tenants in record time. I thanked him and this time, when we later spoke of the conversation, there was no advice that I'd been crying during the entire communication. *Sorry, Sonny Bob, but grief apparently ebbs and flows.*

I terminated the call to Howie and finally took a sip of my coffee, finding it lukewarm. Next on my call list was Buck, my best friend of several years now. It is always wonderful for a single girl to have at least one good, platonic male buddy, although my second best friend Jeannette insists the vibe she gets between Buck and myself is not exactly brother-sister. Jeannette and I met when we were both New York models. A plus size and a ballsy, fast-talking Bronx native, she was currently babysitting my third best friend in the world, my cat Pierre.

Just as it was when I called Buck upon my arrival in New Orleans, his line was busy and I was faced with leaving another voicemail.

"All right, dude," I fairly yelled. "Are you there or where are you?"

Maybe he reconciled with the nurse he used to date and they were making up in Tahiti or some such nonsense.

"Did you get my message that I'm in New Orleans at Gram's?"

Do you even care?

"Well, now, my friend, I'm in New York!"

I paused for dramatic effect, then more rationale thought prevailed.

"Buck, I don't mean to fuss at you. Just checking in. I'm getting ready to fly back to New Orleans. Something tragic has happened. Sonny Bob has been murdered. Hope all is well there. See you when I get back."

I was about to call Jeannette when the detectives returned. They came bearing three steaming mugs. The smell of fresh coffee mingled with the room's aroma of stale smoke and fresh sweat. I fairly grabbed my cup as the female cop placed it on the table. Somehow she'd divined I preferred a lot of cream, and as I took a first gulp the immediate effect was familiar and soothing.

Hospitality accomplished, they got down to business.

The male detective spoke first. "The official cause of death is several blunt force traumas to the head. Cardio pulmonary failure would have occurred because the knife entered the victim's body and collapsed a lung, but the ME reports the victim was dead before the attack by the spear."

"We're told the spear is some sort of vintage Aboriginal spear," the female advised.

"We assume you had it as a decorative piece in your home," from the male.

"The spear? I've never seen it before. And, no, I never had it in my home."

The two detectives looked at each other with what appeared to be a blondes-don't-know-what-they-have-in-their-homes look. *But perhaps I'm being sensitive.*

"Any chance a decorator you hired placed it there and you just have never noticed?" the female asked.

I wasn't being sensitive. I answered, "No" firmly and shot her a this-blonde-knows-what's-in-her-home glare.

"The crime scene," the male detective began, his head cocked and one eyebrow raised, "was found to be immaculate. No fingerprints, footprints, hairs or fibers. Nothing. The perp supposedly didn't touch a thing. What do you make of that?"

Well, gosh, sir, I've always been taught to be neat. Hated to leave a mess after brutally murdering my husband.

Aloud I said in a small voice, "I don't know."

Then the female detective began firing questions at me. Did I know of any enemies of Sonny Bob? Where did he work? Where did he live? What was he doing in my house? Why did the former tenants leave in such a mysterious fashion? Had Sonny been depressed of late or angry with anyone in particular? What about threats to his life, stalker fans, fired employees, old girlfriends?

I could only tell them these were the exact same questions I'd been entertaining and I'd come up with zero answers.

"There was no forced entry," the male detective advised and waited a few beats for this possibly complex fact to penetrate my little blonde head.

"Well, as you know, Sonny had a key and perhaps the killer entered with Sonny," I said. "Forced himself upon Sonny or was someone Sonny trusted and arrived at my house with him or was someone Sonny knew and he let him in at some point."

The detective cut a quick glance at the female, perhaps meant to convey even super models possess some powers of deductive reasoning. He nodded sagely.

I decided to nod sagely myself, just to keep up with this dog and pony show.

"There were no prints on the spear," the male detective further advised.

"Someone wiped them clean." This from the female, stating the obvious. Her eyes were clear, sharp, penetrating. "Someone wiped any prints there may have been on doors, walls and so forth." Her words were crisp, almost plated with anger. *Was this a veiled accusation?*

"If they wanted to remove all evidence, why didn't they just take the spear with them?" I asked.

The female blew on her steaming cup of coffee, raised her head and looked at the male, then at me. "We asked ourselves the same question, Miss Bonnaire."

"Call me Freddy . . .please." As soon as I said it, I regretted it. This was not a social conversation. But it did seem to have the effect of causing the female to drop her glare. I thought I detected a trace of a smile from the male.

"There were no prints anywhere," she repeated, more matter of factly. "Someone was meticulous. We're looking into the footprints but they look deceptive also. Some kind of rubber boots. They may have been two sizes too big for the killer as they appear to drag."

"Drink your coffee before it gets cold." The male being chivalrous.

As I took a couple of sips, the female did the same, then gazed off at some far corner of the room. She looked back at me, and took two more sips.

"When did you first . . ." the male interrupted the silence.

"You said you realized your ex-husband was in some kind of trouble back in New Orleans . . ." The female decided to do some interrupting of her own. "When and how did you come to this conclusion?"

I provided a description of the scenario Gram had recited to me, including as much detail as I could summon from memory at that moment. They advised that unfortunately my grandmother would have to be questioned. I told them I understood this, and would call and prepare her in advance.

The male detective nodded, took a gulp of coffee and cocked his head to one side as he said, "There's one puzzling aspect to this case, Miss Bonnaire. The blows to the head and the stabbing with the spear occurred approximately two hours apart."

chapter 8

MY RETURN FLIGHT to The Big Easy was uneventful. Roland, that prince among men, met me at the airport and drove me to Gram's home on St. Charles Avenue, a redbrick colonial house boasting gothic columns. As her gentleman friend carried my luggage upstairs, Gram fixed a scotch and water for me without even asking. I think she knew recent events called for something stronger than sherry.

"You've been through so much, sugar. How can I help you?"

"Just being here with you, Gram," I said, "helps me enormously. And Roland gave me the addresses and phone numbers of Sonny's next-of-kin and a couple of friends. He said he's already invited them to the funeral, but I plan to contact some of them. To get some kind of closure on this, I need to find out more about Sonny Bob's life. I have a feeling I was clueless about a lot of things. Also, I may learn something to help the New York police."

"Do you think those nasty men who spirited him away are Mafia? Do you think the Mob killed him? Maybe Sonny was mixed up with the Mob. Have the police found DNA?"

Obviously Gram and Roland had been having a lively discussion about my ex-husband's demise with crime-solving flourishes.

"I've asked myself some of those same questions, Gram," I had to admit, "And I think I know of a contact here that may help with some answers."

"A contact? My Lord, honey, you know someone with the Mafia?"

"No, no, gram, just someone who knows Sonny Bob. I'll tell you the minute I learn anything."

It was only a partial lie. I'd long suspected Alex DeCicco had Mob connections, but suspecting and knowing are two different things. Before I left for New York, I'd met with two of his buddies in Metairie and been given a name to contact in Brooklyn. The sad discovery of Sonny's body occurred before I'd made time to pursue that endeavor.

"I'm pretty pooped, Gram. I think I'll get some shuteye now."

"Well, of course, darlin', you do just that. We can discuss the investigation in the morning."

Buck would appreciate Gram's crime-solving instincts. He greatly values amateur sleuths like me, my friend Jeannette and others. At least he sufficiently tolerates us to, from time to time, place us in his employ.

—

The next morning, Roland was gone. *At least I don't think the rascal slept with my grandmother!* And Gram slept late. I took advantage of some time alone to ring up one of Sonny Bob's two known family members: his cousin, Helen Anne.

"Freddy!" Helen Anne fairly yelled into my cell phone. "How good to hear from you! You've been such a doll to bring Sonny home, plan the funeral, host the reception afterward, and even pay for so much of it. Why I don't know what we'd. . . "

"Hold on, Helen Anne. I can't take credit for any of that. My grandmother's friend, Roland Figgins, is the knight in shining armor you want to thank."

"Well, whatever," she sighed. "Your family is just the sweetest bunch. You know Sonny Bob just surely loved every single one of you. . .even after the divorce. . .and, you know, I don't think he ever really wanted that divorce. . .why, he once said to me. . ."

"Excuse me, Helen Anne, I know you must be busy. . ."

I assumed she had her hands full as I could hear her daughter Amy screaming in the background. Gram always referred to little Amy, only six, as "that demon seed." An appellation that was unkind, but not inaccurate.

". . .what I'd love to do is meet you for breakfast tomorrow. Some place quiet where we could chat. I have some questions about Sonny Bob. Would that be okay?"

"Well, of course, honey. You name the place and time. I'm always up early. I'm expecting number four, you know, and I'm. . ."

Oh Lord!

". . .in my eighth month, can't sleep anyway."

—

At nine thirty the next morning, I headed for my favorite breakfast place: Slim Goodies. It is housed in an eighty-year-old building on Magazine Street, right off Louisiana Avenue, and has been in that locale for the past six years.

I entered the restaurant and perched on the nearest seat in the counter section. I was staring down at the floor, lost in contemplation over Sonny Bob and the whole sadness, so the first thing I saw was the sneakers, then the pale green cargo pants, a light blue jersey and finally the great smile, gray eyes and short strawberry blonde hair.

"Freddy! So good to see you! Tell me you're back here for good. Y'all really been missed around here! Where y'all been?"

Kappa, a nickname derived from Katherine, was Slim Goodies' owner and sometimes its hostess.

"These days I hardly know where I am, let alone where I'm living, Kappa, but it is good to be here."

She looked slightly puzzled at my response, and who can blame her, but favored me with a hug.

"Helen Anne's already here." Kappa rolled her eyes for some reason. "Come this way. There's a nice breeze today, and I thought you girls would enjoy the patio."

I followed Kappa outside to find Helen Anne seated at a table under a tree, nursing a Bloody Mary, with Amy, nursing a scowl and looking like she could *use* a Bloody Mary.

Helen Anne rose and gave me a hug. I then bent over to hug Amy, but she quickly shifted away and concentrated on blowing orange juice through a straw.

"Brian's coming to take Amy shopping," Helen Anne offered. "He's running errands but he'll be here any minute."

Brian was Helen Anne's husband, a personable guy who was as tall and lean as she was short and chubby.

We ordered—a crawfish étoffée omelet for me, potato latkes for Helen Anne, and a bowl of oatmeal for Amy, which she promptly converted to a "pretend mountain" on the tablecloth. We concentrated mostly on small talk and occasional gossip tidbits provided by Helen Anne. Fifteen minutes into our visit, Brian, thankfully, arrived and spirited Amy off to conduct brattish behavior at some other venue.

"Helen Anne, Sonny's Aunt Winnie has been notified and invited to the funeral, has she not?"

"Oh yes, your friend Roland was most thorough. Winnie's flying out tomorrow."

"Flying out? She's been traveling?"

The last I'd heard of Aunt Winnie, Sonny's mother's sister, she was living in a trailer in Bywater and barely keeping body and soul together, a lifestyle that rather precluded any kind of travel. . .except, perhaps, from the law had such a thing as debtors prison still existed.

"Goodness, Freddy, didn't Sonny tell you? Aunt Winnie was a character but, you know, she wasn't bad looking for her age and she was interesting as all get out. Winnie met and married up with a rich tourist here a little over two years ago and six months after their wedding he up and died."

"How sad."

"Well, not entirely. He left her a wealthy widow."

"So Aunt Winnie now travels the world, does she?"

"I don't know about that, but she lives well, that's for darn sure."

"Maybe has a house in the Garden District now?" I asked.

"'deed she does. And, like a lotta folks in the Garden District, also keeps a pied-à-terre in the French Quarter."

"Okay, I'll bite, what exactly is Winnie's current situation?"

"That's what I don't understand, Freddy. You not knowing and all because. . . "

I said, "I was fond of her but Winnie and I were not exactly bosom buddies and. . .

"But, Freddy, she lives in New York, in some ritzy building on the west side I hear,

and . . ."

"I didn't know that."

"Sure enough, sweetie, she's 'bout as rich as Donald Trump these days and . . ."

"Amazing."

"Did Sonny Bob know all this?"

"Hell, yes, darlin', for quite a while he lived with her."

chapter 9

Since moving away several years ago, I'd looked forward to a return visit to New Orleans, to seeing my beloved Gram and the city that was to me almost equally beloved. Even after growing up here, I retained a tourist's awe and enthusiasm for its many charms. Although I'd be with Gram this trip, drinking in the distinctive antebellum architecture, gaining pounds on sinfully rich Southern food and getting a buzz from potent Sazerac cocktails was not to be. My sad mission of burying Sonny Bob replaced enjoying the city's languid vibe.

The sky on the day of the funeral was appropriately a tent of pale gray. Roland had arranged for the mass to be held at Saint Joseph Catholic Church on Tulane. It was reportedly the largest church in New Orleans. The Romanesque exterior was bland to my eyes, but the cavernous and elegant interior more than compensated. I don't remember what the priest said. I can't even remember what Aunt Winnie said in her eulogy, only that she wore sunglasses as she spoke and looked as elegant as the church and startlingly different from the Winnie so popular at the trailer park, famous for her menthol cigarette habit and husky laugh. But today's Winnie was the one Sonny Bob last knew. He had actually lived with her in her apartment, The San Remo, at 75th and Central Park West. This was a fact as bizarre to grasp, as it was to imagine that Sonny Bob would have ever inhabited this formal and imposing church in life.

We were a sorrowful little cluster of humanity facing the huge white altar, almost thirty of us. Some elderly musicians who'd known Sonny as a child, several women I knew to be girls who'd gone to high school with Sonny, a twenty-something bartender from the Quarter, and a few other women I didn't recognize. In addition to Winnie, family members were his cousin on his father's side, Helen Anne, and her husband, and little Amy who was blessedly subdued, Gram and me. I did not recognize any of the pallbearers. Were they hired help? Roland would have done that. He seemed to be a man dedicated to appearances, and able-bodied male attendees among Sonny's New Orleans acquaintances were in short supply.

Soon it was time to head for Lafayette Cemetery No. 1, conveniently located on Washington Avenue in the Garden District. A slight drizzle had commenced when we'd been inside the church, and everyone raced to their cars as if the rain preordained another hurricane Katrina.

At the cemetery we waited until all the cars were parked and the mourners could once again gather to make their way down the aisles, led by Roland and Winnie, the latter seemingly assuming a sort of hostess role. Gram held onto my arm and that of one of the high school ladies on her other side. Several burials were in progress. It was a busy place and as eight black men playing instruments turned into an adjacent aisle, suddenly the sun came out. Now, at last, it seemed like an environment appropriate to Sonny Bob—bright sunshine, music, people and intensity. Between the above-the-ground gravestones, I could spy the musicians decked out in white shirts and black suits slowly swaying to the mournful notes of *Just a Closer Walk with Thee.*

"Granted Jesus is my plea-e-e-e." Winnie suddenly softly chimed in, and it was good to see her original eccentricity still lurked behind the façade of the perfect makeup, very elegant dress—its hem nearly sweeping the ground—and stylish picture hat.

The shadow of a nearby angel figure reflected upon an especially large tomb that we passed, and a black wrought-iron fence surrounded it. I hoped the resting place Roland had chosen for Sonny was somewhat less elaborate.

Winnie sidled up to me, her enormous black hat bobbing as she walked.

She whispered, "I would surely like to be havin' a whiskey sour right now if you want to know the truth, shugah."

I realized one thing I greatly missed away from the Crescent City was being called "sugar."

We turned a corner and almost collided with the band members. They must have been on the way out of the cemetery because I heard the last notes of the livelier *When the Saints Go Marching In* and the beginning of *Didn't He Ramble*. Finally, Roland led us to a comparatively quieter area. Sonny Bob's coffin was already in place, covered by a mass of white roses. Gram left my side to stand next to Roland, and the high school woman joined her friends.

"Where yah at, Freddy?"

I recognized the Louisiana greeting colloquium, but not the speaker. As I momentarily bristled at the glib slang and jovial tone on this sober occasion, I took a second look and realized I did know the tiny woman who'd approached me. Lean and wiry, her black hair well coifed and only slightly flecked with grey, she'd once been Gram's maid.

"Good to see you, Anna Mae," I said, *sotto voce*. "I'm so glad you could come."

"Gracious me, Freddy," she whispered back. "Where'd y'all get that tan? You're 'bout as brown as me."

I said absently, "I didn't see you at the church."

"Couldn't make it on time. Sonny Bob's Aunt Winnie had me doin' so much stuff back at the house."

"Back at Gram's house?"

"No, Winnie's house."

"I heard Winnie has a house here."

"Deed she does. Hardly ever uses it, but pays me to keep it up."

"Gram will be so glad to see you, Anna Mae. You'll come back to her house for the reception, won't you?"

"Didn't Mr. Roland tell you? The reception's at Winnie's house. Or I should say, mansion. And I'll surely be around, being as I live there. Katrina done did my own home in and I'm grateful that. . ."

Anna Mae and I ceased our chatter as the priest commenced his eulogy. Roland began distributing a rose from the coffin's generous arrangement to each mourner, eventually assisted by Sonny's bartender friend.

I dropped my rose as I fished in my large purse for Kleenex and as I turned to retrieve it, I caught a glimpse of a woman's light hair, almost sparkling in the sunlight. My first thought was that the hair might be red with blonde glints. I mused that Jeannette had flown in and surprised me by suddenly making an appearance, but the figure in the distance was far too petite to be my plus-sized friend. She wore a black pants suit, her head turned toward Sonny's coffin, her eyes hidden behind very large sunglasses. She carried a small black shoulder bag, which she clutched in front of her. For a moment, she removed her glasses and looked directly my way. She smiled slightly at me, but her expression seemed flat and cold. Perhaps this impression was judgmental. Did I presume her to be a Sonny Bob girlfriend, perhaps during our marriage? Somehow I didn't think so. Her eyes darted toward the coffin, then cut back to me. We locked glances once more. After about two minutes, the small woman turned and walked quickly away.

There was something vaguely familiar about her. *Where had I seen her before and who was she?*

chapter 10

I TRIED TO listen to what the priest was saying, but so many distracting thoughts swirled in my brain. I turned my head and focused on the four couples in our small gathering. All but one couple appeared too conservatively dressed to be friends of Sonny Bob. The husband of the couple in rather Bohemian attire resembled a musician he worked with when we were first married and living in New Orleans, before our move to Manhattan. Another couple, fairly attractive and stylishly dressed, stood apart from the others, giving the priest their full attention. The remaining two couples of my mystery group wore funeral black and whispered among themselves, drawing occasional disapproving looks from Gram.

Aunt Winnie approached me again, gently placing an arm around my shoulders.

"Look over there, shugah. Remember Commanders Palace? Sonny Bob loved that place, used to rave about it all the time."

I gazed to my right at the restaurant with its familiar turquoise and white awnings gracing the white Victorian Building with its turrets and columns and other assorted gingerbread.

"I do remember it, Winnie. Sonny loved the duck, he ordered it every time."

"Mmmmmmm," Winnie said, rubbing my arm affectionately as she savored the memory too. "Ah'm thinkin' hot and sour melted onions over Jack Daniels buttermilk coush-coush with pepper jelly glazed sweetbreads."

I had to smile at her precise recollection. "And we always had turtle soup spiked with sherry first," I said.

"Honey, makes me wish we were havin' the reception over there instead of my house but Hermione's friend Roland planned a wonderful menu for the event and he and Anna Mae have worked so hard. . ."

"Winnie," I interrupted rudely, "I never knew you got married."

"Sure enough, shugah, ah met Charles de Foucauld and it was love at first sight for both of us. A whirlwind romance. And, truth to tell, ah knew he was from France—you woulda loved him, shugah—but I didn't know he was rich till he told me after the weddin' we were going to Hawaii for a month and then to London, Paris and Madrid. Coulda knocked me over with one of them feathers Anna Mae's always wearing. It was a great shock when he died. Some of my so-called friends here gossiped about me, the new wealthy widow. Ah didn't feel wealthy without my Charles. How ah loved that man! Had him buried in upstate New York where most of his kin live, and ah go there once a month but ah. . ."

It was my turn to put an arm around Winnie and render a hug. "I'm so sorry for your loss, but I guess we're talking too much now and. . ."

"You're right, shugah," she agreed, and slipped an arm around my waist, inclining her head against my arm.

The priest concluded his remarks, and we began filing away from the burial site. Gram had explained to me beforehand that Sonny Bob would be lowered into the ground later, after we'd all left. The ceremony over, Winnie took my arm and began chattering once again.

"Hermione told me y'all moved away some time back, honey. Of course. I know you were in New York when. . .when it. . .when the tragic occurrence happened. I also heard you'd been sort of movin' around from hotels and the like for a while. I just want to tell you any time you need a place to stay you gotta come to your Aunt Winnie's. Well, of course, I'm not really *your* Aunt Winnie, but you know, shugah, even before you married ole Sonny Bob I thought of you as kin. Now you gotta promise me. . ."

"I'm honored to have you as my aunt, Winnie, and I may take you up on that offer. As of now, I plan to possibly move into my place in Brooklyn, rather then always renting it out but it will be in a state of renovation for a while and I. . ."

"Well, that's a practical decision, shugah. It's settled then. You'll stay with your Aunt Winnie and there's no if's, and's or but's about it."

I had to grin at her enthusiasm, and I felt very grateful for her offer. The musicians arrived at an aisle adjoining our path once more, their mournful but loud rendition of *St. James Infirmary* effectively drowning out normal conversation, but I had a question I wanted to whisper to Winnie anyway.

"Winnie," I bent down to press my face close to her ear, hoping the enormous diamond earring she wore would not impede her hearing. "Who are those four couples just ahead of Gram and Roland? I don't recognize a one of them."

She put her arm around my waist once more and hugged me close, seemingly delighted to share some gossip.

"That couple with the fella in that large cowboy hat and the girl with him in the long paisley skirt, they used to play in a band with Sonny Bob. Nice folks, they stayed in touch with Sonny for years. That tall fella and the little brunette, that's the Benjamins. Lovely people. Real down to earth even though they *are* British. They surely treat me good. That young couple over there that kinda looks like hippies? They're what we call trust fund kids. Live near my place here in a big ole house. Family had money but they don't do a lick of work. And that young guy they brought with 'em? He looks for all the world like one of them gutter punks here. Probably call his kind gang members in New York, but I don't know what all about that. Gutter punks in these parts squat in abandoned buildings, 'specially one on Decatur Street. Mostly they panhandle during the day but I'm sure they also contribute to New Orleans rise in crime since hurricane Katrina, along with the folks who used to live in the project buildings. Their homes got destroyed so they're desperate."

"Has the crime rate grown that much, Winnie?"

"I hope to tell you! And these days New Orleans folks see a crime and the locals all text each other about it to get the word out. Even if they report it to the police, the public's not always told about it."

"I didn't realize that . . ."

"Well, 'nuff about that, shugah, back to the guests," Winnie continued. "Look over there. You musta met Bella and Dina. Maybe it's been a while. Dina's gained quite a bit of weight in recent years and Bella's added those funny maroon highlights to her hair. She's got perfectly nice dark brown hair. Ah don't know why in the world she. . ."

"I can't quite place them, Winnie."

"You'd of remembered 'em, honey. They're brash, over-bearing and abrasive, everything you're not. You probably haven't seen them for a spell. Ah remember back when you were a debutante at the Mardi Gras Ball. But you wouldn't have met 'em there. Not like their daddy was a judge like yours and they . . ."

"You think I should know them?"

"Well, Lord have mercy, Freddy, of course you must have met them! They're Sonny Bob's stepsisters."

chapter 11

THIS SORROWFUL DAY was proving to be one of constant surprises. One of an inanimate nature greeted me as we disembarked from the limo Roland had thoughtfully provided and stood before a beautiful house on Prytania Street in the Garden District, not far from Gram's home. From the street, it looked larger than the surrounding homes but other than its size, the exterior was not unique: a surrounding black wrought-iron fence, white columns fronting a narrow porch, black doors and black shutters gracing the red brick structure.

We stepped inside and I was immediately grateful for the invention of air conditioning but what was even more impressive was the view of a long staircase to the right, a medium-size oriental rug over gleaming hardwood floors, and the huge, brightly lit chandelier visible in the living room ahead.

Winnie had an announcement for the female guests. "Y'all go on upstairs and feel free to freshen up and leave your purses in the first bedroom on your right. Just make yourselves to home, but hurry back down 'cause we got lots of good food and drink here. Don't we, Roland?"

Roland gave a slight nod of his head, appearing slightly uncomfortable around Aunt Winnie-style exuberance.

It was Anna Mae's turn to grab my arm with whispered comments as we ascended the stairs.

"Is this not the livin' end, Freddy? It's got seven bed-rooms and just as many bathrooms. Well, five are full and two are half baths. And wait till you see the kitchen. It's to die for. Ole Winnie can't cook more than hot dogs herself, but she hired a chef, name's Morgan, and he's a gourmet and a half. Well, ain't that fittin'? I always hear you're a gourmet cook. You and Morgan can exchange recipes. I'll introduce you to him later on."

Anna Mae turned to talk to Gram and I quickly ducked into the closest of the seven bathrooms, grateful to get away for a moment from the collective loquaciousness of Win-nie and Anna Mae. Usually their brand of good spirits was prevalent at funerals where the deceased was extremely old and thus may have been said to have lived a long and full life; but Sonny Bob was only thirty-four and had been *murdered*. I was beginning to think I should be looking for suspects among the funeral attendees.

I fluffed up my hair and freshened my blush, surprised to find my cheeks somewhat tear stained. As I exited, Gram grabbed my hand and squeezed it.

"My turn to go in there, shugah. Wait for me and I'll introduce you around when we go downstairs."

I sat on a small bench and waited as instructed, as the other women placed their purses on the sparkling white bedspread and headed for other bathrooms, their chatter and perfume filling the air.

In a few minutes, Gram joined me.

"Let's go down, honey," she grinned. *Another happy mourner.*

Perhaps I was being morose. People in New Orleans love a party, even a reception after a funeral, and Gram and Winnie were both devout Catholics. They knew Sonny was in a better place, so why be glum? Maybe it had to do with the way he spent his life. Even his free-spirited musician friends came to disapprove of the constant high living and the gambling, particularly since he probably borrowed money from everyone here at one time or another. Perhaps they feel that at last there is calm and order in Sonny Bob's existence and this is a cause for joy. I would rather have seen him first attain this peace in the environs of New York City or New Orleans or wherever.

We made our way to the living room or "the biggest of all the parlors" as Gram called it. Bright white was apparently a favorite of Winnie's as this was the color of the fireplace, the drapes and the molding. The walls were a chocolate brown.

Gram pulled me from this room to what realtors would call the private French courtyard. Here and on a covered side porch, the wake was in full swing. A small combo played softly in a far corner of the courtyard, and both areas boasted carving stations with a long bar on the side porch. Behind the bar stood a very tall black man, with skin like burnished mahogany and kind eyes. He smiled readily as he handed out martinis.

Gram approached him, ordered champagne and introduced us. He turned out to be the Morgan Anna Mae had mentioned.

"So pleased to meet you, Miss Bonnaire." Morgan gave a slight bow.

"Call me Freddy." I smiled, which was becoming easier given all the good cheer surrounding me. "I'll have champagne too please."

Suddenly my arm was grabbed again, this time rather roughly. It was Sonny Bob's cousin, Helen Anne.

"Here, take her," she said, placing her six-year-old daughter's hand in mine, "I gotta go pee."

With that, Helen Anne headed toward the foyer and Amy squirmed from my grasp to run toward the farthest end of the courtyard. I placed my champagne glass on the table and walked slowly in the direction of Amy's escape route. I increased my pace when Amy bounded out of sight and attempted to weave my way with some dignity past the second bar, the carving stations, and a round table laden with casseroles of every description. I smiled and said "hey" to the mourners I knew as I passed them and just smiled at what appeared to be several neighbors who'd joined the crowd.

As I moved in Aunt Winnie's direction, she came bounding toward me, placed a hand firmly on my back and pushed me toward the tall, married couple from England.

"Come on, shugah, I want you to meet the Benjamins."

The male Benjamin favored me with a wide smile and a greeting. The missus thrust her hand forward, bypassing her husband's outstretched hand, and I shook it. She wore a black chiffon dress and her muscular legs were chalk white. Her hair was short and dark with some kind of pale highlights that made me think once again of the strange female visitor to Sonny's grave earlier.

"You must be so grief stricken," Mrs. Benjamin cooed. She had a British accent, but one slightly different from her husband's. "We didn't know Sonny Bob terribly well, but I do know he was very good to dear Winifred." She caressed Mr. Benjamin's arm as she spoke.

"I'd love to stay and chat but I have a little six year old in my charge and I've got to go find her."

Judging from their slightly shocked expressions, I might as well have said I have Rosemary's Baby, the demon seed, to apprehend before she murders the cat. Maybe I said something similar, come to think of it.

I made my way thru the north garden's narrow paths. There was such a beautiful array of flowers you'd think even Amy would be tempted to stop and explore. There were numerous types of azaleas, along with salmon-colored poppies, and cherry and ivory zinnias. In an island section there was a Firecracker plant, its spindly stems and little orange buds providing an interesting contrast. I passed a section of daisies that definitely appeared violated. Some remains of flowers lay dormant, pulled from the ground.

Stopping for a second to view the wreckage and cast an eye about for the little perpetrator, I saw my recent acquaintance making his way toward me.

"Mr. Benjamin! Come to admire Winnie's flowers? I'm still in hot pursuit of Amy."

"Bloody hell, Freddy, 'Mr. Benjamin' is my dad, God rest his soul. Call me what everybody calls me. On second thought, I'm a lawyer so I'm called a lot of things. Keep it simple, call me Sherwood."

"As soon as I find Amy, I'll be back to join the party but till then. . ."

"That's why I'm here. . ." he grinned. ". . . to help you find the spoiled rotten little brat."

"Goodness mercy," I mocked an extreme southern accent. "Did I say all that?"

"You might as well have. Your tone of voice said exactly that."

I led the way past the daisies. "Let's try this . . .," I started to say and then heard faint sobbing.

"Over there." Sherwood pointed toward a large cluster of stately white Spanish Spear Yuccas.

We turned a corner and found a somewhat trans-formed Amy sitting on the ground, her dress and hands caked with dirt. Her little smudged and tear-stained face looked upward toward us.

"I can't get the flowers I want, Aunt Freddy. Yah gotta help me."

"I'll help you get cleaned up, missy. The flowers are not ours to get."

Sherwood took command. "Stand up and let's go."

"Who are you?" Amy's voice switched from pitiful to demanding.

"I'm yours and Aunt Freddy's new friend, little one," Sherwood said gently, taking her hands and pulling Amy up. "Lead the way, Aunt Freddy," he smiled.

I stepped past them to lead us back to the reception area where we would hopefully find the mommie for Amy and some champagne for me. My first wish came true when we'd just progressed about fifteen yards.

"Baby, what you been doin' with Aunt Freddy? You must be hungry. Freddy, didn't y'all get her somethin' to eat?"

I couldn't believe this. Was I about to be accused of child abuse?

"I was looking at the pretty flowers, mama."

"Well, bless your heart. We'll go look at 'em later, sweetie. Right now I'll fix you a nice sandwich."

Sherwood and I stood still momentarily, watching them depart.

"And I'll fix you a cocktail, lovely lady, if you'll allow me to."

This guy was as inappropriate in his rather flirtatious manner as Amy was in her attempts at flower purloining.

"I think I'll go check on Gram first, Sherwood, then we'd love to join you and your wife for a drink."

"My . . . oh, you mean Selah whom you met. Selah's my ex-wife." That disarming lopsided grin again. "We've been divorced almost eight years, but when we parted, my ex decided to remain in the same apartment building, the one where Winnie also resides. Winnie was friendly to both of us, and thus Selah got to know Sonny Bob. When Winnie invited her to the funeral, she jumped at the chance to see New Orleans and enjoy some diversion. Her life's somewhat less than full these days."

I made no comment, simply smiled and excused myself once more and headed for the house in search of Gram. I doubted she'd linger in the garden long in this weather. My first stop was the downstairs sitting room just off the kitchen and there I ran into Winnie.

"Freddy, you little devil, ah saw that big ole good lookin' Sherwood Benjamin making goo-goo eyes at you."

She was sitting on a small rose-colored loveseat, pulling off her heels. "Ah'm gettin' too old to be walkin' around in these things all day. Makes my legs get achey. Well, don't just stand there staring at me. Tell me what's between you and the charmin' Mr. Benjamin, shugah."

"Mostly I'd say is ex-wife is between us. She's rather affectionate toward him."

"Oh pish tosh, as your grandmother would say. They've been divorced like just forever, and she's never found a boyfriend. That's just desperation you're lookin' at."

"I see. She seems to still need him."

"Ole Selah lives in some sorta parallel universe in which she thinks she's still married to Sherwood. The only thing that calculatin' little hussy needs is to get laid, shugah. You pay her no mind."

With that, Gram came out of the nearby powder room. "I heard you all the way in there, Winnie. Now who is it who needs to get laid?"

"Probably all three of us, Hermione," Winnie said, "but right now let's go join our guests."

chapter 12

THEY WERE LARGE men, and looked menacing. Both were olive-skinned and stout, the latter trait seemingly composed of both muscle and blubber. One had black hair and a mostly gray moustache. The other was bald with a small diamond in one ear.

"There's nothing to be afraid of, Mrs. Toussaint."

Gram was nursing what she called her "afternoon sherry." It was actually eleven fifteen in the morning but, as Jimmy Buffet sings, "It's five o'clock somewhere"

The two men making my grandmother highly nervous were actually two New Orleans detectives, commissioned by the New York police to interview her about Sonny Bob's initial disappearance. I sat with Gram in her living room, lending moral support.

We learned gray moustache was Detective Thibodeau and diamond earring was Detective Damien.

We also learned that had Gram been considered a suspect in Sonny's murder, the New York detectives would have flown out to the Big Easy themselves. Apparently, they felt a rather frail elderly lady was somewhat unlikely to have flown to Brooklyn, apprehended Sonny Bob, knocked him unconscious and stabbed him to death. Thus, they allowed the NOPD to assist in their case.

"I understand your exposure to these men was very brief, mam, but just do your best to give us a description. Anything you can think of would be enormously helpful."

Gram had been prattling on about the mean and vicious appearance of the men who spirited Sonny away at gunpoint, that she'd never seen people so horrible looking, that they had no manners and were thoughtless in the extreme. Everything but how they actually looked. Detective Thibodeau couched his questions in a gentle tone. Detective Damien, not so tolerant of a senior's thought processes, was visibly tapping his foot in apparent impatience.

"I like to tell you they tracked a lot of dirt onto my good rug runner over there. Maybe there's DNA in that. Oh, wait, I had Anna Mae vacuum it all up. Well, you're free to inspect the rug if you wish."

Thibodeau inhaled deeply, possibly stifling a sigh. Damien's foot action increased in speed. Gram had given me a partial description of the apparent kidnappers when I first arrived in New Orleans; but I was not the actual witness, so I kept quiet and joined the police officers in the exercise of patience.

"Gentlemen, are you sure you won't have some sherry?" Gram, ever the hostess.

"No, mam," said Damien. "We're on duty."

"Surely I can offer you something. Frédérique, do get the officers some almond cookies."

"We're good, mam." This from Thibodeau. "If you can just. . ."

"Detectives, I'll go get the cookies," I said, rising from my chair. "I bet we could all use some cookies." I surreptitiously nodded at Gram as I stepped behind her chair.

I returned and placed the cookie plate and some napkins on the small mahogany coffee table between Gram on the velvet couch and the antique chairs upon which the detectives and I were precariously perched. Each of us took a cookie, and Gram commenced wolfing down hers.

She took a second cookie and alternated bites with sips of sherry. She held her glass out to me for a refill and picked up a third cookie.

"I know it's hard to remember, mam. But just do your best. Think about what they looked like. Maybe you remember what they were wearing and whether they. . ."

Gram took a healthy swig of sherry, then a quick intake of air and sat up straighter. We were about to observe the remarkable restorative powers of sherry and almond cookies.

"One was about six foot tall, the other was just a little taller than me. Both of them were like you. . .that is, they were muscular, heavy men. They had New York accents," she continued. "And one carried a gun. Don't ask me what make, I'm not well informed about pistols."

At this point, both detectives were wide-eyed at this sudden memory resurgence, and I doubt they faulted Gram for her lack of weaponry knowledge.

Thibodeau was now scribbling notes. "Do you recall anything they said, what names they called each other. . ."

"The tall one called the short one something like Bobby or . . . well, you'll think I'm imagining things . . . but it sounded like 'baby' . . .hmmm . . .although maybe with a 'p.' The. . . well, I won't call him a gentleman because indeed he was not. . .short gangster. . .I'm sorry, but that's what I would call him. . .he kept calling Sonny Bob 'S.B,' and he was wearing a khaki-colored raincoat that was rather dirty. The tall one wore a black raincoat. I remember it looked brand new. They both wore black trousers and very shiny brown shoes. Why they wore brown shoes with black trousers I swear I cannot fathom but. . ." Gram took a sip of sherry. "Well, that's not important. What else would you like to know, gentlemen?"

By now, the detectives wore satisfied smiles. Damien's foot had been immobile for some time.

"You're being very, very helpful, Mrs. Toussaint," Detective Thibodeau said, "Did they say anything else?"

Gram picked up an almond cookie and bit into it delicately. Now that she was a valuable informant, she was not about to be rushed.

"Frédérique, you get yourself some more sherry. This must be very trying for you too, honey."

"I will, Gram." I rose to refill my glass. Gram was on a roll, and I was not about to dispute any request she might make.

"They said something about Sonny Bob owing money, they didn't say how much. He, of course, protested that he was going to pay it back, that he had almost half of it here in a bank in New Orleans. They didn't seem to believe him and got very ugly about it. I've never seen Robert Arthur. . . that's his real name you know. . .so upset. He always was such a relaxed, charmin' young man. He further protested that he knew where he could get it, the money, that is, when they didn't seem to believe he had any funds in a bank here. There really wasn't much conversation after that. They just held that gun on him and pulled him out to the car."

"Did you see the make of the vehicle, mam?"

"The vehicle? Oh, you mean the car those dreadful gangsters were driving? Well, gentlemen, it was pitch black dark outside that night. Something went wrong with our street light and don't think I don't intend to tell the mayor about that. But even so, we should have had some light. Elizabeth Fremont, that's my neighbor next door, she has a beautiful ornate carriage lamppost near her gate but it went out ages ago and she never repaired it. She's so lazy that way. Says it's because she's a widow. Well, land sakes, I'm a widow too but I try to keep things up and. . ."

Damien's foot returned to action. "Did you notice the color of the car, Mrs. Toussaint?"

"In the middle of a dark night? I'd say not. Oh wait . . . when they pulled away, I got a little glimpse. The reason I did was because I was standing at the door when they went down the walkway with Sonny Bob. Looking back, that was probably foolhardy of me. I mean those men were dangerous. But I was just dumbstruck. I stood there with my door clean open and it must have been the light from the hallway that helped me see a little."

Gram took a slow swallow of sherry and just stared straight ahead at nothing in particular, clearly reliving her awful experience.

"You were smart to keep that door open, Mrs. Toussaint," said Damien. "What exactly did you see?"

Gram shook her head in response to some inner thoughts and continued staring, not quite ready to depart from her reverie. Absently, she ran her hand over the velvet softness of the couch. Then, in about five beats, she blinked and turned to Detective Damien.

"You really should have another cookie, Detective," she said. "If you can't enjoy some sherry, you need some kind of nourishment. You know, when Sonny Bob was visitin' me here I would fix him three big meals a day and it just made a new man out of him."

She turned toward me. "Don't you folks eat in New York? Are all of you dieting or something? I never in my life saw such. . ."

"Gram," I said slowly and deliberately, "how would you describe the car those men were driving?" *I was about to join Damien in some toe tapping of my own.*

Gram narrowed her eyes at me and then, also slowly and deliberately, took several sips of her sherry.

"I saw the front of their car, saw one of those little emblems on it. You know those little round things with the points."

"A little round thing with. . .?" I took several sips of sherry myself.

"Oh, you know. Yes, I remember. The three-pointed star."

"A Mercedes-Benz, Gram?"

"My stars, I do believe so. . . "

Broad smiles from the detectives.

Gram continued, ". . . looked like the car your brother owns, Frédérique. But his is red, which is really too flashy for a lawyer and. . . ."

Gram caught herself, ceased her chatter, then matched their grins, undoubtedly feeling self satisfied and important.

"Mrs. Touissant, you've been very helpful," Damien said. "There's just one more thing we'd like you to do."

"Detective," Gram said, "I'm really quite fatigued and . . .

"No, not today, mam. Tomorrow we'll come pick you up and take you to the precinct to confer with our sketch artist."

"Well, I . . ., Gram waved an almond cookie in the air. "I have a hair appointment and . . ."

"It won't take long, mam," Thiboeau said. "Would eleven work for you?"

"Very well, I'll call Tulip and reschedule"

Gram's eyes narrowed. "Yes, my hairdresser's name is Tulip, detectives. And if you make one smart remark about that . . . well, I'm sorry. I just don't want you to think ill of my judgment and my memory . . .that is, because I have a hairdresser named Tulip." She bit down hard on the cookie.

"Mam," Detective Damien said, a smile barely curling his lips. "Tulip and you and your descriptions to us have our utmost respect."

"Well, you jest, sir, but I appreciate that." She waved the cookie in the air once more as if to dismiss them.

"We'll be in touch, mam," Thibodeau said, and they both bowed slightly.

I walked the detectives to the door, we shook hands once more and they left. I returned to the living room to find Gram already peacefully dozing, one last cookie resting on her lap. I was glad to be essentially alone. I had a lot of thinking to do. Gram told the good detectives far more than she'd shared with me the day I arrived. There was something familiar in her dissertation, but I couldn't quite put my finger on it. I took my glass of sherry outside to the back patio, hoping fresh air would clear my head.

A soft sliver of breeze punctuated the August heat and humidity. As I sat on a rattan chair, ruminating and admiring some white roses, a recollection came rushing back to me: Gram had mentioned one thug called the other 'Bobby" or 'baby.' But then she added, "with a 'p.'" She described him as medium height with thick hair. I recalled my recent meeting in a dirty, run down bar in Metairie where I met two associates of my friend Alex DeCicco. Alex had said they'd provide the name of a contact of Sonny Bob's in New York. I met with them and they gave me a name and phone numbers. They never introduced themselves when we met, but Alex had briefly mentioned their names over the phone to me. One was named Gio. But he was tall, with a moustache. The other was short, had a moustache and his name was Beppe. The proverbial light bulb at last illuminated my deductive reasoning. "Baby . . . with a 'p.'" Beppe.

Detective Thibodeau had said, "There's nothing to be afraid of, Mrs. Toussaint."

If the Beppe I met and the Beppe Gram saw capturing Sonny Bob are one and the same, Mrs. Toussaint should be very much afraid.

chapter 13

Outside, evening shadows lay over the French Quarter. We were seated at a window table overlooking Bienville Street. I would have preferred grabbing a bite at Port O' Cal over on Esplanade where you can get the best burgers with baked potatoes, but my companion insisted on G W Fins. Mere steps from Bourbon Street, it was generally considered the best seafood restaurant in the area, and I had to admit I liked the elegance of the high vaulted ceiling and dark wood columns. .

"Miss Frédérique, what'll you have?"

It wasn't our friendly waiter speaking, but rather Sherwood Benjamin, who seemed to be my new best friend in New Orleans. As Sherwood was leaving the wake for Sonny Bob, he hastily issued an invitation for dinner two days hence, and I, just as impulsively, said yes. I certainly had no intention of going on a date while here. I've had enough romantic complications since parting with Sonny: the owner of a French restaurant on whom I had an ongoing hopeless crush, a Native American homicide detective with whom I had a relationship that appropriately would also be deemed hopeless and then there's Buck Lemoyne, my private investigator buddy. I consider Buck just a buddy but my best friend Jeannette has a theory that we're a couple and just don't know it. A hopeless supposition on her part, if you ask me. Do we see a trend here? My love life is . . . well . . . *hopeless.*

"I think I'll go with the Chilean sea bass."

"Great choice, Freddy, but I have a better suggestion."

Sherwood seemed to alternate between calling me Freddy and Frédérique. The latter had a nice traditional vibe to it . . . and I like to think of myself as a traditional type girl . . . but it sounded strange to my ears coming from one of my peers. I usually hear that from Gram, Aunt Winnie and other seniors I know.

The waiter arrived, asking for our drink orders.

"A glass of white wine for me."

"I'll have a scotch and soda," Sherwood added.

"Appetizers?"

"I'll have the smoked oysters. The lady will have the lobster dumplings."

Then he gave the waiter his preferred choice for our entrée over my sea bass selection. The waiter pronounced it an "excellent" selection.

When he left, I said, "Have you ever had a waiter say you've made a lousy choice? I always get such a kick out of that restaurant protocol."

"Come to think of it, I never have," Sherwood smiled. "But I'll tell you another excellent choice. The one I made for you as my dinner companion."

Smooth operator. I smiled back.

"Tell me about yourself, Freddy. Winifred . . . I mean, Winnie . . . sorry, she seems to go by Winifred in New York . . . in any event, she said you're a model. I can certainly see why. Never thought much about that as a career I'll admit, but I imagine it's a fascinating life style."

"Yes and no. I love it, but not too long ago I went through a long period where bookings were decidedly slim."

"Hard to believe in your case. For one, you made quite an impression on Winifred's bartender, Morgan. He thinks you look like some movie star . . . can't recall the name."

"Cameron Diaz?"

"That's it! You must get that often."

"Often enough. Very flattering. To me, at least. Cameron has yet to weigh in on the subject."

Sherwood grinned, he did that a lot. "She's flattered also. Ah guar-rahn-tee it."

He pronounced "guarantee" with a mock New Orleans accent. I can't deny the man has charm.

"You have a slight trace of a southern accent, Freddy, but Winifred tells me you grew up in New York."

Winnie had clearly been doing a lot of telling. "I was born in Paris. My family came to the States when I was nine and settled in Louisiana. When I was seventeen, we relocated to New York. The years we were here in New Orleans, my parents gradually started sounding like natives. It wasn't an affectation with them, they were crazy about their adopted city and their accents were just a side effect of this. I probably picked up some dialect then."

Sherwood returned to his earlier premise, "And modeling? You do think it's exciting?"

"Well, you could say that. It is to me. But I learned pretty quickly that it's not all parties and getting free clothes and getting paid a lot of money. It's also a lot of work, at least more work than the general public assumes. But I have to confess I love everything about it. I even love the way photo studios smell . . . usually cold and damp, with a hint of chemical in the air. You cope with that atmosphere with fresh brewed coffee . . . and donuts, of course. And the camaraderie with the other models. Even if we're in fittings until two in the morning, we don't care because we feel part of the overall creativity. I remember shooting all night in Paris. Sometimes there'd be only one of each couture dress, and we'd be waiting for hours on end for an outfit to arrive. But we'd have great background music playing and nobody complained."

"Commendable. Lawyers, on the other hand, complain about their long hours all the time. My secretary runs off to fashion shows in department stores and the like on occasion. Would she have seen you at one of those?"

"Possibly. And she'd see one happy camper. There's a great energy in runway work. The atmosphere is electric, lots of passion and adrenaline. A nervous buzz is in the air . . . everyone becomes your instant friend . . . photographers shouting your name . . . but how I do gush—don't I?"

"Not at all, Frédérique, it's intriguing. You must meet some famous designers in your line of work."

"Ah, designers! I love to watch a designer work. I watch for days on end to see what some dress is going to be like it it's finished. I've watched many of the great designers do what they do. That's why I'm still loyal to designers that I've known since I was nineteen. A couple of my friends and I have done ads for designers who don't have a dime to their names . . . just because we like their style. Silly and sentimental, huh?"

"Not really. Tell me more," Sherwood said. "Your whole case history. Case history! Do I sound too much like a lawyer?"

"Nothing wrong with that. I have nothing against lawyers. My brother is one and my father's a judge." My turn to grin. "But I've talked enough about myself. What about you? What kind of law do you practice?"

"The very boring kind. Trusts and estates."

The waiter arrived with our appetizers, which looked divine. Conversation stalled for several minutes as we dug in, both of us seemingly famished.

After two dumplings, my hunger was sated sufficiently for me to offer a polite, "I bet that's not a boring field at all. Confess, Sherwood, who are the celebrities you've worked with? Here in New Orleans, you must have clients among the musicians and chefs and . . ."

"Allow me to correct an assumption. I don't practice here. This bloke works in Manhattan. That's one reason I wanted to get to know you. Winnie said you live there and. . . ."

"I'd rather lost touch with Aunt Winnie for a while. The divorce from Sonny unsettled my life for a time and then to go to the place where we once lived and to find . . ."

"I won't go there then, Freddy. I'm so sorry for your loss."

"Thank you. But I don't mind talking about New York. I'm mad about the place. Tell me about your law firm there. I temped for a short time and for a few law offices, I may have been there."

Sherwood beckoned the waiter and ordered a second scotch.

"If you'd been at my firm, I assure you I would have noticed and . . ."

"How you do go on, Mr. Benjamin." I feigned an exaggerated southern accent. I guess we're both hams at heart. "But back to your legal career."

"Okay, Frédérique. I'll start with the name. Are you ready?"

"Should I be taking notes?"

Big smile. I loved the way Sherwood grinned at almost everything I said.

"Probably not. Remember, I told you it would be boring. But the firm name's a mouthful: Peters, Nelson, Benjamin, Simms & Fallon."

"You're a name partner. Impressive."

"It's a good firm I will say. Been around for over fifty years. I've been with them for almost twenty of that."

A busboy swept away our appetizer dishes as the waiter delivered our main course. As we dined on nut-sweet, succulent trout meunière and deep-fried eggplant sticks covered with powdered sugar, I decided Sherwood could dictate my dinner selection any time.

I glanced around. The place was packed, and it was just a weeknight. All the tables and booths were filled. Our entrées arrived and we lapsed into comfortable silence, save for both of us stealing glances out the window to catch a view of strolling tourists and sharing comments on same.

An older gentleman with a white beard and skin the color of mahogany stepped into view, then stood stock still and played a harmonica.

"That's Grandpa Elliott," Sherwood advised. "He usually sings as well I'm told. He entertained on the streets of Quarter for loose change for years, then he got famous via some worldwide musicians project. Now he's internationally known and has his own album out."

I said, "That's wonderful . . . how nice for him!" and returned to enjoying my spaghetti squash, determined to avoid the calories of the mashed potatoes.

As I paused to take a drink and resumed people watching, I saw what appeared to be a homeless man peering in at us. I couldn't seem to avoid looking back at him, it was such an unusual occurrence to experience at this upscale eatery. Suddenly he stepped back as two women came into view. I saw him attempt to grab the shoulder bag of one of them, only to have her execute some kind of karate chop on his upper body. He struggled away from her and grabbed for the purse once more. With that, the woman got him in an arm lock and lowered him to the sidewalk. By now, Sherwood had joined in observing the scene.

"Wow," he said, "who's that woman? I don't want to meet *her* in a dark alley."

The homeless guy rose slowly to his feet and staggered backward, then forward, seemingly determined to complete his mission. The woman made no attempt to leave, her solid frame in an erect posture as if she dared him to try again.

"Sherwood, that woman looks familiar."

"To me, too. It's obvious the poor chap is drunk. Even sober, I don't think he'd be a match for that heifer."

I had to smile to myself. "Heifer" was Jeannette's favorite term for women she didn't particularly care for. I had a brief moment of nostalgia as I mused on how much I missed her, and Buck too. I had no further time to ruminate over this as the action out on the street escalated.

Drunken homeless guy lunged for his prey and Miss Body Builder quickly averted his attack by flipping him head over heels and flat onto his back. A cop and one of G W Fin's waiters appeared on the scene.

"Wait a minute," Sherwood said. "The other woman I recognize. Yes, that's Bella. Absolutely, that's Dina and Bella."

The cop hauled hapless homeless guy away, and the waiter stepped out of view. The two women remained, chatting, then laughing, over the bizarre incident.

I studied them and realized whom Sherwood had identified. Bella was the taller, dark-haired one. Dina was the slightly overweight woman with the light brown pony-tail, our heroine who apprehended the would-be purse-snatcher. They were Sonny Bob's two stepsisters.

chapter 14

"GRAM IS EXPECTING you to come in for a nightcap, but if you'd rather not make a late night of it and . . ."

"Thank the Lord for grandmothers," Sherwood grinned. "I accept her kind invitation. Was hoping it would come from you, but I'll take Gram."

We had finished our meal at G W Fins pleasantly and compatibly, with after-dinner cocktails of Kahula and cream after the drunken-homeless-man episode and were now walking down the slate path to the Toussaint front porch.

"There you are!"

Gram opened the door before I could try my key. She'd obviously been spying from a window.

"I was worried about you, darlin'. It's getting pretty late."

"I'm a big girl," I smiled at Gram. "And I was in good hands."

We stepped inside. Even though the walk from Sherwood's car to the door was relatively short, it was—as usual—a noticeable relief to be in air conditioning once more.

"Well, it seems like there's plenty to worry about these days." Gram moved to get the sherry and I motioned that I'd do the honors. She and Sherwood sat down, Sherwood on the couch, Gram on one of the upright chairs.

"I don't want you worrying about anything, Gram." I placed a tray with the three glasses of sherry on the coffee table. I sat at the end of the couch, opposite from Sherwood.

"Tell that to the New York detectives."

"They were here?" Sherwood said.

"Oh, no, they called on the phone. They mostly repeated what the New Orleans detectives had asked me. I do want to help Sonny Bob, but I'm getting very tired of these sad conversations . . . oh, they did have a new piece of news."

Gram sipped her sherry and then seemed to lapse into one of her reveries.

"And that was?" I said.

"That was simply that poor Sonny Bob had also been hit over the head. With a blunt instrument, I believe they said. And from behind, as if that matters. They seemed to think it happened before he was . . . before he was . . . well, you know."

"Winifred filled me in on the whole story," Sherwood said. "What was Sonny Bob doing in your house, Freddy? Not that it's really any of my business but I just . . . "

"That's all right. It's a perfectly good question, but I don't know the answer. I never changed the locks after our divorce and, of course, Sonny had a key. It never occurred to me to ask for it back."

"Well, honey, that's because . . ."

"Probably because I'm not detail oriented." I smiled at Sherwood. I knew Gram was about to posit her you-and-Sonny-Bob-were-in-love-and-never-should-have-broken-up theory. Of late, I'd been doing a little of that same type of ruminating and it didn't help my peace of mind.

Gram picked up her glass of sherry and rose from her chair. "It's way past my bedtime, if you two will excuse me."

I didn't know if Gram was really tired or my interruption had offended her, but her tone was pleasant and her smile sincere.

I rose and walked her to the stairs. "I'll see you in the morning, Gram. How about my treating you to breakfast at Slim Goodies?"

"I'd like that, dear." She raised her chin and gave me a kiss on the cheek. "And be nice to that darling Sherwood. He's rather good looking, and he's a lawyer you know. You would do well to . . ."

I patted Gram's hand where it rested on the banister. "I'll turn on all the southern charm I'm capable of."

"Oh good, dear. Keep your New York personality at bay and try to . . ."

"I'll charm the pants off him, Gram," I grinned. "Now go to bed."

Gram shook her head. "I will. Just see that *you* don't. Go to bed, that is. With him. Just charm, never mind about the pants off part and don't . . ."

"You're relentless, Gram, but I love you. Can I help you up the stairs?"

"I'm going, dear girl, I'm going."

I joined Sherwood in the living room, planting myself on the chair Gram had vacated.

"I was going to tell Gram the story of the drunken homeless man," I said. "She'd probably find it amusing. At least I guess she would. Neither of us knew till the other day that Sonny Bob had two stepsisters."

"That's odd. Winifred seemed to know all about them."

"I'm surprised they didn't see that homeless man and immediately steer clear of him. Anyone who lives in New Orleans knows to be careful in the Quarter after dark."

'I'm sure they do," Sherwood said. "New Yorkers are savvy about such things too so why those girls wouldn't be cautious in a different city and . . ."

"Excuse me, are you saying Sonny's stepsisters don't live here?"

"Something else that's news to you?" Sherwood almost seemed to smirk. "I can see I need to take you out more often and bring you up to speed. Dina and Bella live in New York, Brooklyn to be exact."

"No, I need to sound out Aunt Winnie more often," I said, then stopped, realizing I'd in effect contradicted Sherwood's suggestion of future dates. I decided I'd better absorb this new information on my own time and that I should change the subject.

"Sonny liked that Winnie was so unconventional." I smiled at the memory of Winnie's former life and some of my and Sonny's get togethers with her.

"Really?" Sherwood rose and brought the sherry bottle over to the coffee table. He topped off our glasses. "Winnie seems like the soul of conventionality to me, a real lady."

"Oh, Winnie's always been a lady in the true sense of the word. It's just that she lived a somewhat bohemian life prior to the one she lives in New York City I'm sure. I'm not implying a lesser life, just a different one."

"She was a wild child?"

"In a sense. She did ride a motorcycle for a time. We didn't see her often I'm afraid. From time to time, she'd invite my mother, Gram and me over to her trailer park. She'd pack lunches and take them and us over to the community pool in her park. We'd eat poolside and enjoy the people watching. Everyone was so friendly and everyone knew Winnie."

"She's popular in New York also," Sherwood said. "But in very different venues. Winifred's on the board of the Metropolitan Opera and the ballet. She gives generously to several charities and, in some circles, is considered to be somewhat of a fashion leader."

I had to laugh. "Winnie was a fashion leader at the trailer park too. She hung out at their pool every day, and she'd color-coordinate her outfit. The rubber floater she used, her flip-flops, her hair clasp, even her beach towel, they all matched the bathing suit she was wearing that day. She had it down to a science. Gram used to turn her nose up at this preoccupation with pool wear. She'd sniff and say, 'I have better things to do with *my* time.'"

"It's good to see you laugh, Freddy. You've been looking as worried as your grandmother these past couple of days."

"I *am* worried. There's something I haven't mentioned. When Gram was interviewed by the NOPD detectives, she remembered one of the men who kidnapped Sonny had a name that sounded like 'baby'. . .and added with a 'p'.' The physical description she provided sounded a little like a guy who . . . well, I met with two friends of mine who gave me a contact name to use in my search for Sonny when I first flew to New York. One of them was named Beppe."

"Obviously you think one of the two Italian gentlemen could be one and the same chap."

"It's possible, and if I'm right, then Beppe lives here, but flew or drove to New York and possibly is involved in the murder of Sonny. The Beppe Gram met had a New York accent . . ."

"Or so your grandmother claims."

"Gram's pretty sharp about such things. The Beppe I met was short and he had a moustache. Gram says her guy was of medium height, no moustache, but her memory could be faulty. Also my Beppe may well have had a New York accent. I'm very used to New York accents and I may actually not have noticed. I was very nervous the day we met and . . ."

"You have friends who make you nervous, Freddy? Not a good thing, my dear." Sherwood fairly scowled.

"Oh, no . . ." I caught myself in my 'friends' white lie. "I was mostly just tired from my flight."

I took a gulp of sherry, and continued. "If it's the one and the same Beppe and he lives here, he may know, or has assumed, the police have interviewed Gram and . . ."

"He may think he can't afford to have her around as a witness."

"Exactly."

We sat quietly for a couple of minutes, sipped a little more sherry, and absorbed this deduction and its implications.

"You're probably worrying needlessly, Frédérique. All those mobster types look alike."

"Maybe so, but I can't dismiss the idea. If there's any chance whatsoever that Gram could be in danger . . ."

"She'll need police protection," Sherwood said.

"I would think so, but will NOPD see it that way? They may think the coincidence is not that big a deal."

"I went to law school with a guy who's practicing here. At least I think he still is. He has friends on the force. I'm sure he'd have some influence in that regard. I'll contact him."

"That would be great. As I told you, my brother's a lawyer. His practice is here in New Orleans, but I don't know if he's tight with the police department. He does corporate law."

"No need to contact your brother. Consider it done."

"Well, thanks, although my brother . . ."

"Your brother and your father, did I see them at the funeral?"

"No, Hank and Daddy are in Hawaii this month with their significant others. But it's dubious they would have attended anyway. They were once Sonny's friends but not for long. After a while they disliked him big time."

"They had bad business dealings?"

"No, it had to do with our marriage. Sonny was quite a gambler, mostly with my money and . . ."

Sherwood leaned toward me and took my hand in his. "I have to tell you, Freddy, how much I admire you. You always sit so straight and seem so calm. There's a stillness about you that is so compelling. Through all this tragedy, you are never anxious or restless. You are obviously a lady who's comfortable in her own skin."

"That's so nice of you to say, Sherwood." *I think I'm starting to like this guy.* "And I believe you yourself have probably been a source of strength for Winnie. She was so . . ."

I heard my cell phone's musical chimes. "Excuse me one moment."

I quickly headed to the hall to retrieve my purse. Grabbing it on the last ring, I breathlessly said, "Hello, it's Freddy."

"Good for you. Just exactly *where* are you?"

"I'm in New Orleans. Sad trip, for a funeral."

"Whose?"

"I thought I told you about it in a voicemail—Sonny Bob's."

"Good Lord."

I was in no mood to reiterate the recent events, so a change of subject was in order.

"How's things in California?"

"How the hell should I know? I'm back in New York. Got a gig here. Jeannette told me you'd been staying at some fleabag hotel in the Village so I crashed there, only to find you'd flown the coop so I . . ."

"Buck, may I call you back first thing tomorrow morning? We have company right now."

"Okay, babe. Check you later."

I carried the phone back into the living room.

"Important call?" Sherwood asked.

"Uh . . . friend from California. Private investigator I know. For some reason he's in New York."

Sherwood shot me a rather puzzled expression, which seemed to contain a hint of irritation.

Then I realized I was grinning from ear to ear.

chapter 15

THE AIR WAS muggy and heavy as I walked Sherwood to his car. I murmured some pleasantries about enjoying the evening. As I thanked him for the wonderful dinner, I realized I was absently looking off in the distance at a weeping willow tree and immediately concentrated on focusing upon this charming, courtly man who'd been so kind to me.

"I enjoyed it too, Frédérique. I'll be in New Orleans for a few more days. What are your plans?"

"I'll be here awhile too. Got to take advantage of this opportunity to visit with Gram. Do you know what Winnie's plans are?"

"Selah and I are her houseguests. In separate bedrooms I hope I need not add. We'll leave whenever she leaves, and she indicated she'll stay about three more days."

"That about jibes with my plans. Maybe we can all book a flight back together."

Sherwood's face lit up in one of his now-familiar lopsided grins. He was about six feet, with gray-blue eyes, a medium build and that pale skin that seems characteristic of many Englishmen. He had a slightly jowly face with close-together eyes under which there were dark circles and a long nose, but these imperfections didn't detract from his overall attractiveness.

Sherwood placed a warm hand on my elbow, bestowing a soft kiss on my cheek. "I'll call you tomorrow if I may."

"You may indeed," I smiled.

He climbed into his car, and I headed swiftly back inside to the welcoming coolness of Gram's house. I hurried up the stairs to my guest bedroom, knowing what I had to do next.

The call was answered after two rings. "Buck Lemoyne here."

"And Frédérique Bonnaire here. I know why I'm *here*. The question is why are you *there*?"

"Hey, kid, can't you add two plus two? You left a voice mail that you were in New York. You sounded like you were in trouble and needed help. Ergo, I'm here in New York."

"I'm touched, Buck, I really am. That's so sweet."

"I'm not being entirely altruistic, my little blonde friend, Martha is out here to audition for a play so I'm doing the usual handholding number."

Martha Fleming is a client of Buck's, a vibrant actress in her senior years who is as charming as she is talented, and that's a boatload. She hires Buck as a bodyguard whenever she ventures out to dangerous hinterlands such as Manhattan. I looked forward to the possibility of seeing her again.

For the next few minutes, I filled him in on the whole story: discovering Sonny Bob's body in my Park Slope home, the police interviews here and in New York, Gram's descriptions, even the funeral and wake details.

"Why do I feel like you're leaving something out?"

I realized I needed more of that sherry so my cell phone and I headed down to the living room. "Just a minute, Buck."

I laid the phone down on the couch, poured myself a glass, and sat down.

"When I first arrived here, Gram told me about Sonny's abduction. The bad guys doing the deed had New York accents she claimed. Their physical descriptions were also, shall we say, rather Italian in nature. I went to college with a guy from here, Alex DeCicco, who may or may not be a wiseguy. So I contacted him and, sure enough, he had me meet with two of his associates who provided a name in New York of a man who knows . . . knew . . . Sonny Bob and could lead me to him. I wanted to help. Obviously, Sonny was in danger;"

There was silence on the other end for about three beats.

"Also obviously, my enlisting your help in solving the murder of your friend Doris gave you delusions of grandeur, Fred."

I had to smile. "I'm sure that's true. It just seemed like the right thing to do."

Another moment of silence. Clearly, my impulsive and impetuous behavior was offending Buck's sense of logic.

"So what's the plan now, Fred? Heading back to Santa Monica when?"

"Heading for Manhattan in about three days."

This time I anticipated the silent intermission.

"I'm here and I'm waiting, my tall, tan, silent one." I couldn't resist teasing.

"You know I'm not tall, but you left out handsome and a number of other adjectives. You also left out *why* you're going back to New York so, I'll bite, why?"

I filled Buck in on the two or one-and-the-same-Beppe theory, about the related possibility of Gram being in danger, about the contact name I'd never had the chance to follow up on and had never revealed to the police, about my need to find out just what Sonny Bob had been involved in and why he'd been in my house.

"You never gave that name to the New York cops? Why in hell not?" The impatience in his voice was now in full throttle.

"Buck, I can explain further another time. I'll call you again when you get back to California."

I used this next period of silence to drain my sherry glass.

"Here's the deal, Freddy. Call me when you know your flight schedule; I'll meet you at the airport and we'll take it from there."

"I know I said I'd visit and spend some time there but right now I'm not going to California."

"Understood, babe. And neither am I."

chapter 16

THE NEXT MORNING I slept later than I'd intended. Looking at the clock and seeing it was already nine, I grabbed my robe and scurried downstairs. Gram was seated at the dining room table, dressed to the nines and touching up her nail polish, a cup of hot tea in front of her.

"Gram, have you already had breakfast? I planned to take you out."

"Haven't had one morsel, darlin', but you and I have other plans. Winnie called and she's havin' a whole mess of people at her place for a sumptuous repast of breakfast. At least that's what she called it, and, you know, you don't say no to Winifred."

I'd been looking forward having some alone time with Gram. "Gram, do we really . . . "

"Yes, we really do, Frédérique. Now hush and go get dressed. Roland's pickin' us up any minute now."

"Roland's coming too?" I'm a little slow on the uptake in the early hours.

"Yes, and Sherwood and that former spouse of his and Sonny Bob's two weird sisters and who knows who else. Winnie never does things by halves. Now go get dressed. Hurry!"

I took the stairs two steps at a time in deference to Gram's sense of urgency, had one of the quickest showers of my life and pulled on black jeans, a gray linen shirt and black suede flats. I slung my purse over one shoulder, stuffed my cell into a pocket and grabbed a hairbrush for additional grooming on the ride over. I raced down the stairs and just as I decided I'd brush my hair in the hall mirror, the doorbell rang and I opened it to a beaming Roland Figgins.

Gram arrived, fairly floating toward us as if we suddenly had all the time in the world. She smiled at Roland, extended her hand and he kissed it. I stood there, still panting from my recent marathon of preparation, my hair sticking out at odd places. Neither of them seemed to notice this. *Young love.*

At Winnie's, Morgan the bartender had become Morgan the butler. As he opened the door for us, we were greeted by a hum of chattering voices, both male and female. Circling a long buffet table laden with silver serving dishes of scrambled eggs, sausages, bacon, and biscuits together with bowls of fruit were Sherwood, his ex Selah, a couple of other women from the funeral whose names I still did not know, Sonny Bob's two stepsisters and a slim, black teenage boy I did not recognize. We three took our places in line, filled our plates, then followed the others out to the patio.

Winnie's patio was not tiny but several round glass tables were pressed very close together to accommodate all the people present and more, she informed us, were on their way. Morgan, in bartender mode after all, brought Mimosas to we new arrivals, and I ended up at a table with Sherwood, stepsisters Bella and Dina, and the teenager who turned out to be Morgan's college-bound son. No elitist Winnie. At the table immediately to our left were Gram and Roland, the unnamed women and Selah.

Winnie rose and walked around the tables, making introductions. Everyone was in a happy, cordial mood, thanks in no small measure to constant refills of our champagne by Morgan. At one point, I rested one hand momentarily on the table, and Sherwood pressed it with his hand. At this Selah leapt from her seat, stood behind Sherwood murmuring something about their flight schedule and ended her brief dissertation with a prolonged caress of his shoulder before returning to her seat. I never ran into Sonny Bob after our divorce, but I could not imagine similar behavior on my part had I done so. Selah baby was truly an enigma. Just then she looked over at me with beady, ferret eyes as if she could read my thoughts.

A moment later, the cell phone in my pocket rang. I grabbed it quickly and pressed it to my ear, feeling somehow guilty at the banal disturbance of this gracious southern morning. Turned out someone else had flight schedules on the brain.

"Hi Buck, what's up?"

"You probably tried to call me with your arrival time, Freddy . . ."

I'd forgotten.

". . . but I've been out of pocket for almost a whole day, so lay it on me, babe."

Out of pocket? Buck's cell was a constant and alive extension of his arm. He never turned it off, or so it seemed, and took calls everywhere. Maybe my private eye buddy had enjoyed a romantic interlude when he wasn't squiring Martha. I dismissed the speculation . . . damn, I could be silly at times . . . and recited my latest flight details and ETA. Everyone seemed to find my call of great interest as conversation faded away as I spoke.

"Friend's meeting me in New York," I smiled. No one seemed to heed this needless explanation, leaving me feeling extra foolish.

Why were Buck's calls invariably so unnerving?

chapter 17

ROBERTO GAGLIANO. COULD the name be any more Italian? Could this whole scenario surrounding Sonny Bob's death smack any more of a Mafia enterprise?

These were some of the questions I was asking myself as I soared through the sky on my red-eye Continental Airlines flight back to New York. I had decided not to wait and fly back with Aunt Winnie, Sherwood and his ex-missus, as interesting as that prospect might be. Buck was proving to be more than a go-the-extra-mile type friend. The least I could do is not waste any more of his time than was necessary.

Arriving back at Gram's after Winnie's breakfast event, I had called Buck with more data, adding, for good measure, the name of Roberto Gagliano, the contact for Sonny Bob provided by Alex DeCicco's friends Gio and Beppe. It behooved me to stop being coy about my mission to find Sonny Bob on my own and share information with Buck. Now, of course, my quest was to find a killer, and the supposition that I was equipped to do that by myself was even more bizarre than the former premise.

A friendly steward brought the scotch and water I'd ordered, and I just sat staring into the drink as if the answers to *who* this friend of Sonny Bob's, this Roberto Gagliano, could be and *what* he could be lay floating between the ice cubes.

There was another puzzling question, albeit a minor one. Who was the mysterious woman who rather covertly attended Sonny Bob's burial? She wasn't at the wake at Aunt Winnie's house and when I later mentioned her to Winnie, she could not recall anyone she knew who fit that description. I decided my need to know was motivated more by romantic jealousy than crime-solving speculations.

I needed to focus on the mystery of the Beppe character and if the bad guy was the local friend of Alex's. If my Beppe was Gram's Beppe and had a part in Sonny's death, he would not be happy about my grandmother's good memory and powers of observation, assuming he'd learned of her informative interview. In the gossip mills of New Orleans, both in the underworld and in general society, such a possibility was highly probable.

And, of course, there lingered the initial questions of what Sonny was doing in my Brooklyn brownstone and what person or persons apparently hit him over the head and then stabbed him. The ornate spear used in the murder was not from my home. Who walks around carrying such a thing? And the most important question of all: *why* did someone want him dead?

I glanced over at the passenger next to me: a slim woman, of about seventy or so, who was enjoying a glass of red wine and reading the *The Times-Picayune*. She was thoroughly absorbed in the sports page, specifically the draft picks for the New Orleans Saints, my favorite football team. I had to smile to myself, thinking she was my kind of woman. The inner smile must have made its way to my exterior, as she suddenly looked up and over at me.

"I hate getting my news from this silly paper," she said. "Forgot my reading glasses to boot. Wish they'd show the news on those TV screens, instead of that ridiculous movie.

If it's not on the Fox evening news," she smiled, "I don't know it happened."

"I'm the same way. Never get around to subscribing to a paper, just pick them up from bubble machines."

"What brings you to New Orleans?"

The funeral of my ex-husband seemed too heavy an answer to lay on this lighthearted woman.

"I'm visiting relatives."

"That's nice. Me too."

"Do you watch Fox news? It's the only channel I ever watch."

"Mostly I surf different channels," I answered.

"I see." She returned to her newspaper. Apparently, my lack of commitment to a favorite news channel left no room for further conversation.

I finished off my scotch and mused as to whether I should have a second. Then I mused further on my companion's conversation, and the proverbial light bulb popped over my head. The short, well-built woman at Sonny's funeral. I *had* seen her somewhere before—she was the newscaster on the street outside my home on the day of Sonny's murder. Did her presence in New Orleans consist of further follow up on the story? What could she expect to find in the way of leads at a funeral?

It had already been a long day, and my drink had made me drowsy. I decided to put a lid on all the cogitating going on in my head and surrender to a nap.

chapter 18

"YOUNG LADY, WE'RE here."

My seventy-something seat companion patted me on the knee to advise we were about to arrive at our destination. I'd dozed off and now I still felt groggy, fatigued, and decidedly regretful that I'd elected to take a late flight, arriving at one in the morning and in New Jersey yet. I'd selected a flight to Newark Airport because I was determined to get to New York as soon as possible and that was the only flight that met my schedule. Buck thought it crazy that I'd amended my original morning flight. He was further frustrated that I'd then be taking a van from Newark directly to my hotel, and he would have to cool his heels and meet me there rather than JFK or LaGuardia. *If I didn't know better, I'd think the man was yearning for a romantic airport rendezvous.*

One pleasant aspect of my resolution to get my life back on track was the warmhearted reception when I contacted Marc Caress, the lovely man who was my booking agent for modeling gigs before I drifted away from my career and became a nomad in the city. I'd left a message for him and, ever gracious, he was not only glad to hear from me but eager to get me back to work.

Another bonus was when he learned of where I'd been staying he advised me of a new hotel in Chelsea between

Sixth and Seventh Avenues on the West Side that catered to models. It was appropriately named Fashion 26, and it was there that I'd made reservations for my return. Howie, my accountant and erstwhile home maintenance provider, had informed me my Park Slope brownstone was not yet in habitable condition so a hotel was the best solution, despite Aunt Winnie's insistence I stay with her.

We landed and I joined my fellow passengers as we slowly filed down the aisle, waddling in Penguin mode, lugging our carry-on's, all of us bleary eyed and rumpled. I'd done this Newark run once before so I knew where to go for the van. I arrived at the shuttle desk, then looked around. It was a more popular time of day to be flying the friendly skies than I'd anticipated and every seat in the area was filled. Mothers were holding children on their laps and one teenage girl sat on her boyfriend's lap. An unoccupied place to rest did not appear imminent. I decided I'd rather get some air than stand around looking hopeful, so I inquired about the locale of the incoming van and headed out, pulling my suitcase behind me.

The temperature was almost cool. An early smell of September was in the air. I never failed to be enchanted by fall in Manhattan, autumn leaves, street vendors roasting chestnuts, the chance to wear cozy coats and sweaters, new shows on Broadway, the whole bit. I stood on the curb, taking in the inky sky and bright lights, for a mere five minutes or so when a light-colored van pulled up and stopped. I could barely make out the driver but I could hear him. He leaned toward the passenger side, calling out "Frédérique Bonnaire!"

I couldn't believe my ears. Now this was personalized service beyond the call of duty!

As I stepped off the curb to approach the van, a side door slid open and two men grabbed each of my arms. I only managed to cry out "What the . . ." before I was pushed to the floor of the van and tape was slapped over my mouth and eyes. I was then rolled to my side, my arms were yanked behind my back, and metal handcuffs clicked onto my wrists. One man sat me up as the other pulled my legs forward, then pushed them back so my knees were in a bent position. One or both of them, it was hard to discern, commenced to tie my ankles with rope.

For maximum in-flight comfort, I'd worn a caftan style black jersey dress and Ugg boots. The first thought that occurred to me as I sat on a rough wooden surface in that hogtied position was that my dress was now up around my hips and my panties were probably showing. What panties had I put on this morning? The black or the see-thru nude? *Clearly I'd spent too much of my life in a profession where appearance was all.*

With my wrists bound behind me, one arm pressed against my shoulder bag, causing its contents to poke uncomfortably against my waist. As I always did when out in New York, I'd crossed the bag's strap across my chest to ward off any would-be purse-snatchers. The goons had made no effort to separate me from my bag so clearly they were not interested in theft of the forty-one dollars and three quarters it contained.

I heard some shuffling, breathy sighing and a crackling sound. The shoe or boot of one of my kidnappers pressed against my hip and I moved myself to the left to avoid his touch. I guessed they were now resting with their mission accomplished, sitting on what had felt like large cardboard boxes that I'd bumped up against when they first tossed me inside.

Kidnappers. I'd thought the word before its meaning really resonated with my conscious mind. The two men were silent. One lit a cigarette.

This dilemma of course brought to mind the abduction of Sonny Bob from New Orleans. I'd lost all sense of direction since being tossed into the van and wondered if somehow these were the same thugs who'd captured Sonny and if this portended that I would be taken back to New Orleans. Such a long trip would be a hideous ordeal in this uncomfortable vehicle, not only for me but for the two cretins who'd grabbed me. I decided it served me better to think about escape tactics than to worry about our itinerary.

Think, Freddy, think! Buck had given me instructions on what to do were I ever attacked. I searched my now headachy brain for some of Buck's tips. *Act confident and authoritative whenever you're in public.* Well, I was right on message there. I'd confidently stepped right up to an unrecognizable van, with no commercial signage on it, and authoritatively responded to a strange driver who somehow knew my name. *Brilliant, Frédérique.*

What further advice had private eye extraordinaire Lemoyne imparted? *Keep your_distance and your cool. Maintain more than an arm's reach between you and strangers, whenever physically possible.* I was a few feet from the van driver at the time of my abduction; but when his goons grabbed both my arms, countermanding our physical intimacy became beyond my control.

Create a scene. If grabbed, go crazy. Yell, flail, fight, scream obscenities or shout "Fire," do anything in your power to draw attention to the situation. Good advice from Joseph Buckley. I guess my "What the . . .?" decidedly lacked dramatic impact.

What else had Buck said? *Run, just run. The odds of escaping without taking a bullet are in your favor. Even New York cops only hit an average of thirty-one percent of moving targets, even when firing from close range.* Well, gosh, that was helpful. At last, some advice I may well need to put into action whenever we arrive at our destination.

Finally one man spoke. "See that cooler over there. Grab me a beer."

I heard the pop of one beer can opening, then another, then the rattling of paper.

"Gonna be a hell of a long ride."

A slightly different voice, must be the second man. *Both men had decidedly New York accents, fluent Brooklynese in fact.*

A paper snap, as if to give emphasis to the damnable travel length.

"Oh, shut up, Beppe, and gimme the sports page."

Beppe.

chapter 19

It is to be assumed that years of modeling preceded by the example of my chic French mother would prepare me to be appropriately garbed for any occasion, *n'cest pas*? However, years of *Vogue* shoots and runway gigs plus the glamorous example of *ma mère* had not provided direction for proper attire when one rides cuffed, roped and taped in a stuffy van on a warm, humid night in Jersey. Because I usually find the temperature on planes to be freezing, I'd added a black sweater to my jersey dress and this now raised my body temperature a notch or two. I could feel sweat beading on my forehead and a dampening under my arms. The Ugg boots, which were great for a chilly plane, were a hot disaster now, and my feet began to itch.

Well, I could at least remedy the revealed-panties situation so I stretched my legs forward from the bent-knee position first dictated.

"Hey!" One of my two charming companions broke the silence.

"What's wrong?" From the other one.

"Nuthin'. She moved."

Control freaks. What did they think I was going to do? Throw myself against one side of a ten-thousand-pound van and thereby escape through an opening?

"Do we got dumb luck or what?" One of my captors posed a question, then giggled.

"Huh?" The other responded. Then, finding some pore in the thick wall of his understanding, he said, "Don't say it's dumb, you idiot. Tell the boss we planned it this way."

"Yeah, but we was just gonna follow her. Who knew she'd walk right into our arms?"

Now they both giggled, and I heard the sound of beer cans popping once more, one of many such pops since my friends first imbibed.

"Where'd yah get them cuffs?"

I now knew one of my hosts was named Beppe but thus far, the other name had not been mentioned. I tried to recall Alex DeCicco's two friends I met with back in New Orleans. Wasn't one of them called Beppe, I asked myself of the umpteenth time, still not believing this kind of coincidence. They never introduced themselves, but the name rang a bell in my throbbing head in which several bells seemed to be currently chiming.

The other of my fellow travelers had a deeper, gruffer voice, so I imagined him to be the larger of the two. In mind I labeled them Mr. Big and Mr. Little. Mr. Big had voiced the cuffs inquiry.

"Ain't they somethin'? My sister-in-law's cousin used to be a cop. Took 'em off him last time they was over. Jerk drinks like a fish, probably don't remember where he coulda left 'em." This, of course, from Mr. Little.

"Look like new." An observation from Mr. Big.

"Dunno. When Henry saw 'em, he said they were Smith and Wesson Model 100 double lock."

"Henry oughta know," Big declared, and they both laughed over some private joke.

"Who gonna talk to her when we get there?" A question from Little.

"Who the hell knows. Frankie R. maybe."

"Not Mr. Big?"

"Nah. You ever met him?"

"Me? Hell no. I dunno if Frankie has. He don't tell me his name, so I just decides to call him Mr. Big. Whatta I know?"

Well, gosh, fellas. We're on the same page after all. All of us are referencing a Mr. Big. Clearly great minds think alike.

After this wry observation on my part, sobriety returned and I mused on the reality of my situation. So someone was going to talk to me. Was this a good sign? Did it ordain that no one was planning on killing me? Or should I assume Mr. Big or some other interrogator would question me, and *then* kill me? This had to be about Sonny Bob. No one else I knew had been murdered lately or had done anything to provoke this type of criminal action against me.

But what about Sonny? I doubted these were concerned citizens bent on vigilante justice with a mission to avenge Sonny's death. Did they possibly not know Sonny was dead and think I could lead them to him? Given Sonny's gambling and often reckless lifestyle, it was very possible he owed money to some shady characters. But what had that to do with me? Had these goons adopted creditor mentality with the assumption that the spouse was now liable for Sonny's debts? Had they been highly inefficient and not checked with Dunn & Bradstreet and determined I *had* no resources?

My attempt at deductive reasoning was interrupted as the van came to an abrupt halt.

"Yah gotta untie her feet."

"Yeah, I know."

"Better take the cuffs off too."

"Hey, what is this? A social event?"

"Beppe, where the hell's she gonna go?"

"Okay, okay. You're right."

Beppe, I assume, performed this mission of mercy. The rope was removed from my feet. It was a relief to bring my arms forward and rub my wrists once the cuffs were off.

The familiar sound of popping a beer can open.

"Why yah stoppin' for another beer now for hell's sake?"

"Hey, I'm gonna relax and drink while she goes."

"Make it the last one. You've had enough."

"Screw you! You've had as many as me, asshole."

I could have joined this fascinating consumption debate, but I was still absorbing the 'while she goes' comment. Where was I going?

The next sound was of the van door sliding open.

At least one of them got out and then pulled me forward from the van and into a standing position. The ground beneath me was cement.

"Hold her while I pee, then I'll take her."

Oh, *that* kind of 'going.' We were simply making a restroom stop.

It was Mr. Big—*my* Mr. Big, not the one who presumably was their Godfather, consigliore or corporate strategist—who spoke. So Little, or Beppe, and I stood together for a few short minutes, his hand tightly gripping my arm.

I tried to absorb my surroundings, the better to describe them to NYPD Blue when my inevitable rescue occurred. It wouldn't be long. Isn't that the way it always happened on *Law & Order?* But there was nothing to absorb. I heard no other voices. Indeed, no other sounds other than a faint suggestion of distant traffic. There were no distinct smells. Detective Goren, *Law & Order-Criminal Intent,* would be sorely disappointed in me.

"You go. I've got her."

Little departed and my opposite arm was grabbed. *Whatever happened to ladies first?* Again, a brief wait.

"What are you clowns doin'?" A third voice. Had to be the driver.

"Takin' a leak, whatta yah think?"

"I'm next."

"Okay, okay. Just hurry it up."

Another wait.

"You guys got beer?"

"Almost gone. Anyways youse is drivin'. Don't even think about it."

"Go to hell!"

Boys, boys. You really should learn to get along.

"Take her."

"Why me?" Little was apparently protesting the assignment of being my ladies room escort.

"Why not you, asshole? Get it done!"

These losers really needed an anger management class.

Little grabbed my arm and quickly pulled me forward a few feet and to the left. I heard a door creak open. I was shoved forward. It was closed behind me. I stretched out my arms and then lowered them and felt the rim of a toilet seat. I turned around, pulled down my panties, either the black ones or the nude ones, and let Mother Nature take her course. What relief. We appreciate the simple pleasures of life in times of duress. I practically felt grateful to my captors for this respite. Is this how Stockholm Syndrome begins?

Being alone in this tiny room also felt like a kind of freedom. I longed to simply remain seated here and somehow wish this whole nightmare away. A knock on the door.

"Hurry it up in there! I know you're not puttin' makeup on."

I could hear them laugh at this. Clearly, they were feeling the numerous beers or were just easily amused. *Think, Freddy, think.* Is there any way to escape at this moment? My mouth and eyes were taped, but my arms and legs were free. Surely this should constitute some kind of advantage. I thought some more. *Act crazy.* That had been one of Buck's admonitions should one get captured or apprehended in any way. I stood up. For good measure, I mussed up my hair, removed the tape from my eyes and then my mouth— painful! —and smeared my lipstick a little.

I yelled. "Open the damn door!"

"Okay, okay!" I heard the door creak open. "Yah can't turn the damn knob yourself?"

"You bumbling idiot!" I waved my arms wildly in a circular motion and shouted. "You bind and gag me, you don't feed me, you don't give me anything to drink."

The two men were mostly enveloped by darkness, but I could see that Little *was* little. He tried to grab my arms and I stepped backward. And Big *was* big, mostly courtesy of a potbelly, and he was the taller of the two. They both darted back and forth a lot, making it hard to discern their facial features, but I could make out they were wearing cut off jeans and tee shirts.

"Where's the damn tape? Get the tape!"

"How do I get the tape? I don't see it."

"Beppe, you moron, in the bathroom. Gotta be in there."

I was learning something every minute. Little was not only little and a moron but he was Beppe. Wherever we were, there were no street or store lights. I couldn't be certain he was the Beppe I met back in Metairie, courtesy of the meeting arranged by my old college buddy Alex, or a Beppe I did not know. How many people could there be cursed with the name of Beppe? In the Italian community, maybe dozens of poor souls.

We appeared to be in an abandoned gas station. Beppe headed to the bathroom.

"You cussed idiot," I yelled. He grabbed one of my arms. I waved the other arm around and bounced up and down. "Why don't you just tell me what you want? Are you crazy? Are you madmen? You're not civilized!" I stamped one foot and then the other. Then I bounced up and down again, danced around in a circle and let out a guttural yell.

I screamed, *"J'en ai ras le bol!"* I was simply adding I was fed up and had had it, but figured it wouldn't hurt to throw in a little French to further irritate them.

"You nutso broad! Beppe!"

"I got it. I got the tapes."

I shrieked and struggled to get away from B gasp. I let out a string of insults, first in English, then French. I rolled my eyes, shook my arms and legs like an out-of-control puppet and spat at them.

"Put 'em on. Put one on her eyes." Beppe did so. I yelled again, and let out a stream of curses while I still could. Big pasted the other tape on my mouth.

They were both strong enough to stop my movements, but they seemed at least somewhat unnerved by all my histrionics. I flailed about and bounced some more.

"Hold still, bitch. You're gettin' on my last nerve." A complaint from Big.

I stopped moving, stopped the heavy breathing I'd adopted and stood still. "Hmph," I said softly through the tape and nodded my head up and down as if to acquiesce. I drooped my shoulders to signal resignation, and held my arms forward, wrists together.

"That's better. Beppe, yah got the cuffs?"

Beppe clamped the cuffs once again on my wrists.

I dropped my head and made crying sounds.

"Oh give it a rest." Big's voice. "Let's get her back in."

They each took an arm, walked me back to the van, lifted me inside. They got inside. I heard the door slide shut. The van's motor turned over, we began moving, slowly at first, then faster.

I was sitting on the floor once again. I raised my knees up and rested my cuffed wrists between them. I lowered my head, made myself as much as possible into a round ball. A kidnapped victim who was now prepared to sleep.

But I'd accomplished the small victory I'd desired. *My arms were now cuffed in front of me, not in back.*

chapter 20

Après la pluie, le beau temps, Gram would say about now. Indeed, it did feel like the storm was over and I was experiencing a kind of calm. After our eventful restroom stop, we seemed to travel for what felt like another hour. We once again stopped, and once again Big and Beppe roughly pulled me from the van and escorted me through a door. In this case, it wasn't a lavatory. I had a sense it was a larger room, although not by much.

They shoved me down to the floor and I sat. There followed a brief conversation as to just what to do with me next.

"We oughta feed her." This from Beppe, my sudden benefactor.

"You want I should get the chef?" Big's retort, and they both laughed.

"Mmmmmmmmmph." This from me, trying to signal I voted for the 'feed her' option.

This was simply met by more laughter.

"We're supposed to go to Frankie's now. He'll know the plan," said Big.

"Should we take her to the bathroom before we go?"

"Whatta yah in love, Bep? Let her sit and pee herself. She gets loony at bathroom stops. We ain't no nursemaids. Let's go, I need breakfast."

I listened as their footsteps receded, then the whoosh sound of what must have been a door opening and closing, as the sound of their footsteps receded.

This was the *calm* period. As in the brief respite in the restroom, being alone felt like a kind of freedom. For some reason, I thought of the period in my life right after I told Sonny I wanted a divorce and moved out of our Manhattan co-op. I didn't hate him or dislike him. I'd simply decided *we* were all wrong. I hadn't lusted for freedom per se, but when it came it felt sweet. Was solitude to be my fate? I seemed to sabotage relationships since becoming single.

Stop this introspection, Frédérique. You'd best concentrate on your current fate.

I knew the first thing I planned to do, but I wanted to be sure Big and Beppe were truly gone. There was no certain way to determine this, save to wait it out a while longer and hope this was the case. Their conversation and Big's plan to go get breakfast was a good indication of this, but I did not feel so cool, calm and collected that I wasn't still in a state of fear.

The good news was that toward what turned out to be the end of our journey, my escorts began slurring their words courtesy of the multiple brewskis. Thus they didn't see the contradiction in their determination to keep my eyes and mouth tightly taped—they applied fresh tapes at our new location—and the fact that my hands were now in front of me, and I could easily remove these restraints. That was my first plan of action, but I wanted to make sure they were good and gone.

I also thought of my cell phone, still in the purse draped across my chest. It was a small, black suede purse that blended into my black sweater. That was the only reason I could deduce that my captors had left it intact. I'd turned the cell off while on the plane, but I'm sure Buck had been frantically pacing the lobby at my hotel and calling me for the past few hours. I thought of it when I was in the gas station restroom. Buck had a new cell phone number, and I didn't know it by heart. It was in my address book, which was in my suitcase, which was still resting outside Newark Airport . . . or stolen. I could also call 911, but what would I say? I had no idea whatsoever of my location, could not even make a wild guess. Maybe this time when I removed the tape from my eyes, something definitive about where I was would be revealed.

Yeah, right, Freddy, you'll just roll yourself out a door and make note of a street address.

In the movies, I would now be in an abandoned warehouse in some remote industrial section, and I had no reason to think my current true-life situation was any different. Why else would they so confidently leave me alone, unguarded?

Maybe I was by water, the sea or the docks. I thought of City Island, a small town at the edge of New York City just beyond Pelham Bay Park in the Bronx and surrounded by the waters of the Long Island Sound. I'd recently seen a film about the area and it seemed quaint.

The heat and hunger had obviously gotten to me. I was now hoping to be held captive by these goons in an area with scenic charm.

About now, Gram would say, *Donner sa langue au chat.* By which she would mean stop guessing, give up. Literally it translates to give your tongue to the cat. Pierre, my red-haired Persian, would appreciate that irony.

Agreeing with my imaginary Gram comment, I decided to focus on immediate solutions. Given my captors' first stop at an abandoned gas station, I was probably now in an abandoned motel. One that boasted a restaurant that had closed down fairly recently, given the remnants of food smells. Every so often I felt a sort of rumbling vibration from the floor. I was probably near a railroad.

The time had come to remedy at least some of my discomfort. I pulled the tape from my mouth. Actually tapes plural, and, boy, did it hurt. My eye area was next. There'd been no mirror in the gas station restroom, and I couldn't tell if that first tape removal had taken off my eyebrows or not. Could I later convince my booker, Marc, that *W* and *Bazaar* preferred a model *sans* brows? More to the point, would I have a *later*?

I pressed my lips together to recapture feeling and lightly patted the surrounding area the way the girls at my favorite nail salon did just after waxing my brows and area under my nose. It didn't really help then and it didn't accomplish much now. *Okay, cease the self-pity and do the eyes.*

I bowed my head and yanked the tape. Owwwww-wch! I pressed my palms against my forehead for another brief recovery period. After a minute or so, I raised my head and looked around. I was in . . . a kitchen.

A kitchen contains knives. It was time for some action. I made fists of my hands and pushed myself up on my knees. From there I pushed, and rocked myself backward to a standing position. As soon as I was upward, I felt dizzy from the lack of food and rest, but I'd anticipated this and had moved next to the cabinet so that if I was inclined to reel backward—which immediately occurred—there'd be something to break my fall.

I stood still for a few minutes to get my bearings and adapt to the now strange condition of actually being upright. The idea was to find a knife and saw away at the rope binding my ankles. I hopped over to a counter containing several drawers. None contained knives. I looked around the room. Silly me, a large wooden knife holder rested on a counter across the room. I managed to hop over to it, despite feeling slightly faint. I chose a knife and lowered myself to a sitting position. I sawed and sawed but the rope was less fragile than it appeared.

Deciding I simply needed more strength to apply to the task, I rose and hopped over to the refrigerator. Fumes smelling like Italian sauces hit me. Behind a large jar was what I'd hoped for—a tall bottle of water. I managed to get the top off and, after spilling a potion, gulped down most of it. I again stood quietly for a few minutes and once more surveyed my surroundings.

There were two doors in the small kitchen, the one Big and Beppe had exited—I knew their departure sounds were to my left—which undoubtedly led to a dining area of some sort and a side door which I supposed and hoped led to the outside . . . and my escape. This was the height of optimism on my part—not that the door led to an outdoor area, but that once outside there'd be some method available to me to get far enough away to be safe. The realistic possibility I hoped for was that there would be surroundings that I could identify and thus call the police, give my location and await a speedy rescue.

It was time to achieve more freedom. Still feeling weak, I sat down on the floor. I could now walk around and see. I could also talk, had there been anyone to listen. I thought about my cat Pierre, safe in the care of my friend Jeannette, but undoubtedly grieving for me. Ever since my divorce, Pierre had become my closest companion. When I was alone at home, I was not really alone. There was always Pierre to talk to and, call me guilty of anthropopathy, he was an intelligent listener and most of the time responded, albeit in his own catspeak.

Okay, Frédérique, your favorite feline isn't here so it behooves you to rely on a certain Cajun, one Buck Lemoyne.

Along with Buck's lectures on what I should do if mugged or attacked, together with a course on shooting guns he'd insisted I take, was a physical demonstration on how to get out of handcuffs. The only problem was Buck baby had a special tool for this. He failed to provide me with one of these and, even if he had, I doubt I'd have sufficient paranoia to be in the habit of toting it around on a daily basis along with life's real necessities such as my American Express card, lipstick and a really good hairbrush.

I then did what any strong, resolute, brave-in-the-face-of-danger woman would do—*I cried.* I downright sobbed and used my three pieces of Kleenex to good advantage.

That catharsis accomplished, I returned to planning and speculated I could go out the back door while still handcuffed, but I didn't want to have that constraint. Suppose my two thug buddies had one of their associates posted outside that door. Like the driver—what had happened to him? I might not be as unguarded as I hoped. My fantasy was to be free of these cuffs and, before venturing outside, to have a couple of knives in my little handbag and one in my hand. It might be foolhardy to think I could thereby overcome possible clones of Big and Beppe, who'd undoubtedly be armed, but a girl can dream.

chapter 21

I CAST ABOUT for something that resembled the wire-type instrument Buck used in his how-to-open-handcuffs-when-you-don't-have-the-key demonstration. The collection of knives yielded nothing that looked sufficiently slender, but I picked up the smallest one available, then sat on the floor to commence the operation. The chain linking the two cuffs was long enough to allow me some maneuverability, but the knife's tip was too large to be effective. I put the knife down knife and leaned back against the cabinets, my head throbbing from the effort and from my continuing hunger.

Oh, Buck, when you thought to provide instructions on how to open handcuffs in an emergency, why didn't it occur to you I just might not have your precise tool at the ready? You were in the habit of often seeming to regard me as a very girly, impractical, stereotypical clotheshorse of a model so why didn't . . .

As I thus peevishly ruminated, my memory slipped back to a spring evening when we were having coffee in an outdoor cafe. The restaurant's music drifted outside—some selection from my favorite Broadway show, *Les Miserables*. In my mind's eye I saw us giggling together. The laughter was in response to something I'd said, and then Buck made a serious comment.

The proverbial light bulb burst above my aching brain as Buck's remark played across my consciousness.

"Of course, Fred, if all else fails, you can use a common everyday bobby pin."

I never use bobby pins, but I remembered palming a few of Gram's to have in case I wanted to ponytail my mop in response to New Orleans' famous humidity. Could I be lucky enough to have them with me? I usually carry purses big enough to contain necessities for a trip to Europe, but today's little suede number was an accommodation to the ease of travel. Still, I turned my cuffed hands to my left and, through a series of twists and turns, managed to get the purse in front of me and then dump the contents out on my lap. Spread out before me were what I expected: a credit card holder, two pieces of gum, some cash, coins, lipstick and a blush compact.

I moved my hand around the bottom of the purse and felt something promising: toothpicks. I held one up for inspection. Possible, but not probable. Too fragile. I rummaged around some more and felt something else: *bobby pins*! Three of them. God bless Gram. The upper rubber end didn't look like a solution, but perhaps the bottom tip . . . then I remembered Buck had addressed this very dilemma.

I did as he'd instructed. After the little tip was clear of the plastic, I bent the end that had been concealed and inserted it into the keyhole.

There was another step. I recalled wondering about it at the time. I took the bobby pin and bent it the other way so that it ended up in an angle.

Again, I inserted the pin into the keyhole, continuing to plumb my memory for Buck's exact words. He had pulled out two casserole dishes and rustled up shrimp amandine and asparagus au gratin that night. Afterward, we'd cleared the dishes, retaining our glasses of chardonnay as we bent our heads over the handcuff procedure.

My stomach rumbled on cue at the memory of food, and my head pain felt like it had spread to my very teeth, but I persevered.

What did Buck say next? *Think.*

I remembered: "On the very edge take the bobby pin and bend it down. This will release the latches that will open the jaws of the handcuffs."

Think some more, Frédérique.

"If you have a double lock, put the bobby pin in the keyhole on the other side, release the double lock, turn it around to release the latches and open the jaw."

Buck had gone through this procedure twice, and apparently my concentration had been complete and, thankfully, uncompromised by the wine.

I followed these steps. The jaws opened!

I was free! Now there were no tapes and my arms and legs were unrestrained. But Big and Beppe could return at any moment. I'd been lucky they'd stayed away this long. It was time to dive for that door and get the hell out of here. If I found myself on a deserted highway, I'd just have to run, not walk, toward the nearest sign of civilization. I was hardly in shape for a jog, but in the midst of danger, you had better fake it.

I opened the door and received the shock of my life. As it turned out, I needed only to walk a few steps and hail a cab.

I was on a street in the middle of New York City's Little Italy.

chapter 22

THE GARMENT DISTRICT in New York City is approximately one square mile bordered by the Javits Convention center at the extreme west, the James Farley General Post Office, Penn Station and Madison Square Garden in the center, and the Empire State building in the east. No longer the textile-manufacturing hub of the U.S., it remains the fashion capital for designers, couture houses and showrooms. In this area are the domains of designers such as Nicole Miller—who never looks her fifty-eight years, much less like a mogul with an empire of clothes, eyewear, perfumes and a bed and bath line—along with Anna Sui, Oscar de la Renta and Calvin Klein.

It was in this neighborhood that I made my hotel reservations for my return to New York City. The name of the hotel was Fashion 26 and it was located on 26th Street, a combination of facts easy to remember even in my present altered mental state. So it was with great confidence that I caught a taxi on Mulberry Street and directed the driver to my memorized destination. If he was less than impressed with my messy hairdo and wrinkled clothes, to say nothing of a crying need for a shower and deodorant, a client who promptly supplied a precise name and address surely appeased him.

My cabbie maneuvered smoothly and skillfully through the usual Manhattan bumper-to-bumper traffic but then came to a screeching halt in front of my hotel—an action

I took to signal, "Get out, lady, and get out fast!" I had exact change for his charge and tip, so I was able to comply. On the way, I'd called the hotel and learned Buck had waited all this time in the lobby, so I was just as eager to exit his taxi and run into friendly, welcoming arms as he presumably was to be rid of me.

I paid my fare and fairly ran to the door of the hotel. Immediately as I entered the lobby, I saw Buck rise from where he'd been sitting and rush toward me—a five foot eight vision of salt and pepper crew cut, broad shoulders, muscles and California tan.

"Oh, Buck, you don't know how good it is to see you!" I wrapped my arms around him in a fierce hug.

He hugged me back with equal vehemence and then added some fierceness of his own—in his glare. Pale blue eyes blazing, he clutched my upper arms and held me back from him. "You smell like a rental car. Where the hell have you been?"

I'd left a message with the front desk when I'd called from the cab but had merely said, "I'm running late."

"Buck, I'm so sorry. I didn't expect you to wait for me. Something happened that . . ."

"And you look like hell, by the way."

"Thanks, buddy." I inhaled deeply and caught my breath, this unanticipated angry reaction oddly providing me with a kind of calm. "You don't look so hot yourself."

Buck could match me in the rumpled department. His tweed jacket, blue dress shirt and khakis looking . . . well . . . like he'd slept in them.

"Okay, babe, explanations later. Let's get you checked in."

Fashion 26's lobby was ultra-modern with white tubular lights hanging from the ceiling. Behind the front desk was art in the form of a large, square frame containing rows and rows of spools of thread in red white black, blue and yellow with gray interspersed here and there. After I got my room number and card key, Buck steered me toward a huge winding staircase, which led to the Rare Bar & Grill. Once we were seated, we both buried our heads in the menus.

"Burgers are good here," Buck offered.

"Everything," I said breathlessly, "looks good enough to eat." I had to smile at my own lack of originality.

"*You* look good enough to eat," Buck looked at me seriously and intently.

"I thought," I grinned again, sense of humor returning, "that I looked like hell."

"That too."

I'd first met Buck a little over three years ago when we both lived in New York and he provided security at some of the fashion shows where I did runway work. His comments were his way of saying he was happy and relieved to see me. I well understood Buckspeak by now.

Buck laid his menu down, and I continued to peruse mine. "What in the world is a deep-fried Oreo?"

"Have no idea, Fred. Decide what you want and then tell me your life story—at least, the last eight or nine hour's worth."

A waitress arrived with glasses of water and, despite his burger recommendation, Buck referenced his New Orleans roots and ordered a barbeque brisket po' boy. I ordered something they called their M & M burger. The description declared it consisted of caramelized shallots, cheddar cheese, apple-smoked bacon and—best of all—was flambéed in whiskey. The latter was something I could definitely use right now.

"Drinks?" she asked wearily. *Perhaps she'd been waiting for me also?*

We said "iced coffee" in unison.

She left and Buck studied me again, as if he hadn't seen me in years.

"I'll let you eat first, Fred, before I demand a full account of you and your recent whereabouts, so just chill."

"Oh, okay," I couldn't help but smile. "But here's something for you to chew on, no pun intended."

"I'll bite," he didn't smile. "No bad pun there either."

I took a sip of water and inhaled. "I was kidnapped."

"Not funny."

"Yeah, I had a hard time finding the humor in it also." I glared at Buck. "Since you think I'd joke about such a thing, you're going to have to listen to the whole story on an empty stomach."

I took a few more gulps of water and proceeded to describe my harrowing experience from beginning to end, starting with Gram's detective interview, my own abduction and even including my crazy act at the restroom stop. Our food arrived, but I continued, taking small bites of my whiskey burger so as not to interrupt the flow of my true-crime adventure. I ended on the note of my smarts in getting myself re-cuffed with hands in front and my skill in ultimately getting free of my handcuffs.

"You were lucky, Fred. Lots of criminals are dumb, and you fortunately ran into two of the dumbest."

"Something else is fortunate. If my Beppe is Gram's Beppe, then he's not in New Orleans where he can terrify her but here in New York."

Buck cocked his head, then shook it despairingly. "For the moment."

chapter 23

"LOOK!" BUCK FAIRLY hissed as he spoke. "Do you see anything familiar? Do you see any*one* familiar?"

There was nothing familiar about the dim lighting nor the low ceilings painted a soft fresco pink. Sprays of flowers were placed here and there and the tables consisted of squares of slick white marble. I looked around and spied what primarily looked like a bunch of dark suited lounge lizards and twenty-something women cloaked in eye shadow and desperation as they headed for the upstairs bar. Not a single soul that resembled Beppe or Gio—the latter the questionable associate of my friend, Alex DeCicco.

After lunch, Buck and I had repaired to my hotel room. We flopped onto the king-size bed—both of us in a state of exhaustion—and shared a much needed and platonic nap together. *Did I mention it was platonic?* When we awoke, we grabbed a cab for a late-night dinner at Kenmare, an Italian restaurant on the fringes of Little Italy. It was already nine o'clock but, lucky for us, the eatery Buck chose stayed open until four a.m., like so many New York City haunts. Buck was eager to get back to the scene of my escape. Me, not so much. Even though it was on the same street, I was fairly certain we were not in the same restaurant where I'd been in bondage for a period of time, but I couldn't be sure and

Buck was determined to commence detective work this very night.

Buck ordered the veal cutlet, which was pounded thin in the Milanese style and garnished with fresh-made salsa verde and wedges of lemon. I chose the grilled lamb T-bones, which were soaked in a honey marinade and scattered with nuggets of toasted orzo. It was a pleasant dining experience, but no thugs with a predilection for kidnapping models at airports showed their dark heads nor bushy moustaches.

Mission unaccomplished, Buck put me in a cab back to my warm bed at Fashion 26. I once again fell into a deep sleep, awakening at ten o'clock the next morning as my cell phone began to play merrily, and a loud, high-pitched voice that *was* familiar greeted my eardrums.

"Frédérique! Where in the name of all that's holy have you been!?" *It certainly seemed to be the question of the week.* "I've been calling your cell, it won't accept new messages. I've called your hotel. I even called your friend Jeannette somebody who was talking to someone named Pierre at the same time I was trying to converse with her. And a cat was meowing in the background the entire time. It was madness, sheer madness! It's just three days until Fashion's Night Out and I have you booked. You have to go for fittings. There was one yesterday, and I was told you didn't show up. Are you quite mad!? Have you forgotten where you are and what this week is? I'm simply going out of my mind and . . ."

The diatribe continued. This latest inquirer was Marc Caress, my modeling booker, in case you haven't guessed. It was actually a relief to be pulled into the world of my profession and away from the recent dark happenings surrounding the death of Sonny Bob. I let Marc talk on a little longer. He needed to get his understandable frustration out of his system. When he veered from the subject of my absence to gossip about a particular designer, it was time to step in.

"I'm so sorry for what I've put you through, Marc. I won't burden you with the details, but it was a family emergency. It's over now, I'm fine, and I'm ready to work. Do I have a fitting today?"

Today? Good grief, Frédérique, try an hour ago! This one today is not for Fashion Week. Never mind, they're probably waiting for Gisele also. Get your high-priced little rear over to Oscar's and then call me when you get there."

chapter 24

"DON'T GO IN the bathroom. The designer and his assistant, they in there. Doin' lines of coke."

The advice came from one of the seamstresses I've gotten to know.

The chatter from her sister sewers was a bit less sensational. "The hem is missing." "Cut a centimeter shorter." "Bring up the sleeve a little." "The lining is sticking out— it got shortened too much." "We worked till three a.m. this morning— then he added a new dress and a new shirt . . . Paul, we have to cut a skirt."

A producer had a request, delivered in a shout. "I want coffee . . . now!"

I smiled to myself—grinned actually—so happy was I to be back in the familiar, frenetic, hairspray-filled atmosphere that attends a fashion show. I took in the scenery: metal racks of dresses, each boasting square white cards with numbers, white wood folding chairs, a small Asian woman stitching on a green and orange ball gown. Air conditioning hummed from the south wall of the tent and blew across the room in gusts. Piles and piles of pocketbooks lay scattered on the various rectangular tables along with bottles of Fiji and Evian water.

One of the male assistants, obviously not interested in designer water, swigged from a bottle of vodka. Everyone was feeling the pressure.

A model strolled in a circle, using a runway walk, to test the length of a white strapless gown dotted here and there with red flowers and blue leaves.

Shannon, one of the show's producers, flitted about making notes on a clipboard and conferring with people, always conferring. Shannon was tall with long, ash-blonde hair and wore black leggings, a black tank top under a loose black jersey jacket. She intermittently checked the cards attached to the gowns and re-applied her lip gloss. Many producers and staff of fashion shows feel obliged to be as well dressed as the models that grace the runway—making for a very attractive scenario.

In another corner, a fair-skinned model with light brown hair sat in one of the folding chairs as a man in a crisp white shirt attended to her upsweep. She wore some sort of gray shorts outfit and knee-high gray patent boots. As White Shirt added a blonde fall to the back of her hair, she sipped iced tea from a tall plastic cup and checked her Blackberry.

A new model entered the room, nude but for a black lace and beige thong. She modeled a dress, then changed into short jean cutoffs. She stood braless for several minutes, oblivious to the three men in the tent, and they to her.

Debi Stein, the person in charge was a slim woman in her fifties. She wore a medium gray gabardine dress, slim belt, full skirt. At her throat were three layers of ruffled rows, which strongly resembled paper ribbons once you've run a scissor over them to make them curl. Surely, that was not literally what that was—or was it?

A male assistant joined in the stitching of a gown. He wore a black and white print cotton shirt, a gold belt, and bright Kelly-green pants. His dark, spiked hair was blonde at the tips.

Debi's main assistant was a gorgeous tall blonde, swathed in white jersey with a beige fringed scarf wrapped around her hips. She spent most of the time engaged in intense conversations on her cell phone.

The models were always smiling and occasionally blew air kisses as someone new entered the tent. The youngest assistant, Sarah, wore a black and gray mini skirt and a mustard jersey top. She, too, mostly conferred with people.

Producer Shannon stopped pacing, sat at one table and discussed procedure with the designer, describing the runway moves of the various girls. Then they launched into a lively conversation about the music. Shannon was, with some exasperation, advising, "The music must have high beats per minute count with a solid backbeat, a B-52 sound system complete with fifteen-inch speakers on stands and subwoofers" and concluding with an emphasis on "a mix board and Ipod cable, a sure SM microphone . . . and the finale, the finale."

The air conditioning was now approaching frigid, but staff, models and designer all remained calm and smiling. A photographer in a safari jacket posed the designer next to a rack of gowns.

Someone helped me into a strapless fuchsia gown punctuated by red and fuchsia ruffles at the hem. *It was good to be working again.*

The blonde in white jersey said, "Can I steal everybody for a quick rehearsal?"

I lined up with the other models at a side entrance to the stage. We all wore our hair in thick buns in preparation for the show, but otherwise were garbed in our street clothes of jeans and tank tops.

As we strolled, by turn, down the runway, Shannon was at a mike, instructing "hold" as we reached the runway's end.

"Line them up from the top now, please Gail," she intoned.

"Okay, stand by music."

"Let's do the lighting cues now."

"Not so fast."

"Color shift, go."

"Anna Jean, hold. Beautiful. Nice and slow, Freddy. Slower."

"Beautiful. That's a good pace, Karen. Perfect."

"Michelle, right down the middle, you're off to the right. Beautiful."

"Margo, can you go a little faster. A little more elegant, like you're floating, a little more regal."

"Tamara, that makeup's beautiful."

"Slow down, Sienna. Beautiful."

"You need to slow down Anna Jean. Way too fast."

The music blared from speakers on each side of the stage. Black folding chairs, with red labels on the front row chairs indicated reserved seats. Large video screens loomed on either side of the long, white runway.

Shannon was still bossing. "Karen, you're the last girl so you are going to hold at the back of the stage . . . finale music . . . too close together . . . all come down the center . . . this is the wrong order . . . Sophia's not in the finale . . . spread yourselves out. Beautiful. Look where you are—get a frame of reference for where you are now. Shift and move left and right. You'll alternately step to the left, right, left, right so Coleen can walk down the middle."

Crew members stuffed shocking pink tissue into each seat's swag bag.

"Leave the color up, so just the white light comes up." Our friend Shannon again. "Karen, you will not wait for color. You will not get a complete blackout, Karen. You will just turn and hold. Finale music, go. Models, go. Beautiful."

A voiceover practiced announcing the designer, "Ladies and gentlemen, Colleen Quen."

Shannon was happy. "Good job, girls. Gorgeous."

It was show time!

Typically, at a fashion show, the first row is for V.I.P.'s like Anna Wintour, editor of *Vogue*, and various other celebrities.

In this case, actress Sarah Jessica Parker sat next to Wintour who sported her signature sunglasses, her classic bangs and bob and a short-sleeved print dress. Sarah J. wore a bold coral dress, matching sandals and a chunky necklace. On her wrist sparkled a multicolor Fred Leighton cuff. Some of the others in the same row were Victoria Beckham, Maggie Gyllenhaal, Jennifer Lopez, Halle Berry, Nicole Kidman, model Kate Moss and the ubiquitous Olsen twins.

In the second row, the designers and some journalists reside. Today's lot were Calvin Klein, Donna Karan, Jeremy Scott, Tom Ford, Sonia Rykiel, Tory Burch and Stella McCartney. There were probably several journalists, but I only recognized Susie Menkes. Rachel Zoe, stylist for many movie actors, was also in the second row.

In the remaining rows were various people connected to the fashion industry and standing room consisted of fashion students.

On the sides of the enormous tent, the photographers began arriving.

Now fully decked out, we lined up once again.

Shannon was whispering directives. "Ladies . . .be serious . . .like soldiers . . .no smiling."

At my cue, I strolled out, wearing an orange taffeta ball gown that I loved. It had a long slit from the knees down and billowed at the sides. I felt confident, happy.

I had on my "game face" and kept my gaze straight ahead but as I turned, my peripheral vision revealed something disturbing. At the end of the runway and back a few feet were two eleven-foot tall aluminum light trees. The base of the tree on the right was shrouded in comparative darkness and crouched next to the tree's base was a person. It appeared to be a man. Whoever he was, he was close to the runway. I could not make out features, but the figure's shape *looked a lot like the short member of my recent captors.*

chapter 25

IT STARTED WITH a loud and determined banging at the front of the house. The night before I'd had a bad dream after spying what looked like a suspicious character lurking near an exit at yesterday's runway gig—memories of Sonny Bob's bloody back . . . of the spear . . . of my frightening van abduction . . . visions of someone invading my Gram's home in New Orleans. I'd decided that an antidote to these fears would be a late evening trek to my Brooklyn brownstone to observe the renovation progress for myself, despite Howie's passionate insistence that he was performing "weekly on-site inspections." I took a break from my tour to have dinner out and then, feeling especially tired, decided to crawl into a bed and spend the night.

The hour was now very late, or early to be more precise, as it was almost two in the morning. I crept barefoot toward my front door in the darkness, calculating if and how I could look out the curtain-less windows without being observed. A column of moonglow poured across the living room, suggesting that insufficient cover would render my curiosity a dangerous indulgence.

I stood inches from my front door, and the loud knocking increased in speed, a definite indication my caller was probably frantic, possibly angry, and certainly bold.

Should I call Buck? He was scheduled to attend the cast party for Martha's beau, Erskine Varney, an aging character actor but one who was—like Martha—still vibrant and employable. I hated to interrupt that, plus he'd technically be working—on the job. *So who should I call?*

A neighbor? *I don't know my neighbors.*

The police? Would Brooklyn police take "loud door knocking" seriously? *Fuhgedabout it!*

When I first awakened, I was almost too groggy to be frightened by the relentless pounding. Now, as more clarity presented, I felt vulnerable. And not only because this sleepover was unplanned and I stood nearly naked in a flesh-colored thong. I'd grabbed a towel from the bathroom to cover my chest area, thinking my possible visitor might see this and comment that my mammary glands were so deficient that a hand towel would be adequate for the job.

Just as I thought of such commentary, I further mused on who'd make such a rude observation; and it helped me identify, even in my dulled state, the voice I heard seconds later.

"Damn it, open this freaking door!"

I did as instructed. The tall intruder stood before me, huge halo of hair, darting eyes, a large object hanging from one hand and the other was suspended in the air mid-knock.

"What are you doing here?" I demanded, not unkindly.

"What the hell are *you* doing here?" was the retort.

This dialogue was not going to get us anywhere, so I simply sighed and with that the interloper grabbed me tightly.

"Oh, Jeannette, it's so good to see you!" I said from the depths of her bear hug.

"Girlfriend, you're a sight for my big, beautiful green eyes yourself."

'They're big, all right, and so is that hairdo," I said, beckoning her to step inside.

Her head full of red curls stood out like a seventies afro.

Jeannette dropped her bag on the floor. "What can I say, the damn New York air makes it a little wild."

"That look passed a little wild forty miles back and arrived at bizarre."

"Are you gonna keep criticizing my appearance out of obvious jealousy or are you gonna invite me to stay overnight in this . . . this . . ." Jeannette's head of bobbing red curls turned slowly as she scoped out her surroundings. "This strange residence here"

"It won't look strange when it's . . . never mind that, who's watching Pierre while you're here?"

Jeannette frowned. No, glared at me. "I stand here tired, thirsty and all you can think of . . ."

"I'm so sorry, I'm sure you left him in good hands," I said, giving her a quick hug and picking up her black duffle bag. "Come with me to the kitchen."

We made our way down the long hallway, and I snapped on the kitchen ceiling light. Jeannette planted herself on a chair next to the round glass table with sighing and groaning appropriate to having just crossed the Sahara desert as opposed to enjoying an expensive cab ride from Manhattan, which turned out to be the case.

I opened the fridge and held up two small bottles of Evian water. "This is all I have, Jay. I wish . . ."

"That'll do, Freddy. No, you take one. I don't need 'em both."

I sat and downed a healthy swig. "As happy as I am to see you, Jay, I have lots of support here and you didn't have to . . ."

"Oh, don't get all altruistic on me, girl . . ."

Altruistic? I didn't know Jeannette knew the meaning of the word. I mean *literally*. Her habitual profanity and Bronx accent tended to obscure the fact that she has a fine mind. Then she read mine.

". . .and, yes, I know what *altruistic* means and, no, I'm not just here on your account, blondie."

"No, no, no, Jay. I am glad you're here, whatever the reason." I smiled sweetly. Then I glared with alarm. "Wait a minute . . .who's taking care of Pierre?"

"Our favorite red-headed cat is probably purring in Winnie's arms as we speak. She's probably . . ."

"Winnie?"

"Yes, Frédérique, your dear, darling southern-as-the-day-is-long Aunt Winifred, which is what she seems to prefer to be called these days, by the way. Beats me why she thinks . . . "

"You've been to see Winnie?"

"Who says blondes are dim? Girl, you pick up on things with lightening speed and . . ."

"Why?"

"Why are you so quick? Well, I guess it's all that higher learnin' at NYU, not to mention the years in France and abroad. They say extensive travel gives you . . ."

"I mean why are both you and Pierre here, and you know it."

"We now come as a set. We truly bonded while you were gone. We have long, meaningful conversations, him and me. I regale him about my love life just like you do. Turns out he's a very patient listener, being so used to your whining on the subject, and he . . ."

I waxed stern. "Cut the comedy."

"Okay." Jeannette grinned and took the four huge gulps required to empty her water bottle. "I have big news," she began, "and no cracks about the *big* part."

Here in New York where we first met, Jeannette had started out on track to become a high-fashion model but a swift and permanent weight gain graduated her to plus-size work. It was still a somewhat sore point.

She took my water bottle and swallowed the last of its contents.

"Sorry." The grin again. "I just . . ."

"Please . . . talk!" I remained in stern mode.

"I spoke to Marc and he . . . "

"You talked to Marc?"

"Whadda I just say?"

"Marc? Marc Caress? My booker?"

"Gee, he didn't mention the part about how you owned him, but yeah, *your* Marc. Can I finish?"

"Do so . . . and get to the point."

"Okay, so Chanel's reopening this store they got in SoHo, and they're launching a big ad campaign about how they're gonna feature plus sizes. Well, I'm not gonna be in the ads themselves. That's gone to Miss I've-Cornered-the-Market Crystal Renn . . ."

Jeannette allowed herself a momentary bitter smirk, ". . . but I'll do a runway they've got scheduled in two weeks in conjunction with the whole deal and Marc says . . "

"*My* Marc?" I smiled to let her know my humor had returned.

"Yes, of course, queenie, *your* Marc . . ." She smiled in return." . . . and he said to me 'my darling girl, you'll soon be as big as Renn.' And by big he didn't mean . . "

"I know," I said, still smiling. "He means successful and I've no doubt of it."

"Marc don't doubt it either, girlfriend. He says Saks is about to carry plus-size clothes. and who's on board to design this stuff? None other than the likes of Armani, Oscar . . . as in de la Renta . . . Dolce & Gabbana, Donna Karan and . . ."

"Well, Donna's always designed clothes that are some-what forgiving. Maybe I can relax and gain all the weight back I've recently lost and . . ."

"I was gonna add Fendi, and, no, you don't, missy. Don't you go gaining nothin'. Stay outta my field. You're nice and skinny. I see you gain an ounce, girl, and I'll . . ."

"Relax! Kidding!"

I patted her hand. "So I called Winnie and told her I'd decided to spend the night here and she told you. I've put clean sheets on the double bed in the guest room, and we can share that. There's a king-size in the master bedroom but I don't want to . . ."

"I know, I know. I heard." It was Jeannette's turn to pat my hand. "I wouldn't expect you to go back in there."

I turned my head away and swore I heard the neighbor's dog mournfully howling once more. The still musty smell of the kitchen was getting to me.

"Let's go upstairs, Jay. We both could use some rest."

We rose in unison. She picked up her bag and followed me down the hallway. I stopped and headed back to the kitchen to turn out the light.

Jeannette swiftly turned and followed me. "Leave it on!"

I gave her a puzzled look. She gave me a fearful one.

"And the hallway and the living room lights too!" She was fairly yelling.

"Jay?"

She looked around, a worried crease between her eyebrows.

"There's something I didn't tell you."

chapter 26

BEPPE VITALE WAS not having a good day. First off, he'd been summoned to Frankie's headquarters, an office behind a small restaurant on Montague Street. Not a good sign, especially since it was
a weekend and Frankie usually reserved that time for his family.
The other irritation was that cars were parked bumper to bumper
all over the popular commercial street in Brooklyn Heights, and
he had to leave his car two long blocks south of his destination
and walk over in the driving rain. He couldn't find either of his two
hats that morning and he didn't own an umbrella.

Pulling together the collars of his thin olive-green raincoat, Beppe bowed his head and hunched his shoulders
forward, as if doing so would somehow deflect the incessant downpour. He glanced up momentarily to look ahead
and view the large glass windows of a couple of outdoor
cafes with patrons sitting inside and chatting and laughing
happily, soothed by being away from their jobs and feeling
dry and warm and full of good food.

He mumbled to himself, cursing the "yuppies" and the
fact that they couldn't stay away from Sunday brunch even
in a rainstorm.

He finally reached the restaurant. The door was open,
but no one was inside so he reached into a side pocket and
drew out a cigar. Frankie didn't allow smoking around him,
and Beppe needed one of his beloved stogies as morale
reinforcement before entering his boss' inner sanctum. He

took a few puffs and a few deep breaths, then headed to the men's room to relieve himself and lose the cigar.

"Yer late!" Frankie bellowed. Beppe was actually earlier than the appointed time, but he understood Roma had to assert his authority.

The room was lit solely by an oversized table lamp. Frankie's desk was a long rectangle of dark knotty pine. It overwhelmed the tiny room. The walls consisted of fake wood paneling. A heater hummed from one corner. Stacks of newspapers spilled over the seat of one of the two chairs facing the desk.

"I got an explanation about yesterday, Frankie. What happened was . . ."

"Can't wait to hear it, moron. Does it beat the way you and Gio bungled things with Sonny Bob? Is it better than the losing the Freddy broad outta the van story? 'Cause I'm writin' my memoirs and I need to hear something interesting."

"Frankie." Beppe spoke the name in a whine. "I was parked across the street from her Park Slope digs day n' night. Finally, yesterday—yah know it was just yesterday, right?—at five o'clock in the evening, she shows. I was waitin' till she turned out the lights and it'd be dark and her neighbors would be in bed and . . ."

Frankie stood up from his desk and began to pace. He was almost as short as Beppe with dark brown, slicked-back hair. On this day, he wore a starched white shirt and a yellow paisley tie given to him by his daughter, Caitlin. He'd dressed up to take the family to early morning mass, and he was eager to return home and enjoy the great meal he knew Sophia would make. Lately his daughter had been chiding him about his grammar. He wanted her admiration and respect so he was trying to remember not to drop his g's as she had mentioned and not say 'don't' when the correct word was 'doesn't.' If he did all this, pretty soon the boys would be laughing behind his back, but screw 'em. Caitlin's opinion was far more important. She was a beautiful girl, tall and slim like her mother, and smart too. Now, instead of sitting in the big leather chair in his den and going over her homework with her, he'd come out in the rain to meet with this retard. Alex DeCicco had called from New Orleans that morning and when Alex wants answers, you move.

He turned as he paced and gave Beppe a brief look. "DeCicco says to me, 'This MacGyver's on my back, Frank.' Alex says, 'He's payin' me mucho bucks to get this dough, in addition to my cut of the whole bundle.'"

Beppe understood this MacGyver to be the man he and Gio referred to as Mr. Big.

Frankie had told Beppe that he didn't know who this Mr. MacGyver was, only that MacGyver wasn't his real name and that he was owed a lot of money by Sonny Bob Bonnaire and he knew for a fact that Sonny had a secret stash of funds somewhere. In a rare moment of sharing, Frankie had confided that he was certain Alex had referred to MacGyver as 'she' on one occasion. They'd laughed together at this and then the moment of camaraderie was gone, and Frankie had given Beppe stern lecture number one hundred and fifty as to the seriousness of this particular job.

"Okay," Frankie said. "Go on with your story, and make it good."

". . . so's I get outta my car when it's dark," Beppe continued, "and I'm headin' for the door, see? Next thing you know, a cab comes roaring around the corner and some big, tall dude gets out. He's got some kinda little duffel bag and walks right up to the Freddy chick's door and starts bangin' on it. He sure as hell looks like he's armed, Frankie, so what I gotta do? You said Alex said . . ."

"He *looks* like he's armed?"

"Yeah, right. You said Alex said not to hurt this broad. How I gonna pull that off in a two-against-one situation?"

"Yah know what? I don't much *care* how. Bonnaire is dead . . . which don't matter . . . as for his money, he was probably too high to know himself what he done with his stash . . . but that ex-wife of his knows where the dough is. So figure it out!"

Frankie rubbed his shoulder. This damp air was not helping his arthritis. He increased the speed of his pacing and pondered. *Alex don't . . . doesn't. . . . want this girl hurt in any way and yet I gotta do my job. But if I gotta hurt her, I'll do it. Tell Alex some kinda accident story. If I gotta kill her to keep my boys safe, I'll do it. Alex needs me. He ain't got no other reliable people here and he can buy my story or shove it.*

Beppe longed for another cigar or, better still, a beer. Frankie had never told him to sit down, and he stood in all his wetness, dripping on the fake Oriental rug and wondering, if he took his raincoat off, it would be okay to take a chair.

Beppe scowled inwardly. He was constantly being jerked around by this particular job. First, Alex says the money's in New Orleans and he'll handle the deal himself. Then he changes his mind, says it's in New York and he knows this for a fact.

Frankie stopped pacing, stood stock-still and stared at Beppe for what was probably seconds but seemed like an eternity to the object of his gaze. Suddenly he commanded, "Sit!"

His employee did so.

Beppe smiled inwardly at this new courtesy. It probably meant Frankie would chat with him some more about future projects and maybe give him a monetary advance on this one. He could go home, watch football, and maybe take Gloria out to dinner if the rain lets up.

Frankie took his suit jacket off the back of the tall, ornate chair behind his desk and shrugged into it. He pulled a long, black umbrella from a brass container.

"Sit there, Beppe. And think!" He moved toward the door, and yelled at Beppe's back. "Think about how you gonna pull this off and not blow it. Think about how bad it's gonna be for you if you blow it one more time. Get some help on this one from now on. Get Sal or Timmy or even Boris. No, make that Timmy. Get Tim Ryan and get the Bonnaire broad in here."

Frankie coughed and slammed the door behind him.

Beppe sat in the chair, alone in the shadowy office, and did some of the recommended thinking and pondering. He wondered why Alex hadn't just grilled this Freddy himself when she was in New Orleans and why he and Gio had to meet with her. Then he remembered that Alex had them meet her so they'd know what she looked like.

Sam must have the hots for this tall, skinny model broad, he mused. Even before Sonny was killed, Alex thought the model might know where his dough was, so why not get what she knows outta her in Metairie and then whack her then and there?

He wondered why Frankie had decided he should now pair up with Tim Ryan on the Freddy deal. He wasn't a big fan of the hippyish looking Timmy with his long blonde hair and that damn fuzzy moustache.

He felt a headache coming on from trying to figure out Frank Roma . . . and Alex DeCicco, too . . . for that matter. So he switched to wondering if Dallas would beat Minnesota and if the injured Brett Favre would be back in shape for today's game.

So, Frankie said *think,* did he? Roma and DeCicco were nuts, and Favre was probably healthy again. It was the best deduction his cogitating could produce.

chapter 27

HE FAVORED ME with a mega-watt glare, looking me up and down with disapproval. Then he circled around me, taking slow, measured steps. The hostility in the air was palpable. I hoped downright hatred was not in the mix. If he felt unjustifiably wronged, would I have to anticipate some future and ultimate retribution? I couldn't imagine such a thing but, as he squinted his eyes at me in obvious displeasure, I feared the worse.

My cat, Pierre, was angry with me.

"Go off and leave me for weeks on end and then I'm deposited in this strange place with this strange woman and you're not there either. Now you come waltzing in, all smiles and wanting to pet and hug. Gimme a break," he seemed to be saying.

After my stay at my Brooklyn brownstone, complete with Jeannette's startling news that someone had been lurking in the darkness as she banged on my door, announcing her arrival, we'd both managed to hit the sack in the guest bedroom and sleep like babies. As daybreak came, however, eager for the perceived safer environs of Manhattan, we'd fairly flown down the street through a downpour of rain, clutching a shared umbrella, to the subway and the destination of the forty-second street station. Once there, we grabbed a quick breakfast at a diner near the theater district and hailed a cab to Aunt Winnie's spacious and insistently luxe apartment on Central Park West.

Winnie had answered the door herself with Pierre standing next to her right leg, in full victim attitude.

"Shugah, it's so good to see you both. Buck doesn't seem to think it's safe for you to go gallivanting around and staying in places all by yourself . . . well, even with your lovely friend with you. Why you two could have . . ."

"Buck?" I intoned. "I haven't heard from Buck in a coon's age, as Gram would say. Has he called? Left any messages? When did you talk to him? Was he actually here?" I sounded hysterical, even to my own ears.

"Pay no attention to her," Jeannette said in a world-weary tone, dropping her overnight bag onto one of two red-tufted chairs standing on either side of the front door. "She's sooooooo into Buckley Lemoyne and just doesn't know it. That's freaking lovelorn complaining you're listening to."

I nodded toward Jeannette. "That's the jet lag talking," I said to Winnie. "Buck is my buddy, my pal."

"Right now, darlin', ah'm just concerned that you two are here safe and dry. Take a breather from all this huntin' around for Sonny's killer. Buck told me all you've been up to, that kidnappin' and all. Why do you think we have NYPD Blue? Do they call the police that these days or is that just from that TV show? Well, no matter," Winnie babbled on. "Sit yourselves down and rest. Ah'm making some yummy corn chowder soup. Perfect for a rainy day."

"May I use your phone, Winnie?" Jeannette asked. "Gotta find me a hotel until I decide where I'm gonna live. Yes, Freddy, I said *live*. Don't look at me like that. Your Marc says he can get me a lotta gigs. Beats starving back in L.A."

Winnie shook her head vehemently in the negative, and I remembered back in the trailer park in New Orleans when she wore her lovely gray hair streaming down her back as opposed to its current very short, chic length.

"Ah'm delighted y'all are going to get work, Jeannette, but there'll be no going to hotels, at least for a while. This place has four bedrooms, plus a den with a sofa bed. Ah'm sure we can choose a room for each of you. No, Frédérique, close your little mouth and don't bother protesting. Ah have spoken." Winnie grinned at the uncharacteristic imperiousness of her last comment.

"There, it's settled," Winnie further declared. "Now, come with me to the kitchen and help me with this soup." She paused as she caught me staring intently at her with a half smile. "Just what you lookin' at, shugah?"

"Nothing, Aunt Winnie. It's just lately I haven't seen you dressed so informally. It's refreshing. I mean plaid and denim? I'm glad the loveable, down to earth Aunt Winnie still lurks beneath all the glitz and glamour."

Winnie puffed out her chest and stretched to her full five feet three. "Ah'll have you know this is a *fashion* plaid shirt," she sniffed. "Some Japanese designer, from a store in SoHo. And who says one can't be glamorous and *also* loveable and down to earth? You should have learned that from your stylish late mother, God rest her soul."

"You're so right, Win. Mom was all those things, and more."

"Okay, shoo now! You girls go get cleaned up . . ."

"Excuse me," Jeannette laughed. "We showered before we came here."

"Well, I'm sure you did, darlin', but you both look . . . a little damp around the edges. Go dry your hair and take off those wet shoes, and then get in the kitchen and prepare to work."

Winnie turned on the heels of her designer sneakers and headed toward the kitchen. Pierre, who'd been surreptitiously snoozing nearby, rose, turned on his four little heels and followed her.

In three beats, Winnie stopped, whipped around and faced us. "Oh, here's how we'll do it. Jeannette, you take the bedroom with the lime green walls. Freddy, you take the one with the chocolate brown walls. Just go down that hallway, you'll see them. They each have their own bathrooms." She eyed our feet once more, "For heaven's sake, get *dry!*"

We did as instructed, with me accomplishing the "get dry" edict before Jay. I returned to the living room and just stood still—not only to admire Winnie's beautiful dusty-orange silk bishop-sleeve curtains against the lapis-blue walls but also to watch the rain sluice down the eight huge windows overlooking Central Park. *Winifred de Foucauld has certainly done all right for herself.*

Jeannette joined me when I was about four minutes into my distraction. "Spectacular, isn't it?" she said. I nodded.

We stood watching a little longer, with almost religious reverence, until Winnie called out "Girls!"

"Sonny Bob would have adored a place like this," I said as we headed to the kitchen.

"Sonny Bob couldn't have *afforded* a place like this, girlfriend."

"There was a time that would have been my guess too, Jay, but I'm now beginning to think he had more money than he let on."

I almost became swallowed up once more in ruminations—this time over the possibility that Sonny had savings or investments that I didn't know about. Why else did the thugs in New Orleans grab him and run? Sonny owed a lot of people money and they all seemed to know that at this point in his life he was dead broke. It would stand to reason that the kidnappers are the ones who killed him. But why? Broke or not, he's no good to them dead. Also, why kidnap *me?* If the Beppe who, with his accomplice, spirited me away in a van was the same Beppe as Alex's friend in Metairie, how does that add up? Does Alex DeCicco not know the true nature of these men? So much didn't make sense. I needed to talk to Buck about this. I needed his advice, but he was caught up in Martha Fleming's schedule. Just doing his job, I reminded myself.

We three passed what was left of the morning pleasantly and compatibly, sitting around the long butcher-block table, chopping onions and celery, dicing bacon, scraping the kernels from the cornhusks and chatting.

"Why do you suppose, Winnie, that Sonny never told me he had two stepsisters?"

"Oh, ah can answer that, honey. Bella and Dina had a falling out with Sonny for . . . well, for a few years actually. They thought, once he got so successful, he oughta be spreading the wealth around—specifically to them—and when they saw that wasn't happening they were piss ant mad!"

"Did they feel entitled to his money because they'd grown up together?" I asked.

"Ah think they only lived under the same roof for about three or four years." Winnie placed the bacon in a heavy pot, covered it, and warmed to her subject. "But, listen, those little low-class witches were *born* feeling entitled. Learned it from their mother ah think. Heard she was a real pistol and helpless as the day is long."

"Where are Sonny's father and his real mother?" Jeannette asked.

"Sonny's mother died of cancer years ago," I answered. "His dad, Victor Bonnaire, was a widower for about four years and then married Dina and Bella's mother. Then, about five years ago, Vic was killed in a car wreck."

I placed thyme leaves, dried marjoram leaves, and some of Chef Paul Prudhomme's Vegetable Magic into a small bowl and shook it up.

"Is Sonny's sister Dina always so morose? I know I mainly observed her at the funeral but still . . ." I added a tablespoon of dark brown sugar to the mix. "I never saw her crack a smile . . . or act very friendly, for that matter."

Winnie took a sharp knife and began to dice the peeled potatoes.

"You're right on the money, honey. Don't you never mind her, that girl is permanently pissed. Lord knows how that fits with her working in sales and all. Think she'd scare the customers away."

"What's the little heifer sell?" Jeannette asked. She'd looked the recipe book over and was getting heavy cream and a large container of chicken stock out of the fridge.

Winnie wiped her hands on her apron and began putting some of the ingredients into a large pot. "Ah must say, she's got herself a lil' store out in Brooklyn on Atlantic Avenue, called Antiques and Treasures, something like that. Sonny Bob gave me those two oil-on-wood bird portraits in the dining room from there, gave 'em to me for my birthday."

Winnie covered the pot and sat down, with a sigh.

"Dina does all right, from what ah hear. And that husband of hers has a job, forget exactly what he does. They don't seem to be hurtin' for money. But you know some people, they just get real greedy for more."

"Dina sounds like a piece of work," Jeannette offered.

Winnie nodded. "She's put together a darn nice antique store though. I've gone there a few times. Pretty much runs it herself, too. Oh, she has a young girl come in and help out two or three days a week. Met her once, Sonny Bob brought her here. Pretty little thing. I think *she's* the one with the sales ability."

Winnie rose. "I'm gonna get us some liquid refreshment to have with this lunch. Okay with you girls?"

"Sounds great," I said.

Winnie opened a low cabinet boasting rows of bottles stored horizontally. "Oh," she said, rising quickly and bringing up a bottle of white wine with her. "Ah almost forgot, a girlfriend of mine got a 19th-century spool chair and two Samurai swords from Dina's shop."

"Any chance Dina carries Aboriginal spears?" Jeannette chuckled.

I glared at Jeannette at this dark—and certainly inappropriate and tasteless—attempt at humor.

Winnie uncorked the wine. "Oh," she said breezily, and innocently, "she carries antique daggers and spears and such galore."

chapter 28

MARTHA FLEMING THREW open the paneled Giambattista Valli coat draped over her shoulders to reveal a black velour tracksuit above dainty black sequined sneakers. She entered the room accompanied by her usual aura of drama that electrified the atmosphere as if the room's lights had just acquired extra wattage. Martha was of medium height and slim. Her still-brown hair was worn close to her head and as short a man's. Somewhere along the way in her life, she'd decided hairdos were a bother and now used wigs on stage in whatever style was appropriate to the character she was playing. Martha had just come from her evening Tai Chi class, and I had a hunch her purposeful and energetic stride—which certainly belied her eighty-one years—suggested that some dramatic news or exclamation would follow. I was not to be disappointed.

"My dears, the most fabulous thing has just occurred." She patted the air with one hand, her long coral fingernails gleaming. "I must tell you that . . ."

"You got the role!" Buck added an enthusiastic note of his own.

"Buckley, if you'd just let me finish, I will . . .

"You got *another* role?" I said. I normally hate people who interrupt but—what can I say—as reputed, enthusiasm is contagious.

"My, my, my," Martha frowned. "It seems I'm not the only diva in this room. Calm down, kids, and let the actress speak. I'm the one who's entitled to try and grab the spot-light."

"Pay no attention to them, Miss Fleming," Jeannette intervened. "They're just star struck."

"Thank you, my dear, and do call me Martha."

She plopped down on a chair, dropped a large Bar-ney's of New York shopping bag on the floor and threw her cell phone onto a nearby couch. The spacious living room of her suite was warm with lamplight and boasted two large vases of white roses.

"It's been such a long day . . . I'm parched . . . I hate to ask, speaking of divas, but would someone order some Perrier from room service?"

"Your wish is my command," Jeannette offered and headed for the phone. She was meeting Martha Fleming, star of stage and screen, for the first time and was clearly impressed.

"Isn't this a divine hotel?" Martha rhapsodized. "Do you know the other day Erskine ordered vodka at three in morning? He had the gall to add, 'ASAP' and they brought it immediately and with a smile."

She giggled, perhaps remembering a romantic inter-lude that accompanied the vodka incident. Buck appeared to frown, but if you're in your eighties and have romantic interludes, I say you're entitled to a giggle.

"And furthermore," she added, "its one of the few places without those nasty little intruders." She was referring to the recent infestation of bedbugs in many of Manhattan's hotels.

"Martha, the news?" Buck prompted.

"Yes, yes, of course. Here's the big news . . . alert the media, as my nephew would say." She finally laughed. "I'm going to Florence for a month!"

She threw her arms in the air and her fashion signa-ture—an array of matching bracelets on both wrists—made tinkling sounds as she did so.

"Sounds exciting, Martha. You're in a play over there?" I asked.

Martha leaned forward and popped a grape into her mouth from a bowl on the coffee table before replying.

"Oh my child, acting is not *all* I do. Don't you recall my telling you I've begun designing handbags?"

"Yes, actually, I do—*I didn't*—and . . ."

Buck said, "You're talking about Italy?" *Who says we're slow on the uptake?*

"Is there another Florence?" Martha had the grace to smile at herself. In fact, grin. "No less than Braccialini is going to manufacture my handbag and I'm going over there to oversee the process," she continued. "When it's done, they'll have them in their SoHo store on Broadway. Exciting, *n'est pas?*"

"*Chouette! Formidable!*" I agreed. Martha does not really speak French, but it wouldn't hurt to indulge her on this momentous occasion of her latest achievement.

"Well, actually . . . ," Martha crossed her legs and adopted a prim position. ". . . I got a lot of help from a professional designer. Also named Martha. No relation."

"No relation?" I said.

"Well, yes, because we're both named Martha."

"Ah," I replied. *Don't try to understand the logic of an actress.*

"Maybe you know her," Martha offered. "She goes to all the fashion shows. Her full name is Martha Napier."

"Napier . . . maybe I have. In her twenties, very pretty blonde?"

"*Mai oui*, that is her."

"I've seen her with her husband at parties. He's a media consultant."

"Well, I've never met him but I'm sure I shall. They'll be going to Florence also. I can't wait to see the finished handbag. And, *mon dieu*, with my name on it!"

"Put me down for two!" Jeannette said.

"That's so darling of you," Martha responded, "But they'll sell for nine hundred and ninety five dollars, sweetheart, so

I'll persuade the Braccialini people to give me some free samples, it's the least they can do."

"The best news is . . . ," Martha continued as she pulled off her sneakers and substituted heels gleaned from her shopping bag, ". . . that Erskine will be coming with me."

Shaking one sneaker in Buck's direction, she added, "Good news for you, my current guide and protector, yes?"

"Well, yeah," Buck said. "You're sure you'll be all right?"

"Of course I will, dear boy. Erskine will go everywhere with me and anywhere he doesn't go, young Martha Napier will accompany me. She looks strong and fit." She giggled again. "Together we'll fend off any overzealous fans."

Buck was having dinner tonight with the divine Martha and, at her request, he'd invited me to join them. I'd asked if I could bring Jeannette and Buck agreed, saying he was certain this would be fine with his client.

By pre-arrangement, we three had arrived early at the Michelangelo, an elegant hotel near Rockefeller Center. Jeannette and I had copped a tour of her one-bedroom suite before Martha was scheduled to make her appearance. I loved the country French decor of the bedroom itself with its blue and beige accents and a sleigh bed in natural pinewood. Most impressive, to Jay, was the Italian marble bathroom, complete with a huge oval bathtub and imported shampoo and lotions in large containers as opposed to the usual tiny hotel size. I'd toyed with the idea of pilfering the latter, but that would be just too tacky. Besides, the future had begun to look positive for the resurgence of my modeling career, also for Jeannette's, so we needed to abandon our recent inclinations to "think like poor folks," as Gram would say. Or, more likely, she'd raise my harmless purloin to the level of theft and recite, *bien mal acquis ne profite jamais*.

Now we sat with Martha in the parlor of her suite. Between this and the luxury of Aunt Winnie's apartment, we two struggling models could become quite spoiled. At

Buck's suggestion, Jay had added white wine and beer to Martha's room service order for imported water.

As Jeannette and Martha became engrossed in a conversation about shoes, it fully sank into my consciousness that, with his client's escorted departure for Florence, one Buckley Lemoyne would be free for other projects.

I moved to the chair where Buck was sitting and sat on the floor at his feet, the better to share a confidence.

"You'll be going back to California soon," I said.

"Is that an order?" he deadpanned.

"It's a question, of course." I was in no mood for one of his battle of wits.

"I have other things I have to do in this city," he advised.

"Like what?"

"Things." He *was* in the mood for the wit battle.

"Oh, well, when you explain it like that."

I waited.

Buck remained silent, cocking his head and looking down on me with a half smile.

"Okay," I rose somewhat and leaned on the arm of his chair. "I have something I need help with and I'd like you to stay," I whispered.

"My answer is 'yes' since you put it like that and also since you're begging."

"I'm not *begging*," I snarled, still in a whisper.

He lowered his face to a couple of inches from mine, then kissed me on the cheek. Nodding downward, and suppressing a grin, he whispered, "Babe, looks like you're on your knees to *me*."

A short, stocky figure slithered back thru the shadows to a destination three blocks from the Michelangelo, jammed his gun once again inside the back of his belt, and climbed into the driver's seat of a gray Ford Focus. Complications tonight. He'd make his move another time.

chapter 29

THE FIRST THING I noticed was the shoes. They were a medium brown with a rounded toe, but the distinguishing factor was that I knew they were by Edward Green—handmade and from England. My dad, the judge, has a couple of pairs and they cost nearly a thousand dollars. I could visualize my father's shoetrees now with the inscription 'Edward Green, Bootmakers, Northampton.' These looked a bit incongruous, paired as they were with dark blue jeans, a red flannel shirt and a fleece-lined navy windbreaker. One item that did match the pricey footwear was the gloves lying on the table in front of him. They were calfskin, butterscotch in color.

The next thing I noticed was the book he was reading—*Austerity Britain*. "Impressive title," I smiled.

"Frédérique . . . Freddy, there you are! I was beginning to think I'd hit upon the wrong place."

I looked at my watch. "I'm actually a little early."

"Yes, of course you are," Sherwood said. "It is I who decided to be earlier still. Just so eager to see you."

This lovely man says all the right things. I leaned down and kissed him on the forehead.

Sherwood had dropped by Winnie's last night, heard her exclaim about all the stress I'd been under of late and offered to take me to dinner tonight. He'd actually suggested Cafe des Artistes, one of the older French restaurants in New York City—established in 1917—chic, expensive and romantic. But I had an appointment with Howie, my accountant, in the Ft. Greene section of Brooklyn and thus had suggested Roman's, a very down-to-earth neighborhood Italian restaurant just blocks from Howie's home office.

As soon as Sherwood agreed, I realized how self-indulgent I was being but I let the plans stand. I realized it once more when I saw his sweet attempt to 'dress down' for a Brooklyn eatery and thus fit in. He looked so dear in blue jeans, but with highly expensive British shoes, that I nearly kissed him again.

He was sitting in the outdoor section of Roman's—amid less-than-elegant surroundings, not helped by cabs driving by and exercising their horns, a lot of sidewalk traffic, many walking dogs, not to mention the soot in the air.

"Would you rather be inside?" I asked.

"Yes! I just didn't want to miss you." He stood and placed his hand on my elbow. "By all means, let's go."

We entered the restaurant, greeted by a buzz of voices only a few decibels less than the outside noise. The tables were worn and mismatched, but the lights were low and in their beams the decor of white subway tiles almost glittered. We were seated and given menus.

I'd been here before and knew what I wanted to order, so as Sherwood perused the menu I examined his book.

"It's a stuffy read," Sherwood offered. "All about the years 1945 to 1951, as Britain got over the second world war. Nobody had a thing to eat in those days, but Brits love to tighten their belts anyway. Probably makes us feel superior."

"I don't know about the superior part, but I do admire your country. You've been through a lot and survived with such nobility."

"I dare say that . . ."

"And one Brit in particular that I know is an exceptional representative." *Hey, I can be suave too.*

"Should I blush about now?" Sherwood asked, adding his lopsided grin.

"No, that's my territory. Right now, while I read about other superior Brits," I smiled, "You look the menu over."

Sherwood did as I suggested, but I didn't exactly immerse myself in *Austerity Britain*. There were too many other things on my mind of late. I opened the book and attempted to study it, but my attention drifted. I thought about the odd figure standing by the exit at the fashion show and the other lone figure Jeannette had spied outside my brownstone. The latter could well have been a home-less person, a neighbor arriving home after one too many at a local bar, any number of explanations. The person at the runway gig was more weird. The photographers were all collected in a certain place. The show's staff was back-stage. All the attendees were invited guests with reserved seats. Fashion shows are well-oiled machines, no reason for anyone to be out of place.

The waiter appeared, breaking my reverie, and we sim-ply ordered "the house red wine" as their numerous listings of wines and unique cocktails offered too many choices.

Sherwood returned to a study of the menu. "I don't know what to recommend to you, Freddy, since I'm not familiar with this place and . . ."

"Oh, I know what I'm going to have—their striped-bass fillet. They serve it in this great buttery wine sauce with car-doons and green olives."

"Sounds good," Sherwood said, although he looked skeptical and maybe a bit taken aback by my indepen-dence, as he returned to the menu. I'd come to regard my English friend as someone who liked to be in charge, but that's just what I need these days. And if that's the price to pay for his wonderful attentiveness, I could have worse problems.

Which led me to dwell again on those worse problems. I looked around and realized in my walk here from Howie's I'd not had the fear I'd felt of late that someone was con-stantly following me. Maybe not being alone but here with a healthy, strong-looking male was the deterrent. I'd taken a brief walk with Buck after our dinner with Martha and company and felt safe, not stalked, then too. Perhaps this was my imagination, or a constant bodyguard was the answer. I couldn't take Sherwood or Buck along as I raced around to the modeling gigs Marc was beginning to schedule with a near frenzy, but I could attempt to be in their company as much as possible. Buck might be impatient with this idea, but I was beginning to get the feeling Mr. Sherwood Benjamin would not object at all.

I did not succeed in putting all of my worries aside. "How well do you know Sonny Bob's stepsisters?" I asked.

Sherwood's mind seemed to be elsewhere. "I detect that you have a slight southern accent."

"Yes, I spent most of my growing up years in New Orleans. Picked it up there."

"Well, you know, you have a wonderful voice," Sherwood said.

I smiled and started to open my mouth, but he continued. "When I first saw you from afar at the funeral—so tall and slim and youthful—I decided you probably had a high-pitched, little-girl voice. I'm sensitive to voices, so these things occur to me. But yours is low, sensible, strong."

"Wow, that's a lot of adjectives for a voice. Thank you, Sherwood, that's a nice compliment."

He smiled, proud of himself the way men are when they know they've pleased a woman.

"I was saying—about Dina and Bella. You've met them before?"

"Who? Oh yes, the sisters. Well, they seem to be quite fond of Winifred—your Aunt Winnie—and, living as I do in the same building as Winnie and visiting with her fairly often as I do, I've run into them any number of times. Why do you ask?"

"Oh, no reason in particular. I was married to Sonny Bob for four years and knew him for six and I never knew he had stepsisters."

"Mysterious fellow, your Sonny Bob. Correct? Well, Sonny himself used to say the sisters were a greedy lot—particularly Dina. Such a stern woman, totally without charm in my book. Don't fancy her at all." He looked back down at the menu, then added, "But that's just my opinion, don't want to influence you, my dear."

"Oh, don't be concerned, Sherwood. Just curious. I formed a first impression that's all. I don't really give them much thought."

Then I proceeded to do exactly that. Dina was short and stocky. She had the same build and height as the mysterious Beppe, as well as I could recall him. Could she be my Brooklyn stalker and runway intruder? The thought seemed bizarre.

Our wine arrived, and I quickly took a large, enthusiastic swallow in an unconscious attempt to dispel my senseless paranoia. Sherwood took a sip of his and his eyes seemed to widen at my unladylike gulp.

"She owns an antique store, you know," he commented.

A vision of the store's display of spears played in my mind.

chapter 30

THE BUILDING WAS larger than I'd anticipated and didn't look anything like I'd imagined. It was a dull red, with the exception of the gray stone that surrounded an arched front door. The area containing the archway undulated from the main structure, as did one section to its left. Ivy grew over and above the doorway and more thickly on the area to the right, which boasted a tower, giving a castle-like effect. All in all, it more resembled a vintage private school than what it actually was—the 88th police precinct in Park Slope.

A wrought-iron fence bordered most of the building, facing a parking lot currently occupied by two blue and white NYPD vehicles—a squad car and a van—and a black Lincoln town car. Assuming there'd be no vacant parking spots, Buck and I had parked his rental car two blocks away. It was a bright, sunny day with a hint of fall in the form of a slight, cool breeze, so we didn't mind the walk to our destination.

"A friend of mine at the ninety first gave me the low-down on this guy," Buck had said when he picked me up in front of Winnie's apartment house.

He was referring to the Brooklyn detective who had interviewed me right after Sonny's body was discovered. Apparently Buck didn't check out his female partner, as she was not mentioned, and I didn't ask. They'd probably given their names to me at the time, but I was too much in shock to absorb this, and I couldn't have told you what either of them looked like. Buck did some checking and learned I'd met with a Detective Patrick Brennan. He said the female detective had been transferred and was no longer on the case.

We entered the lobby and went up a staircase to the second floor, where we were directed to wait in an interview room. It was small with white walls and blue molding and the air felt oppressive. I was wishing I hadn't left my water bottle in the car, when the man of the hour himself appeared.

Buck had said of Brennan, "He's a bit of an independent cuss I hear, doesn't play by the rules."

I'd started to ask how those characteristics would benefit our particular case, but decided to wait and judge for myself.

Brennan was a big guy, at least six four. He looked—well, a messy Russell Crowe in a role as a reporter came to mind. He had a medium build, but I suspected the tweed jacket when unbuttoned would reveal a bit of tummy, and he wore a blue dress shirt, open at the collar with a striped tie knotted at a halfway point. Khaki pants pooled a little around his ankles, and I could swear he wore no socks with his scuffed brown loafers. All of it—you guessed it—quite rumpled. But at the same time fresh and clean looking. Hair was cut short and neat and, though it was flecked with a lot of gray, I placed the face around forty or so, maybe even thirty-eight.

We remained seated as Brennan shook Buck's hand first. "Hey, Lemoyne, hear good things about you from Captain Bowler. Private eye now, huh? Good for you. Might look into that myself some day."

"And Miss Bonnaire." Gray-green eyes whose gaze was like a laser. "Nice to see you again."

Brennan didn't smile during these pleasantries, but his voice was cordial.

I decided a smile was in order so I offered one up, adding, "This building you're in is most impressive, Detective. I love the . . ."

"Built in 1893," Brennan said glumly. "Oughta be gutted."

Make a note, Frédérique, no patience with small talk.

Buck spoke up. "Freddy didn't fill you in on a couple of extra aspects to this case . . . Pat . . . are you called Pat?"

"Actually, Clint," Brennan said.

Buck and I had no comment.

The detective filled in the silence. "Middle name's Clinton. Like the president."

"Here's the story, Clint," Buck began. "Back in New Orleans where . . ."

Clint eyeballed me. "You guys need coffee?"

"Not me," Buck said. "It started . . ."

"Me," I chirped. "I would."

Brennan's long frame rose quickly from his chair and out the door.

Buck looked at me, his forehead slightly wrinkled in irritation. "This guy's all business," he said, as if in a warning.

"He can be whatever he wants to be, but I'm parched," and I raised his wrinkled forehead with one stern scowl.

Two minutes later, Brennan returned, bearing three small plastic bottles of water. "Pot's empty, they're making new. This is quicker."

"And much better," I beamed. "Thanks so much."

Seeing his grimace of irritation, I frowned at Buck.

Buck matched my frown with a light smirk plus two forehead creases and began again. "Sonny Bob was grabbed by two thugs in New Orleans . . ."

He recited the full circumstances of this, together with as much description as we had of the bad guys, their car and all of Gram's comments. He then moved on to my van heist, again with all the details I was able to report and concluded with his own deductions on these two acts and their possible perpetrators.

Brennan drummed his fingers on the metal table, then took a couple of long swigs of his water bottle. He looked squarely at Buck. "There's just one thing . . ." Worry in his voice.

"Is there a problem?" Anxiety in mine.

The detective turned toward me momentarily. And frowned. *A lot of that going around.*

Brennan returned his attention to Buck. "Kidnapping is a federal offense . . ."

"Means FBI." Buck finished his thought.

"Exactly. But doesn't have to. Not for now. These grabs were not hard-core kidnappings. No one harmed. Well, Sonny Bonnaire of course. Ultimately. But not the girl. No ransom demand. I caught this case as a homicide and I'm good with it staying that way."

The girl? I'm sitting right here in front of him and his first thought is *the girl?* Clearly, I had not made much of an impression on one Detective Brennan.

Brennan and Buck continued chatting along the lines of how the so-called kidnappings were not that relevant to solving the murder—not on a level of importance making it imperative to "call in the Feds." Adding, "Not yet."

I allowed myself a minute or so more to stew over Brennan' rudeness and hoped, although the plan was for the three of us to work together and cooperate going forward, this interview would be our last. In addition to being a maverick, as Buck stated to me earlier, he'd heard Clint—the *prince* formerly known as Patrick—was highly competent and well respected in the department. I reminded myself that this trumped any lack of charm or breeding and began to relax.

As Detective Brennan proceeded to share possible theories of his own, Buck's cell phone chimed its Zydeco tune and he answered.

"Lemoyne here."

Then, "Yes mam!"

"Right . . .of course . . .of course . . .no problem. Where?" He looked at me and shrugged. "Yes mam, be there in a mo'."

Buck slapped the phone shut and stood up. "Martha needs me by her side—like now. She needs someone to get her organized and to the airport in the next couple of hours or so. Erskine can't do the honors, he's in some kind of business meeting. He's going to meet her at JFK. We gotta split, Fred. I'll drop you off."

"No, you've got a time crunch. You go. I saw a subway station when we walked over, I'll catch that."

Buck knew that after this meeting I wanted to go to my brownstone and check on things. He felt obliged to take me there, but I could tell Miss Martha needed his prompt presence more. He was going to run into rush hour traffic and he didn't need a side trip to my place on top of that.

Buck opened the door, saying, "Thanks, Fred" and "Be in touch, Brennan" as he swiftly exited.

Before rising, I started to collect my large purse from the floor and then my water bottle when Clint Brennan leaned forward slightly, giving the table a firm pat with one hand.

"How 'bout dinner?" he said.

Outside, in the most distant parking slot next to a boarded-up Chinese restaurant, a gray car pulled out and headed home. Its driver felt confident in abandoning the tail tonight.

chapter 31

BEFORE ME WAS the answer to one all-important question from our meeting with the good Detective Patrick—*call me Clint*—Brennan. We had entered the Washington Avenue Italian restaurant chosen for our dinner "date." I had excused myself to go to the ladies room while Brennan got a table. After I brushed my hair and freshened my lipstick, a waitress led the way to where Clint was seated. My curiosity was satisfied: Clint sat sideways in his chair, legs crossed, and there they were—his socks were flesh colored, so my new cop friend was not actually bare legged.

Il Porto had a certain rustic elegance: simple wood tables and chairs with the backs painted black, a brick archway and a column of seaside mural just below the ceiling. Almost all the tables were filled and aromas like marinara sauce filled the air.

"Want wine?" Clint asked.

'That would be nice, if you'll join me."

A waiter appeared, and my somber companion ordered two glasses of 2007 cabernet sauvignon. "That okay?"

"Sounds great," I said.

Brennan seemed to feel no obligation to make small talk. He looked around the room, presumably scoping out the other customers. Maybe looking for fellow cops. Maybe observing whether officers' wives, their girlfriends—*his* wife or girlfriend?—were among the customers.

"Thought we needed to talk more," Clint said, as if he read my mind and was clarifying that this was not a date. "And you looked hungry. I know I am," he added.

I looked hungry? Was this a commentary on how thin I am? Hard to figure out these men-of-few-word types at times.

I studied the menu and Clint simply surveyed the room some more. Buck had mentioned that I felt I had a stalker, maybe that was the purpose of his concentration.

The waiter returned with our drinks and we ordered. *Penne il porto* for me, which translated to shrimp and asparagus in a pink vodka sauce and *vitello alla sorrentino* for Clint, a meal of veal scaloppini topped with mozzarella, eggplant and proscuitto.

The waiter left and the strong-silent one spoke.

"So you're a model?"

"Yes, I am."

"Like it?"

"Love it."

Usually I lapse into an entire monologue when asked that question. I rhapsodize about the travel a career in modeling affords, the beautiful clothes, the fun of working with designers and other models and throw in a humorous anecdote or two, but I wanted to see the reaction of Mr. Monosyllabic to short responses similar to his own.

'You're one long drink of water."

"Five, ten to be exact."

"Wear heels much?"

"All the time."

"My sister wanted to be a model."

"How'd she do?"

"Didn't work out."

"Oh?"

"Too short."

"But you're so tall."

"Step sister."

"I see."

Clint took a sip of wine. "Carry a camera with you?"

"Not usually."

"Start doing it."

"I need a hobby?"

"Need a photo of your stalker."

"Think that's do-able?"

"Rarely, but worth a try."

"Do I need a bodyguard?" *I knew I didn't but wanted to see what he'd say to this.*

"You scared?"

"Maybe a little."

"Right to be."

"Never alone."

"Good. Buck with you?"

"Buck and another male friend."

"Good."

"Grandmother okay?"

"So far."

"Someone live with her?"

"She has a beau."

"A beau?"

"That's what they're called when you're eighty-two."

"Lives with her?"

"No, but around a lot."

We both sipped our wine frequently during this chat. Then the waiter came with our dinners. Clint was right: we were both famished, and now neither of us wished to talk. The food was filling and delicious. We both ate fast and when we were almost finished, Clint ordered another round of wine. He hadn't asked, but a warming refill was just what I wanted as, like many New York restaurants, the air conditioning was on a meat-locker level. Presently the waiter came to collect our empty plates, and asked, "Leave room for dessert?"

"Not me," I answered.

"How 'bout chocolate ravioli with raspberry sauce?" This from Clint.

"Chocolate ravioli? There is such a thing?"

"Oughta try it."

"I will try it."

"Very good," the waiter said and left.

Clint went back to observing the restaurant, particularly the entrance.

I should have brought a good book.

"See anyone you know?"

"Some buddies."

"Go say hello."

"No need."

Our desserts arrived and we devoured them with the same speed as dinner.

"Coffee?"

"Sure."

Clint waved at our waiter and lip-synced "coffee."

We consumed our caffeine slowly, mine with cream, Clint's, black.

"There's one thing we forgot to tell you," I said.

"I had a feeling there was. Shoot."

"After Gram told me about the night of Sonny Bob's abduction by two men who looked like thugs, I reached out to a former college friend of mine living there in New Orleans, a Alex DeCicco . . ."

Brennan nodded at the mention of Alex DeCicco, meaning, I was sure, that he knew the name.

". . . and when I did so, Alex had me meet with two of his boys—he called them business associates—dark, swarthy Italian types. We met in the back of a low-class restaurant in Metairie."

"Purpose of meeting?"

"They were going to give me the name of a contact in New York who would help me find Sonny."

"What Alex say when you met him?"

"Sam? I never actually met with him, we talked over the phone."

"Sam couldn't just give you contact name?"

"I didn't question it at the time. When the description Gram gave me of the two men who spirited Sonny away sounded like they could be Mafia types, I thought of Alex because there'd been rumors during the last few years that he was mob connected."

"You didn't question Alex's meeting setup?"

"No, who knows how and why Mafia types operate. I was just thankful for some help, from any source."

"Now you realize you met with them so they could see what you look like, and now they might well be your stalkers."

"Exactly," I said.

"Definite possibility," he concurred.

The waiter came and warmed up our coffees. I recited the one-and-the-Same Beppe theory. Clint was slouched back in his chair, watching me speak in his own languorous fashion. Despite his habit of keeping a watchful eye on the entire restaurant, when I was actually talking he was a focused, attentive listener.

"Contact name was?"

"A Roberto Gagliano."

"What happened when you met Gagliano?"

"I never did. Before I made the time to call him, I discovered Sonny's body and the mystery of his whereabouts was, sadly, solved."

"DeCicco describe Gagliano to you?"

"No, but the guys in Metairie gave me two of his phone numbers. One home, one work. They said it was best to use the work number."

"Don't suppose you memorized them."

"No, but I have them with me."

I lifted my purse off the floor, unzipped it and fished around in the cosmetic bag where I knew I'd stashed the sheet of paper with the phone numbers. I handed the note to Clint. He looked at it and began nodding his head as if to say "yes."

"Knew it was this guy. Just wanted to confirm it."

Now we were getting somewhere. Brennan must be impressed with me at this point. I'd supplied some valuable information. Obviously a gangster he already knew about, but he, of course, would not know his connection to my case.

I smiled. "You know of this person?"

"Sure do."

"And you know of his background? What he does?"

"All of it."

"Wonderful. Tell me."

Just then something else—in addition to the fact that he wore socks in the color of nude—revealed itself about the reserved Detective Brennan. They were white and fairly even, albeit slightly buck: his teeth. He was highly amused by the response he was about to provide.

Clint grinned and said, "Rob Gagliano is an undercover cop."

chapter 32

AUGUST SLIPPED AWAY and September arrived. Central Park began to sport rusted foliage—the maple tree leaves turned red and the American elms burst forth in a brilliant yellow. We still had the occasional warm Indian summer day, but cooler, gusty breezes were making their presence known.

Marc Caress was keeping me busy with magazine shoots mostly and just enough runway work thrown in to provide variety. He found some of the latter for Jeannette also and, through her own connections, she found some print work. The two of us were happily, and gratefully, bivouacked at Aunt Winnie's, as was Buck. Winnie had heard Buck grumble about his rented room in the Village and then about his mid-town hotel and had insisted he, too, move into one of her guest bedrooms.

He didn't protest, asserting this made it all the easier to keep tabs on me and keep me safe. I didn't expect him to go with me to my modeling assignments, despite the fact that I often felt followed, even in broad daylight. But he was often unavailable on some evenings and my days off. I didn't confront him on this, figuring he was busy with more pressing P.I. work.

In fact, Buck was making a concerted effort to drum up business. His birthday was September 9th and he threw himself a party at Sardi's and invited many of Martha Fleming's friends and Broadway co-stars from past shows, along with a smattering of other show biz types: directors, agents, even some stagehands. It was held upstairs in the Eugenia Room where the world-famous cartoon drawings of the likes of Lucille Ball, Kevin Bacon, Michael Douglas and others lined the walls. An artist sat in a corner with an easel doing similar renditions of some of the guests, and a photographer took an individual shot of everyone upon their arrival. The booze and hors d'oeuvres flowed and, all in all, it added up to a successful networking venture for Private Eye Lemoyne.

Clearly, Buck was planning on extending his usual New York stay for as long as it took to find Sonny's killer, so he had every right—and certainly need—to do everything he could to drum up additional business.

I had to admit it would also be typical of Buck to do some sleuthing on Sonny's behalf on his own, without worrying me with the particulars. The police, via Detective Clint Brennan, now had all the facts. I needed to quit stressing, all we could do was wait.

The work on my Brooklyn brownstone was proceeding slowly. Currently my accountant Howie, the main overseer of the project, was in a dispute with some of the men employed by the contractors and they'd gone on a work stoppage until it was settled.

Howie told me not to worry about the repair progress. Buck told me not to worry about anyone following me. I called Gram in New Orleans regularly and she quoted *à cheval donné on ne regarde pas le dents*, which roughly translates into "don't look a gift horse in the mouth" and must have referred to the benevolence of Aunt Winnie's free room and board despite the fact I'd not mentioned my living arrangements but rather whined about my fears to her. There are apparently no French proverbs for worry over stalkers and kidnappers.

On the brighter side of the news—and a circumstance that was doing a great deal to keep most of my worries at bay—was the fact that one Sherwood Benjamin, Esquire was calling regularly and squiring me around town. Better still, he would be flirtatious and attentive but never crossed the line and pressured for more physical contact nor did he take for granted I'd be available whenever he called, although that was usually the case. He seemed to respect that, ex-husband or no, with the murder of Sonny Bob I'd just lost a person of some importance in my life's history. Sherwood was a lawyer, not a bodyguard, but I felt safe in his presence. The sense that I was being followed was absent whenever we strolled around town, leading me to conclude that my stalker was a figment of my imagination. But then I'd spend a day on my own and my antennae bristled with suspicions once again.

It was on one of my assignment-free days that I awoke to a quiet apartment, donned my favorite years-old lime-green terrycloth robe and headed to the kitchen for a breakfast of hot tea and croissants. The apartment was a little stuffy, as Winnie had decided we were close enough to October to turn up a little heat now and then. I was perusing the *New York Post* and planning a day at the Metropolitan Museum of Art when the lady of the house invaded my tranquil morning.

Winnie has some of Martha Fleming's flair for drama. She fairly flew into the kitchen, her beige taffeta robe rustling in the breeze she created. She carried Pierre in one arm and waved a card in the air with her other hand.

"Freddy, shugah, you're finally up. This must mean you're not working today. Well, that's wonderful because I need you. I mean I *really* need you, honey. Now don't say no. I don't mean to impose . . . well, yes, I guess I do . . . but haven't I the right now and then? Don't answer that, just listen. This is a catastrophe!"

I smiled. "I'm all ears, Winnie. And it's nice to be needed, whatever it is."

Winnie stopped abruptly, gently placed Pierre down on the floor and fanned herself with the card. "I do believe this menopause is gettin' to me, shugah. Forgot to take my hormone pills this week. I better sit down first."

Winnie is sixty-eight and rather past the age for menopause from what I've heard, but it seemed to make her feel good to refer to it frequently. Rather past the age for taking hormone pills too but I hear that's what many southern women do.

Pierre padded over to his milk dish, took a few dainty gulps, then raised his little head and glanced back at Winnie momentarily as if to say, *cool your jets, lady.* He padded out of the room, content to miss whatever the latest crisis might be.

"Let me get you some tea, Winnie."

"Thank you, honey. It's been so wonderful having you and Jeannette and Buck here. I'm gonna miss y'all when you're gone."

"We love being with you," I said as I poured.

I warmed my own tea and said, "What seems to be the problem?"

"Oh, my child, what doesn't? As you know, ah'm one of the co-chairs of the planning committee for the opening night gala of the New York Philharmonic."

"Of course." *I didn't get the memo.*

"And, as you know, it's *the* event of the year . . . it's really what starts the season here."

"I do." *Why does no one tell me this kind of vital news?*

"Well, shugah, there's more than one co-chair and just late yesterday ah found out the names of the others." She waved the card in the air again.

"A lovely bunch of philanthropic souls I'm sure." *Social climbers all.*

"Some of them are not really music lovers at all, Freddy."

"They're not?" *I'm shocked.*

"No indeed. And some of them are, well, not in our league."

"I would imagine." *What league would that be? Baseball league? Basketball league?*

"One name in particular will surprise you no end."

"I'm sure that's true." *Who would that be? Madonna? Lady Gaga?*

"One other co-chair is Dina Hutton!"

"Sonny's stepsister?"

"Yes!"

"I am shocked." *I am shocked.*

Winnie's tea had cooled somewhat while she was talking and now she downed it in three quick gulps.

"Pour me some more, shugah, and if you want to put whiskey in it, that's fine too."

"I don't know if that's a good mix at this hour, but more hot tea is coming up."

I turned on the flame under the copper kettle and stood, waiting.

Pierre padded back into the kitchen, raised his head and gave me an inquiring look, which I didn't think meant, *what's this I hear about a co-chair?* but rather, *are you gonna give me some grub, toots, or not?*

I opened a can of Fancy Cat and spooned its contents into Pierre's bowl. Once the water was hot, I got a teabag and renewed Winnie's tea. "You get along with Dina. It won't be a problem."

"Well, the get-along part is yet to be proven, sweet girl, but there's a more immediate problem."

"And that is?"

"Dina talked me into having lunch with her today. She had the gall to suggest the Four Seasons—as if she could afford *that*!"

"She knows you'll pick up the check, Winnie."

"She does indeed. And she's bringing her sister Bella too. For what reason ah can't imagine."

"For another free lunch."

"You got that right, honey. I don't know how I'll cope with the two of those . . . those . . . never mind."

"You'll do fine."

"Well," she sighed, "Ah know ah will because, Freddy, y'all are coming with me."

With that, my cell phone rang and I retrieved it from the pocket of my robe. Was I to be saved by the bell? Hopefully, this was Marc with a last-minute gig.

"Hello," I said.

"Free for dinner tonight?"

"Why, I believe I could be but . . ."

"Pick you up at six."

"Seven?"

"See you."

If I didn't recognize the voice, the cadence was familiar.

"Who was that, shugah?"

"Detective Patrick, aka Clint, Brennan."

It was going to be an interesting day.

chapter 33

"IT'S GREAT TO see you again, Miss Freddy." This from Winnie's bartender, chef, chauffeur, butler and all-around handy man, Morgan. "It's great to see you too, Morgan. How's your son?" "Back home, going to LSU." "That's wonderful." Morgan had pulled up in Winnie's black Bentley as he'd drawn transportation duty to the Four Seasons.

Morgan expertly threaded his way through the usual noisy mass of cars, limos, numerous taxis and pedestrians with an exaggerated sense of entitlement when it came to adhering to walk or don't walk signs.

"Tell me again, Winnie, why this lunch with Dina is so necessary."

"Well, darlin', you said yourself ah have to get along with the little runt. So when she said, 'let's get together and discuss the gala, just you and me,' what could ah say? Of course, it's just a ruse to get me to tell her how it's done. She's got some relative who's on some other board or another who's important and got her this spot because, heaven knows, she's not exactly high society."

Morgan coughed.

"Well, shugah, neither am I for that matter. But you know what ah mean. They're simply not nice people, didn't speak to Sonny Bob for years until eight or nine months ago and . . ."

Winnie warmed to her subject and pontificated further on the various reasons the sisters lacked grace, style, breeding, manners and on and on. But I was distracted, fascinated as I was by Morgan's cough. Inwardly, I was grinning to myself. Was it deliberate? Was it meant to remind Winnie of her own humble beginnings? And where did a chauffeur/chef/bartender get such nerve? If it had been a warning cough, I greatly admired Morgan, even as I was astounded at his gall.

We pulled up to the Seagram building on 52nd Street, and Morgan came around to the back of the car and helped Winnie out and then me. "Have a pleasant lunch, ladies."

"Thank you, we will," Winnie sang out as she walked rapidly to the entrance. We took the elevator up to the second floor and got out.

"The de Foucauld party," Winnie told the maitre d'.

He ran his finger down a list of names in what looked like a guest book.

"I'm sorry, Madame, there's no such name here. Perhaps . . ."

Winnie interrupted. "Try Hutton."

"Ah yes, here we are."

He beckoned a waiter over, who said, "This way please, ladies."

As we followed, I whispered to Winnie, "Hutton?"

"Dina's last name." She virtually spat the words out. "Wouldn't you know!"

Dina and her sister, Bella, were already seated at one of the tables near the huge floor-to-ceiling windows. I expected them to stand in deference to Winnie's age, but they didn't. They did smile . . . well, Bella did. They'd already ordered drinks and were chatting away. They wore no makeup, and Dina had pulled her light-brown hair into a ponytail. We sat down and joined them. Winnie began chirping away about the weather.

When the waiter came, I thought our orders were indicative of our personas. The sisters, both of whom are a little overweight and, according to Winnie, abrasive, ordered the spicy spaghetti. I, as a model ever a slave to calorie count, ordered the ahi tuna seaweed salad, and *noveaux riche* Winnie chose a dramatic dish—the beef tartare that, the menu advised, would be prepared tableside.

Conversation progressed pleasantly enough as Dina asked questions about the chef for the gala's post-concert dinner—someone with the impressive name of Kurt Gutenbrunner, just where the dinner would be held—Arpeggio Food and Wine in Avery Fisher Hall, just who was Wynton Marsalis—Winnie took a deep breath and answered, "An American jazz and western classical virtuoso trumpeter and composer and Artistic Director of Jazz at Lincoln Center."

New to being rich or not, Winnie had clearly absorbed cultural knowledge, and I was impressed. Not enough to fully listen to the rest of the conversation as my thoughts wandered, as they were wont to do these days, more absorbed as I was in the facts surrounding Sonny's murder than anything else.

The real new knowledge that most impressed me was that Roberto Gagliano was not a fellow mobster buddy of Alex DeCicco's but in reality an undercover cop. It meant I could erase one name from my list of suspected stalkers. And maybe Gagliano was reporting regularly to Detective Brennan—Clint—and with his inside knowledge this case would be solved very soon, or at the very least Roberto could identify whoever was following me. Buck seemed casual, even dismissive, of my stalker suspicions but I remained convinced.

My next musing had to do with the possibility of ordering a glass of wine—we'd all ordered iced tea—when Winnie excused herself to go to the ladies room.

As soon as she was out of earshot, Dina leaned toward me and said, "Has Winifred discussed Sonny Bob's Will with you?"

The woman is nothing if not subtle.

Bella leaned forward in her chair also. I was afraid if the answer was 'yes,' they might both leap across the table and into my lap, such was their obvious urgency.

Fortunately, my answer was, "No."

"She told us you hadn't seen it, so we thought she might have at least discussed it with you," said Bella. "Sonny was always talking about his Will. Making jokes about it really. Remember what he said back last winter, Dina? I laughed my ass off over that one."

"What makes you think Winnie knows anything about a Will? I'm not so sure he even had one."

"Well, Sonny Bob lived with her for a time. I think he confided in her."

"I wouldn't know anything about that, and we haven't discussed it. I think we're both more concerned with the nature of Sonny's death."

They sat back in their chairs, nodding agreement and mumbling insincere comments along the lines of "Of course" and "That's most important."

"I hear you own an antique store, Dina," I said.

Dina looked distressed that the conversation about Sonny Bob and money had been interrupted but answered, "Yes, on Atlantic Avenue in Brooklyn."

"That must be so interesting. Winnie said you have a marvelous collection."

Winnie had said no such thing, but the sisters hadn't cornered the market on insincerity today.

"I do my best," Dina said. She had begun to look down-right glum over this change of subject.

"I've always been fascinated by spears. Especially exotic ones. Do you carry any?" *Neither had they a monopoly on a lack of subtlety.*

Dina looked extremely uncomfortable. "I have a couple of Japanese ones, mostly I have daggers," she said.

"Daggers are very popular," Bella offered. "People like to give them as gifts." Bella's voice contained a smile and she seemed unperturbed.

"You have some Aborigine spears too, don't you?" I asked Dina.

"Yes . . . that is, I think so. I haven't done a full inventory in ages." Dina's response was sullen. She had fallen into the kind of full sulk I'd observed before. She looked around the restaurant with some impatience before adding, "Most collectors seem to prefer Italian daggers."

Dina didn't seem curious as to why I posed this question. I couldn't decide if this was due to her usual self-absorbed indifference or something else.

Winnie returned as the tail end of the sentence was spoken. "Prefer Italian what?" she asked, then answered her own question. "Men? Oh, my dear, I prefer French like my late Charles. Now there was a wonderful man, and he . . ." Her eyes suddenly looked watery and her voice began to crack. I patted her arm.

"I'm sorry," she said, shaking her head.

"Don't be, Winnie. Would you like dessert?" I said.

"Ah think ah might," she answered.

Bella said, "I'll wave the waiter down."

"Excuse me, I'm going to make a pit stop too," I said, and headed for the ladies room.

Later, when Morgan picked us up and we were alone in Winnie's car, she filled me in on the conversation that took place when I was absent.

"The girls weren't hesitant to talk about how they just hated the idea that you might inherit all of Sonny Bob's estate, shugah, ah never heard anything like it."

"I'm not surprised."

"Bella said you should never have divorced him and that you'd probably take his money and go shack up with someone. Dina said you looked like a flakey blonde and you'd probably donate a hunk of it to Greenpeace or some such thing. They don't even know you, honey. I don't understand all that venom. I was too shocked to speak. I wish I'd told them to . . ."

"It's okay, Winnie, don't upset yourself."

"Well, it's just awful the way . . ." Winnie let out a sigh and then looked at me intently.

"Listen, when ah was in the ladies room, did they talk about me?"

"No, Winnie. We just made small talk."

I lied to spare Winnie's feelings and because my thoughts drifted again—this time to Dina Hutton's extreme consternation and change of subject when spears were mentioned.

"Who the hell is that driver?" This from a small figure crouched behind a wheel, following Morgan's smooth cruising through heavy traffic. *"Looks like dat guy from the New Jersey people. This prick's gonna be trouble, I know it."* He made a note to tell Timmy.

chapter 34

GLORIA VITALE STOOD outside of the small beauty shop where she worked in Queens, about to enjoy the first of many smokes of the day. She lit up, tossed the match onto the street, stuck the cigarette in her mouth and buttoned the long, pink coat sweater she was wearing against the morning's chill. It was a Monday, and business would be slow. Her first appointment wasn't until eleven thirty, but she'd come in early in case there were walk-ins. Besides, she wanted to have some time alone, to think. Traffic was heavy as people were still driving to work at this hour and the combination of exhaust fumes and general city soot wasn't the most pleasant environment for reflection, but at home her two young daughters and Beppe provided too much distraction, even though Beppe wasn't home much these days. That was one of their issues.

Beppe ran a couple of bakery franchises for his friend Alex DeCicco and, especially lately, the pastry business seemed to demand all sorts of hours and travel. Back and forth to New Orleans yet. It's not that Gloria hadn't entertained some suspicions prior to these past few months. The money Beppe brought home, or more accurately, the amounts he spent seemed to rise and fall in a way that had no bearing on bakery sales and certainly bore no relation to the current general economy from what Gloria understood from the television news.

Two skate boarders whizzed by, nearly knocking Gloria down. She swore to herself and tossed the butt of her cigarette out onto the street, fished in the pocket of her sweater for her pack and lit up another.

"If life didn't make me so nervous, I wouldn't smoke so damn much," she said aloud to no one in particular.

Beppe even chided her of late about her drinking. He'd taken her to a dinner at Frank Roma's home. He'd insisted she and their daughters oughta get to know the Romas. That Louise and Jenny would enjoy getting to know Roma's daughter, Caitlin—even though their girls were ten and twelve and Caitlin Roma was eighteen years old. Just one of many things Beppe said and did that made no sense. Frank was always bragging to Beppe about Caitlin and she had to admit she could see why. Caitlin was a gorgeous looking girl, skinny and very tall. On this occasion, Gloria had downed one too many glasses of red wine to calm her nerves.

Frank's wife, Sophia, seemed to adopt a superior attitude, as did Frank. Beppe had said the Romas ran about three bakeries for DeCicco. Owning one more bakery than the Vitales entitled them to put on airs? It's not like Roma was Beppe's boss, or anything, but he sure acted like it. That had also made her stop and think. Gloria had never finished high school, but she wasn't dumb, she noticed things, *everything as a matter of fact*, and so much didn't add up these days.

"Hey Gloria, Betty brought some donuts. Are yah comin' back in?"

One of the other operators, Sally Salvatore, had stepped outside, her elaborate blonde upsweep nearly coming undone from the wind. Gloria's own black hair was caught up in a short ponytail.

"Thanks, Sally. I'll be in soon."

Gloria thought about Sally and her other friends. She'd worked here since she was seventeen and she loved everyone in the shop. When she met and married Beppe, he tried to get her to quit and work closer to their home in Brooklyn, but she wasn't about to. And that was the other problem: friends. More specifically, Beppe's friends. Not just the snotty Frank Roma and his wife, but the new one, Tim Ryan. He, too, seemed to look down on Beppe. Gloria had to smile to herself. *And not just because he's tall and skinny and Beppe is short and chubby.* He didn't look a bit like any of Beppe's other friends. Ryan had a big nose, and she hated his blonde, stringy hair, the way he wore it to his shoulders and his bushy moustache. He'd come over to the house for a drink about three or four times now and seemed to always be arguing with her husband.

Betty came out with a caramel covered donut. "Here, you gonna stand out here freezin' your ass off, you might as well not be hungry on top of it." She left as swiftly as she'd arrived, clutching the top of her hairdo.

Gloria took a grateful bite, chewed, swallowed, then took another drag on her cigarette. Does Beppe have any friends like that? Maybe that Roberto Gagliano. He'd been to their home a couple of times and at the Roma dinner party too. He was friendly and down to earth. She noticed Frank and Beppe always called him Roberto, but he'd refer to himself as Rob. *Gloria noticed everything.*

She dropped her cigarette on the ground, crushed it with her toe, and concentrated on the donut.

Gloria mused, *I keep eating and drinking like I have been lately and I'll weigh three hundred pounds.* Which made her think again of tall, thin Tim and his visit two days ago to their home. Beppe had received him in the closed-in porch just off their dining area. The room he called his den on such occasions, but the one Gloria called the girls' homework room at all other times.

She'd brought two beers in for them and, unthinkingly, left the door slightly ajar. Just enough so that minutes later when she went to retrieve a platter from the dining room armoire, she'd heard their raised voices.

"Sam said, don't harm a hair on her head," she heard her husband say.

"Hell, Beppe. Alex's there and we're here. This Mr. Mac-Gyver said follow her. But if she doesn't lead us to the dough, grab her, take her somewhere and grill it outta her. Then go get the money. If it's not where she says, beat it outta her. If it is, go back and whack her. Nice and clean."

Gloria heard Beppe belch. "You're nuts, Ryan. When this job is over, MacGyver is history. We ain't workin' for no Mr. MacGyver, or whatever his name is. Our job is to do what Alex wants. You wanna be in deep doo-doo with Alex?"

"Listen wiseass, right now Alex's workin' for MacGyver. If we get it done the way MacGyver wants it done and as fast as he wants it done, we'll be in solid with Alex. DeCicco's not gonna worry about details once he gets his share," said Tim.

Then either Beppe or Tim slammed the door shut. More out of anger, Gloria was certain, than to not be overheard as she'd been silent as a cat in the dining room and visually obscured by the open armoire door.

"Don't sound like bakery business to me," she'd whispered to herself at the time.

Later that evening, after she got the girls to bed, she'd revisited the scenario she'd witnessed and decided to file it all away in her memory bank for the time being. Soon it would be Thanksgiving, and then Christmas. Not the time to stage a confrontation with Beppe. In the meantime, she'd go about her business, continuing life as usual. *And she'd notice everything.*

chapter 35

THE DAY WAS closing down, and pink and orange ribbons laced across the evening horizon. When we arrived at our destination, I saw that it was a plain, but good-sized, house in Brooklyn—on Schenectady Avenue in East Flatbush, to be precise. There was a shared driveway with a garage and deck, and I eventually learned it had a large formal living room, a larger-still formal dining room with a spacious kitchen boasting loads of cabinets. Upstairs a wide hall led to four full-size bedrooms. Three bathrooms, a finished basement with a separate laundry room completed the layout. A realtor's dream. Just not what I expected as our dining destination.

Earlier Winnie's house phone had rung, and it was Clint. True to his gracious, if abrupt, invitation to dinner, he'd arrived ten minutes before the agreed time of six o'clock and was announcing that he was downstairs, parked, and waiting for me. I'd fully expected that I needed to plan to be in front of the apartment building, on the sidewalk at six, ready for his arrival. The early arrival and call was, in a way, an unexpected courtesy from Detective Brennan.

When he initially called, Clint had not included any advice as to how to dress. I was tempted to throw on jeans and be ultra casual, but maybe he'd reserved at a somewhat upscale restaurant for our second date, or meeting, confab, or whatever it was, and I'd be insulting him were I to dress down. I opted for something middle of the road. At least it was unremarkable in the book of this clotheshorse. It would possibly be termed outrageous by a more sensible woman. If I were entirely honest with myself, outrageous was probably what I was aiming for. Anything to shake a few extra syllables out of my less-than-loquacious new friend.

I sifted thru some of the clothes I'd splurged on since my return to New York and came up with a Louis Vuitton short knit coat and matching belted shorts in a black and white tweed design. The shorts were very short and—as if that wasn't bad enough—I added stiletto-heeled black suede pumps. I was aware it would be entirely possible that I'd be a tad overdressed for wherever Brennan was taking me. I was yet to learn I'd be inappropriate in spades.

When I got in the car, I noticed Clint's formerly worn-looking loafers had taken on a new shine. A good sign.

He said, "Hey," as I slid onto the seat.

I said, "Hey," back.

Knowing Clint, our dialogue might have ended there for the entire ride, but I'd come prepared with a topic of conversation.

"You know," I said, "I've been wondering about something. As Buck probably told you, I deliberately contacted an old college friend of mine in New Orleans who is said to be connected to the Mob and I met with his friends who absolutely meet anyone's definition of Mafioso, but I'm still having a hard time grasping this. I mean I thought the Mafia was a thing of the past."

"They're definitely diminished in number and power," Clint said, "But there're still remnants around. All the big five families are understaffed, you could say. Most of the top honchos are in prison. Some are still running their businesses from there."

"You say they're understaffed?"

"Yeah, the Bonanno family no longer has an underboss or consigliore, same with the Luchese and DeCavaleante families. The Columbo family has a guy who's technically the street boss. He's been in bad health for years but manages to function in their business, yet stays out of trouble. Most of these guys are in their 60's and 70's."

"But the ones I know," I said, "are from New Orleans. I'm not naive about some of the rumors about political corruption there, but I didn't think there was much of a mob presence."

Clint turned his head just briefly to glance at me with a look I couldn't fully decipher and then returned his attention to the road. He was wearing khakis and a black V-necked sweater over a light blue dress shirt. Wherever we were going, they didn't require that male customers wear a jacket. I looked around, realized we were headed over the bridge for Brooklyn, and wondered if before long we'd be back at the cops' favorite Il Porto.

"On the contrary, Freddy, New Orleans was the first home of the American Mafia. And you a former Big Easy girl," he chided, smiling slightly but still looking ahead.

"No kidding?"

"Yes, mam. Back in the 1800's there was a small Sicilian colony of 'em in New Orleans. During the Union occupation, a gang headed by a guy named Agnello was trusted by the Union to keep things under control along the French quarter docks."

"Amazing."

"Interesting anyway. Not long after that, a guy named Macheca was running the underworld. He wasn't technically a Mafioso, but he established a family, name of Matranga. After him, a bad guy called Giuseppe Esposito escaped from the authorities in Palermo, left Italy for New York, ended up in New Orleans and took over. He also put the Provezano family in charge of the docks there. They had family wars and some leaders died off, but the Mafia thrived and continued."

We took a left turn and I realized we were not headed in the direction of Il Porto, but I was enjoying the ride and the evening breeze drifting through the car windows and was not about to demand to know where we were going.

"More recently," Clint continued, "There was a Carlos Marcello and . . ."

"Now *him* I've heard of," I said, proud of myself.

"Yeah, for a long time he was really the most powerful Mafioso in the United States."

"I would think that would have been John Gotti," I said.

"Most people would. Marcello kept a far lower profile than Gotti."

"I read a book about Marcello and his possible connection to the assassination of President Kennedy. But wasn't he shot dead or something like that?"

"Nothing like that. He got out of prison, got Alzheimer's but lived out his years in his mansion."

"Really? He probably lived in the Garden District, and I didn't even know it," I chuckled.

"Nope. Lived in a white marble, two-story house overlooking a golf course in Metairie."

In my mind's eye, I suddenly saw a visual of my own recent experience in Metairie, with DeCicco's thugs. I was in the heart of Marcello's empire and didn't know it.

"Are you telling me Marcello's mob is still alive and active?"

"Not really. His son's around, word is he's legit. There's a restaurant that was a long-time hangout for Marcello called Mosca's. It's still in operation."

I had to admit I was fascinated and made a mental note to visit it during my next trip.

"Don't tell me it's in the Quarter?"

"Nope, in Avondale."

I was impressed by Clint's knowledge, not to mention getting complete sentences out of him for once.

"You certainly know your mob history," I said.

"Like I said, it's interesting."

I was still gazing at him with school-girlish admiration when he pulled into a driveway. It was then I saw the large but unpretentious semi-detached brick home.

"We're here," Clint announced.

"Is this where you live?"

"Nope."

"I don't mean to be nosy," I said teasingly but with undisguised apprehension, "but you said we were having dinner."

"We are." Clint said. "My Aunt Pearl lives here."

He got out of the car, came around and opened my passenger door.

He grinned. "She throws a big family dinner here every Monday."

chapter 36

A JOVIAL GENTLEMAN in his late fifties, as tall as Clint but with a much wider grin, opened the door at our knock and greeted us. Immediately behind him, I glimpsed a staircase to the right and to the left a grandfather clock and a long, faded rug runner in some kind of colorful design that cascaded down a narrow hallway. From distant rooms, I heard the din of voices joined with some squeals and giggles, obviously from small children. A hint of smoke filled the air, together with the more pleasant aroma of food cooking.

"This is my uncle, Seth Brennan," Clint said. "Seth, this is Frédérique Bonnaire."

"Frédérique!" the uncle exclaimed, "a pretty name for a very pretty girl!"

"Thank you, please call me Freddy."

"Freddy," Seth said, "You're a big one . . . by that I mean a tall lady, aren't you now?"

"You and I are tall, too, Seth, so height is not something new around here, is it?" Clint said sullenly.

"Oh, no offense intended, I just . . ."

"None taken," I said and extended my hand and shook Seth's.

Clint gently touched my back, saying, "Follow me. I'll get us some drinks."

We threaded our way through the living room, which was dominated by a long, brown velvet couch that seemed to have seen a stain or two from spilled drinks in its time, and a dining room boasting a round mahogany table with mismatched chairs. Clint stopped for introductions here and there. Everyone seemed very polite, at least no one did a double take over my attire. The guests were wearing jeans if they were on the young side, pants suits or dresses if they were over fifty. This was clearly the gathering of a big Irish clan. A few of the elders had a brogue.

Our path ended in the kitchen where I met Aunt Pearl—at about five, three, she was almost as wide as she was tall, with beautiful gray hair. She had merry blue eyes with deep squint lines around them, indicating she, like Seth, smiled a lot. From the fridge, Clint grabbed a bottle of beer for me and a can of Pepsi for himself, as Pearl and I made small talk.

Clint said, "Excuse us," and we left for the dining room. Dinner was buffet style, and after handing me a plate, Clint wandered off to talk to some men across the room, leaving me to mingle on my own. I filled my plate, then carried it and my beer to an armchair covered in faded maroon velvet next to the bench of an upright piano. The living room walls were lined with bookshelves that were jammed with a combination of hardbacks and paperbacks, all looking slightly worn, thus well read. It was a warm home that clearly put comfort ahead of style. I loved it.

It was not hard to like the other guests either. A few made it a point to walk over and chat with me. The topic was usually Pearl's wonderful stew. A woman named Beth commented on some of the ingredients—mushrooms, herbs, beef gravy and ketchup. A teenager named Alice advised that it should always be made with oxtail soup, preferably a brand that she spelled out as K-n-o-r-r. And Seth dropped by to tell me even curry powder was included, a fact he clearly found remarkable, as did I. By the end of the evening, I felt I could go home and duplicate the main dish.

When I finished eating, I took my plate into the kitchen where Pearl was still busily at work. I chatted with her and then she did a lot of insisting when I declined a slice of apple pie, but I won in the end. I did accept a cup of tea and stayed to sip and talk longer, all the while wondering what Brennan had in mind with this unusual visit and just when I'd actually get a chance to talk to him. As if reading my mind, he appeared at one of the kitchen doors, crooked a finger at me and said, "Come on," adding, "Excuse us, auntie."

I put down my teacup, nodded at Pearl and followed the peripatetic detective down the hall to the main entry and up the stairs. We continued along the wide upstairs hallway and, as we walked, I peeked through the open doors at the several bedrooms, all consisting of a decorating melody of flowered wallpaper, flowered bedspreads, and floral slipcovers on chairs—none of them burdened with an attempt to match each other.

Clint was walking at a fast clip and in no time he opened a door for me to enter.

"It's a bathroom!" I said.

"It's the only guarantee of privacy."

"What if someone. . ."

"They'll knock."

I'd figured out by now that Brennan was a tad unconventional, but this was a bit much.

"Go on," he said impatiently, as I hesitated.

For a second, I entertained the fear he might really have some kind of standing-up version of intimacy in mind, but I didn't have long to ponder this, as he pulled me inside and pressed me down on a dainty white metal chair with a plush green cushion. As bathrooms go, this was sparkling clean with a white tub and sink, a white shower curtain adorned with forest green fishes, a large shag rug in the same shade of green and an aroma suggesting some kind of perfumed cleanser. Brennan closed the lid on the commode and sat down.

"How's your week been?" Clint asked. "Any stalkers?"

I *did* appreciate that he took this issue seriously. Certainly, Buck did not.

"When I'm running around on photo assignments, I scarcely have time to notice," I confessed, "and I won't have any more runway gigs until next week. The rest of the time, I've been with Buck or riding around in Winnie's car. Speaking of which . . ."

"That's good news."

I was determined to tell Clint about Dina, her antique store and its supply of spears, but I felt self-conscious about the idea. There were antique spears available all over the city, as well as the internet. Would I sound like a ridiculous amateur sleuth? I decided to frame my report as an amusing story.

"Well, a funny thing did happen this week. You see, my aunt is a co-chair for some gala benefiting the New York Philharmonic and . . ."

"Cut to the chase."

So much for humorous anecdotes.

"Okay, I will." I spoke sternly and fairly glared at Clint, but this seemed to escape notice. "Winnie and I met with Sonny Bob's two stepsisters, one of whom is Dina Hutton, the owner of an antique store in Brooklyn. She stocks antique spears. When I asked about this item, she seemed to be noticeably uncomfortable and irritable. That's the story."

'That's fairly interesting."

"It *is?*"

"Did you read any of the newspaper reports on Sonny's murder?"

"I was pretty distracted at the time. I didn't take the time to actually . . ."

"We didn't release the information about the spear to the press."

chapter 37

It was the third quarter. The score was New Orleans Saints, nine, San Francisco 49'ers, fourteen. San Francisco called a time out. It was Saturday morning, and Pierre and I were watching a football game Buck had thoughtfully taped the night before. After the cozy dinner at the home of Clint Brennan's Aunt Pearl, it was back to work for the remainder of the week with two photo layouts for *Vogue* and one for *Bazaar*. No assignments today, but I'd risen early anyway. Winnie had announced she was "fixin' to go" to her summer home in Southampton for the weekend for one last hurrah before cold weather permanently set in. Pierre and I had breakfast and were now in the den, nestled on an overstuffed salon sofa that was covered in gray mohair. My little feline buddy dozed next to my hip and I nursed a second cup of coffee. I'd heard Buck come in very late last night, so it was not surprising that he would sleep in. It was almost eleven o'clock but Jeannette also had yet to wake up, and I was feeling impatient about that—because I had a surprise for her.

Commercials came on, and I hit the mute on the remote. And thought. About spears and death, about Mafioso thugs, about the small figure lurking in semi-darkness at the fashion show, and about a heartbreaking funeral in New Orleans. Ruminating on the last factors in the list reminded me of another small figure—the petite woman at Sonny's funeral. I'd eventually put an identity to her image when I realized she was the newscaster next to the ABC van on the street outside my brownstone on the night I reported Sonny's death. But I'd yet to come up with her name. I made a mental note to take time to watch the ABC evening news soon or, at the very least, google their website on my laptop. I hoped she'd meet with me and reveal just why it was important to show up at the funeral.

Drew Bree threw a completed pass to Colston Marcus. Third down, inside the five.

I turned my attention back to the game just in time. I got up to warm my coffee. Pierre stirred and followed me into the kitchen. I re-filled his water dish and topped off my cup. We returned to the den together. Pierre is a devout Saints fan.

Touchdown! David Thomas made the TD and the score was Saints, sixteen, Forty-Niners, fourteen.

The game went on and I tried my best to concentrate on it.

Reggie Bush caught the ball and ran it back to the thirty-five yard line of San Francisco. The commentator said something about 'really critical mistakes by the forty-niners . . .

Good.

I watched as the score climbed to 19 to 14, New Orleans, then 22-14, New Orleans. I could breathe a sigh of relief.

I pulled Pierre onto my lap, thought about my laptop and realized it was in my Brooklyn brownstone. Looking up the little lady reporter would have to wait, unless I was home tonight in time to catch the evening news. I also realized I was still a bit sleepy, and I closed my eyes and stretched out on the couch, rearranging a pillow and Pierre to do so. My nap lasted a mere ten minutes.

"A nail biter," the announcer said. "Score is now 22-22."

This jarred me awake once more, and I put Pierre down on one end of the couch and made my way toward Jeannette's bedroom. I heard no movement from behind the closed door and no shower sounds coming from the adjoining bathroom. *Wake up, Jeannette! Between the game and you, I'm going through too much anxiety.*

I quietly headed back for more football. Pierre was now off the couch and sitting upright on the floor. He looked my way as I entered the den as if to say, "Are you planning to sit still for once and watch the game so I can relax?"

"Yes, I'm here to stay now," I advised, and sat down and sipped my lukewarm coffee.

There's a framed quote in the office of my dad, the judge, about patience. I gulped down the rest of the coffee and tried to remember it.

Il n'y a point de chemin trop long à qui marche lentement et sans se presser: il n'y a point d'avantages trop éloignés à qui s'y prépare par la patience.

The translation is: There is no road too long to the man who advances deliberately and without undue haste; there are no honors too distant to the man who prepares himself for them with patience.

Well, I wouldn't say my surprise involves honors, but I did wish one Jeannette Sullivan would start advancing deliberately.

A color commentator described 'the swirling wind in San Francisco' . . . then 'the kick is good!' The Saints had won 25-22!

I yelled, "We won!" and bounced up and down on the couch. Pierre merely cocked his head briefly in my direction, did a half victory lap around the coffee table and laid down, his head resting on his front paws. He always celebrates Saints' wins with more restraint than I do.

"What in hell is all the commotion?"

Jeannette appeared at the den's door, red curls sticking out in an electric halo, clad in black jeans and a blue tee shirt, a cup of coffee in one hand.

"Jay, you're up and you're dressed! Wonderful!"

"I don't know how wonderful it is. I'm thinking of going back to bed."

"No, you can't. We're going out to my place. I have big news. I think you're going to like it."

"I already like your place."

"No, I mean I want you to see it."

"I've already seen it."

"Not lately. Howie got all the furniture that was damaged out of the place."

"Great. I think I'll get more coffee and take it back to bed."

"No, you can't. I want us to go to Brooklyn."

"How can we do that? Morgan drove Winnie out to Southampton late Thursday. They won't be back until early Sunday."

I burst out laughing. "Boy, are you spoiled, girlfriend! Now you only travel when chauffeured by Morgan? Ever heard of subways, missy?"

"Okay, okay. I'll go, but only if we go shopping. Are you going to replace some of the furniture? They've got great antique stores on Atlantic Avenue and . . ."

"Ouch. Don't mention that kind of store and that street. Not now." I frowned, then took a deep breath.

"Well, we could go to Bloomingdales then. And have lunch at that little place named Serendipity, or whatever it's called."

"Eventually, yes. I'll probably need one or two new pieces."

"Frédérique, from the looks of that place, you'll need more than one or two."

"Well, the furniture is part of the big news. What I plan to do about it, that is."

Jeannette finally sat down. "I give up. Your creative juices are in a rage, and you're going to get some lumber and build your own."

"Nooooooo, I'm going to get my stuff out of storage, load it onto a truck and put all of it into my Brownstone—put down roots again as it were. I've been calling Luke Jefferson's cell to see if he can help with this, but I keep getting voicemail and he doesn't call back. I hope he's okay . . . Buck hasn't said anything about him lately . . . maybe he's on a long truck run and . . ."

"Luke's probably on a truck run to some podunk town in North Dakota, and why in the world would you want to bring your good stuff for renters to abuse? Part of it's your grandmother's antiques . . . and when you get new tenants, they'll probably destroy it. They might have a passel of little rug rats like the Bishops and . . ."

"You're not listening, girlfriend," I smiled. "There will be no new tenants."

"You're selling!"

"No," I waved my empty cup in the air, "I'm staying!"

"You're staying?"

"Yes!"

"As in living in one place?"

"Yes!"

Jeannette grinned, leapt from her chair and gave me a bone-crushing hug.

"I'm so happy," she said.

"Me too," I said. "I mentioned to Winnie weeks ago that I was very seriously thinking of this, but I swore her to secrecy."

"Well, it worked. She sure as hell didn't say a word to me," Jeannette said, then looked at me intently and added, "This is a good decision, Freddy. Get a fresh start," she said seriously. "And those Brooklyn digs are really your home."

"Forever and ever," I said. "And the other news, Jay, is I want you to come live with me in Park Slope. There's plenty of bedrooms and bathrooms, loads of closets, and you'll . . ."

"Wel-l-l-l-l," Jeannette drew out the word, her gaze downward, her expression sad. "I was getting used to sleeping on Winnie's Porthault sheets."

Then she looked up and grinned. She shouted "I accept!" and hugged me again.

I picked up our cups. "Let me get us some more coffee to celebrate and seal the deal."

When I returned to the den, Jeannette was sitting on one end of the couch and smiling to herself. Pierre was sitting at her feet and seemed to be smiling too, although it may have been a grimace, indicating, "No one consulted *me* on these plans."

I put both mugs on the gold-leaf French coffee table and sat on a straight-back chair next to Jeannette. She picked up her coffee and took a small sip. I did the same.

"And pretty soon . . . ," Jeannette spoke slowly and deliberately. ". . . I'll have a surprise for *you!*"

chapter 38

THE SKY WAS sunny and bright, the air crisp and cool with a slight breeze, so the weather was favorable. But Saturday itself was a mixed bag of good and . . . not bad . . . but dubious factors. I had been in a robe and pajamas when I broke the news to Jay that I planned to stay in New York so I took a quick shower, toweled off and was just stepping into a pair of olive-green cargo pants when my cell phone rang. I quickly pulled on a pair of black Ugg boots before answering it, as my feet were cold.

"Hello."

"It's a beautiful day but here I am working in my office. The only thing that will make things bearable is if you'll agree to have lunch with me."

"I'd love to, but I'm sort of committed to spending the day with Jeannette."

"Then bring her with you, by all means."

"That's very sweet of you."

"Where would you like to eat?"

"Hmmmm . . . oh gosh, I don't know. I'm drawing a blank here. It's been a sort of eventful morning . . . I've got to shift gears before I can think. You pick."

"My brain is preoccupied right now, too, and I'm still waiting for a phone call before I can leave. How about you come down to my office and then we can decide."

"Sounds good. You're on 57th Street, between fifth and sixth?"

"Yes, the Corcoran Building. Eighth floor. There'll be no receptionist, but I'll have Catherine leave your names with the lobby."

"Catherine?"

"My secretary."

"Great. We'll see you then."

Jeannette wandered into my bedroom as I was pulling a long-sleeved gray jersey over my head.

"Who was on the phone?"

"Our lunch date," I grinned.

"Buck?"

"Nooooo. Guess again."

Jay had a black coat sweater on. That looked like a good idea, so I pulled a similar one from my closet, put it on and wrapped a long gray angora scarf around my neck for warmth and style.

"The tall, crazy detective."

"Not exactly crazy, but no."

I added some gold bangle bracelets and put my cell phone in my large, gray purse.

"Oh God, the Brit."

"Why do you say it like that?"

"What kind of a name is Sherwood?"

"One you better get used to."

"I'm used to Buck."

"If I didn't know better, I'd think you have a crush on Buck yourself."

"No. But you could do worse."

"It's not that," I said, "Buck is a wonderful . . ."

Jeannette turned abruptly. "I'm gonna call us a cab."

I followed her out and down the hall as she retrieved her cell from a table in the entryway. I stood in front of a wall mirror and checked my hair, then lip-synched the address per Jay's prompts once she had the taxi company on the line.

"They'll be here in five," she said.

"Will you be warm enough?"

"Think I need a scarf?"

"Wouldn't hurt."

"Wish I had one like yours."

"Take my black one. Third drawer down in the dresser."

I was going to wait by the door, then I remembered something, and followed my friend into my bedroom.

"Hey, you said you had a surprise."

"Yeah?" She pulled out the scarf, wrapped its long length twice around her neck, and rummaged through my jewelry box.

"Well? What is it?" I smiled.

"I'd rather show you, than just tell you."

"Okay."

"Doing that involves some travel." She retrieved two silver cuff bracelets and put one on each wrist.

"Wow! Sounds interesting."

"I think it's interesting, and then some."

She looked me up and down. "Do you have any more Uggs?"

"There's a brown pair in the closet."

Jay found them and traded her sneakers for the boots. "Let's go."

"*Travel?* How far? Paris? Milan?"

"Oh, get serious. Some place in New York. That's all I'll tell you."

We went out the front door, locked it and pushed the elevator button.

"You don't look happy about this surprise."

"The important thing is that *you'll* be happy about it."

"Now I *am* intrigued."

"Good."

"But you still don't look happy."

"I'm not enthralled about lunch with the Brit."

The elevator stopped, and an elderly gentleman got on, so I let the subject lie.

chapter 39

PETERS, NELSON, BENJAMIN, Simms & Fallon occupied floors five through nine of the tall, gray midtown office building. The lobby guard handed us a plastic card so that once we got off on the eighth floor we could gain entrance through a hallway door and proceed to Sherwood's office, which we did. The hallway lights were dim and the atmosphere was a bit creepy in its near silence. Business offices—particularly law offices for some reason—seem strange and forbidding when devoid of their usual hum of activity and personnel. I spied a young associate or paralegal pouring over a stack of thick gold, red and black volumes marked Martindale & Hubbell, and heard the muted clicking of a distant copy machine spitting out its product.

We stepped out of the hallway and into what was obviously a secretarial area immediately preceding lawyer Benjamin's domain. A silver metal plate on the desk read *Catherine Trabill*, but no Catherine was in sight. We sat ourselves down in two client chairs and waited. Five minutes later a petite woman with very short brown hair wearing a black skirt and a short-sleeved jersey shirt in chartreuse exited Sherwood's office, closing the door firmly behind her.

Jay and I stood up.

"Hi," I smiled. "I'm Freddy Bonnaire. We're here to see Sherwood."

Catherine sat behind her desk and, while keeping her eyes focused on her computer, responded, "Mr. Benjamin is on the phone. It will be a few minutes." She had an English accent, but one slightly different from Sherwood's, more Liverpudlian.

We sat back down.

In above five beats, Catherine stood up.

"You have a beautiful office here," I said. "Great combination of colors."

"Yes, Selah likes it," Catherine said. She picked up a file folder and headed for the hallway. "I'll be back in a couple of ticks."

Jeannette and I looked at each other. "Don't know why she'd mention the name of his ex-wife, do you?" I said.

"Right cheeky of her," Jay said in her best *faux* British accent. "And also no doubt because she's an insensitive piece of work."

"Selah?"

"Her too from what I've heard, but I meant Catherine baby. Bitter because she looks like a frog."

"Really, Jay, the proper term is *crapaud*."

"Let me guess, that's French for . . ."

"Toad," I supplied.

"What's the skinny on Selah anyway?" Jay asked. "Winnie tells me Sonny Bob owed her money."

"Entirely possible. Seems Sonny owed half of New York."

"So Sherwood's supposed to do something about that? That why she calls the dude all the time?"

"She's not possessive, Jay. She's just . . . "

"Winnie also says Selah had an affair with Sonny."

". . . lonely." *Or not.*

Jeannette's eyes darted about the room. "Don't they have any magazines around here?"

"Sherwood shouldn't be long. He knows we're here."

"Does he? I didn't see toadie buzz and announce us."

Jeannette got up and walked around behind Catherine's desk. Pressing the intercom button, she said, "Miss

Crapaud has stepped out, Mr. Benjamin. Miss Bonnaire and Miss Sullivan are here."

She fast tracked it back to her seat just as Sherwood opened the door and looked out, his cell phone held to his ear, and a puzzled expression on his face.

A second later, his face morphed into his charming, lopsided smile and he held up his index finger, giving us the one-minute sign.

"Let's talk about what color I should paint my living room," I said. "Maybe we can take the subway there after lunch and make some decisions."

"Should we call and have Selah join us? She's apparently an expert on decor."

"Glad to see your sense of humor's returned. Can't wait to hear you explain the Miss *Crapaud* comment to Sherwood."

"I'll be a *veddy* proper English woman during lunch, don't you worry."

"That'll be a good trick for a *veddy* improper chick from the Bronx."

"You just watch. I'll . . ."

Just then, Catherine returned. She sat behind her desk, took some papers from a drawer and began shuffling through them, never glancing our way.

Jeannette had paused. She spoke again, pretending to continue her original thought. "I'll have shepherd's pie or maybe some very proper fish and chips." Again, delivered with an English accent.

This got Catherine's attention and she looked up at Jay, but only for a nanosecond.

I glared at Jeannette. She shrugged her shoulders.

Catherine opened her mouth, looking as if she was about to deign to announce us, but Sherwood opened the door once more and beat her to the punch.

"Come on in, ladies. Good to see you. Catherine, hold all my calls, please."

Catherine merely turned her head in his direction quickly and then back, which I take it is the universal secretarial sign for agreement to that request.

Again, Jay and I sat in two client chairs, this time those fronting Sherwood's desk, which was an impressive number, its carvings probably done by hand. It sat on top of a large Persian rug and was backed by mahogany bookshelves joined by a low cabinet in the middle. Above the cabinet was a replica of a seascape by the English painter, Turner.

On a side table sat a silver tray and tea service. A proper Englishman, my friend Sherwood. I hoped Jay would not see this and make any clever comments.

"I thought we'd go to Nobu, it's just a couple of blocks away. Sound acceptable?" Sherwood said.

"Sounds great," I said.

He shrugged into a Mackintosh jacket in blackwatch plaid that had been draped over the back of his chair. Buck wouldn't be caught dead in such a jacket, but on Sherwood it looked perfect. He stepped in front of us and led the way out of the office and down the hall to the elevator.

Jeannette whispered, "Sort of a hipster British grandfather look, don't you think?"

"You better mind your manners, missy, is what I think," I hissed.

—

It was a lovely Japanese restaurant with walls in golds and greens and modernistic versions of birch trees as part of the decor. The menu was pricey, but we all chose the sushi lunch special, which kept the order simple and the bill reasonable. Our meals and the bottle of white wine we ordered arrived, and conversation commenced pleasantly, with Jeannette querying Sherwood about his background.

"Born in Blackpool in Lancashire I was. It's a seaside town, heavily dependent on tourism—has been for decades."

"Really?" Jeannette said. "And me, I thought I knew all the tourist spots in Great Britain."

I seriously considered favoring her with another glare, but our host appeared unperturbed.

"Oh yes," Sherwood said, "Documents have been discovered that testify that the reason Blackpool escaped heavy damage during World War II was because Hitler had chosen the town to remain an unspoiled leisure attraction after his planned invasion. Planned to vacation there one day apparently."

"Fascinating," Jay said.

"In the decade after the war, tourists swarmed there to the tune of about seventeen million a year."

"Amazing," Jay gushed.

"But then things went downhill," Sherwood continued. "The decline of the textile industry led to an abandonment of week-long vacations and the rise of package holidays lured our visitors abroad where the weather was more reliably warm and dry."

"A shame," Jay said.

"Well, retailing has been boosting their economy in recent years, but tourism remains their main focus."

"It's all so interesting," Jay cooed.

Sherwood looked away momentarily to pour himself more wine, and Jeannette winked at me, pleased with herself.

He took a healthy sip and then leaned forward, looking Jay square in the eye.

"I'll get you a book on Blackpool, young lady . . ."

Jeannette beamed. "Why, that would be . . ."

"And then," Sherwood added, "You won't be taking the mick with me."

Jay's eyes simply widened.

Sherwood took another swallow of his drink and said, "That's British slang for pulling someone's leg."

"Touché!" I exclaimed, and gently kicked Jay under the table.

Sherwood's retort pretty much silenced Jeannette Sullivan, and for the remainder of the time, he pumped us for details about our modeling careers and various travels. To all this he dedicated rapt and sincere attention, in contrast to our redheaded companion's earlier posturing.

After finishing our food and enjoying a lot more wine, Sherwood hailed a cab for us but not before depositing a chaste kiss on my cheek.

Lunch had ended up being a three-hour affair, and afterward neither Jay nor I were in the mood for a long subway journey to Brooklyn. The taxi pulled up in front of the entrance to Winnie's building. Sherwood had paid the driver, so we just hopped out, eager for naps or at least some mindless down time in front of the tube.

As we got out of the elevator, we saw that Winnie's front door was ajar. We stepped inside and saw her standing by the entryway table, studying a small piece of paper. When she turned to look at us, she looked white as a ghost.

"What's wrong, Winnie?" I asked. "You're home early."

"Oh," she said absently, "A party was cancelled. But that's not the problem."

"What is?" I asked.

"It's Buck. He's gone."

chapter 40

THE FASHION SHOW would be viewed on huge screens in Time Square. The designer, Narcisco Rodriguez, is known as a minimalist, but that doesn't translate to mean general *preparations* are simpler. It would be a long evening for those of us behind the scenes. As is typical under such circumstances, the backstage dressing room buzzed with equal parts excitement and angst.

Someone shouted, "The lining is sticking out—it got shortened too much."

A seamstress, in tears, lamented, "The bib dress is still in trouble."

"Bring up the sleeve a little."

"Collette, when you do the narration, call this 'Wall Street banker meets velvet *du jour.*"

We'd done the rehearsal, and now fittings were being perfected.

As I sat in a chair in front of a stand-up mirror on a table and let someone I'd never seen before apply makeup gently to my face, I took in the various visuals and the snippets of conversation.

"I know I could have done better." From the designer's assistant.

A tall brunette chewed gum furiously and strolled around in a strapless fuchsia gown punctuated by red and fuchsia ruffles cascading from her neck to her waist, encircling her hips and continuing down her left side to the hem.

"The black carpet is gone!"

"She and her agency are excited about the brand."

"Put water on the floor, in place of the black carpet."

Gradually it all came together.

"Girls, line up now."

I heard the orchestra begin.

"Good show everyone. Have fun," the designer said.

Once again, it was exhilarating to be involved in runway work and to experience the great distraction, however temporary, it provided from the inconsistencies in my day-to-day life. Buck had left Winnie a note, but a cryptic one. We were all puzzled. And Jeannette had some sort of surprise for me, but one she seemed reluctant to reveal.

"Freddy, let's go!"

I was next.

I walked down the runway at the proper pace, enjoying the music and the bright lights. I looked straight ahead but directed my gaze peripherally as much as possible until I could actually feel my eye muscles strain. My goal was to detect any suspicious characters lurking by side exits. No lurking was in evidence.

Maybe in the audience itself?

I glanced at the front row. Two predictable attendees were there—Sarah Jessica Parker and Anna Wintour. Gwyneth Paltrow also graced the first row, looking gorgeous as usual. Katie Holmes was there, as were two of the Kardashian sisters. Kate Hudson looked ravishing in a white pants suit and next to her sat Rachel McAdams and a tall, stunning black woman I didn't recognize.

I *did* recognize all of the designers in the next rows—Vera Wang looking like a perfect little doll with her long, dark hair, Nicole Miller and several other high-profile types like Donna Karan—who'd just celebrated twenty-five years in the business, de La Renta—as in Oscar, who'd started his label back in 1965 and was known for his love of life and of people, Burch and Rykiel.

I returned to the dressing room and was helped into my next outfit. And the next, and the next and so it went.

Finally it was over. All the models kissed both cheeks of the designer. Everyone was exuberant and relieved.

One Frédérique Bonnaire was especially relieved, as not among the throng of guests nor in the dark corners was there anything—more precisely, *anyone*—alarming. No short, stocky figure had been anywhere in the theatre.

But one was now in the dressing room—walking toward me.

"How did you get in here?"

"Well, hello to you too, Freddy. I have a friend who got me in. The show, that is. I got back *here* when that freaking sentry they have posted out there was distracted. You looked wonderful, by the way."

"Thank you, but I don't think you came back here to tell me that."

"No, I didn't. I think we should talk."

"Here?"

"Of course not. I'll grab a chair and wait while you change. I have my car outside. We can go somewhere quiet."

"Look, I've had a long day. Can we do this some other time?"

"There's no time like the present, as they say. I think you and I have some mutual interests."

"I don't mean to be rude, but I can't think what that would be."

"And I think it's pretty obvious. Hurry up, get your clothes on. I'll drive you home afterward."

"After what?"

"After we talk, of course. Look, don't get paranoid. It's just a civilized talk."

"As I said, I'm too tired right now for a talk, civilized or any other kind."

"I don't feel like waiting for some time when you can pencil me in your damn appointment book. We'll do it *now*. It's necessary."

"It's not necessary. Call me and we can do this another time."

"You're being difficult and I don't see why. I came here with a simple, reasonable request. Want me to help you get those boots off? Stick your foot up."

I thought of other places I'd like to put my foot, but instead I calmly said, "Look, I'll call you and we'll schedule another time. I'll have Alex show you the best way to a street exit."

"I'm not going anywhere. Stop being such a pain-in-the-ass diva. Change your clothes and let's get out of here."

I leaned forward, spoke slowly and enunciated each word with force. "Leave-now-or-I'll-have-Security-throw-you-out."

"You're despicable!" was the retort and the short, stocky figure turned and left.

I meant it. I was not in the mood for conversation.

Especially with the pushy, presumptuous Dina Hutton.

chapter 41

THE TERRITORY IS now well known as Southampton where Aunt Winnie and a host of celebrities, like actor Michael J. Fox, have homes. Not the settling of the land itself but an important part of its history was initiated by a humble town clerk named William Pe letreu via his discovery of a cache of small cloth sacks containing rolls of paper. These papers were minutes of town meetings going back to 1641. They documented that the Shinnecock Indians had been pushed off their ancient lands by town proprietors.

Pelletreau did not have an abundance of sympathy for his Indian brethren but his diligence was responsible, in part, for a lawsuit, which eventually honored the Shinnecock claim of ancient burial grounds. The Shinnecock were recognized by the United States government in June, 2010 after a 30-year court battle.

In any event, the area is now known as the Shinnecock Hills Golf Club, a victory of sorts for the white men whom Pelletreau in his day characterized as "grasping, unscrupulous and avaricious." In other words, *greedy*.

It was to this town that Morgan was driving me, Jeannette and Winnie on a slightly overcast weekend, as Winnie's previous "last hurrah visit" to her home in the popular Long Island vacation spot turned out to be the next-to-last "hurrah."

The previous week had flown by in a blur of photo shoots and fittings. Jeannette had been busy too, so when Winnie proposed we take a brief respite from the city, it sounded perfect. There were no compelling reasons to stay in Manhattan. No progress seemed to be afoot on Sonny's murder. At least, no new information was forthcoming from the laconic Detective Brennan.

As for Buck, I'd called his number repeatedly, only to get voicemail each and every time. He seemed to have fallen off the face of the earth. He'd initially come to New York to provide protection for Martha Fleming, but Martha was off with her boyfriend to Florence. Then he claimed he'd stay here to help find Sonny's killer, but I certainly saw no action from Mr. Lemoyne on that score.

Since Sherwood lived in the same apartment building as Aunt Winnie, he had dropped by several times for coffee or a drink—with ex-spouse Selah frequently buzzing his cell during these visits—but no invitations for this particular weekend had been forthcoming.

Winnie sat up front with Morgan, chattering away to him about her social engagements for the upcoming week. Jeannette and I sat in the back, and Jay dozed for most of the trip. I tried to focus on a paperback mystery but, more often than not, gazed out the open window and enjoyed the cooler and cooler breezes as we sped down the Long Island Expressway to Captain Daniel Roe Highway to Sunrise Highway and right onto North Sea Road and then Main Street in Southampton where we were to have lunch.

Per Winnie's directions, Morgan aimed the car for 75 Main and a restaurant called—75 Main. Going by that name, the owner was obviously an ancestor of the pragmatic and literal little town clerk, Monsieur Pelletreau.

We were famished and lunch was quickly ordered but, once consumed, we relaxed and leisurely nursed cups of hot tea. Eventually Winnie paid the check and rapidly led us out of the restaurant and onto the street.

"Shugah, between the ride and lunch, we all been just sittin' for almost four hours. Let's us walk around and stretch our legs. Morgan, you're welcome to come with us."

"I'll just take a nap in the car, Miss Winnie, if it's all the same to you."

"Jay," I said, "You up for a walk?"

"I'm up for shopping and this street looks like prime territory for that," Jeannette answered.

Despite the energetic tone of her initial invitation, Winnie strolled very slowly down the street. She stopped often to look in store windows. The display in one dress shop called out to both Winnie and Jeannette, and they went inside to see if they should spread the wealth.

"I'll just walk on ahead a little and then circle back for you guys," I told them.

I continued down the street, at Winnie's pace as it turned out. Someone who looked a lot like Rene Zelleweger passed me carrying two paper containers of coffee and I swore I saw Matthew Broderick on a street corner. Other than my real or imagined celebrity sightings, there were only a few other pedestrians on the sidewalk, thus the atmosphere was peaceful and I felt especially mellow.

But minutes later, I had another feeling—that someone was following me. *Out here? Miles from the city?* What I believed I saw dart into a Chase Bank was a short, stocky man. *Frédérique, you're cracking up!*

I could see myself years from now in a psychiatrist's office.

Miss Bonnaire, what exactly precipitated this complete nervous breakdown you speak of?

Well, doctor, it began in a van with a short, stocky man.

I see.

And this short, stocky man attacked you?

He kidnapped me.

And how did that make you feel?

Kinda hemmed in. Frightened, of course.

I see.

And he raped you?

No.

And how did that make you feel?

That I wasn't raped? Well, I guess fortunate.

I see.

But he administered physical and brutal harm upon your person.

No.

And how did that make you feel?

Well, not being a big fan of brutality, again I felt relief.

I see.

He kept you locked up for weeks or months on end.

No. I escaped.

I see.

But I think he still follows me to this day.

How does that make you feel?

Violated. Mostly scared.

I see.

So I still have an inordinate fear of short stocky men. Can you help me?

Ve vill cure you immediately, Miss Bonnaire. They have wonderful pills for the short, stocky man syndrome. Here, I'll write you a prescription.

I continued down the street. I was getting far afield from the dress shop, but, knowing Winnie and Jeannette, they'd be awhile and I still had enough energy to head back quickly if I lost track of time. The air was chilly, the formerly gentle breeze had upgraded to a healthy wind and the sky began to darken slightly, but I pressed on, feeling a need for exercise and a just as compelling need to clear my head.

The sidewalk ahead of me was completely empty so when I heard footsteps behind me, my head whipped around despite my less paranoid intentions. I thought I saw a man behind a tree. A short, thickset man. *Of course.*

I slowed my pace down even more. *Don't show fear.*

I continued on for about half a block. Then I couldn't resist—I glanced backward. Well, maybe it was more than a glance. Maybe it was a stare. Maybe I stood stock still and intently eyeballed the area behind me. But such discrepancies don't count.

I saw no short, stocky individual or individuals. All I saw was a tall, slim guy, about thirty or so, stroll casually by me. I stood and watched for a few seconds, then continued walking. Tall/Slim continued walking and then circled back to a long white wooden bench and sat down.

Clearly he was someone enjoying, just like me, a leisurely walk around town. He had dark blonde hair to his shoulders and a sort of unkempt moustache. Definitely not a Mafia type. I hurried past him and as I turned a corner, I heard someone call out, *sotto voce,* but still discernible, "Tim!" Definitely not a Mafia name.

I decided to continue on around the block and approach Winnie's dress shop from the other direction. That would take about five minutes, which should dovetail perfectly with when the girls would be finished snatching up purchases. I window shopped but walked briskly and nearly collided with Morgan.

"Miss Frédérique," he said, "How come you all by yourself?"

"Just went for a walk," I smiled. "The girls are down the street. Follow me."

We walked just a few yards and were passed by the tall, slim guy apparently named Tim coming from the other direction. I smiled at him, and he smiled back. We continued on our way, and I felt foolish for worrying about my safety in this pastoral little seaside community.

chapter 42

JEANNETTE AND I had risen early after an especially sound sleep—must have been the sea air—and, after bagels and coffee, had taken second cups into Winnie's newly redecorated library in her white clapboard Southampton home. We'd just traded sections of the Sunday *New York Times* when Winnie swept in, dressed to the nines in a navy pants suit with a cluster of gold necklaces at her throat and a navy Chanel purse. Her short, thick gray hair was somewhat teased on top with a side bang almost covering one eye.

"Good morning, gorgeous girls, I'm so glad y'all are up. Guess where we're all going? . . . no, wait . . . first, how do you like the new library?"

"It's beautiful," I said. "I think I recognize the blue and white print of these chairs, and they're so cozy and . . ."

"Well, they're in a print by Oscar, shugah, so of course they're magnificent."

"Oscar, as in de la Renta?" Jeannette asked.

Winnie ignored such a plebeian question.

"The print wallpaper in the middle of those two book-cases is also by Oscar. I just love the red, blue and yellow against white," she gushed, "so fresh looking and . . ."

"Why the painting of a bull, Winnie?" Jeannette said.

Winifred de Foucauld, newly of New York, New Orleans and Southampton, took a deep breath, and decided to ignore that question also.

A change of subject was in order. "Auntie, you said we were all going somewhere?" I reminded her.

"Yes, of course, honey. It's Sunday and we're going to church, where else?"

I knew Jeannette was groaning inwardly, but I said, "The big Catholic church on Hill Street?"

"Well, that's very nice, but ah had in mind a marvelous church called St. Andrew's Dune Church. It's practically a historical landmark and just everybody goes there. Around 1879 they added onto a lifesaving station and made it into a church. Isn't that amazing? Like ah say, everybody goes . . . oh, now, it *is* Episcopal so if you'd rather . . ."

"Winnie, I'm ecumenical at heart. Doesn't matter. We'd love to . . ."

"I second the motion," Jeannette interrupted, obviously anxious to make up for her Oscar and bull gaffes.

Winnie picked up a framed photograph from the bottom bookshelf above one white cabinet, solemnly contemplated it for several seconds, and then turned the picture of her late husband so we could see it.

"The bull painting, Jeannette," she said, her voice cracking slightly, "is by Allan Ryan, an animal and wildlife artist. He lives near here in Bridgehampton. Ah met him at some charity function when Charles was still alive. Ah bought the painting for Charles since his sign is Taurus. He loved it."

'That's sweet," Jeannette said. "I love it too."

At that, Winnie grinned. "Y'all are so full of it, Jay . . . but that's okay . . . hurry up little girls. Go get dressed!"

We hotfooted it to the upstairs guest room we shared and took a cue from Winnie's sartorial choice. I chose a pants suit in black and Jeannette quickly pulled herself into one in gray. I grabbed two long ropes of pearls and handed one to Jay. Our conservative dress would surely pass muster with Winnie, and as we descended the stairs, I could see from her happy expression that it did.

We all climbed into her black Bentley—me up front with Morgan this time—and took off.

"Just where *is* this place?" Jay asked.

"Near Coopers Beach," Morgan said. "Kinda old church, Miss Jay, but lots of society folk like it. Sits on sand dunes with the ocean on one side and a fresh-water lake on the other."

I feared Winnie's *nouveau riche* sensibilities might be offended again at the 'society folk' comment, but she just cheerfully remarked, "It's unique, very inspiring."

The drive passed quickly. Morgan pulled up to the main entrance. People milled about in front and along the sides of the church. It was a frame building in brown wood with tiffany windows, and boasted two steeples. I took a deep breath to experience the aroma of salty sea air.

"Are you coming in, Morgan?" I said.

"No, mam. I'll just wait. I'll be parked over there to the right."

The service passed pleasantly enough, the sermon interesting, the choir seemed devout and boasted an excellent soprano soloist. As we all filed out, I surreptitiously glanced about, trying to pick out a celebrity here and there. No luck.

I did spy one familiar face— the blonde guy from Main Street with the unruly moustache. The wind whipped his hair away from his face, as he stood next to a car, and I could see he wore a small gold earring. I couldn't see the driver, but they could be locals or possibly weekenders like us. Southampton must be like a small town if you lived here full time, I mused, and thought about the charm of such consistency and familiarity. I hoped Winnie would invite me down here often in the future.

Morgan saw us and drove over to where we stood. Soon we were back at Winnie's house.

"Ah'm ready for hot chocolate or something stronger," she called out, as she walked toward the front door, Morgan giving her a supportive arm. "How about you girls?"

"I vote for the something stronger," Jeannette said.

I saw Morgan walk away. "Come on in with us, Morgan," I said. "It's getting cold out here."

"Thanks, Miss Freddy. I'm heading out to a church I go to here."

Something about Morgan looked lonely and forlorn as he hunched his shoulders and headed back to the driveway.

"Where is it?"

He stopped and turned toward me. "Called Community Church." He resumed walking, then turned back and added, "It's a Baptist church, over on Reverend Raymond Lee Court."

"Wow, that's a mouthful," I teased. "Maybe I should go with you, make sure you don't get lost."

Morgan stopped again and grinned. "That would be great, Miss Freddy. You're most welcome."

Once again, I climbed into the front seat next to Morgan and once again, we headed for a church. The small white clapboard church was packed, and we sat in the back. The choir was very enthusiastic and the hymns we sang had a definite beat. The pastor demonstrated an amazing skill for quoting long passages of scripture by heart. After a half hour or so, he seemed to be winding down when I received a call—and not one from a higher authority.

"Morgan," I whispered, "where are the restrooms?"

"It's complicated, Freddy," he whispered back, "you have to go thru that side door and around back. It's the only way to get there."

"It's an outhouse?"

"No," he smiled, "just a flaw in planning. But let's us go out the front door. We're closer to that, won't disturb folks."

"That's fine, but you don't have to leave too."

"No problem. I'll show you the way," he said.

We rose and gingerly stepped past a young couple with a toddler who merely smiled and didn't seem to pass judgment on our early departure, and finally past two women in their sixties or so, who didn't disguise their frowns.

We exited out the front and Morgan led me to the edge of the building where we turned left toward the back of the church. I looked to my right and watched the sand and sea grass flow with the breezes and the ocean foam lace softly at the water's edge. The sun was just behind a massive smoky gray cloud.

We stopped at the door marked Ladies, and I went inside. It contained three stalls, one of which was occupied. I stepped inside one of the empty stalls and seconds later, I stood up and discovered the handle was stuck. As I was wrestling with it and audibly sighing and swearing, a short, rather chubby black woman of about thirty-five or so exited the adjoining stall, washed her hands, then appeared beside me, holding my stall door open. She had a very pretty face and wore a heavy green sweater over a print dress. A short-handled brown purse hung from one arm.

"Can I help you, miss?"

"Oh!" I think I blushed. Anyway, it sounds good to say I did. "Pardon my French. I can't get this to . . ."

"Here, I know about that one. You gotta jiggle it."

"She jiggled with complete success and I thanked her.

We stood in front of the mirror together. I washed my hands and examined my face. She smoothed her pixie haircut, but I decided it would the useless to try to do anything with my tousled hair, only to step outside and have it become windblown once again. I brushed some lint from my jacket, opened the door and stepped out, with my jiggle benefactor immediately behind me.

Morgan was right outside the door. "Howdy, Miss . . . you know, I've forgotten your name," he beamed. "I'm . . ."

His words were interrupted by a loud sound. The woman's lips had already begun to form a reply but they instead broke into a scream.

I'd focused my attention on her as soon as Morgan addressed her and now I gently touched her soft round shoulder. "Can I help you?"

My own words seemed drowned out by the noise of the relentless wind. It whipped the skirt of her dress against her thighs.

She was now shrieking hysterically. Both of the woman's hands were pressed against her cheeks. Her wailing was extremely loud, so I shouted.

"What's wrong? Can I . . ."

She looked at me, then pointed to the right of us.

There on the ground, curled into a fetal position, a thin line of blood trickling across the sand . . . lay Morgan.

chapter 43

THE TWO POLICE detectives looked at me with what appeared to be shocked expressions. They were not quite ready for my response even though, as cops do, they had heard just about everything in the course of their work. Or perhaps they hadn't, given that in this beachside village even the police precinct resides on a street with the whimsical name of Windmill Lane. Their building had an A-line green roof with the words *Southampton Police Department and Justice Center* traveling over the white stucco front above an arched entranceway supported by two pillars of slabs of gray stone. It was here that they'd taken me and the woman in the print dress—who turned out to be named Ellie Norton—in their squad car which had departed the scene at the same time as the ambulance had pulled away, punctuating the Sunday calm with its raucous sirens, and carrying its sad cargo of Morgan's dead body.

Earlier at the hospital there'd been paper work, questions and a lot of needless waiting. No *wondering* though—Morgan had been shot and an ambulance had born him away. The local cops had insisted we accompany them to the precinct rather than remain at the hospital.

Now three of us sat in a small interview room. Detective James slouched back in his chair and just regarded me strangely. Detective Wilson leaned forward on his elbows, squinting his eyes, his head cocked. They were men of medium height and medium build with dark brown hair,

and light vestiges of summer tans. They wore sports jack-
ets—one navy, one a beige tweed—and ties in pastel colors. They had just advised me that Morgan had died of a
blunt force trauma to his head.

I was in a state of shock myself, but apparently not so
much so as to refrain from being irreverent as I sarcastically
commented, "This is getting old."

They were talking, something about Morgan's family,
but I was distracted. Who was this mystery killer? Did he get
up each morning, shower, dress and say to himself, "Wallet? Check. Driver's license? Check. Credit cards? Check.
Comb? Check. Blunt object with which to murder people?
Check." *Was it the same person who took the life of Sonny
Bob? Or a random copycat? Who was this monster?*

"I'm sorry," I said, and I could hear my voice begin to
crack. "It's just . . . it's just . . ."

I put my head in my hands and felt my cheeks become
wet with tears, my shoulders tremble.

I heard the door suck shut and several beats later open
as one detective left and returned with a cup of coffee for
me. It was hot but it was black. I hate black coffee, but that
was trivial. I hated what this day had become more. I took
a sip and it burnt my tongue.

"Another friend was recently killed the same way," I told
them, by way of explanation for my weird comment. Then
I briefly recited the highlights of Sonny Bob's murder. They
looked at each other and then at me, seemingly puzzled.
Sonny was out of their jurisdiction.

But of course, they asked, "Do you think the two events
are related?"

What am I, a detective?

"I don't know what to say. I don't know."

They said something about communicating with the
NYPD.

"You wanted to know about Morgan's family," I said. "I
know he has a son in college in Louisiana. When I get home,

I can find out about his address and so forth and also about any other family or friends in the area."

I had called Aunt Winnie on my cell, merely telling her something had come up and we'd be home later. This was not the kind of information I was going to impart to her by phone. I told this to the detectives. They seemed impatient about any delay, but I would not be dissuaded.

Earlier they'd told me that Ellie Norton was in an adjoining interview room. They would question her when they were through with me because she had the great advantage of witnessing the entire event.

"I'll have someone drive you back to your car, Miss Bonnaire," Detective James said.

"Can you tell me what the lady . . . Ellie Norton . . . said?" I asked. "What did she see?"

Wilson stated the obvious, "We haven't spoken to her yet. If you'll call in tomorrow . . ."

"I'd rather wait if you don't mind."

"It could be a while. We have a police woman in there now, trying to calm her down and . . ."

"I'll wait."

"Fine," Wilson said. "You can wait in here or out by my desk."

"I'll go sit outside."

We three exited the small room. They turned left to enter the other interview room, and I turned right and headed down the hall to the adjoining area of desks, carrying my mug of black coffee. I found Wilson's desk and sat down in the molded plastic chair next to it. Time passed. I thought no profound thoughts, came up with no brilliant conclusions about all that had happened recently, merely surveyed the room, studying the objects on the desk tops and the people milling about. Lights were on as it had already become dark outside.

Presently I saw Wilson approach his desk. He was walking slowly, ambling in fact—*just another bloody, heartless killing in his Southampton week*—carrying a mug of coffee, undoubtedly black.

He didn't sit down, but remained standing. "We came up with nothing, but we'll talk to her again. Right now we need to get both you ladies home."

I remained seated. "What did she say? Did she see the person who hit Morgan?"

"She did and she didn't. She's pretty shook up, make that extremely shook up. She isn't sure if he's short or tall. He wore a khaki raincoat, that much she remembered. He was bent over as he attacked Mr. Foster . . ."

Foster. I never knew Morgan's last name.

"Are you all right, Miss Bonnaire? Can I . . ."

"No, I'm fine. Please, go on."

"She's pretty sure he's a white guy but he wore gloves . . . at least she thinks he did . . . so she didn't observe much skin. You can see that . . ."

I stood up. "Thank you. I'll go home now. I need to talk to Winnie . . . to Mr. Foster's employer."

"Boyd!" Wilson called over to a young uniform cop, standing nearby.

Detective James appeared, his hand on Ellie Norton's elbow as they made their way toward us.

We walked outside with Officer Boyd into the chill of late evening and got in his car.

Ellie and I sat rigidly in the darkness of the back seat. Her right hand was resting on the seat between us. I placed my hand over hers and we rode together in silence.

—

I asked that I be dropped off at Winnie's. I'd figure out how we'd collect her car from the church tomorrow. Boyd agreed and asked for directions. We arrived and I thanked him. I patted Ellie's hand, then gave it a gentle squeeze and got out of the car. I walked up the brick path, got out the key Winnie had given me and opened the door to bright lights and the sound of a television coming from a distant room. I locked the door behind me and dropped my purse on the floor.

"Shugah, is that you? We're in the den."

"It's me, be right there."

I considered making tea for us first, then decided against it. No sense delaying the inevitable. Then reconsidered. I wanted to provide the solace of hot tea. I walked to the archway of the den.

"I'll fix us some tea, Winnie."

"Good lord, honey, you look like hell. Where y'all been? You and Morgan hit a bar? Sit down, sweet girl, ah'll go fix us some tea."

I sat down on the soft couch and didn't argue, hugging one white embroidered cushion to my chest.

"You got here just in time," Jeannette said. "*Blind Side_*is about to start. I've seen it but Sandra Bullock is so great in . . . what's the matter, girlfriend?"

I just shook my head.

"Hey, why the tears?" Jeannette got up from her chair and sat next to me. "Is it that damn Sherwood? I know he didn't ask you out this weekend but Winnie said something about running into him in the hall and he had a bad cold and who cares anyway? I can't stand British accents myself and that freakin' ex-wife of his is always . . ."

"Jay, stop. Please. It's not that. Wait till Winnie gets back."

Winnie returned with a tray bearing three heavy china mugs that she placed on the round glass coffee table in front of us.

"Forgot somethin'. Be right back," Winnie sang out as she turned on her heel and left the room.

Where was she going? My nerves are stretched to the breaking point.

In only a couple of minutes, she reappeared with goodies on a blue and white china plate.

"Oatmeal cookies," she announced.

"We girls gotta have some nourishment. Jeannette and I went for a hike today and, Freddy, shugah, you look like you been walkin' the town too. Now tell us what you bought and what . . ."

I held up both my hands, palms outward in a stop gesture. "There's been an accident . . ." I began.

chapter 44

FOR THE OUTSIDE shutters, Jeannette and I agreed on French blue. We decided on a cream color for the walls of the living room. The dining room would have my 18th-century rustic Spanish table with antique French chairs in a cocoa brown so matte beige walls would be a perfect backdrop. We both thought one of the kitchen windows should be done in stained glass with the walls painted a vivid yellow. I selected a plain white-walled background for my bedroom as my bed's headboard is in classic red toile and I planned to hang panels I'd found in New Orleans in muted blues and greens, add a couple of chairs slip covered in the red toile and include an iron day bed covered in a blue and white floral. I was happy with all our selections save for the walls of what would be Jay's bedroom—I could not talk her out of the choice of a pale tangerine. Go figure.

All of this was a frivolous but necessary enterprise. I'd driven us home from Southampton, there was no more to be done there. Plus practical business commitments called out to us. Jeannette had fittings on Monday and I had a runway gig that evening.

On the ride back, we called Gram on my cell with the sad news and asked to speak to her gentleman friend, Roland Figgins. We needed some information from him.

"He's due here in about twenty minutes for dinner, honey. Give me your number and I'll have him call you immediately."

Eventually we made funeral arrangements for Morgan to be transported to New Orleans. More correctly, we merely initiated them as when Roland called I asked him for a contact name in New Orleans, he insisted on taking over.

"Sadly, I'm getting rather good at this, Frédérique," he said. "A neighbor of Hermione's fell and broke her hip three weeks ago. With no kin to contact, save an aging cousin somewhere in Nevada, the honors fell to us."

"That's so wonderful of you, Roland," I told him. "And Winnie will be flying out. She's going to break the news to Morgan's son in person."

"That's probably best," he said. "Winnie's a kind soul. I also understand from Hermione that she's paying for all the hospital expenses."

"She is indeed a good soul. She's always . . ."

"I have to ring off now, Frédérique, Hermione's calling me. She's taking the news rather badly. We both are. We're very fond of Morgan."

I said, "Goodbye and thanks so much for everything, Roland," and heard him click off without a word.

Today was Thursday. I had nothing going on and Jay just had a morning fitting, after which she grabbed a taxi and met me at my brownstone as she'd agreed to help make some decisions as to colors so the job of painting could commence. Since she was going to live with me, it seemed only fair to make her part of the whole process.

Before I left for Brooklyn, I'd grabbed a tote bag and filled it with hot dogs, rolls and cokes—complete with jars of mustard and ketchup—purloined from Winnie's kitchen so we could eat quickly in the midst of our decorating. Neither of us had stopped for lunch, so now we sat on the floor on throw cushions devouring an early dinner.

"Freddy, girl, I gotta say you set a fine table. Comfortable seats, the best in paper towels for napkins. I could get used to . . ."

"Jay," I said somberly, "There's gotta be a connection to Sonny's killing."

"The police in Southampton are on it, girlfriend. Stop trying to play detective. I'm getting another coke, you want one?"

"No, I'm good."

Jeannette returned with two cokes and handed me one in spite of my refusal.

Maybe she's right, maybe I need lots of caffeine to figure all of this out.

"Someone got killed because of me, Jay. Because he was with me. I can't help but think that."

"I think so too, Freddy. I just don't know what we can do about it."

"I know who could do something about it." I gave her a fierce look. "Your great and good friend Buckley Lemoyne. And where *is* he these days?"

"Martha came back from Florence early. I thought I told you that. And that dude she's goes with . . . Erskine somebody . . . he got himself another Broadway role. Check *that* out. Martha didn't get her role, but he did. These old people in your life, Freddy . . . Martha and your grandmother . . . they've got it goin' on. They're doing better than we are."

"Jeannette . . ."

"Maybe we should look into that. My dad's got a tee shirt that says *old guys rule*. I wouldn't mind a date as good looking as Erskine and Roland seems to be so nice plus he's loaded and . . ."

"Jay, I'm going to call Buck," I announced sternly. "He supposedly stayed in New York to help me and where the hell is he? I'm being followed, someone close to me got killed and he doesn't answer the messages I leave on his phone. And this is the man you think I should have a relationship with? Hand me my cell over there . . . thanks . . . if I have to leave fifty messages, I'll get to the bottom of . . ."

Jeannette had looked startled mere seconds into my diatribe. Now her eyes widened further and she shook her head at me. Then she grabbed the cell phone from my hand. She stuffed it in her jeans pocket, gathered up in a paper towel the remains of her bun and her coke and stood up.

"Go get your coat, Miss Frédérique, while I call a cab. It's time to show you my surprise."

chapter 45

FIVE MINUTES INTO our taxi ride, Jeannette and I did a monetary reality check and decided to be dropped off at the Atlantic Avenue subway station rather than pay the freight all the way into Manhattan, the location of Jay's surprise. We paid our fare, headed to the station, thru the turnstile and hopped on the B train, which arrived minutes after we arrived on the platform. It was early rush hour so we had to stand all the way but eventually we disembarked at a stop in the East Village.

We left the station and walked along the border of Tompkins Square Park to 7th Street, which turned out to be our destination. The sun was beginning to set and cast a golden glow over an area that otherwise looked very pedestrian with a typical New York row of apartment buildings in either ornate gray granite or plain red brick. The block had a healthy amount of trees—mostly small—with a few medium sized ones just large enough to have their leafy boughs extend over the narrow street.

Jay led the way to the entrance of one of the gray numbers, through the door and over to a ground-floor apartment.

"Here we are!" she smiled happily.

Jeannette fumbled in her purse, took out a key and unlocked the door.

We stepped into a long narrow room with floors that were a dark polished wood. A tall fichus tree stood in a large terra cotta pot to the left and two generous French doors graced the opposite wall. A medium-sized library desk jutted out from the right wall with a rolling chair behind it. Two ornate straight-back chairs stood in front of the desk. The wall was plain just beyond the fichus tree with a large modernistic painting in the center. It was a short wall and it jutted off to the left, revealing a hallway.

"This has a nice open air feel, Jay, but who . . .?"

"Just follow me."

The small living room consisted of more hardwood floor and white walls, only in this instance a gold and white rug was in the center and dark mahogany furniture warmed the area up somewhat. Two sofas and two chairs were a very light beige and traditional in design. Two stacks of packing boxes, yet to be opened, stood off to a corner. But the real focal point was the walls—they were a deep, wet-looking red.

"Can't miss these walls," I said.

"Is that too much?" Jay grinned. "And guess who painted 'em? He had to use umpteen layers of marine paint and . . ."

It suddenly struck me that Jeannette had opened the door with her own key.

"Jay, you got your own apartment! Why in the world didn't you tell me? And why did you agree to live with me? I can manage on my own. Were you worried about me? Of course you were. It's this damn situation, being followed and all. Jay, don't feel you have to sacrifice for me. This place is wonderful. You deserve it and . . ."

Jay grinned. "If you'll stop talking, I have something to tell you."

"Well, okay, lay it on me."

I sat down on one of the chairs and then I saw them— two red Chinese lacquered chests, pushed together to form a coffee table. I'd seen them before. In Buck's house in Venice, California.

"You bought Buck's chests. Or he gave them to you? Must have really cost to have them shipped out here. But they *are* nice and . . ."

"They're not mine." A smile was in Jay's words and she spoke slowly, for effect. "And this apartment is not mine. This is Joseph Buckley Lemoyne's apartment."

"He's renting this apartment while he's here?"

"He's moved lock, stock and barrel into this apartment."

"All his stuff from Venice is here?"

"Every pillow and spoon."

"This is Buck's apartment!" I said.

"That's what I'm telling you. Did you pick up on the desk and client chairs when you first walk in?"

"His office."

"You got it."

"This place looks like a co-op. He's buying this apartment?"

"Well, yes."

"No!"

"Yes. You know Buck, he's always been careful with money, invests, buys property, stocks, that kind of stuff. He's one smart dude. But then I keep telling you that."

It still wasn't sinking in. "So he's buying this apartment?"

"Did I stutter? Matter of fact, he's buying this building, my friend."

"No!"

"You gotta stop saying that."

"I call this crazy," I said.

"I call it commitment myself," Jeannette said. "There's beers in the fridge. Want one?"

"I think I *need* one, yes!"

Jay returned with two bottles of Samuel Adams and handed one to me.

We gently chugged our beers and slouched back in our chairs. Jeannette looked like contentment personified and something in me felt the same way.

"So Buck has moved here permanently."

"Nothing gets past you, shugah, as Winnie would say."

"What brought on this decision?"

"Gee, I don't know. My guess is you're being here made him think about it some time ago and then lately when you've been in trouble . . ."

"But what about his L.A. clients?"

"You know show biz types. They travel to New York a lot. Plus he knows loads of people here. And he's used to flying from coast to coast. The only difference is his headquarters will be here instead of that weird thing he calls a house in California."

"The beach house in Venice? I rather liked that place and . . ."

"Anyway, missy," Jeannette interrupted. "This is what's had Buck so preoccupied. Getting this real estate deal and more New York clients and what not. I've been in touch with him all along. He swore me to secrecy, but I told him we had to let the cat out of the bag some time and the sooner, the better, so he gave me a key and left it up to me."

"I am touched. It doesn't explain his cavalier attitude about my being followed, especially on the heels of my van abduction, but what can I say? Maybe he thought Morgan would be my protector."

"I don't know the 411 on that either, except I know Buck. If he seems like he thinks there's nothing to worry about, he must have a reason."

We lapsed into silence and drank our beers, lost in our individual thoughts, but I knew we were both contemplating the swift turn of recent events and our new lives in the city so nice they named it twice.

Oh, if that were the only thing we had to worry about.

As if phones could read minds, my cell rang.

"Hey, dinner tonight?"

"I actually had a pretty early dinner."

"How early?"

I looked at my watch. A little over two hours ago."

"Time to eat again. Pick you up in half an hour."

"Wait! I'm not home. Jay, what's the address here?"

Jeannette recited it and I told Detective Brennan, "It's 265 East 7th Street, apartment G."

"Got it."

The phone went dead.

"Wait," Jay said. "I can guess who that was. John Wayne."

"John Wayne?"

"That's what I call your detective boyfriend who talks in shorthand."

"He does that, but he's hardly a boyfriend."

"You have dinner dates with just every cop you run into?"

"They're not dates."

"Whatta you call 'em?"

"I call them meetings—to discuss Sonny Bob."

"Ah ha, that's all that goes on?"

"Girl scout honor."

"You were never a girl scout."

"So sue me . . . oh rats! . . . I'm sorry, I should have told him you're coming along."

"No, I'm not."

"Of course you are. I want you to."

"Want all you wish, Frédérique. I'm taking a subway back to Winnie's to break the Buck apartment news to her. I think she'll be tickled. We'll have a few drinks and watch *Dancing with the Stars*."

—

Jeannette walked to the nearest subway. She noticed a weird-looking little guy talking on his cell phone while sitting on a stoop, looking shifty eyed, like he didn't belong there or thought he was being followed.

"Now Freddy's got me paranoid," she mumbled to herself. "Hell, she's the one some dude is tailin'. I gotta get outta here. Hope Winnie is up for vodka tonics."

The weird little guy had been pretending to talk on his cell. Now he dialed his boss and reported in.

chapter 46

"You should know that right now this is only for Android phones, so a guy or gal's packing a smartphone of a different nature, they're safe—for now. But you've got an Android, so here's the facts. You could be in the shower. Maybe you're doing a fashion show and you're distracted. The reality is that during a vulnerable moment, someone can take your phone, download this application, have it run silently in the background and then monitor from their phone every text message you send without you being the wiser."

We were sitting in a restaurant walking distance from Buck's apartment called Against the Grain.

The name fit my slightly eccentric dinner companion.

The place was about the size of a hallway. Clint said it was fairly new and the ultra shiny woodwork and gleaming tin ceiling testified to this. The menu boasted seventy brands of beer with names like Porkslap and Old Chub— recommendation enough I suppose for a cop type.

Brennan was describing a new application called Secret SMS Replicator.

"So you think that's how the person following me always knows where I am?"

"Possible. You said there's no one who knows your schedule who's suspicious or who you don't trust. But you also said there's usually someone or other you text about your appointments, shows, places you go, so all the data is there on your phone waiting to be found."

"What can I do about it?"

"You could always try to get the drop on this bad guy and deactivate the program remotely through a secret text password."

"Sounds complicated."

"Easier to get a new phone—a regular smartphone, nothing fancy—and keep it on your person at all times. If you're in a show or somewhere you can't do that, leave it at home. Locked up in a place no one knows about."

"I can do that. What should I do with the phone I have?"

"Give it to me. See how the bastard likes following me around for a while," he smiled.

I pulled my cell out of my purse, stretched my arm across the table, the phone in the palm of my hand.

Clint placed one hand under mine and with the other picked up the phone, holding my hand seconds longer than necessary. His large hand felt warm.

A waiter finally appeared. "Hi folks. Can I get you drinks?"

"Beer," Clint said, a mischievous glint in his eye.

"What kind, sir?"

"Surprise us."

"Very good," the waiter said and left.

"Purpose of our meeting?" I asked.

"Update from you."

"I'm afraid I do have an update." I started to tell him about Morgan.

"Read about it," he interrupted.

"It made the papers here?"

"Southampton's a playground for Manhattan society types like your aunt. Not to mention the acting community and a certain supermodel. So, sure, what goes on there is of interest."

"I don't call myself that."

"Supermodel?"

"Right."

"Good. I like modesty in a victim."

"I seem to be that, don't I?"

"You were kidnapped."

"I got away."

The waiter returned, put two Miller Lights on our table. Not an imaginative server.

"Are you ready to order?" he asked.

"Braised short ribs for me," Clint said.

"Me too," I said.

I pointed to the Miller label. "We obviously don't look like exotic types to the waiter."

"At least I don't," Clint smiled.

I took a sip. "Do you think Morgan's shooting is connected to Sonny Bob?"

"Yep."

"And thus to me?"

"You bet."

"Why?"

"Hard to say at this point. To warn you, scare you."

"About what?"

"You've got something someone wants. Money? Information? You tell me."

"Money does seem to be the question, but I don't have the answer. Sonny Bob may have left some money lying around. I don't know how he could have accumulated much, but it's possible. I don't know where it is. Don't have a clue."

"They don't know that."

"They?"

"Whoever's following you, of course."

"They're hoping I'll lead them to it."

"Bingo."

"Shooting Morgan for no good reason . . . they're extremely violent. Would they harm me?"

"Not until after you've given up where the money is."

"So they'll just keep following me until I produce what they're looking for."

"Or until they get impatient. Then they'll try to kidnap you again and get the information out of you."

"That's a pleasant prospect."

"They tried it once."

"I was lucky once. I might not be again."

Our food arrived and Clint stopped talking, dug in, and ate as if he hadn't eaten in a week. *And also as if he didn't have a care in the world.*

"Don't let the fact that my life is in danger ruin your appetite."

That made him laugh and he nearly choked on his meat. He took a gulp of beer.

"We're working on your case, Freddy. I haven't found anyone to arrest yet. When I do, you'll be the first to know. Meanwhile, that's why I'm keeping in touch with you."

"I *do* appreciate that."

I decided to adopt his enthusiasm for our meal and took a bite of my food, then a sip of my Miller's.

My turn to smile. "Do you take all of your case victims out to dinner?"

"Yes," he said, straight faced.

What other kind of answer did I expect?

chapter 47

FOR SEVERAL DAYS after meeting with Detective Brennan I was running around Manhattan on Go and Sees. Go and Sees in the modeling business are meetings you have with either fashion editors, photographers, catalog clients, advertising clients or even executives from advertising agencies. They are mostly the chore of younger models just starting out, but not always. Marc, my booker, had decided there'd lately been an unacceptable lull in the pace of my gigs and so I needed to let more of the industry know I was alive and well, living in one place in New York and very much in business.

These types of casting calls can be draining and depressing, but I was having a ball. It's always a good idea to be talkative and outgoing on Go and Sees and I was having no trouble with that as I felt exuberant—thrilled to be out and about without the sense of being followed with the subsequent danger of being mugged, spirited into a van or any and all other threats potentially ending in my demise.

It's totally acceptable to dress casually for these meetings so my days had the added advantage of seeing me in a tee shirt with layers of jersey tops and sweat pants and sneakers. I ran around, lugging my portfolio, a street map, a bottle of water and a supply of my comp cards stuffed into my large purse. Comp cards are composites, usually 8 ½ x 6, with shots of a model in different poses, your measurements, dress and shoe sizes and contact info for your agency. It felt a little strange to be hawking these again, hopping on and off subways and racing about like a novice but the compensation of feeling glad to be free and alive was more than enough.

The sun was shining, the air was chilly but not overly cold, the sidewalks were, as usual for this time of day, packed with people. It's a fallacy that New Yorkers are always rushed and stressed out. I saw nothing but smiling—often laughing—faces as I made my rounds. People, like me, glad to be alive and employed and living in one of the most fascinating cities on earth. I was used to the crowds, the pushing and shoving, and the grime of the aged subway stations. I fell in love with all of it all over again.

Only when I stopped to grab a salad for lunch or had to play the waiting game in some reception area did I have time to reflect upon senseless tragedy involving Morgan, the killing of Sonny Bob and the grief that so many of their friends and family were experiencing. Not to mention the concern that my perpetrators had not actually given up on me. Would they simply lie in wait . . . at my Brooklyn home . . . or Aunt Winnie's. Per Clint's advice, I was varying the times of my coming and goings, using back or side doors at Winnie's and staying away from my brownstone entirely, handling the directions to the painters by phone and hoping for the best.

It was two o'clock on a Friday afternoon and I had no more appointments for the day. I had a dinner date that night with the ever-charming Sherwood, and I was looking forward to it. I was not in a romantic muddle as in the past. Clint Brennan had his own brand of charm but he was nowhere as interesting as Sherwood. And Buck, the friend that Jeannette was forever insisting was my true soul mate, was making himself scarce. I had to be impressed if he'd moved to New York because of me—Jeannette's contention—but it was sure a long-distance devotion if that were true. He'd called a couple of times over the past two weeks to check up on me, but that's all. I didn't ask if he'd learned anything new about Sonny's murder and he didn't offer anything.

I'd seen a cream-colored sequined top in the window of Bloomingdales that would be perfect with the pants suit I was going to wear to dinner tonight and was planning some shopping before taking the subway back to Winnie's when my cell rang.

"Dear girl, I see by your schedule that you're through for the day. What a relief, *n'cest pas*? You must be famished."

"It's only a little after four, Marc," I sighed. But then I had to smile. "Is this your way of sugar coating that you've scheduled me for a last-minute appointment? Okay, where is it?"

"My darling, when one says *famished*, one is speaking of food. I'm inviting you to an early dinner. There's someone I want you to meet."

This had all the earmarks of a blind date but, if so, it would be a first for Marc. As dramatic as he could be, he generally stuck to the business of being my booker and delved into my private life less that most agents.

"I already have a dinner date tonight and . . ."

"Cancel it, young lady, there are more important matters to consider so meet . . ."

"Such as?"

"Excuse me?"

"Marc, what more important matters?"

"Oh, well, not that your social carrying on's are not significant, my darling, but think of it as a favor to *moi*. Haven't I resurrected your career? And in spades, I might add."

"Who is he, Marc?"

"Oh how I despise it when you adopt that world-weary voice, Frédérique. I'm not giving away my little surprise. Meet us at Cafe des Artistes at five. *Ciao*."

Marc abruptly hung up.

I wasn't getting weary of the world but I *was* becoming a bit impatient with dinner dates disguised as something else, *a la* Detective Brennan, for instance. And also of being rather controlled, again like Officer Clint.

I decided to head for the lobby of the nearest hotel and sit and relax and decide what I really wanted to do. The nearest hotel happened to the The Plaza. Nothing but the best for this girl when she decides to cogitate. As long as Donald Trump didn't wander by and have some alternate dinner plans for me, I'd be free to contemplate my evening options.

I walked two blocks, up the steps, through the hotel's main entrance, crossed the shiny cream-colored floor and planted myself in a soft leather chair.

I could call Marc back, state firmly that any little tête-à-tête he'd planned would have to wait another day and hang up suddenly—as he had. I considered this for a nanosecond and then, people pleaser that I am, dialed another number.

A pleasant voice with just a trace of Brooklyn accent answered. "Good afternoon. Peters, Nelson, Benjamin, Simms & Fallon."

"Sherwood Benjamin's office please."

"Just one moment."

Three beats later, "Mr. Benjamin's office."

"Hi Catherine. Is Sherwood in?"

"Selah?"

"No, Catherine. It's Freddy. Is he free? This will just take a minute."

"Who is calling please?"

"Freddy. Freddy Bonnaire. We met a week or so ago. I was in with my friend and . . ."

"I thought you sounded like Selah. I believe he has to go over to her place. Her dishwasher is broken and . . ."

"Has he left yet?"

"Well, no, he hasn't."

"Could I please speak to him then? As I said, this will just take . . ."

"One moment."

Since Sherwood's ex-wife Selah has an English accent, it was hard to justify Catherine's confusion, but who knows? Selah was an ever-present entity in the practice of dating Sherwood as she often called when we were having dinner with . . . well . . . with things like broken dishwashers. She obviously had yet to cut the matrimonial cord.

Sherwood's voice came on. "It's the most beautiful model in New York City, or anywhere else for that matter."

"Gosh, you keep getting me confused with other people," I said. "This be just one very exhausted worker bee."

"Don't tell me you're going to cancel on me," he said.

"No, not at all. I thought I'd ask where we're having dinner tonight."

"I had in mind Masa. Would you like that?"

Masa is a very elegant Japanese restaurant on Columbus Circle in midtown. *Très* expensive, at least as much so as Cafe des Artistes, so I knew I'd be on equal financial footing in my suggestion.

"I have a business appointment at Cafe des Artistes. Could we eat there instead? Say around six thirty? Then I'll be through with my meeting and I'll be all yours."

"I like the sound of that last part," Sherwood said, and this time I could hear a grin in his voice.

"Well," I said, "I'll let you go. I know you're busy."

"I am indeed and I'll be able to accomplish even more now that my morale has been boosted by talking to you."

"Thank you, Sherwood. See you soon."

We hung up simultaneously.

I sat back in my chair for a few minutes and basked in the glow of just having spoken to my new friend and the pleasant anticipation of the evening ahead with him, then made my way outside and let the doorman summon a taxi for me, forsaking yet another subway ride.

Back at Winnie's, I called and arranged for a cab to pick me up around four forty five. A little before four found me enjoying a long, hot shower, then washing and blow drying my hair and finally switching from the beige pants suit I'd planned to a wool camel with a white jersey blouse and a necklace at my throat that was a thick cluster of gold leaves and pearls. I pulled on suede camel boots and went down to the lobby.

The taxi was ready and waiting out on the street and in no time dropped me off at the restaurant. I went inside and was immediately hit with nostalgia. The atmosphere of dark, low lighting, beautiful arty murals and lush accumulation of plants in front of the windows was impressive on its own, but my reaction had to do with other dinners with Sonny Bob. He'd taken me here often when he could ill afford it—and many times as not on _my_ dime, although I didn't know it at the time. But that didn't lessen the fact that we had some beautiful moments here.

The air felt like ice to me. New York restaurants are always air conditioned to meat locker level in the summer but we were inching toward November now. I saw more people starting to file through the front door. Maybe the collective body heat would soon compensate.

Lost in my reverie, I almost didn't hear the voice coming from a nearby corner.

"Frédérique, over here."

At the same moment, a waiter appeared at my side, smiled and led me over to Marc's table. He was sitting alone.

As I sat down, he took my hand, kissed it.

"Punctual as always. I do love that in you, Frédérique."

Marc always called me Frédérique in public as opposed to Freddy, which he used over the phone. Guess he considered it part of my image building. Or his. Whatever, it is quite all right with me. It beats Fred, which is what Buck always calls me.

The waiter reappeared and we both ordered white wine.

"Okay, so where is this guy you want me to meet?"

"Guy? Who said anything about a guy?

Marc whispered. "I do believe you're as bad as the younger, oversexed models. At thirty-one, Frédérique, I do expect you to have more of a life."

"Hey, I believe I'm doing a favor for you here. That's what you said. So no lip from you, my friend."

"Just joshing, dear, you know that. You're the prize possession in my stable, in every way. You know that. You're not only lovely outside, you're just as . . ."

"Okay, okay," I smiled. "Seriously, where is this person? I have a dinner date right on the heels of this meeting and I can't be held up."

"She'll be here any moment. I'm sure something unavoidable happened to make her a little late. She's really a very . . ."

"She?"

"Yes, she. Her name is . . ."

"You're fixing me up with a she?"

"Frédérique, are you listening?" Marc frowned. "I said nothing about fixing you up, as you put it. I want you to meet a wonderful young model who . . ."

"You're replacing me?" My latent insecurity kicked in.

"Are you quite mad? Of course not!"

"Well, then what . . ."

Marc took a long, deep breath and sat up straighter. "One word," he said, "Roshumba."

Our drinks arrived, giving me time to recover my dignity and confidence. We each relaxed and took long swallows.

"I see," I said.

Roshumba had been an established model with Marc's agency when I was first starting out.

At the time, Marc had said to me, "Here's the secret to success, Miss Toussaint. Pick a favorite model and adopt her as a role model. Copy her good habits and career moves. And you might even learn from her mistakes."

I'd nodded silently. I was far more shy in those days.

"So who do you choose?"

I nodded in the negative, shrugging my shoulders.

"Very well, I'll choose for you. Roshumba. I'll introduce you tomorrow. She's successful and wise and, most importantly, she's very kind. She'll be happy to mentor you."

And indeed she was, all of that and more. She was a striking African-American woman, even taller than my five foot ten, wore her hair cut short to her head and treated me like a younger sister. I can't imagine what I would have done without her.

"You want me to show the ropes to your new protégée."

"Exactly, my dear. Who better than you? She's not your competition. She has an entirely different look. She's exotic. You're more girl-next-door."

"Thanks. I think."

I took a sip of wine and turned to gaze around the room. I immediately saw a tall girl, about my height, maybe an inch or so shorter, with long dark hair, walking toward us. She had a long face like a Matisse painting, big brown eyes, a small rosebud of a mouth. She wore a white tee shirt on which was sketched in black the head of a woman wearing dark sunglasses. On one lense were the words *My future is so bright. I gotta wear shades* was on the opposite lense. *Nothing like self confidence.* With this, she wore black tights, slouchy black suede boots, and carried a heavy wool black jacket.

"Mr. Caress, I'm, like, so sorry," she sputtered as she arrived at our table. "I, like, took the subway. Daddy told me I should take a cab but I called one and it didn't come on time so I just headed out and, like, wanted to get started."

She stopped in her breathless recitation to look over at me. "Oh-h-h-h, you must be Frédérique Bonnaire. I've seen your pictures and Marc . . . Mr. Caress . . . told me all about you. I'm already, like, a big fan and . . ."

"My child, do sit down," Marc said.

She obeyed, smiling happily.

"May I order you a wine?"

"Mineral water," she said.

"Of course," Marc said. "Silly me." He summoned the waiter, placed the order.

We three proceeded to discuss the modeling business in general and then moved on to specific assignments and goals for her, with Marc doing most of the talking.

After almost half an hour of this, Marc said, "Well, it's wonderful of you to meet with us. I know you have another engagement so we won't mind if you excuse yourself."

Thinking Marc meant me, I started to say something when our young friend rose from her chair, saying, "Yes, I do. So super to meet you Miss Bonnaire. I can't wait to, like, meet with you again. It's gonna be so great."

She paused and just stood for a moment as if she was not quite sure what she should say next, but Marc was already on his feet. He planted light kisses on both her cheeks and said he'd walk her to the door.

By the time he returned, I'd ordered second glasses of wine for both of us.

"Isn't she amazing?" he said.

"I'm sure she has a future," I said. "By the way, you never mentioned her name."

"Her father's Frank somebody . . . reputedly an important businessman in . . . ," Marc sniffed and pursed his lips as if hit by a four odor, ". . . of all places—Brooklyn."

"And her name is?"

"Caitlin Roma," he smiled.

chapter 48

TIM RYAN PULLED his 2004 gray Ford Mustang onto the driveway of a duplex house on Fifty-Third Street in Brooklyn. Killed the motor, locked the car, and ambled toward a side door leading to the home's basement. Once inside, he turned on the overhead light, tossed his keys on a scarred wood table by the door, headed across the damp, cluttered room toward the small refrigerator standing on a chest of drawers and drew out a bottle of beer. He thought of turning on the television but it was not quite time for the football game to start and dinnertime would interrupt his viewing pleasure anyway so he decided to just sit and drink. And think.

What he thought about, for the umpteenth time he had to admit, was how much he hated living here in his parents' house. Hated being called to dinner like a schoolboy, hated his cramped quarters and, most of all, his dad's incessant nagging.

Ryan's basement apartment reeked—as it always did—of acrylic oils and turpentine. He was an artist by profession. "By obsession," his dad was fond of saying. A not very successful artist. The few galleries he approached had no interest in exhibiting him. He tried to sell to people he knew—his old high school classmates. The women had shown polite interest but made no purchases. The guys were less than flattering, some of them calling his work bizarre or gruesome. Money was scarce and thus he languished in this miserable hovel in his parents' home. He worked now and then at a local hardware store when they needed help, waited tables for an uncle when he was shorthanded, drew unemployment checks in between.

Ryan relaxed with his beer, grateful for the break in his routine. Soon he would have to make up something about his day when he confronted his parents. They thought he was currently working part-time in a women's dress shop in the lower east side to supplement the income from his art. Income that was largely non-existent. They never visited him there, nor had they even asked the name of the shop. Making the journey from Brooklyn to the area of the fictitious store would not be an obstacle. They never planned to visit him at his job because they were ashamed. His father had been a construction worker before he retired, as had his mother's father and her grandfather. They both considered that occupation some kind of holy family tradition. In the world they lived in, the only honorable way to make a living was working with one's hands, and they didn't mean wielding a paintbrush and they certainly didn't mean selling women's clothes.

He looked to his left at the dimly lit set of stairs leading up to the kitchen. He could smell the aroma of cooking food, and soon there'd be two knocks on the stairway door—his father's signal that dinner was ready. He felt like Pavlov's dog each and every time it happened.

He rose to get another beer, took a passing glance in a mirror at his stringy hair and decided he was tired of his own negativity. There was one good thing about this house. It was two doors down from Frank Roma. The man who was going to enable him to flee this situation. Who had gotten him one job six months ago that paid a big chunk of change and was employing him for the last two months on a job that would net him even more dough. That and a few more jobs like it and he'd have his own apartment. Hell, he'd have his own studio.

It had started last winter. Snow was coming down hard outside. It was a weekend and one of the rare occasions when he was spending some time in his parents' living room, primarily because his own TV was on the fritz. There'd been a knock at the front door and this tall, thin girl with a beautiful face stood there.

"My dad's shovel broke and he was wondering if you had one he could borrow."

Tim Ryan smiled, an occurrence that was just as rare as his keeping company with his family. He looked at the girl and her big eyes and dark hair. She was about seventeen or eighteen and in the looks department she was definitely a ten. He'd like to get in her panties so if she wanted a shovel, by God, she'd get a shovel.

"Wait here . . . no, come on in for a minute," he said. "I'll be right back."

She stepped inside, smiled shyly at his parents and they began introducing themselves.

Ryan all but ran downstairs to the basement, quickly decked himself out in a heavy, quilted jacket, knit cap and leather gloves.

He returned to the living room and said, "Come with me" to the girl.

She nodded a goodbye to his parents and followed him out the door, down the steps toward the back of the house. He opened the garage door and retrieved two snow shovels.

"Your dad needs to shovel snow? I"ll help him," he said somberly. He'd forgotten to smile.

"Oh, you don't need to do that," she said. "I don't want to inconvenience you."

"Why not?" he said.

She laughed as if this was some kind of a joke.

"My name's Caitlin, by the way. Yours?"

"Timothy." Maybe she'd appreciate the more formal version of his name. He didn't know. He wasn't big on social skills. His father told him that all the time and his mother seemed to more or less agree.

All that seemed like a lifetime ago. Now he was in thick with Roma and his Italian buddies. They all seemed to like him, to his great surprise. After dropping by Roma's house whenever he could find an excuse, it soon became clear that Caitlin Roma didn't share their feelings. He asked her out for coffee once and she actually giggled. The rotten little brat. He'd show her one of these days, but the time wasn't right. It wouldn't be for some time. He needed to get more bread out of her old man, until he had a sizeable stash of his own.

Right now, he had to concentrate on that Bonnaire woman. In his opinion, the Italians wasted a lot of time trailing her around. Did they think she'd walk up to an ATM machine one day, draw out millions and they'd luckily be standing nearby, apprehend her and be suddenly rich? Or she'd stroll around Central Park, armed with a treasure map, go to a particular tree, dig a hole near it and pull out a chest overflowing with hundred dollar bills? These freaking Guineas could be so dumb. They talked tough but most of 'em had crap for brains.

Now they'd finally decided—or this mysterious Mr. MacGyver had decided for them is what they admitted—that they didn't necessarily need to take her in alive. Why he wasn't sure. They hinted someone stood to get a lot of the bread if she died. Not all the money, which was the reason they'd tailed her to get their hands on everything Sonny Bob, the dead country-western singer, had, but still a sizeable pile. The deal was MacGyver would pay some Italian down in New Orleans first and he, in turn, would divvy up some of the spoils with Frank Roma who'd pay Beppe Vitale and himself. Roma was as greedy as the next guy but once at his office Tim had heard him arguing on the phone with someone named Alex about knocking off Freddy Bonnaire. He didn't really want to do it. That was obvious.

One of these days, Tim Ryan knew he'd have his own operation. Run things like Frank, rake in all the dough from jobs like Frank did. He'd already begun some independent action and he knew he was twice as smart as Frank. There was that weekend he'd aimed at the Bonnaire broad but hit the black dude instead. He'd effed up, no question. Would have been better if he'd killed the black driver, making himself a made man—and thus rising several notches in the hierarchy of Roma and his cohorts.

The knock on the door came. Ryan got up, slowly climbed the stairs and thought about killing the Bonnaire woman. He had no problem with it.

chapter 49

AUNT WINNIE AND I were sitting in her spacious kitchen, enjoying an early morning kibitz over cups of hot chicory coffee. The rest of the household was in a more active mode. Jeannette was shuffling through the rooms, mumbling something about misplacing her boots. Buck had paid us a visit and was pacing through the halls—his image was visible through the kitchen door every couple of minutes—on his cell phone. Pierre padded in and out of the kitchen periodically, to catch Winnie's chatter no doubt. I'm afraid he has a certain fondness for gossip. I had just told Winnie about the recent angry dressing room appearance of Dina.

"Oh, shugah, Bella and Dina, them two are both a pair of ball busters. Their own father—God rest his dear soul—used to say so. You pay her no never mind, you hear?"

"I'll try, Winnie. Still, I keep wondering what she wanted to talk about. No, no, don't look at me like that, I'll stop worrying. I promise. Thank heaven I have Sherwood in my life. He's a real . . .

"Well, that reminds me, honey. That floozy Selah . . . that trollop . . . asked me for tickets to the New York City Ballet. Hellfire, it seems she knows I'm on the Board. Well, the Advisory Board. Well, that is, I used to be. Until last week. And you know what happened? They . . . all those hoi polloi . . ."

"Why do you call her a trollop, Win? She can be annoying, yes, but . . ."

"Didn't dear Sherwood tell you? She ran around on that boy like crazy."

"Cheated on him?"

"Like a house afire, with some personal trainer from her gym. Not to mention the Sonny Bob affair."

"She had an affair with Sonny?"

"Honey, ah spoke plainly I do believe. Drink you some more of that coffee. You'll feel sharper."

"At the risk of sounding clueless, I'll ask—did she have a relationship with Sonny when I was married to him?"

"Oh, goodness gracious no. Give your dear ex a little credit. No, this was after the divorce, but she *was* married to dear Sherwood at the time. Frankly, ah think Sonny Bob just hung around for the money."

I took a couple of gulps of coffee to illustrate to Winnie that I was working on the sharpness factor before saying, "The money?"

"Honey, she loaned him mucho dollars. She once mentioned how much, but I've forgotten. And, believe me, it was a *loan*. Sleeping with that darlin' hunk or not, I know for a fact she wanted her wampum back."

Another name to add to the list of the usual suspects who might want revenge on Sonny Bob.

I was anxious to change the subject. "Back to the ballet, are you able to get comp tickets? I only ask because Jeannette would love to . . ."

"Honey, comp is the only kind of tickets Selah Benjamin understands. She's been tradin' on the fact that Sherwood's my friend for ages. But, listen, ah'm about to pitch a hissie fit over a much more important issue that ah gotta take care of this morning."

Winnie rinsed her coffee mug in the sink and announced, "Ah have to pack."

"Where are you going?" I followed her down the hall in order to ask my question, as she took off like a bat out of hell.

Winnie turned abruptly to look at me, her face contorted. "They threw me off the Advisory Board, that's why ah have to leave town."

I trailed her into her bedroom. "I don't understand."

"They plumb kicked me off, shugah. Put some little actress on in my place. Sarah Jessica somebody."

"Sarah Jessica Parker?"

"That sounds right."

"I always liked her."

"Well, *don't* like her any more!" Winnie commanded.

"Yes, mam."

"And this week," she continued, "they're havin' their gala—the one ah helped plan, ah might add."

"Then don't you want to go? Sherwood and I would be happy to take you."

Winnie took a deep breath and puffed her ample chest out. "Ah wouldn't give them the satisfaction! Hellfire, honey, ah'm goin' to Southampton and rest up. Buck's arranged for a driver for me—he's such a doll—Buck, that is, not the driver. Haven't even met him. No matter. I'm just happy to get out of this hypocritical town."

I returned to the kitchen. Jeannette was sipping juice and talking to Pierre.

"I finally found my damn boots," she said. "Forgot I loaned 'em to Winnie. They were in her room. Boy, has she got a mad on! Plus you got me talking to this damn cat."

She suddenly looked down at Pierre. "Sorry, I didn't mean that." She bent down and stroked his fur. "Gotta go. Got a fitting. See yah."

Jeannette took off for the front door with the same zest as Winnie's departure.

Right on cue, Buck strolled into the kitchen. He was rather dressed up for Weekday Buck—shiny black penny loafers, pressed black slacks, blue and white striped shirt, black and white tweed jacket.

"I've been instructed to make fresh coffee for you, handsome."

"That had to be Winnie," he said, "Woman's a jewel. She needs to boss you around more often."

I threw the used filter in the trash, got a fresh one, and emptied coffee from the small grinder into it. Set it on Brew. The kitchen was extra warm this morning and smelled of coffee and Winnie's perfume.

Buck was already seated at the long marble table. I joined him and sipped from my mug that I'd left there. It was a little cool, but I didn't mind. I was just happy the house was finally quiet and I realized I was happy to be in Buck's company. It felt like I hadn't seen him and talked with him in ages.

"So Winnie tells me you have news for me."

"I do. Been doing some research on your behalf."

"About Sonny Bob? What is it? Does it lead to . . .?"

"Ah'm goin', children." Winnie appeared at the kitchen door, resplendent in a copper-colored raincoat and matching boots.

I rose to give her a kiss on the cheek. "Be careful and have fun, whatever you do."

Winnie kissed me back. "Buck, ah only have this lil' ole bag and ah'll carry it down. You didn't tell me the driver's name."

"No, I didn't." Buck smiled. "He'll tell you. You'll like him."

Buck rose to walk her to the door. By the time he returned, fresh coffee was ready and I poured it into mugs for both of us.

"So, pal," I said, "the news?"

"Thank God you confide in Winnie," he said. "You haven't brought me up to speed on a lot of things. I hope you share more with the good Detective Brennan. Do you? How much *do* you share with Clint baby, by the way?"

I ignored the inference of the last question. "Get to the point, Buckley. What did Win tell you?"

"All about the mysterious woman at Sonny's funeral and how you eventually discovered she was a news anchor, the one on the scene when you discovered Sonny, and how you wanted to question her but hadn't gotten around to it."

"That about covers it. Do you know the answers to any or all of those questions?"

"No, Frédérique, but we're gonna find out tonight."

"Tonight? Tonight I think she's on the air."

"After."

"After her newscast? Do you think it's a good idea to go barging in and . . . ?"

"No barging involved. Joseph Buckley Lemoyne, private eye extraordinaire, has located her after-hours haunt. We're gonna ambush the good lady there."

"You know she'll be there this night?"

"Know exactly when and why."

"And you found this out how?"

"Worked the Lemoyne charm on her assistant."

"Deadly, that Lemoyne charm," I smiled.

—

"It's north of Little Italy," Buck told our cabbie. "On Lafayette, between East 4th and Astor Place."

"Got it," the driver said.

"*I* don't got it," I said. "You haven't even told me the name of this place."

"Butter."

"No, seriously."

"It's called Butter. Big celeb spot these days. And on Monday nights, Sherry Devore—that's the reporter's name by the way—and other journalist types hang out there. This particular Monday night she'll get there early because she's got a date."

"Ah ha, there *is* some barging involved—as in on Ms. Devore and her date."

"Nope, it's a business meeting. Her assistant tells me dates are rare in Sherry's life. She's getting there early to get some liquid courage and hob nob with her colleagues. *That's* when we make our move."

I leaned over and planted a kiss on Buck's cheek. "I take it back, you're brilliant."

He moved closer to me, placing his hand on my knee. "I could get even more brilliant."

"You could," I whispered, "But you're a gentleman through and through, sir, and you won't."

Buck just smiled, leaned forward, inched a little over to his side, sat back and relaxed.

We rode the rest of the way in comfortable silence.

Just before the taxi slowed and pulled over to a curb, he said, "So what's up with this Sherwood character?"

"We're here," I smiled.

"Saved again from giving me a straight answer," he frowned and paid the driver. We got out, hurried through the cold air to Butter's front door.

"She'll be in the Gallery Room," Buck said, and led the way through a second glass door.

I don't know what television journalists wear in their off hours so I'd donned a heavy white sweater and black tights. Added my Michael Kors Python boots for a little style and topped it off for warmth with a lined and fur-trimmed royal blue raincoat Winnie—tired of my penchant for wearing nothing but neutrals—had given to me as a gift a month ago.

The long room looked to be a New York version of Western decor. Padded rust-colored benches lined two walls, fronted by small pale oak tables and chairs whose backs looked like slices from Redwood trees. Delicate vases with flowers rested on each tiny table—not exactly a rustic touch but, hey, this is New York City, not Wyoming.

"That looks like her, right?" Buck said, nodding toward a short, compact female sitting by herself at the next to the last table.

She was wearing a kelly green turtleneck, white pants and beige boots, with gold bangle bracelets hanging from one wrist. In this better light, her hair proved to be a medium-length champagne blonde, teased into soft swirls framing her head like a perfect sculpture. A rather big nose and a strong mouth didn't quite fit her heart-shaped face, but the overall effect was attractive. One hand wrapped around a thick glass that appeared to be a tall gin and tonic with a twist of lime. With the other, her long French-manicured nails tapped nervously on the table, signaling impatience over something or someone.

"I'm sure that's her. Good job," I said.

"I'll sit here." Buck indicated the row's first table, "You go join her."

I shrugged out of my vivid blue raincoat, handed it to Buck and headed toward Sherry.

"Miss Devore, I'm Freddy Bonnaire. If I could have a few minutes of . . ."

"I recognize you," she said. Her voice belied her small stature. It was deep and raspy.

"May I sit down? I'll just take a very few . . ."

"Sit!" It was a definite command. She looked around, left and right and toward the door.

"You want to know what I was doing at your ex-husband's funeral, right?"

"Among other things."

"Here, take this." She shoved both hands into a large open purse and pulled out a narrow spiral notebook and a pen.

"It's not crowded now," Sherry advised, "but that will change in a few minutes. Take notes, act like you're interviewing me about a career in broadcasting."

And I thought I was paranoid.

Her glass was almost empty. She took several small sips and nervously looked around again.

I wanted to ask if someone was following her. Maybe we could join forces and share a bodyguard.

"I dated Sonny Bob for a short while, okay? After your divorce, of course. Not when you were married. Let's get that straight."

"I have no reason not to believe you. Do you know anyone who would want to harm him?"

"Boy, you get right to the point, don't you?" Sherry smiled.

"Well, I usually . . . "

"Sherry, baby." A slim, elegant man in his mid-fifties appeared at my left, carrying a bottle of beer. He grasped her wrist with his free hand. He had salt and pepper hair and a small goatee.

"Hi Harry, haven't seen you here in a while," she said.

"Only stopped in for a quick drink and to make some phone calls," Harry replied. He sat down at the table next to us, on the padded bench.

"You know, Sher," he continued, "Euripides said clever women are dangerous women. I think he had you in mind."

"Oh, let it go, Harry," she said.

Harry just smiled, pulled his cell phone from the pocket of his black leather jacket and commenced dialing, then talking.

Sherry ignored him, turned to me and leaned forward. "News anchors must have their pulse on global, social, political and cultural movements," she said. "We're always looking for the next big trend or history-making happening."

She paused to finish off her drink. "We anchors need to be able to think on our feet. Sure, we read a lotta stuff off a teleprompter but if there's something late breaking, a producer may feed it into our earpiece and we gotta be able to relay this immediately in a way that is clear and concise. And usually succinct—that's very important, to be succinct."

She leaned back and added, "You know, be economic with your words."

In case the clueless model in front of her didn't know the meaning of the word succinct.

I pretended to take notes.

Sherry beckoned the waiter and pointed to her drink, indicating a refill. "When we're on the air, our main function is to introduce stories and videotaped segments or live transmissions from on-the-scene reporters."

Harry put down his cell and leaned toward us. "When not on the air, it's to purloin their colleagues' stories, by fair means or foul."

Sherry scowled at him briefly, then turned back to me. "I'm assigned to the evening shift right now but working hours can vary a great deal, especially if there is a late-breaking development. At times we need to be ready to go on the air with virtually no time at all for advance preparation. A typical day is one that has the potential to change drastically at a moment's notice . . ."

I scribbled away and was actually enjoying that she was so informative.

". . .so news anchors," she said, "need to be able to maintain their composure and think on their feet . . ."

"Or in her case" Harry directed his words to me, "with her penis." Turning to Sherry, "You did grow one just before the Senator Simmons case. Right, madam?"

I just gave him a blank look. It wasn't hard since I had no idea what he was talking about. Sherry gave him a more creative look, try venomous.

"Sit somewhere else, Harry."

"Ah, that reminds me of when we worked for the same boss," Harry said, addressing his remarks to me again. "*New York Times*, to be precise. She used to tell everyone where to sit at the staff meetings. Organized everybody. A top sergeant extraordinaire." He leaned closer to me and whispered, "Small, but mighty." And grinned.

With that, Harry pocketed his cell, took one last swallow of his beer, gave Sherry a combination salute and bow and headed out the door.

"That was interesting," I said.

"Sorry 'bout that," Sherry said. "But he does have a case. Which leads me to why your Sonny Bob and I broke up. He said I was too bossy."

"He hasn't been *my* Sonny Bob for a long time."

"Oh . . . well . . . we lasted five months. I'm sure your record beat that."

As Sherry predicted, the room had filled up quickly. Three beats after Harry left, two women took his table. They must have also been reporters because Sherry returned to *faux* interview mode.

"Anchors usually have a degree either in journalism or in communications," she said. "Television news is highly competitive. Just a BA won't get you anywhere. When you're first hired, you may do a lot of grunt work . . ."

I was now weary of this dialogue. It was using up precious time. "When is your date arriving?" I asked.

"I'm meeting him in the Birch Room. I should leave about now."

"Just tell me, Sherry," I said. "Who do you know who would want to kill Sonny and are you investigating the case on your own?"

She did the furtive looking around bit again. "Murder is extreme. I can't imagine anyone who would do that . . . no matter how much he . . . I don't know."

"You said *he*. Do you have someone in mind?"

"Just a figure of speech." She stood and picked up her purse and a white jacket that had been bunched behind her. "Gotta go."

Sherry put a twenty on the table. "We'll talk another time."

I sat there with the notepad and pen still in front of me. Buck waited a minute and joined me.

"Get anything?" he asked.

"Absolutely nothing," I said but I thought . . . *She knows something. I can feel it. And she's afraid of something . . . or someone.*

chapter 50

"I'M SO GLAD to be in America, my dear. We do enough shows in Paris, don't we? The small, slim man garbed in a black suit and tie with hair as white as his high-collared shirt was directing his attention to a tall attractive woman who looked down on him fondly. "And, oh, speaking of you-know-who, she was my guest in Saint-Tropez last month." he continued. "Well, you know how I like to operate. From Friday night until Monday morning, I like to be alone. I was, of course, sequestered in the right side of the house and she had a perfectly lovely room on the left. She couldn't leave our running into each other by chance, which is my preference. She simply followed me all over the place."

"How awful for you," the woman exclaimed but she laughed heartily as she said it.

The conversationalists were designer Karl Lagerfeld and Diane Kruger—a still-stunning beauty who'd formerly been his fashion model and muse. The actress Keira Knightley suddenly joined them and in a minute or two Diane drifted away.

I felt rather like drifting off myself but I stayed rooted to my spot behind the fashion show's curtain, peeking through the slit I'd created to observe the rich and famous people who'd arrived early. I was already encased in painfully high-heeled sandals that pinched my toes and a beaded dress that weighed a ton.

I should have stayed in the dressing room but I needed a breather from my little shadow of late, Caitlin Roma. Marc's idea of breaking her into the modeling world was to have her accompany me everywhere but the bathroom and together we'd been trekking to my runway gigs and photo shoots for the past eight days.

Today Caitlin showed up at the coffee shop on Fifty-Third Street that was our daily meeting spot with her hair lightened to the exact color as mine and trimmed to my length.

Now I can be paranoid about my stalker and about being replaced career wise also.

I eavesdropped again. Karl was regaling Keira. "When I came to Chanel—and I've been there for twenty-seven years you know—there were no archives. I made the archives, so now I don't have to look at them. Besides, my job is not to be inspired by what Coco did, but to make you believe this is what she would do. I've done Chanel now longer than she did. I don't owe her anything except to continue to create clothes that sell."

Keira appeared as enraptured as Diane had been, but I decided one Frédérique Bonnaire needed to go sit down while she could. Soon the ballroom would fill with the expected one thousand plus attendees and a symphony orchestra would begin playing Bjork.

I headed for the dressing room to slip out of these five-inch heels for just a minute and chug down cold Perrier only to find Caitlin modeling my royal blue raincoat and experimenting with my cosmetics.

"Honey, you're welcome to my makeup but please take that coat off first. It's a gift from Winnie and I wouldn't want . . ."

"Oh, I'm so sorry, my bad!" She blushed deep rose, which only served to make her look prettier, quickly shrugged off the coat and carefully draped it over the back of a chair.

"Can I borrow this lipstick?" Caitlin's embarrassment didn't last long. "You have two tubes of it and I think it could, like, look good on me too."

"Certainly, take it. But would you do me a little favor?"

"Anything," she said breathlessly and I had to smile at her eagerness.

Am I really thirty-one and was I ever that young?

I sat down and unbuckled the strap to the left sandal. "Put these on and walk around in them. Maybe it'll break them in a little."

And maybe you'll get a firsthand taste of a bit of the downside to the career you aspire to.

I took off the other shoe and handed them to her. I had to admit she did an admirable job of walking up and down the three aisles of dressing tables, only bumping into models and dress racks a couple of times. Me, I padded back to my post behind the curtain.

Karl had remained in his spot. By turns, Jessica Alba joined him followed by the omnipresent fashion show attendees Sarah Jessica Parker and Gwyneth Paltrow, matching Lagerfeld with equal star quality.

My eyes scanned the huge room for other celebrities but what caught my eye was a tall, slim man with shoulder-length hair and a funny moustache. He was standing with a group I knew to be students from the Parsons School of Design and Fashion Institute of Technology. I never recognized one student from another but there was something familiar about this guy. He was chatting merrily with one of the females but she didn't appear receptive.

I heard a clicking of heels and Caitlin suddenly appeared next to me, encircling my waist with her arm and giving me a slight hug.

"Do you want your shoes back?"

"I guess I'd better," I smiled. "I've been rubbernecking and it's almost time."

Caitlin looked thru the curtain opening, now curious herself.

It was silly but I thought I'd ask. "See that skinny guy talking to the little brunette in the big lavender sweater?"

"Yeah," she said, and before I could pose my next question she answered it. "I really can't see his face, but he, like, looks kinda familiar."

"Does he?"

"I guess."

"Where have you seen him?"

"Dunno," she said and leaned down to pull off her shoes, already bored with the subject.

But I wasn't.

"Caitlin, my Aunt Winnie is having a sort of memorial service for my late husband at her home tonight. Would you like to come with me?"

"I sure would." She was breathless again. "Who'll, like, be there?"

"Possibly a few well-known people," I said. "Maybe you'll enjoy it."

And maybe I was inviting my little friend because just maybe I was afraid to leave here alone.

chapter 51

FRANK ROMA'S HOME office had its own door to the outside and it was thru this that Tim Ryan entered, having received a voicemail on his cell that his boss wanted to see him by seven that evening. He never could figure out Frank's peculiarities—sometimes he was content to do business by phone, most of the time he worked out of his Brooklyn Heights office and other times, like now on this damn rainy night, he wanted to meet at his house. None of it added up. Maybe he thought his office got bugged every so often and these home visits were necessary until the de-bugging took place. Who knew? At least that runt Beppe wouldn't be there. Maybe Tim could score some extra points with Roma, leading to maybe more bucks and better jobs.

Frankie had said he wanted a report on the tailing of the Bonnaire woman and he hinted that Beppe was now out of the picture. Tim was never sure if he and Bep were doing double duty and Frankie didn't trust either of them to do the job right. Now his solo position seemed confirmed, and he felt empowered and expansive.

Tim stepped inside the small, cozy office, grateful to feel warm, hoping to feel dry again in minutes and hoping to be offered a drink. Like his Heights office, Roma had a massive mahogany desk way too big for the size of the room. The room was made to look smaller still by dark wood paneling and over-sized red leather furniture. Bookshelves lined the wall behind the desk and the tomes it contained were a few dictionaries, textbooks and several rows of romance novels, the covers of which were worn at the spines, some torn, as if they'd been read and re-read. Tim doubted Roma was a fan of the latter. They were undoubtedly his wife's, but placed there to fill up space and make Frankie look intellectual. There was also an oriental rug similar to the one in Frankie's other office, but the overall effect was neater, cleaner. Must have been Mrs. Roma's influence. *Or maybe that of that bitch of a daughter of hers, Caitlin.*

Tim rubbed his moustache vigorously as if the action could dispel the memory of the young woman he wanted but could not have. People were always telling him to get it trimmed. He thought it made up for his bad skin and couldn't bring himself to alter it.

His boss had his phone to his ear and motioned Ryan to help himself to one of the beers sitting in an ice bucket on a side table. Tim did so and then sat down to drink and await the end of the call.

Frankie was nervously pacing as usual—this time lumbering about in thick gray socks, and clad in a white wife-beater tee shirt and navy sweat pants, waving a cigar around as he talked and stopping periodically to sip from a glass on his desk that looked like it contained whiskey.

Tim slipped off his soaking wet boots. Since Frankie was shoeless and he was getting the sense he was the number one man on the Bonnaire gig, he could afford to take liberties. *What's he gonna say?*

Suddenly Roma stood still and let out a stream of curses. "Yah gotta be kiddin'," he said, just as he grabbed the glass on the desk again, spilling the nearly full contents down his pants.

He looked down at the damage and cussed some more. "Get a hold of Gio and get this fixed. Got it?" he said into the phone, then slammed it down on his desk.

"I gotta go change. Cool your jets for a while."

"Trouble?" Tim asked, as Frankie opened the inside door to a hallway.

"Not your problem," Roma growled and slammed the door behind him.

Whatta piece of work, Ryan thought.

He sat for a few minutes and finished his beer, started to reach for another and thought better of it.

He got up, sat down at Frankie's desk and began to study the various papers and notes strewn about. He reasoned that if Roma suddenly returned, he'd say he was about to use the phone. He heard Roma's wife calling him, and then what sounded like the two of them talking. He figured Frankie had been delayed.

There were all kinds of slips of papers with phone numbers on them, the sports page of the *Times*, a racing form, household bills. A large crystal ashtray brimmed over with cigar butts and the stink filled the small room. Off to one side was a large framed photo of Caitlin, her brown hair flowing over her shoulders.

In the center of it all was a long yellow, lined pad with more numbers and doodles on the margins. Frankie seemed to have the habit—probably to calm his nerves—of drawing stick figures. Also printing people's names over and over. One set of these multiples stood out and drew Tim's attention immediately. The first two words were Mr. MacGyver.

Mr. MacGyver. Tim knew that was the alias they used for the hotshot who was in cahoots with Alex DeCicco in hiring Roma to take care of the Sonny Bob Bonnaire matter. What was interesting was the name right next to the lineup of Mr. MacGyvers. *It had to stand for the true identity of this honcho.*

Ryan's heart began beating thunderously in his chest. He lifted the pages of the long pad and tore off a piece from the last page, which wouldn't be noticed. Grabbed a pen, wrote the name next to MacGyver, unzipped the pocket of his jacket and stuffed the note inside. Re-zipped the pocket. He didn't trust his memory for a thing like this.

He quickly returned to his chair, grabbed a second beer and thought about what he could do with this information.

Frankie was taking his sweet time getting back to office but Ryan didn't care. He sipped his beer slowly and was happy.

Fifteen minutes later, Roma returned and sat down at his desk with a fresh glass of liquor. He began to grill Tim as to where Freddy went, the times of day of every appointment she had, who she saw and more details than Tim thought reasonable. But Tim wasn't agitated. He answered calmly and pleasantly, even when Roma cursed and complained.

When the meeting was over, Ryan pulled on his boots, stood and shook hands with a still scowling Frankie Roma. He stepped outside and pulled the collar of his jacket up, not even minding that a mist of rain was still coming down. He was content and optimistic.

He had a valuable name and he knew what he was going to do with it.

chapter 52

CAITLIN AND I grabbed a cab and the driver made good time, despite the continuing onslaught of rain. We were early for Sonny's memorial and Winnie was still in full decorating mode, buzzing about, placing pots of flowers here and there. Also in full chatterbox mode.

"Hi shugah, and who's this beautiful young thing?"

She could have left out the young part. I glanced at the hall mirror to see if my face had a jealous green cast.

"Aunt Winnie, meet Caitlin Roma, the next top super-model," I smiled.

"Well, hi," Caitlin said, adopting the breathless thing again. "I'm just so, like, thrilled to, like, meet Freddy's aunt."

Winnie frowned slightly.

Apparently, like, youth had, like, quickly lost its charm.

"Nice to meet you too, dear," she said rather formally.

"Listen, y'all put your coats in the little parlor just off the hallway," Winnie said, somewhat irritably. "Yes, ah know you can put yours in your bedroom, Freddy, so don't get your knickers in a knot. I want out guests to see coats in there when they come down the hallway so ah don't have to tell 'em where to put 'em."

We did as we were told and returned to the living room to a frowning Winnie, maybe still a little unnerved by our early arrival.

Then her excitement over her current task prevailed and she brightened, "There's matches over on that table. You two can help me light all these candles."

"Wow, candles are, like, everywhere," Caitlin said, heading for the matches.

I picked up my own supply from the bowl holding Winnie's collection of matchbooks from all of New York's better restaurants.

We lit the candles. I realized they were scented as aromas of pine and cinnamon commingled in the spacious living room. But I had another observation. "Winnie, I've never seen so many tulips. Where in the world did you get them at this time of year?"

"Oh, honey, tulip season has gotten longer and longer because Franco said they have hybrids or somethin' now-a-days."

"Franco?"

"The florist over on seventy-second. My, how that man can talk. He told me yellow tulips originally meant hopeless love. That's why ah got a few of those—because your Gram says Sonny was still pining away for y'all." She sighed and looked around. "Now, white tulips, according to Franco, are a way of sayin' 'I'm sorry.' That's why there's that whole cluster next to the fireplace. Ah think your Sonny Bob would want to say that. Goodness knows, he had his share of problems and drove some folks crazy and owed a lot of . . . well, we won't go into that."

Winnie picked up two pots and placed them on top of her grand piano. "You'll notice though that most of the tulips are like these—pink—and you know why?"

She didn't wait for an answer. "Because pink tulips represent the finer things in life. Wouldn't you agree that Sonny Bob was like that? Didn't that boy just dearly love to have the finer things in life? 'Course he did."

Winnie crossed the room to the large box holding the pots of pink tulips, picked up one pot, and then paused, her eyes suddenly brimming with tears.

I walked up to her and put my arms around her. "You've done a wonderful job, Win. Sonny would be so very, very pleased. All the posters on the walls of him, that arrangement of photos on the coffee table. It's all very special."

"Well, he was very good to me when he lived here, that boy." She handed the pot to me and dabbed her eyes. "You finish puttin' these around please. Ah gotta get the CD's. Ah'm gonna have Sonny's singing playing the whole time. The caterer's bringing someone to help with that, even though that's not their job. Isn't that sweet? Lotta people were fans of Sonny's."

"You've got a lot of extra chairs around I've never seen before. They look beautiful."

"Oh, they're antique chairs from Dina's shop. Ah sent the doorman to pick 'em up earlier when he wasn't on duty."

"How nice of her," I said.

"Hell, honey, she's chargin' me fifty dollars to rent each one of 'em, so it's not all that nice."

Glad to see Dina hadn't stepped out of character.

I placed the last pot of tulips on an end table and, as if on cue, the doorbell rang and the stream of people began.

Sonny's stepsisters, Dina and Bella, arrived first with their spouses. Sherwood arrived next and graciously took over bartender duty. His ex, Selah, arrived seconds later as if her antennae alerted her to his presence. She bee lined over to him, ordered a drink, thanking him effusively. She then pulled up one of Dina's slim antique chairs, placing it two feet from where he stood and sat down.

Is there such a thing as an umbilical cord from first marriages?

Booze and all manner of exotic hors d'oeuvres flowed freely.

Some plus-size models Sonny and I both knew arrived with Jeannette. My booker, Marc Caress, arrived with an entourage of his top model clients. Once Marc had introduced all of them around by name—Zoey, Sadie, and Casey— to everyone present, he and Caitlin sat on a small couch together for the remainder of the evening. Twenty minutes after the model surge, a slew of residents in the building—mostly married couples—arrived, undoubtedly invited just because they were Winnie's neighbors. Buck came with Martha Fleming, who wore a simple black pants suit and tamped down her diva inclinations, opting for a respectfully demure demeanor.

Last to trickle in were about twenty musicians Sonny had worked with, most with their significant others. One of them—a guitar player named Floyd—took over CD duty from the catering staff and turned up the volume.

I was trying to talk to Sherwood—Selah had left her post to chat with one of the single musicians—but Sonny's music filling the air was distracting.

They played *Country Strong* from a recent movie. Sonny had never sung that song, but I guess Winnie wanted to be *au courant*. Then *Love Don't Let Me Down*, a favorite of Sonny's.

It was followed by *Ring of Fire, Walking the Floor Over You* and then Sara Evans' *A Little Bit Stronger*, and that was the one that really got to me.

"Tryin' to ignore the hurt," Sonny's twangy baritone wailed.

". . .made me think of you . . .I'm done hopin' we can work it out . . . lettin' you drag my heart around . . . I know my heart will never be the same but I'm tellin' myself I'll be okay . . . even on my weakest days." The lyrics that hit home a little too closely droned on, ending with a robust chorus of "I get a little bit stronger."

Sherwood excused himself and left my side. He walked over to Floyd and whispered in his ear for a minute or two, then returned to me.

Immediately *King of the Road* reverberated through the house, followed by *A Boy Named_Sue*. It appeared a sensitive, thoughtful Sherwood had divined my distress and ordered some light-hearted fare. *God bless him!*

Sherwood returned to my side and began telling me about a new client of his who was especially eccentric and demanding. It was an interesting anecdote, but I was feeling emotional and not in best listening mode. My eyes circled the room and I spied Selah. She had been standing with Jeannette and her friends, all of them chatting away. I'd never actually talked to the woman, I must get Jay's impression later.

The guests were all certainly in a light-hearted mood. The endless quantity and consumption of liquor undoubtedly aided this, together perhaps with the fact that it was months since Sonny's funeral and mourning had been accomplished.

Mercifully soon the party broke up and everyone left en masse, much more quickly than they'd arrived. Jeannette began ushering her model pals to the front door, Selah included. I waited for her at the edge of the vestibule.

"So what's Miss Selah like? I noticed your cozy little group chat."

"Oh, that woman!" Jeannette said. "Couldn't stop talking and wanted to know all about the lives of plus-size models."

"Can't blame her. Did she say anything about Sonny Bob?"

"You mean did she admit she had an affair with him? No, but she did slip that he owed her money."

"I've heard that and . . . "

"Selah's just so annoying to have around. Not too bright in my opinion."

"She must be fairly smart for Sherwood to have married her."

"That chick's not articulate. Every other word is 'you know.' I went to the store and . . . you know . . . bought a new handbag and . . . you know . . . it was so expensive so I . . . you know . . ." Jay began to giggle over her own mimicry. "I come from the Bronx and I talk better than that. Don't I?"

"Indeed you do. Come, help me shuffle out the rest of these people. Winnie looks tired, she needs to turn in but she won't leave the party until they do."

Marc was the last to leave, first thanking me profusely for inviting Caitlin.

"I was happy to," I said. "Could you please take her home? Or at least put her in a cab. She doesn't know the neighborhood."

"I was about to do just that," Marc said. "Looked all over for her, can't find her. Guess she left on her own."

We said our goodbyes and minutes later I discovered not only was Miss Caitlin gone but so was my royal blue raincoat she'd admired.

The little snitch, I smiled to myself. *Well, I'll get it from her tomorrow.*

chapter 53

IT WAS SUPPOSED to be a quiet, reflective day, the day after the memorial for Sonny. Winnie had been well intentioned in her plan to honor Sonny but the gathering in her plush living room had seemed more like a cocktail party than a wake. Or maybe it was just me and the fact that I had not completed mourning—or perhaps even begun the process, and was feeling guilty. In any event, I had no assignments for the day and planned to stay home and contemplate my navel, as they say, and just do some reading.

I pushed off the covers and shuffled to the window. It was still overcast but no rain. If it stayed clear, maybe I'd take myself to the Metropolitan. I was long overdue for a shot of art and culture.

Right now, I'd had a little too much to drink the night before and had not slept well so the first order of the day was coffee. I couldn't immediately find my robe so I pulled on the first covering I saw which was an oversized beige cardigan sweater laying on a chair and made a barefoot journey to the kitchen. Jeannette and Winnie were already there, sitting at the glass table, dressed and sipping from lipstick-stained mugs.

"Well, honey, you're finally up," Winnie said.

"And the famous model's not looking too super this morning," Jeannette grinned, then laughed out loud. "Super model. Not looking super, get it?"

"Even in my vegetative state, Jay, I got that witticism, if you can call it that. I'm extremely sleep deprived. What's *your* excuse?"

I immediately regretted my surly response. I observed the scene before me more closely. Winnie and Jeannette were dressed up, but wearing comfortable sneakers. Their purses sat on one end of the kitchen counter. All signs pointed toward an imminent shopping spree and Jay was undoubtedly giddy with excitement at the prospect of commercial enterprise with the master consumer that Aunt Winnie had become.

"Shugah, she's just trying to cheer you up. No need to be so fussy. Sit yourself down. Ah'll get you some coffee."

"Thanks, Winnie. Sorry, Jay, I didn't mean to be so . . . that's my cell ringing in the bedroom . . . I better . . ."

"Sit still, blondie, I'll go get it. You're in no shape."

In seconds, Jeannette returned, holding the cell phone aloft and whispering, "She says she's a reporter. I take it all back, you *are* famous."

"Hello."

"Freddy, it's Sherry Devore. I'm at Beth Israel Hospital, the one at 10 Union Square. You're gonna want to get down here."

"Sherry, who . . .?"

"Grab a cab. I'll meet you in the emergency room . . . if not there, the lobby."

Who was hurt . . . and why couldn't Sherry at least give me a name? I've heard of journalistic sensationalism but her curt phone call was carrying it too far. I showered in record time, toweled off and found Jay had laid out clothes for me on my bed—tank top, sweatshirt, corduroy jeans, a lined vest and a nylon windbreaker. I pulled on all the clothes and the Ugg boots, also supplied by Jay, and hurried to the front door and the elevator.

A taxi was humming by the curb the minute I stepped through the lobby doors. I slid inside, gave directions and breathed, for what felt the first time in twenty minutes.

I scanned my brain for the name of someone who Sherry Devore and I both knew—someone who would advise her I'd have an interest in this crisis and thus prompt her call.

Buck.

—

Cars were jammed near the hospital, and my cab was grinding forward at a snail's pace so I had the driver let me out as soon as I saw the half-moon overhang announcing Beth Israel Medical Center above its main doors. The air was cold and humid and filled with exhaust fumes and traffic noise. I heard Sherry's microphone-amplified voice before I could see her and knew immediately that I would not be meeting her in the emergency room and not in the lobby.

The ABC remote van was parked as close to the hospital's entrance as legally possible and a sizeable crowd of onlookers had gathered, businessmen with briefcases, students, a couple of bike messengers, a few young mothers with children. Sherry Devore stood, her posture military erect, wearing a white turtleneck beneath a navy wool suit, its brass buttons matching the gleam of her light hair even in the day's gloom. A cameraman stood in front of her capturing a head shot, as she held a microphone and spoke forcefully in her now-familiar gravel voice.

I gently elbowed my way through the crowd to get a closer look. What I got a first look at was an even more familiar face, and I grabbed the familiar arm.

"Shhhhhh, did you just get here?"

"I got here minutes after Sherry called me. What are you doing here? Did she call you?" I asked.

"Listen, she's explaining."

I kept my grip firmly on Buck's arm and focused on Sherry.

"*. . . Witnesses said they saw a crazed straphanger push her into the side of a moving train. The attack has some train riders today on fearful alert.*

"Her? Who's *her*? Is it Martha? Is she . . ."

"No, babe, not Martha. Just listen."

"*At a little after eight o'clock a B train barreling into a Manhattan subway station nearly killed eighteen -year-old Caitlin Roma. But she didn't fall in front of the train. She was pushed.*"

There was a pause as a clip of the subway platform was aired showing a woman with gray curls, clutching her purse to her chest, avowing, "It's scary It really is."

Sherry continued, "*Roma was standing on the 42nd Street subway platform when she said a suspicious looking man came creeping up on her. Roma told police when the train pulled into the station the man pushed her into the oncoming train. The impact sent Roma flying back onto the platform. She suffered broken ribs, a broken left shoulder and left arm and a crushed sinus cavity.*

One witness snapped a picture of the man said to be the alleged attacker but police have yet to make his identity known.

Caitlin Roma is the daughter of Brooklyn entrepreneur Frank Roma."

I was aghast at this attack upon my little friend. But even in the midst of this calamity, I was aghast at something else: Buck had grown a moustache. Trust Lemoyne to find a way to upstage the drama of any event.

"I have to hand it to ace reporter Sherry Devore. Few people in Manhattan, or probably Brooklyn, know Frank Roma is under suspicion for mob-type illegal activity. She wants to let the law enforcement types know she's on to them," Buck whispered, a satisfied smile on his face.

"Never mind that," I hissed. "I want to see Caitlin, let's go."

"Hold on, Fred. Sherry's gonna take us to her. Let's go wait inside for her."

Reluctantly I let Buck lead me around the perimeter of the crowd. We pushed through the heavy plate-glass doors to the lobby. As we stood there waiting, I had time to absorb this late-breaking revelation about Caitlin's parentage. Was it true that her father was mobbed up? Marc couldn't possibly know this. What action, if any, should we take about this? Just as I was rebuking myself for having these concerns when poor Caitlin lay wounded, I saw Sherry hand off her mike as the crowd disbursed. The ABC van slowly attempted to angle into traffic and gained access just as Sherry walked through the doors and greeted us.

She was actually grinning. "Hear my opening? 'A late evening commute turned into a near death experience for a young Manhattan model'. Luckily, I got a few words out of the girl before she lapsed into unconsciousness again and found out she was a model. Then I thought I recognized your raincoat, Freddy, from the night we met. I mean, who can forget a fur-lined bright royal blue raincoat, right? Then I got a cop I know to show me the contents of her bag and a note with your name and phone number was in it."

"But what got you here in the first place?" Buck asked.

"Ah, same cop—who shall remain nameless, by the way—called me soon as he I.D.'ed. her. He and I have an arrangement, let's say." She was still smiling. "Is this my lucky day or what? I'm telling you, I think . . ."

"Sherry, what room is she in?" I was eager to get on to the more important task at hand rather than sharing in the exultation of Ms. Devore's reporting coup.

Sherry frowned, she could hear the impatience and irritation in my voice. "This way."

We followed her to the nearest bank of elevators, pushed the UP button and got in seconds later. Disembarking onto the third floor, our nostrils were hit with the aroma of disinfectant saturating the cooled air like an old sponge.

Sherry marched briskly, with great purpose, ahead of us until she reached room 32-B.

A tall, heavyset black nurse stood next to Caitlin's bed. She had a warm smile beneath chipmunk cheeks and long-lashed brown eyes, her black hair pulled back into a neat, small bun. She looked at Buck.

"Are you the father?" Her voice had a Jamaican lilt.

"No, I'm not. We're friends."

"She's sleeping now. I can't let anyone in but next of kin. Visiting hours are . . ."

"Has her family been notified?" Buck asked.

"Of course. Some time ago. I'm sure they'll be here any minute. Now if you will . . ."

"We're leaving," I said. "When she wakes, if you remember, would you tell her Freddy came to see her and I'll be back?"

"Certainly. I'll try to." The nurse looked quizzically at our reporter friend as she slipped past her and placed her business card on the nightstand.

"For when she wakes up," Sherry smiled. "She may want to call me."

A cast was on one of Caitlin's arms, her head and face swathed in bandages. I wanted so to stay with her and hold her hand until she awakened. The suspicion that this was somehow my fault, that I was somehow responsible, danced around the edges of my still shocked brain, but I couldn't articulate just why at that moment.

We made our way toward the elevators. The DOWN light pinged above the elevator and we got in for our ride to the lobby. It was there that another familiar face and form was before me. He was pacing back and forth where the elevator banks cornered to the main lobby area.

I ran into his arms and he looked almost as shocked to see me as I was to see him.

"Sherwood!"

chapter 54

THE SKY WAS a glowing light blue from the sudden emergence of the sun and the first long shadows of afternoon had replaced the gray, wet morning. Frankie Roma stepped from the cab that had delivered him from Beth Israel Hospital to Montague Street in Brooklyn Heights, but his mood did not match the new brightness of the day. He'd been let out at a corner and he walked the half block to the small Italian restaurant that rarely provided food and rarely had customers but served as a front for his office. The bustle of pedestrians, the deep, somewhat muffled rumble of traffic and the sound of distant sirens were more annoying than usual. He unlocked the restaurant's narrow front door and then locked it behind him.

He'd called a cab as soon as he got the news about Caitlin. He didn't trust himself to drive. He was worried and upset and angry. Now that he had seen her and been assured by her doctors regarding her full recovery and lack of any permanent damage or scarring, he still felt upset and angry, mostly angry. But he maintained his wits. Even in the cab heading back to Brooklyn, he had the presence of mind to make an important call on his cell phone. To put the wheels in motion that would redress this awful act of harm perpetrated upon his beloved daughter, to exact revenge.

Blessedly, his wife Sophia was in Philadelphia visiting her aunt. He'd called her about Caitlin's accident the minute he heard but urged her to stay there for the time being. He convinced Sophia that he'd take care of everything here and that her aunt, who was recovering from a triple bypass, needed her much more at this time. Stay another week, he'd advised, and then come home and pamper and care for Caitlin. He'd take good care of their little girl this week.

On the ride from Manhattan he thought about his involvement with Alex DeCicco. They had first met in college—New York University—during the brief time in both their lives when they'd each envisioned a far different future than the ones that evolved. Roma signed up for a hodgepodge of classes, vaguely working toward an eventual commitment to a major in business, maybe an MBA. DeCicco was majoring in history. Why history, even Alex did not seem to know. Frankie speculated it was because he came from New Orleans—a city with a unique and colorful past all its own. Maybe that sparked a curiosity about the past in Alex, but Frankie never asked. They met in an off-campus coffee shop when Alex was seated alone at a table for two and the only available empty chair in the place when Frankie arrived was the seat at Alex's table. They'd hit it off immediately. Both came from relatively poor families with fathers who were blue-collar workers. They talked about their courses and college life. When they began meeting regularly, the talk turned to their need for money, for their families' need for money. One thing led to another and in the course of their weekly bar hopping they met people who could supply money in less than legitimate ways. The temptation was too great, their aspirations too ill defined, their moral fiber too tenuous, to resist. Alex said he met Frédérique Bonnaire at NYC, a fellow student, but Frankie had never met her and didn't remember DeCicco ever mentioning her during that time.

Now he walked through the silent, deserted restaurant and unlocked the door to his office, relieved to be alone and to think. He shrugged off his raincoat and suit jacket and tossed them on a visitor's chair, loosened his tie. Even during his shock when notified of Caitlin's condition, by force of habit he'd dressed as he usually did. He'd snatched a suit at random from his closet and quickly selected the first tie his eyes lit upon from the lineup on the closet door, even then following his personal edict that he should always look the part of a successful businessman.

He turned on the large lamp on his desk and went to a side cabinet, retrieved a bottle of scotch and poured an inch into a short, heavy glass. Drank it down. Started to refill the glass, changed his mind and took the bottle to his desk. He reached into a side drawer of the huge desk and withdrew his latest favorite cigar—The Maximus from the Diamond Crown line. Observed with pleasure the El Bajo sun grown wrapper harvested on a plantation in Ecuador. Pulled some matches from a middle drawer and lit up, then savored the flavor which lingered somewhere between a cappuccino and a double espresso—not too delicate and not too intense.

Roma leaned back in the huge worn brown leather chair behind his desk and realized that these habits, which usually brought him great satisfaction and soothed his soul, were not working today. His little girl's injuries worried him, but his main fear lay in how close his Caitlin had come to death. Someone would be made to pay and, even in his current state of anxiety and anger, he drew some measure of comfort from the swiftness and thoroughness of the plan he had already hatched and set into motion. Worry and fear aside, this is where his anger had worked for him as it often did.

But this was not the time for contemplation and self-congratulation. This was the time for checking and double-checking the plan. He sat up straight and set the cigar on a small crystal ashtray. Then Frank Roma picked up the phone and dialed a number he thought he would never have to use.

chapter 55

THE THREE OF us headed for Steak Frites, a restaurant near Beth Israel. Sherwood had comforted me in the hospital lobby and, using his cell, dialed his favorite florist and ordered flowers sent to Caitlin in my name. As if this wasn't gracious enough, he invited me for an early lunch. I considered the latter a benevolent gesture as I was wearing no makeup and a less-than-stunning multi-colored layered outfit Jeannette had concocted. I gave him points for wanting to be seen with me. Not so graciously, Mr. Buckley Lemoyne invited himself along for the meal. I don't know what my expression was when he did so, but Sherwood managed to smile and say, "Jolly well, old chap. Do join us."

I felt, under the circumstances, his response evidenced the same British resilience that helped us win the world wars.

We entered to exotic aromas and the sight of a long bar already bulging with laughing singles determined to find hookups even on their lunch hour. Across from the bar, one wall was lined with a cushioned bench boasting a busy pattern of black and yellow, fronted by oak-colored tables. Between this and the bar were several tables of four but Sherwood took my hand and headed quickly for the tables for two. He sat me down on the couch and slid in close to me. Buck was left with the task of swiping a nearby table chair in order to join us. Chalk up one for barrister Benjamin.

A waiter in a starched white shirt appeared as soon as we were seated. I ordered an appetizer, the Maryland

jumbo lump crab cake. My male companions—their appe-
tites clearly undiminished by Caitlin's near tragedy—ordered
butcher's cut steak sandwiches, fries and merlot.

The waiter left and I shifted slightly, feeling the warmth
of Sherwood's thigh next to mine. As if he could read
minds, Buck's knee suddenly pressed against mine. His gall
prompted me to consider saying something especially nice
to Sherwood, so I did.

"I'm so glad you're here," I said, turning to face my Brit.
"It was very sweet of you to come to the hospital."

"Not at all," Sherwood replied. "I heard the news and
knew Caitlin from seeing her at Winifred's party. I thought
you might be at hospital."

I just smiled—sweetly—at him as the waiter brought
the wine and food.

Buck did the pouring honors, and I thought I detected
a restrained frown as he narrowed his eyes and pressed his
lips together. For someone who'd been absent when I was
being continually stalked and needed a bodyguard, he
was certainly Johnny-on-the-spot where Sherwood's presence was concerned.

The three of us finished our meals in silence, the waiter
returned and swept away our dishes. We ordered coffee.
We sipped in silence also, the horror of the attack on Caitlin
finally kicking in to our collective consciousness.

Buck still looked somewhat vexed. It might explain the
next remark he made out of the blue.

"Hey, Fred, remember when we both lived in New
Orleans. It was about three in the morning, we were walking back to our hotel on Bourbon Street via Toulouse, and all
of a sudden, a guy blowing on his saxophone starts following us, playing some Charlie Parker number. Only in New
Orleans, right?"

I shot Buck a look as I thought, *no such event ever
happened.*

If Buck's remark was meant to make Sherwood jealous, it didn't have the desired effect. He just smiled slightly as he caught the waiter's eye and lifted his cup to indicate a refill, leaned back and surveyed the restaurant, then did a full body turn on the bench to face me.

"I have a proposition for you," he said.

Buck leaned forward and frowned.

"Whoa, Sher, buddy, you gonna do this right in front of me?"

"Not the meaning you have in mind," Sherwood said evenly.

"Oh no?" Buck grinned.

"A matter of semantics," Sherwood said. "I just . . ."

"You anti-semantic bastard." Buck laughed at his own quip.

Just then I wanted to render a swift kick—maybe two or three—to the solar plexus of one Joseph Buckley but there was no leverage for this in my current position. I settled for a different form of revenge.

"Buck, lose the moustache." I said it with all the vehemence I could muster.

It had the desired effect. Buck's mouth dropped briefly, he sat back and took a gulp of wine.

Sherwood merely shook his head slightly at Buck with a smile and turned toward me again.

"My proposition," he continued, "is that you come abroad with me."

Buck opened his mouth and I knew some mimicry was about to spout forth so I found a physical response this time and pressed my knee hard against his.

He widened his eyes and wiggled his eyebrows as if he'd decided it was a sign of affection, and said "whoa" again for no apparent reason.

Unperturbed, Sherwood added, "I have to go to North Yorkshire for a wedding—a client's—and then to London on some business. Ending up in Hong Kong for more business.

I want you to come with me. Most of the time I'll be staying at the very large home of another client, there's plenty of room there for you and I think you'll love the house and the gardens. Very therapeutic."

It was my turn to do the mouth-dropping number and then to lean back in contemplation.

"Fred's been to London mucho times," Buck injected.

I don't think I'd ever seen him act so sophomoric.

I raised my cup as Sherwood had done to signal for more coffee, and to give myself a moment to think.

There was no question I needed a change of scenery. There was no question my presence in New York seemed to wreak devastation and some additional deductive reasoning had been swimming through my brain since we'd visited Caitlin's hospital room. She'd recently adopted my hair color and she was about my height and build. She'd been wearing my bright royal blue raincoat in the subway. I'd been wearing that coat all over town every day for more than a week during the unremitting rain. It seemed very possible Caitlin's attacker thought it was me on that subway platform. I wondered if Buck had come to the same conclusion and I glanced at him quickly, searching his eyes. But they looked a blank icy blue, or maybe an intense jealous green is what I was seeing. I returned my gaze to the bar as I thought some more.

Sherwood showed no impatience but did fill in his itinerary.

"I'm leaving three days from now so you'll have plenty of time to pack. I'll have my secretary make all the arrangements. We'll stay in a hotel in London the first night. She'll get you a room . . . *Buck grinned shamelessly at this point* . . . and I'll try to get us seats together on the plane. I booked way ahead of time, so this may not be possible. But other than that," he smiled, "You'll have every comfort and convenience and I won't leave your side."

I felt a surge of gratitude for Sherwood's wonderful offer. And something else. I shifted and as I did so I felt our thighs touch, closer than before. The French call it *coup de foudre*, an instant and intense feeling of love.

"What flight, what day?" Buck said in a demanding voice.

My friend, the control freak.

Again, not the least bit flustered by Buck's temerity, Sherwood rattled off the departure and return dates, flight times, even flight numbers, talking faster than I've ever heard him speak.

"Okay, okay," Buck said and shrugged. "Just asking."

He hadn't taken notes of course and looked as if he totally realized he'd been bested and was resigned to surrender.

Then he recovered, "But, like I say, Fred's been to London. Been there, done that."

Continuation of Lemoyne at his juvenile lowest.

I had a retort of my own. I turned fully to Sherwood and said, "I never tire of London, and I like Yorkshire very much."

"Good," he said, absolute glee in his voice. "It's settled and we'll . . ."

"But like I say . . .," Buck interrupted again and I was sure a repetition of the fact that I've been to England was about to spring forth, so I had something to add.

"And I've never been to Hong Kong."

Sherwood grinned happily.

I did not know it then but we would never make it to Hong Kong.

chapter 56

I HAD A lot to do in the three days preceding my departure for London with Sherwood. There was a hastily scheduled gig in which I substituted for a model slated to be in a show produced for the young designer Martha Napier. The model was out sick, sick but Martha was thrilled, as she put it, to have "a participant of your stature" fill in. Martha's clothes are young and edgy and she loves texture as much as I do so it was a total pleasure. She even gifted me with a short wool skirt with tweed panels for my trip to London. There was a more important job for this time period than packing and getting fresh highlights and a manicure and pedicure, although I managed to give all these high priority nevertheless.

This highly crucial project, which I ended up scheduling for the third day, was to contact Detective Brennan and inform him of what I'd begun to call the-raincoat-connection involved in poor Caitlin's subway accident. I had thought to send a card and more flowers after my aborted hospital visit but now I wanted to propose a visit to see Caitlin with the good detective.

It was a Friday morning. I was to leave JFK with Sherwood tomorrow, and Caitlin was to be released from Beth Israel the next day also. I sat in Winnie's kitchen with a cup of hot green tea, cursing myself for my selfish procrastination and hoping the penalty would not be an unavailable Clint. I dialed his cell.

"Brennan here."

"Bonnaire here too. Hear about the Caitlin Roma subway accident?"

"Nope."

I filled him in.

"So you know her. Sorry about that. This have something to do with Sonny's case?"

"Big time."

"Interesting. Dinner tonight?"

"How about lunch, but first a visit to see Caitlin in the hospital."

"I'm sure she told her story to the cops who caught her case. Something new?"

"Other than the little fact that she was wearing my raincoat and looks a lot like me and could have been mistaken for me in a dimly lit subway and thus her attacker's intent was really to kill yours truly? No, nothing more vital than that."

I'd broken my rule to stick to Brennan-like less wordy communications but I didn't care—he was being obtuse.

"Gotcha. I'll pick you up in twenty."

"That's okay, Clint. I have an errand to run first. How 'bout I meet you there in thirty."

I gave him Beth Israel's address although I was certain it wasn't necessary. However, I really wanted to keep this strictly business and, to me, that little gesture signaled this.

"That works too. See you."

I dressed in jeans, butterscotch Uggs, a heavy white turtleneck and a navy pea coat. I had no errand so I simply took the elevator down to the lobby, exited and walked to a subway station three blocks from Winnie's apartment, jumped on a train to Fourteenth Street and walked the remaining blocks. The sky was filled with the white light of a winter sun, the air was crisply cool and I was filled with optimism that I would fly off with Sherwood tomorrow, leaving Clint Brennan firmly in charge and on the cusp of finding Sonny's killer who would undoubtedly be one and the same as my stalker and Caitlin's villain.

Beth Israel's street greeted me with the usual stream of pedestrians of every stripe, stalled traffic, taxi drivers leaning on their horns. Standing outside near the curb, his face turned upward to catch the sun's warmth was Clint. When I was about two feet away from him, I saw that his eyes were closed, the very picture of the blasé, seen-it-all, just-another-day police detective.

"Working on your tan?"

He smiled ever so slightly. "Thinking deep thoughts about your case. Working on solutions."

I wanted to wax sarcastic and say something like *glad to hear it as you haven't come up with anything substantial or concrete so far,* but I restrained myself.

Instead I said, "We may be nearing a breakthrough. Whatta you think?"

And instead of replying, Clint lightly touched my elbow and steered me through the wide glass doors, to the elevators. In seconds, an UP elevator arrived. We entered, its only occupants.

"Gotta talk to the girl first," he said, just before the doors opened on floor three.

It seems men of few words also sparse out their commentary.

I led the way down the hall to Caitlin's room, surprising myself at how well I remembered the route from the emotion-packed night of her accident. She was sitting up in bed, one arm was still in a cast but there were fewer bandages around her head. Copies of *Vogue,* *Elle* and *Marie Claire* were spread out on the blanket before her.

That's my girl, ever the ambitious supermodel-to-be.

"Hey, girlfriend," I said, "You're looking wonderful. How do you feel?"

"Freddy, how great to see you!" Her voice sounded hoarse, somewhat thin, but the eighteen-year-old enthusiasm remained intact. "Your friend Buck's been to see me. He's like so nice, really cute too. Do you . . ."

She stopped speaking. Clint, it turned out, had stopped at a fountain for a sip of water and was just entering the room. Her eyes wandered up and down all six feet four of him, taking in the rumpled tan raincoat, black wool scarf, construction-worker boots and she probably noticed the five o'clock shadow. I didn't know if he'd match Caitlin's concept of a real live New York police detective, but for the purposes of this interview but he'd have to do.

"This is Detective Clint Brennan," I smiled. "He just has a few questions for you."

Her mouth opened, but before she could speak I thought I'd better explain.

"I don't want to alarm you, Caitlin, but we . . . I . . . think there may be a connection between your subway attack and my ex-husband's death"

Well, that's leaving the drama out, Frédérique. Why don't I just invent something about her life being in danger now for good measure?

Clint read my mind. "Nice low-key start, Bonnaire."

He pulled up a chair, shook Caitlin's good hand gently. "Glad you're in good shape, Miss Roma." He smiled.

I felt nature's call and really had to excuse myself even though it would look like a very transparent attempt to remove my presence after my *faux pas.*

"I'll be right back, guys. You two get acquainted."

I scurried down the hall, asked the first nurse I saw for directions to the ladies room. The strong antiseptic smell of the place obliterated any desire for breakfast, but I longed for some hot coffee. I drink green tea because it's supposed to be healthy, but it's good ole nasty caffeine that keeps me going. I spied the appropriate door, tried the knob, it was empty. Stepped inside and locked the door behind me. After taking care of business, I fished a brush out of my large beige bag and used it to smooth out my windblown hair.

It was a single-occupant restroom and I welcomed the solitude and the opportunity to figure out what I was going to do with my day and, in particular, the next hour or two. It didn't take much figuring. I knew my presence wasn't necessary for the interview with Caitlin, and I also knew I didn't really have much interest in having lunch with Brennan. I decided to play the busy-model-getting-ready-for-a-transatlantic-flight number, plead errands again and take my leave. I walked back down the hall to 32-B, planning my dialogue. As it turned out, I needn't have rehearsed.

As I entered the room, Clint was sitting back casually in his chair but he did hold a long, slim notepad in one hand and was making some scribbles. Caitlin was leaning forward on her cast, looking intense and seemingly focused and even enjoying the interrogation. She straightened up when she saw me, but didn't smile.

Clint turned toward me. "Getting things covered here," he said. "But do you mind if I beg off lunch? You probably got things to do too."

"Well, sure. And I do have a ton of stuff to do. Caitlin, you'll be okay?"

"Yeah, right, Freddy. I bet I see you at work soon." She gave a quick grin.

"You bet, I hope so. Real soon." I stepped close to her, bent down and gave her warm little cheek a light kiss. "See you."

I turned and walked toward the door.

"And, Freddy I, like, know who pushed me!" Her tone and expression radiated elation.

I stopped dead. "You do?"

Caitlin tucked her chin in and regarded Brennan, looking suddenly repentant over her outburst.

"Who?" I said.

Clint looked at me intensely. "Not a done deal yet," he said. He turned back to Caitlin and added, "Getting there."

I didn't move, still shocked.

Brennan turned again toward me. "See yah."

I considered staying, but thought better of it. This was, after all, police work. I managed a smile.

"I'll be away for a while," I said to Caitlin, "but I'll keep in touch." I gave a tiny wave.

She repeated the small smile.

I left, feeling satisfied that things were in Clint's capable hands, determined to stifle the question pounding in my brain—who? who? who?

chapter 57

KIMBERLY CHEN CHONG awoke much later than was her habit. It was just as well. Her boyfriend of three years had already left and she had no plans for the day, other than to visit her beloved *mu qing*—mother—in a nursing home on Long Island. It was her greatest joy, the weekly visits to see her mother. Usually her boyfriend came with her and drove her there but today she would take a cab to the station and then the train to Manhasset. Then another cab to the assisted living community. It was not her favorite thing, to go alone. But it must be done. Sometimes they visited twice a week. Again, her boyfriend was respectful of the Chinese devotion to family, to an elderly parent. Her father had passed away and mama was all she had. There was a sister in Missouri and a brother in Chicago and she and her boyfriend flew there two or three times a year. Chen Chong was a simple person. She had few passions in life but one she did have was to spend time with her family.

Kim—her family and girlfriends knew her as Kim, her boyfriend called her Kimberly—loved a quiet life. She wrote poetry and her boyfriend had his business commitments and dinners with old friends. She had two girlfriends she'd met in a New School poetry class in the Village and they got together for lunch every Thursday. Once in a while she had dinner with one or the other, or both of them together. Her boyfriend never joined them on these occasions.

The two of them were happy with their separate lives. Although she never called it that. It never occurred to her to do so. She was shy and insular by nature, but happily so. There had been enough drama during her family's transition from the port city of Yingkou in northwestern China to New York City five years ago. Yingkou and Manhattan had in common a humid climate and, of course, a proximity to water but there the resemblance ended. Her father had died a year after their arrival, throwing the small family into further turmoil.

She had secured a position as a waitress. It paid the rent for a small apartment she shared with two acquaintances, but she hated it the job.

Kim reached over to the empty space on the massive bed and patted the side where her boyfriend usually slept. She would shower and have some breakfast and then dress. There was no hurry. The plan was to have lunch with her mother and spend the afternoon. She took a quick, cold shower, dried off, pulled a long, gray tee shirt over her slim frame, and stepped into a clean pair of panties, then jeans. She found a rubber band in a drawer, secured her long glossy black hair into a temporary ponytail, and walked barefoot to the kitchen. She would have some steaming hot Chunmee tea and a hard-boiled egg. Maybe some yogurt, no toast.

Her boyfriend liked her thin and she was determined to stay that way. She didn't want children. She saw what having four children did to the figure of her sister in Chicago and she did not look forward to that. She was taller than the rest of her family, something else her boyfriend liked about her. He never mentioned marriage and that was fine with her. Their status quo suited them both.

Kim filled a small teapot with water and turned on the burner. Fetched an egg from the refrigerator, sat down at the round wooden kitchen table and began to peel off the shell. As she did so, she surveyed the room and through the open kitchen door to the dining room beyond. The furnishings in the spacious apartment were all very formal and today, she mused, all very dusty. Their maid had been absent for over a week due to the flu and housecleaning had been neglected. Her boyfriend did not like her to bother with this but today she had time to straighten up a bit and she really must do so. With the way such infections went, the maid might well be away for a second week and she wanted everything perfect for him.

When the teakettle whistled, she poured water into an ornate china cup and added the teabag. She salted her egg, finished it and sipped a little of the tea but didn't finish it. She was eager to make the place look better so she got a dust rag and a spray can of furniture polish from a cabinet and attacked the dining room first. From there she sprayed and rubbed the surfaces in the den and then the living room.

Suddenly a ringing sound pierced the quietude. It was unfamiliar and Kim realized it came from her boyfriend's office. It was a separate line and she never used it. She let it ring. Whoever was calling could leave a message on the answering machine. It was undoubtedly a business call. All calls to her came in on their bedroom phone, a separate number.

But the ring reminded her she really should dust his office. She'd do the bedroom and the small sitting room attached to the bedroom last. Kim entered the dark office. The heavy gold drapes were drawn. She considered opening them to bring in some daylight but decided to leave them be. He liked them closed, so why bother? She turned on a floor lamp near the door and the desk lamp so she could see what she was doing. She polished the mahogany file cabinet, the two side tables and finally the desk, only moving a few things aside on the latter, careful not to disturb what might be a meaningful arrangement. The air in the room smelled like his cologne.

As she dusted the tall brass desk lamp, she noticed the blinking red message light on the black console phone. She sat down on one of the two antique visitors chairs facing the carved mahogany desk. She usually didn't take messages for him but this perhaps should be the exception.

It might be important. He'll probably check in with me on my cell today because he'll know I'm on Long Island for several hours. Maybe I should be prepared to tell him what this message is.

Kim leaned forward and pressed down on the message button. It was a man's voice. He sounded fairly young and very agitated.

"MacGyver? Are you there? It's Ryan. Where the hell are you? I tried your cell. It's shut off. Pick up, damn it! Got a call from Roma. He said, 'Tim, I gotta see you right away.' What's up with that? I don't have a good feeling about it. This is your baby. You said you settled everything. I gotta know. I ain't going to no meeting till you tell me what the deal is. Call me, MacGyver, and I mean now!"

The caller recited what he said was his cell phone number and commented that he knew MacGyver already had it. Then he repeated the number once more.

"Call me, MacGyver, or our deal is off?"

The caller swore, seemingly to himself, and hung up.

Kim sat back in the chair, mystified. Why did this caller think her boyfriend's name was MacGyver? It was clearly a wrong number. On the answering machine, her boyfriend's voice had come on, announcing his name clearly and bearing his distinct accent and providing the home number. The caller had of course heard the greeting, which was delivered slowly and clearly enunciated. So why had this rude man with the uncultured voice left a message if the name was wrong and unfamiliar to him? She mused on this but came up with no rationale answer, save that western ways continued to be a puzzlement.

She did conclude that this man definitely sounded as if he'd keep calling until he got satisfaction so perhaps she should return the call and inform him of his error. It was something she was not accustomed to doing. She only used her phone to contact her family and friends. But hours and hours could go by and this insistent man was likely to ring the phone off the hook in his determination. Plus he sounded like he was in some kind of trouble. It was the right thing to do to advise him he had reached a wrong number.

Kim played the message again and carefully wrote down the cell number on a small notepad. In her mind, she rehearsed what she would say.

As she considered writing down her response, the ringing began once more. Kim recoiled from the phone as if it were a dangerous object and didn't pick up. Three more rings and the call went immediately to the answering machine. Her boyfriend's message repeated.

This time it was his former wife. Her familiar voice droned into the stillness. Something about being displeased with her current dry cleaner and asking where she should go and where he took his clothes. Kim smiled in spite of her current state of mind. This was a call she was used to—this woman's silly, senseless excuses to call, to be in contact.

Kim shook her head, then rose to leave. She would finish her tea and make a grocery list before advising the unknown caller he'd made a mistake. She needed to first summon up courage before placing a call to a stranger. She got as far as the door and the phone rang. She froze in place, again not making a move to answer but allowing the ringing to continue until the machine's greeting kicked in.

Now she heard the caller's voice in real time as the same man's angry words and harsh voice filled the air, punctuated by frequent swearing.

It was frightening. He'd heard the machine's message announcing the correct name and phone number twice now and yet he persisted.

Kim abandoned her good intention of contacting the caller. She'd lost her nerve and never recited the short speech she'd intended to deliver. She had planned to say, "Sir, as our greeting informs, you have reached the home office of Mr. Sherwood Benjamin. He is an attorney and he's gone to England on business and his name is not Mac-Gyver."

Again, the phone rang. The recorded greeting once more, then another insistent message from the ex-wife. And, again, she was not annoyed. She merely shook her head and let the message play out. Kim knew her boyfriend was completely devoted to her. He had enhanced her lifestyle greatly. She lived in a luxurious apartment and had financial security beyond her wildest dreams.

But her gratitude was counter-balanced by other factors. Her boyfriend rarely dealt with his business affairs at home but on those occasions when he did, she had overheard just enough of his telephone conversations to learn he often berated his fellow partners, speaking to them in a profane and disparaging manner. Kim knew little about the business world, but she also overheard things that led her to suspect he engaged in practices that were less than ethical. This was not what she had been taught by her father, who was a man of honor in the old country.

She had another concern: her boyfriend always took the calls from his ex-wife and usually attended to whatever household chore or minor problem she required. But when he hung up from speaking to her, he was less than flattering. He would curse to himself and refer to her as a "dumb shit." In Kim's culture, this betrayed a profound disrespect for women in general. She knew that many people blamed Confucius and his philosophies for the ostensibly lower status of women in China.

Perhaps, she had mused to herself, *but in the old country, they recognized women's honor and power in their given role.*

Thus, Kim's gratitude and respect had its limitations. She bore some allegiance to another man who first provided an opportunity for her to survive in her newly adopted country, the United States. He gave her a job as a waitress in a restaurant he owned when he overheard her fairly begging, without success, for the same employment at the one of the man's favorite restaurants, Fat Choy. At his own establishment, an Italian restaurant, she'd met her future beau. She had subsequently introduced her new lover to her benefactor. They seemed to hit it off.

Kim mused on this memory from time to time, declaring to herself that her first loyalties were directed to the man who had initially made life in America possible, who to her knowledge had always behaved like a gentleman, a man of honor. She thought about him today and the phone call she'd received from him and the request he'd made of her. And she knew it was the right thing to do to help her good friend, Mr. Frank Roma.

chapter 58

WE HAD AN early flight so when Sherwood rang Winnie's doorbell at seven in the morning I was awake and dressed. I had my bags— well, they were Winnie's Louis Vuitton luggage on loan—already in the hallway. I hurried to the door, coffee cup in hand.

"How's my favorite traveling companion?" Sherwood beamed his lopsided grin at me.

"How sweet," I beamed back. "And you're mine. Come on in."

"I've called a cab and I'm here to get your bags downstairs, Freddy, then I'll go fetch mine."

"Okay. There they are. Let me get my coat and I can carry the small one."

Winnie suddenly swept into the room, already perfumed, her taffeta robe rustling.

"My dears, no need for a cab. A limo service town car is downstairs and waiting for you. It's my little gift for your trip."

I felt rather surprised and self-conscious. It wasn't like this was a honeymoon trip and, much as I appreciated the gesture, a gift was hardly in order.

Sherwood looked taken aback also but managed a tight smile and picked up the bags. "Right you are," he said, placing the bags in the elevator and holding the door for me.

"I'll take the other lift up and get my things. You'll be all right, Freddy?"

"I'm fine. Take your time."

Sherwood moved into the next elevator as it pinged its arrival and Winnie took over his position of holding my door open. She apparently had a goodbye speech planned. Despite my growing feelings for Sherwood, I sought to downplay any romantic notions Winnie might entertain.

"Winnie, you didn't have to treat us to a limo. I feel bad enough using your good luggage. This is just a business trip for Sherwood and I'm just sort of a guest and . . ."

"Oh, shush, shugah, what good is my being so all fired filthy rich if ah can't do things for those ah love. And ah can't take full credit. It was Buck's idea. He can be the sweetest . . ."

"Buck's?"

"Yes, honey, now don't you go fussin' about that. We all love you and want you to have a wonderful time. Y'all been through so much lately."

I put down my small bag and gave Winnie a hug and a kiss on the cheek. "Thank you again. For everything you do. You're very dear to me."

"Don't go gettin' too mushy on me. Save it for those nights in London." She let go of the elevator door and as it slid to a close chirped a final "Love you."

"Love you too, Win," I managed before it sucked shut.

I arrived at the lobby level and slid the two large bags out, still carrying the small one, and waited for Sherwood. He arrived three minutes later with two large bags in a camel-colored leather. Deposited them on the lobby floor and frowned.

"So where's the limo driver? Isn't it his job to get in here and lug our cases to the trunk?"

"I'd say so. Let me go and see what's up."

Sherwood started to protest but I was already out the door. It was another cold but sunny day. The car's motor was running and I motioned for the chauffeur to roll down the window. I peered into the car's dim light. I could tell the driver was a big man. He cast his eyes downward, his cap hiding his face. Undoubtedly aware of his oversight and embarrassed.

"We've got bags inside. Could you give us a hand?"

"Glad to." He had a high-pitched voice. "Get in the back please."

Limousine protocol would normally dictate this dude would get out and open the door for me but it was a bit too chilly and windy for me to argue the point. I got in.

Then his performance improved. In record time, he got some of the bags out on the street, opened the door for Sherwood, scurried in and retrieved the remaining bags. We turned into the flow of traffic and roared off to JFK.

By mutual agreement, Sherwood and I foreswore any attempts at conversation, hunkered down in our seats and dozed off and on during the ride. It made the journey go faster and we were almost there when I reached for the warmth of Sherwood's hand. My touch awakened him, he sat up and smiled.

"You're going to love this plane, Freddy. It will be quite an experience."

I didn't know quite what to make of that remark. A plane ride is a plane ride and flights abroad are, if anything, tiring and tedious.

"If it goes as quickly as this ride, I certainly will," I smiled. "But you do know I've flown over to England and especially Paris many times before."

He looked away and laughed, turned back to face me.

"Of course, I know that." He patted my hand. "But have you flown Emirates? That's where the special experience comes in."

"Emirates? That's our airline? I could have sworn you said we were flying British Air."

I was thinking of when we were in the restaurant and Buck was rudely pumping Sherwood for details.

"No, you're mistaken. I'm sure I said Emirates. I use them all the time. But no matter. You're in for a very pleasant time and there's no one I'd rather treat to all this than you."

—

We'd boarded the plane that Emirates airlines called its A380 and—Sherwood was right—it was an amazing piece of aircraft. The flight attendants were especially gracious but, apart from that, the process of getting settled on board was much the same as on any flight. People jostled down the aisles, relieving themselves of hats and coats and sometimes boots, murmuring to each other or the staff. Sherwood checked that I was settled and okay in my seat and asked if I had a good book to read. I showed him my copy of Jean Rhys' *Wide Sargasso Sea*, which I'd begun in New York, and he declared he was going to immerse himself in that day's London *Times* and made his way back to his own seat.

I listened to the high-pitched whine, which signaled the engines were spooling up for takeoff. Then the familiar rattling one always hears of things being jostled in overhead bins and other parts of the cabin due to engine vibrations on takeoff. Then a thump beneath the floor following takeoff as the landing gear goes up into the belly of the plane and the doors to the landing gear bay are shut. We became airborne and as the pilot throttled the engines back and we were cruising, the engine sound calmed from its earlier whine to a hum.

After a nap of almost two hours, I stood up, stretched, and decided to go for a walk. Sherwood was seated four rows behind me in an aisle seat. But then all seats in this luxurious business class section were aisle seats. Sherwood had actually apologized that we were not in first class, extolling the amenities that existed there in private cabins. Each contained a twenty-three-inch TV screen, a personal minibar, your own vanity table, mirror and wardrobe. Every seat had a built-in massage system and, as if all that weren't enough, you could order meals from their a la carte menu at any time during your flight.

Even in business class, our seats converted to flat beds but Sherwood had dozed off sitting up, his head cocked to one side, a sleepy smile curling his lips. I bent down and kissed his forehead lightly. He didn't stir.

My destination was the bar in business class but I decided to check out the economy section first, as I felt flying "coach" in a luxury plane such as this one must be something to see. In economy, the gray cushioned seats were four across and boasted pillows and blankets in either coral or lavender. I continued along the gray-carpeted aisle. Suddenly a cool hand grabbed my arm. The touch was gentle but just firm enough to halt my progress.

"Excuse me, aren't you a model?"

The query was made by a slim woman of about thirty or so. She had dark, curly hair pulled back into a bun. Her face reminded me of the French actress Leslie Caron. Caron, I believe, is around eighty now, but I remember her when she was young from videos of old movies my mother used to watch.

This younger "Leslie" was wearing black tights above a cotton top in a lime green that resembled an artist's smock. Around her neck, a linen scarf in graduating shades of coral had been looped twice over, tied in a knot and pulled to one side. The smock was unbuttoned halfway, revealing a black jersey halter underneath. Big, round silver discs hung from her ears and a huge silver ring with a black onyx stone gleamed from her left forefinger. The sleeves of her smock ended at her elbows and on the inside of one forearm, I got a quick glimpse of a tattoo that appeared to be a lion inside some kind of star. Little black ballet slippers were on her feet.

"Yes, I am," I smiled. I didn't know what else to add. Maybe she'd seen me on a magazine cover or in a show. I was sure she just wanted her curiosity satisfied and I needn't recite my resume so I started to continue on my way, but her grip stopped me.

"I'm a stylist," she continued. "You know, I work with the photographers and set up shots. I remember you from some magazine layouts I did—I think one was for *Vogue*—quite a while ago. I remember hearing you speak French to someone on a couple of occasions and it impressed me because my mother is French but I've never picked it up."

She's essentially an artist, I thought to myself. *Explains her colorful appearance.*

Her face still wasn't familiar so I just smiled and looked at her, still not knowing quite where to take this conversation.

"My mother is from Alsace-Lorraine," she quickly filled the silence. "Sadly, she didn't make much of an attempt to teach me the language and I know only a few phrases whereas I should . . ."

I realized my chatty new friend needed companionship, so I interrupted and said, "I'm headed for the bar in business class. Why don't you join me?"

"That's okay. You probably think I'm nuts but I just couldn't help saying something to you. I'm alone, but you're probably traveling with someone."

"I am, but he's dead asleep and I could use some company. Come on."

She grinned happily and immediately stood up to her full five feet, two. "I'm Kendrick Levine."

"Freddy Bonnaire."

I led the way and we joined about a dozen other people imbibing although the hour was still early. We bellied up to the half-moon shaped bar and ordered from a slim young man in a starched white shirt, tie and beige vest—a bloody mary for me and red wine for Kendrick—then took our drinks to one of the small round tables. The other passengers consisted of two men in Arab headdress, several men in shirts and ties and two couples in their twenties or so.

Predictably, we talked about the fashion industry plus our travel experiences to Paris and Milan. Like me, she was now headed to London. In her case, for an interior design gig. Neither of us wanted a second drink and I wanted to get back to Sherwood so I let the conversation wind down.

"I should get back," I said.

"Oh, of course," Kendrick said. "Let me give you this." She handed me one of her business cards.

"Thanks. I'm sorry, I don't have any cards with me."

"That's perfectly okay," she said. "But maybe if you have free time we could do lunch in London."

"I'd love that. We're staying at the Lanesborough Hotel on the edge of Hyde Park. I'll call you."

My promise was sincere, but Kendrick looked a little embarrassed. "Only if you have free time," she repeated.

"I'm sure I'll have that. The friend I'm traveling with has some business stuff to take care of there so I'll be on my quite a bit."

"Wonderful," she smiled, "*à bientôt.*"

Kendrick looked around and appeared a little confused. "Let me walk back with you," I said, feeling she perhaps didn't know the way.

"Thanks," she laughed.

I took her back to her exact seat and then made my way out of her section. Lost in the glow of my bloody mary and the pleasure of making a new friend, I did not notice the very tall man with narrow designer glasses also seated in economy—a face that *was* familiar to me and one that would have been very significant.

chapter 59

OUR TIME IN London was a pleasing wave of activity. The first day we took a rented Range Rover to Aldborough, North Yorkshire. We took the M1 to the A1, passing many trucks—or lorries, as Sherwood called them—on the motorway with the occasional petrol station. The weather was grey, damp and cold with slush on the roads. The trip took a little over four hours but it passed quickly to me, fascinated as I was by the scenery. From our road, we could see industrial towns with modern estates and rows of old terrace houses. Ancient hand-made stone walls artistically separated fields and lonely farm houses. Glimmers of life could be seen from afar and, here and there, historic English pubs. The most bucolic view in Yorkshire was the sheep dotting beautiful rolling hills that were covered in snow.

We headed for St. Andrew's Church for the wedding of Sherwood's client, which was followed by a lavish reception at Castle Allerton. I relied on Ralph Lauren for both events, wearing a silvery jacket, brown suede skirt and a lace scarf looped around my neck for the wedding itself and a strap-less silver tissue lamé evening dress with a full skirt for the reception. With each outfit, I wore a different version of a leather belt with a huge metal clasp in the center boasting a steer's head. If guests didn't suspect I was American from my accent, they'd figure it out from my cowboy belts.

Sherwood looked exceptionally handsome, decked out in full morning suit and tails. The suit was a dark charcoal gray with a black waistcoat, a blue tie and a crisp white shirt. He left me for a period during the day to attend the traditional pub stop for the ushers. When I went to fetch him at The Ship Inn, I received quite a few open-mouth stares. I didn't care. There were maybe thirty people in the bar, mostly men. The guys at Sherwood's long wooden table seemed to be having a wonderful time, full of many pints of ale. Sherwood was anxiously looking around for someone when I entered. I doubted it was me he was expecting. He and his companions didn't appear to need rescuing by a female. I waved from the door. He waved back. He continued searching the room but smiled and relaxed when I approached. As for me, I'd had enough wedding for the day and was anxious to return to the warmth of the Range Rover.

Back in London, Sherwood had business meetings for the next three days. In the evening, we'd meet up again, dining one night at Clos Maggiore in Covent Gardens—I had the braised rabbit and he had duck breasts—and the next two dinners in Mayfair at Quaglino's and then Indian food at Tamarind. It brought back memories to be in the Mayfair district. My last trip to London, I'd done a charity fashion show in the ballroom of Claridge's there.

Over wine one evening, Sherwood commented, "The next time I bring you here, we'll have to take in a wonderful retreat—it's called Coworth Park and sits on 240 acres of private parkland near Windsor Castle, just a forty-five minute drive outside of London."

The next time I bring you here—hmmmmmm, I liked the sound of that.

As he was preoccupied with work, Sherwood insisted that during the day I "get out and roam the city" as he put it. I did so, having lunch with Kendrick, bonding with her and having a wonderful time shopping with a little sightseeing thrown in for good measure. I'd been fascinated with Kendrick's appearance on the plane and she didn't disappoint during our London sprees, wearing her curly hair in a wild Afro-like style one day and green satin jeans another.

We took the number 22 bus to King's Road and browsed in all the upmarket—Brit term for upscale—clothing and antique shops, buying nothing. We finally spent some money at the chain store Warehouse—Kendrick getting a cocktail dress with a tropical bird print for £65 and me, a beige lace blouse for £55.

We treated ourselves to lunch at the Kings Road Steakhouse and Grill, an elegant but unpretentious little restaurant with art deco touches, cream leather, crystal chandeliers and huge mirrors. Having worked up an appetite, we each had the ten-ounce rib eye.

One morning the three of us had brunch at La Caprice where I spotted designer Zac Posen and afterward Kendrick and I had our hair done at the Richard Ward Salon in Duke of York Square in Chelsea.

On another day, Sherwood accompanied us as far as the door of the exclusive, members-only Brompton Club in Knightsbridge. It was located underneath the white-walled Kensington Hotel and the Italian doorman gave Kendrick's attire a dubious look. Sherwood pressed twenty quid into his large, sweaty palm and in we went.

The club was beautifully decorated even if its clientele were a bit stuffy. We lingered well into the afternoon, appreciating it would be our one and only opportunity to be there. I told her of my upcoming trip to stay at a mansion— The Rawleigh House on Glastonbury Way. It came up after we'd had several glasses of wine and we giggled hilariously over our attempts to pronounce *Glash-thom-berry*.

Each night I invited Kendrick to join us for dinner but she declared she had a special friend she was also visiting and always declined. The fun we had almost—*almost*—quelled my insistent fear that I was once again being followed. I tried to employ rational thought and recited mantras to myself: I was safe with Sherwood . . . if I had been followed back in New York, it was undoubtedly those Mafia types... it was highly unlikely trips to Europe were ever on their agendas no matter what the circumstances.

Mantras-schamtras, I was happy when the day arrived that we were to drive out to the client's house Sherwood had described. He had mentioned that it was in a secluded area near Winchester.

Try stalking me there, Beppe, or whoever you are.

Again, we took the black Range Rover and, in less than an hour, made our way down a long narrow driveway that arched just off the main road and twisted and turned its way through piles of rock and trees bent by the now fierce wind. We arrived at a mansion with a stately elegance reminiscent of a grand European manor. It had a gray stone exterior with limestone trim, decorative carvings and various different window styles. It stood alone on how many acres I could not gauge but if there were any neighbors, they were not visible. The whole place was quiet and white, the stark landscape relieved only by clusters of fir trees on both sides.

As it turned out, our arrival was just in the knick of time as the gentle snow began to evolve into blizzard proportions. Evening was upon us, the sky charcoal with faint ribbons of gold. Sherwood pulled up and I stepped out into the raw, cold air. The intense wind whipped at my clothes and hair as I made a lame show of attempting to help him with the luggage. Gallantly he pointed to the door which was painted a dull antique red, ran ahead and opened it for me enter.

Once inside, we changed from our travel garb—in our separate bedrooms—and met up in the vast living room. The house was a bit chilly so I'd layered two tank tops under a jersey hoodie. Sherwood was infinitely more elegant in a green smoking jacket with quilted lapels.

We rested from our trip in front of the telly in time to hear that the "violent winter snowstorm" had crippled London's roads, subways and buses and all but shut down many parts of Britain. Winter had come howling across the U.K. like a frigid monster.

The report continued to advise that no buses were running because of "adverse and dangerous driving conditions," most of the subway system was closed and large sections of the railroad network had shut down. Further, that more than 3,000 schools across England and Wales were closed, airports were closed, or beset by delays, and about twenty percent of Britain's workers failed to make it to work, adding that the storm would cost the economy several billion dollars. The news anchor's recitation was followed by several man-on-the-street interviews, all eliciting a barrage of complaints from stranded travelers asking why the government seemed so ill prepared for the bad weather, when everyone had known for several days that it was coming.

A clip was then shown of the prime minister declaring, "We are doing everything in our power to ensure that services—road, rail and airports—are open as quickly as possible." The next image was the mayor of London who, the narrator advised, rode his bicycle to work, insisting the city had "done pretty well in what are absolutely extraordinary circumstances." The screen then cut to a man identified as a subway stationmaster who asked that his name not be mentioned.

"No grit, no salt—everyone's late to work. Lots of people didn't make it at all," he said angrily. "It was only by sheer fortune that some of us did. There was one bus and one train from my area. They're telling us to take cabs to get home."

I very much sympathized with the snow-bound Brits but as Sherwood thoughtfully and expertly built a fire in the library fireplace, then left to make hot tea, I felt a warm sense of comfort and ease. More importantly, I felt surrounded by an isolated and impenetrable cocoon of safety and protection.

Earlier that day, a very tall, somewhat overweight, black man walked briskly thru the falling snow to a car rental office in London. He had been following Frédérique Bonnaire, all over London. Now she and the pasty-faced lawyer had changed course. So had he.

chapter 60

JOSEPH BUCKLEY LEMOYNE stood in front of the tall, narrow windows of Winifred de Foucauld's spacious Central Park West apartment. He took a wrapped cigar out of the pocket of his Hawaiian shirt, then put it back, remembering Winnie's no-smoking edict. It was early morning and he'd let himself in with the key he still kept from his temporary stay there. He had things on his mind and he wanted to talk to Winnie. But the mistress of the house was still sleeping and was hanging in the air, obscuring the usual view of Central Park and the buildings beyond. He'd brought some Cajun boudine and sausages to fix for Winnie's lunch. He'd started a pot of coffee and was waiting for it to brew. As its aroma wafted into the living room, Buck turned to his inner thoughts.

His current introspection led him to a contemplation of his name. Family legend was that he was a descendent of Jean Baptiste Lemoyne, a French explorer, colonial governor of Louisiana, and founder of New Orleans.

Amazingly prestigious background for an ex-New York cop, Buck thought, not for the first time.

His family had lived in New Orleans and, like gypsies, moved back and forth from New Orleans to New York for years. They spent just enough time in Louisiana to pick up southern tastes and habits and long enough in Brooklyn to become a family of New York cops. Now he, in similar nomadic fashion, divided his time between California and Manhattan.

A section of mist began to part and Buck believed he could see the skyscraper housing Sherwood Benjamin's office. He'd heard of his firm—Peters, Nelson and so forth—and had nothing against them. He had never heard of Sherwood before he entered Freddy's life and had plenty against *him*. He knew nothing of Benjamin's legal expertise or ethics. It was enough to raise his shackles that he seemed in romantic pursuit of the woman Buck secretly loved.

At least it's a secret to absolutely no one except the lady herself—another thing he contemplated, not for the first time.

A saving grace for his dilemma of the heart was the fact that for the last several months Buck had been distracted by a far more urgent matter—the fact that Freddy had been kidnapped and escaped and seemingly tailed constantly thereafter. Without her knowledge, he'd put his truck driver friend from California on the case. Luke Jefferson, a substantially built black guy, was following Freddy wherever she went. Luke was about six foot four with skin the color of coffee and cream and normally stood out in a crowd but he was smart and agile enough to overcome this and, so far, had remained invisible to Freddy herself and, by all indications, to any of her stalkers also.

Suddenly his reverie was punctuated by a whiff of Chanel perfume and the rustle of taffeta.

"Buckley Lemoyne, you sweet boy, you've started both breakfast and lunch for this poor ole lady, haven't you? Hellfire, come here and give me a big hug, shugah."

The day with Aunt Winnie had begun.

—

It was Saturday and very few attorneys or staffers were lurking in the hallowed halls of Peters, Nelson, Benjamin, Simms & Fallon. Outside, the sky was gray, the air was cold and it was sleeting. Inside, the offices were also uncomfortably chilly. One of many reasons George Fallon resented being one of those few in residence. He shuffled some papers in the middle of his desk relating to his own practice of entertainment law and gazed glumly at the stack of folders that had nothing to do with his clients or show business or anything remotely related to his own area of expertise.

He thought of that phrase, *area of expertise*. Some of his fellow partners would undoubtedly snicker at the choice of words. Six months ago, he'd received what was essentially a warning from the firm's executive committee, saying in a nutshell that he hadn't been pulling his weight financially, that his billable hours were low. He'd composed what he considered a masterful memo repudiating this, citing several instances of his assistance with corporate law cases, his long tenure and loyalty to the firm and stopping just short of whining that he had two teenage daughters to send to college in the very near future. It had worked. His colleagues were, for the most part, a sentimental lot and he knew this. They didn't really want to can him, but his low contributions to the firm's coffers stemming from fees from only a handful of musicians and frequently-out-of-work actors necessitated some notice and resolution.

George looked to his left at the rain-speckled windows of his office, viewing his reflection—longish gray hair, stooped shoulders, rumpled sweater, faded jeans and all. He was tall. He was also good looking and considered by some to look like an older version of the actor George Clooney. Several of the young female associates he'd worked with would concur with this assessment. He cut his glance once again to the new project he'd been assigned and the formidable stack of files it represented. None of the young lovelies would assist him with this particular endeavor. It was—he was told as if he were not quite bright enough to deduce this—to be held in the strictest confidence.

Wearily, George's long, slim fingers pulled the top file from the stack and opened it. He could not delay any longer addressing the task at hand. At least he didn't have the burden of proving *if* his friend, the lawyer in the office next to his, had stolen from the firm or even how much. *He simply had to produce admissible evidence that Sherwood Benjamin had embezzled and diverted money from the firm's funds to his personal account.*

—

Off the FDR Drive at East 93rd Street on the edge of the East River, several people were standing around in the ice-bright morning sunshine looking at a body on the ground. But Patrick Clinton Brennan, his eyes narrowed, his mouth downcast, was unobtrusively examining another body. That of the petite female partner recently assigned to him. Detective Phyllis Harper wore a worn-looking navy pants suit with a camel car coat. She moved away from the officers who were standing and was crouched beside a uniform as they examined tire marks on a muddy area several feet away.

"The marks have been degraded somewhat but this appears to be pretty standard looking tires," she commented.

"Yeah," agreed the male cop. "Probably a midsized sedan."

Clint's interest in Harper was strictly professional. She was thirty-something, skinny, but busty, with a pretty face. These attributes mattered little to him. He resented her existence. Brennan noted that the cop next to her was prematurely bald. Harper had prematurely white and gray hair.

Phyllis looked up at Clint.

"Vic whacked elsewhere and dumped here."

Harper had once lectured Clint about the value of forensic entomology—the study of insects associated with a human corpse that will show, among other things, if the body has moved to a different site after death.

She'll probably bag a bunch of bugs before she leaves today, Clint thought.

The M.E. piped up. "Body temp puts the T.O.D. sometime between six and seven a.m.".

"This one's not a floater, detective," the cop chimed in.

A likewise brilliant deduction. They deserve each other. Why the hell had they transferred Wanda?

Wanda Jane Williams had been with Clint for a little over two years. She was an affable good ole girl from some Podunk town in Ohio. Just wanted to put in her time. Anything Clint did and any way he did it was fine with Wanda. Now this snippy little hotshot had come along. He'd been around her just long enough this week to know she considered herself some kind of expert in many aspects of law enforcement and, the truth was, she wasn't much of an expert on anything. He could see in his captain's eyes that he felt much the same way. Still, he'd foisted this self-important bitch upon him with atypical fanfare and obvious enjoyment.

Suddenly Brennan was aware of a rush of freezing wind coming off the water. He averted his attention from Harper and looked around. The photographer was doing his job, standing back and aiming his high-resolution digital camera at wide-angle shots of the area first, then moving closer to take in the trash and debris around the lifeless form curled into a fetal position. Phyllis Harper had joined a CSI technician. They were dropping cigarette stubs they found nearby together with some soil samples into clear plastic evidence bags.

To their right, he spied old Mike Foster, juggling a pad of graph paper, a pen and a retractable steel measuring tape. He was one of a dying breed. These days few police departments use sketch artists. Most used software such as Identi-Kit or Faces 4.0 when taking statements from witnesses. These programs were fast in mixing and matching facial features and hairstyles, making it easier to identify suspects. But Foster was the captain's cousin and so he was kept on payroll.

As if on cue, Phyllis walked up to Brennan and announced, "Someone's swept the immediate area to obliterate most of the footprints. Pretty much worked too.

Must have used something from that collection of dry brush over there."

Clint just nodded. Harper was too much of a chatterbox for his taste. He scarcely concealed his annoyance.

The coroner's wagon arrived next on the scene. Burt Easley got out, approaching in his weary, looping gate. He was younger than Foster, but looked worn and light-years older. Coroners put in long hours, but are salaried and don't reap overtime. Easley was here to take the body to the lab. He was a thin man with a gray complexion. A plaid wool scarf was wrapped snug around his neck but his overcoat was open and flapped furiously in the cold wind. Easley gave a tired wave to Brennan. .

Clint's gaze returned to the dead man. When he first arrived, a uniform had advised no wallet or other identification had been found on or near the victim. Not surprising since the subject was completely naked with twenty-dollar bills stuffed into every orifice of his body—a well-known Mafia message indicating the deceased had been guilty of excessive greed. As for identity, Brennan thought, *let 'em figure it out for themselves*. He already knew the body lying on the cold, wet ground was a Frankie Roma employee, one Timothy Ryan.

—

Dina Celine Hutton parked her car in a lot off Atlantic Avenue and swiftly began the three-block walk to Antiques and Treasures. Her usual sour mood was enhanced by a particular fury this chilly, blustery afternoon in Brooklyn. Her best friend Trina, who worked in the bakery next door, had called her cell, advising that a cop was inside her shop and that his black-and-white had been parked outside for some time. It was her luck that the police would come sniffing around on one of the days her poor-excuse-for-an-assistant Lindsey was manning the store. Dina knew Lindsey had addiction issues and knew she sometimes crashed overnight in the store but she worked for peanuts and the customers all liked her so her occasional alcoholic or drug forays were considered tolerable.

I don't think this is about that dumb kid getting busted for pot, Dina thought. *I've got a feeling this is about Sonny Bob. I don't know why, but nothing's felt right about his death from the beginning. Not that being murdered ever's right but this has been a pisser. I know what Sonny made from the sale of his condo, and I also know damn well whenever they find the jerk's last will and testament he'll have left everything to blondie . . . miss super model Frédérique. I wanted to talk with her, reason with her that his sisters deserved some of the dough but she was too important and busy to give me her time and then Bella talked me out of pursuing it further. She was right. It was better to go talk to his lawyer the way we did. He wasn't much help but at least we're sort of on record as rightful heirs.*

Dina arrived at her destination, yanked open the door, pushed it closed with her ample derrière, then stepped into the long, narrow shop. Immediately she did a rare thing. She smiled.

"Officer," she said cheerfully, "Welcome to my store. But what brings you here? Do we have a shoplifter? That's been a problem lately."

Lindsey and the cop looked in her direction, startled, as if they hadn't heard her come in despite the tinkling of the bell attached to the door. They'd been grinning at each other, Dina realized, and the cop seemed more engrossed in Lindsey's long, dark hair and charcoal smudged blue eyes than he was in any interrogation he was conducting.

"Dina! Hi!" Lindsey exclaimed. "I was just talking to Ray . . ." She giggled. ". . . I mean Officer Holmes about the spears we have."

Dina blanched. *What in the world is this chick talking about?*

"He showed me a photo of a spear and it looks exactly like one that's from a set of four we've got."

"I don't see the point of . . ."

Lindsey quickly ducked under the counter, reappearing with a half-moon shaped holder boasting three spears and a fourth empty square hole, and spoke before Dina could finish.

"Gotta be the one missing from this thing, right?"

"I don't know. There must be dozens of such . . ."

"Lindsey's memory has been really helpful," Officer Ray Holmes interjected.

'Yeah," Lindsey beamed. "I remember the day I noticed it went missing. And I know it happened that day because I'd just brought it up from the basement and put it next to that purple bowl."

"You remember all that?" Dina marveled. *Even when you're high?* she wanted to add.

As if she read her boss' mind, Lindsey said, "I remember I'd been drinking nothing but coffee all day that day. And lots of water so I felt really cool."

She frowned and added, "And sharp."

Officer Holmes had been looking at Dina as Lindsey spoke. His body language said he dared Dina to challenge the young woman's assertions.

Lindsey ran her fingers thru her long hair and continued. "I remember it was raining and really quiet here that day. God, I was going crazy. Only about three people walked in here the whole damn day."

"That's what I mean about Lindsey's memory," Holmes smiled. "She remembers them all."

"And who were they?" Dina asked.

"Well, your friend Trina dropped by. I thought she knew it was one of your days to not be here but . . .?"

"Who else?" Dina said sternly.

"The guy from the record store who always hits on me. I've never known his name . . ." she looked coyly at the cop. "But he sure knows mine and . . ."

"One more person, right Lindsey?" the cop said.

"Oh, right." She looked at Dina. "That guy who lives in Mrs. de Foucauld's building."

"Sherwood Benjamin?"

"Gosh, I'm awful at names but I think so. And his wife . . . her name is Sheila or something like that . . . she came in too."

"That would be Selah. Short brunette?"

"Yeah, that's her. Well, actually, she came in after he did and left before he left. He said she was, like, stalking him lately, and he made sure to let me know she was his <u>ex</u>-wife." Lindsey giggled, and tucked her hair behind one ear. "I think he was kinda, you know, interested." She beamed up at Officer Holmes and he shook his head, as if in agreement.

Inwardly Dina also shook her head, in exasperation at Lindsey's presumptuousness but mostly at Selah's desperate behavior. *Selah had an affair with Sonny Bob. Five will get you ten, she's in his Will too and champing at the bit for every dollar.* Aloud she said, "And they had British accents?"

"Yeah, they did," Lindsey agreed. "Usually I think that's kinda cute but . . . "

"That would be Sherwood and Selah Benjamin. They live on the upper west side." Dina confirmed, looking at the policeman.

Holmes smiled.

The police had not released to the general public that an Aborigine spear had been found in Sonny Bob Bonnaire's body so the cop's interest had little impact on Dina Hutton. She strutted out of the shop as quickly as she'd come, her main concern that there'd been low sales on the day in question.

chapter 61

SHERWOOD AND I no sooner had our tea, enjoyed the warmth of the fire and lazily reminisced about the wedding we'd just attended than it was time for dinner. He announced the housekeeper had left the day before and was not likely to return because of snow conditions but she'd left a lamb stew for us. I offered to warm it up and make a salad but Sherwood insisted on doing the honors. He assured me that the freezer was well stocked and "even *sans* cook" we'd have plenty to eat and that nothing would involve either of us putting together complicated meals or be burdened with a lot of domestic chores. I wasn't worried—I was thoroughly enjoying this change of scenery and the opportunity to bond with my British friend.

Outside the snow was coming down in large, wet flakes. I was happy to be comfortably ensconced in a large, over-stuffed chair covered in beige corduroy and happier still that it was located very near the fireplace as most of the mansion was chilly and drafty. I took in my immediate sur-roundings: the huge Oriental rug in a large pattern in black, beige and orange, the various chairs covered in prints or red leather. The gilt-framed painting over the fireplace of a woman standing in a living room was an odd note, as was the choice to paint the fireplace itself in a royal blue.

I wondered why Sherwood had not shown me around when we first arrived but then I remembered my French mother's comment that Europeans don't automatically give guests a tour of their living quarters the way so many Americans do.

Sherwood came out from the kitchen, wiping his hands on a dishtowel.

"Soup's on, m'lady. Come and get it."

We ate in the kitchen, rather than the very formal dining room. Knowing Sherwood, I would have definitely guessed we'd dine in the latter, but the man was proving to be full of surprises.

"The stew is excellent," I said.

"Can't take credit," Sherwood said. "Have some rolls and butter. It's all I was able to rustle up I'm afraid. If you'd like a salad, I could . . ."

"No problem. I eat salads constantly in the States. This is a great change."

"I hope all of it will be a change for you, Freddy," he said earnestly. "And productive."

"Productive? I'm just having fun, Sherwood. I've been working non-stop lately. Not nearly non-stop enough to please Marc, my booker, but . . ."

"Yes, I know."

He paused to spread gobs of butter onto a muffin. I followed suit, calories be damned!

"Did London remind you of Sonny Bob?"

The question caught me unaware. "Not really. I went on a tour with him once that passed through here but . . ."

"London is where he and I met," Sherwood interrupted. "I was here temporarily in the firm's London office and he was on holiday."

Sherwood's mood was serious and intense. I wanted to hear about his own early life in England, his growing up years, not reprise the sad Sonny saga right now.

"I know you were born in Blackpool," I changed the subject. "Did you and your family get into London much?"

Sherwood didn't answer immediately. He merely regarded his wine glass for several seconds, then raised it to his lips and took a long swallow.

"I think Sonny kept money in a bank here. Do you know anything about that?"

Where was this conversation going? I'd heard enough about Sonny and the inheritance issue from his greedy stepsisters.

"No, I don't know anything about that. Is it important?"

"Well, I'm his lawyer. He should have told me things like this but Bonnaire could be evasive at times, to say the least."

Bonnaire? It was the first time I'd heard him refer to Sonny as anything but Sonny Bob and what was this lawyer thing about?

"I didn't know you were his lawyer," I smiled, as yet unperturbed by these revelations. "I thought you simply knew each other through Winnie."

"Yes, we met once again when I dropped by Winnie's one day. She's a most outgoing woman and we'd become friends just from running into each other on the elevator. Your husband eventually hired me as well."

Now Sonny is my husband in the present tense. So far, this was not the romantic dinner I'd envisioned.

Sherwood's right hand rested on the table, wrapped around his wineglass. I placed my free hand over his.

"Let's not talk about Sonny right now if you don't mind," I said softly. "It's a very sad subject to me." I gave him a warm smile.

Sherwood took a gulp of wine and began vigorously buttering a fresh roll in quick, rapid motions.

"Unfortunately, it's a subject I *must* address, Frédérique. Winifred is the executrix of his will. I'm sure it's of interest to her also."

We may not be eating in the formal dining room but formality is obviously the order of the evening. Frédérique and Winifred?

"You must have . . .," Sherwood began, then didn't finish the sentence. "Are you through? Let's adjourn to the living room. I'll get the bottle."

I glanced at his bowl. He'd only eaten half of his stew. I'd fairly licked my own dish clean.

I took my glass into the living room. This time I sat in the middle of the red leather couch, propping an orange cushion behind my back. Sherwood came in, placed his glass and the wine bottle on the small, brass coffee table and then stoked the fire to a fresh blaze. That accomplished, he picked up his glass and sat in a cushy corduroy chair, not on the couch as I'd hoped.

Maybe if I let him get off his chest whatever was bothering him . . ."You started to say something," I ventured.

Sherwood bent his head and contemplated his wine for several seconds. The only thing remotely relaxed about this evening thus far seemed to be my friend's frequent pauses.

"I was going to say you must have been to London with Sonny Bob, gone around town with him, on errands, gone to his bank."

Sherwood's voice retained its terse, gloomy tone and his approach was hardly subtle. What was this all about?

"What's this all about, Sherwood?" I let my voice match the sternness in his.

He looked almost startled at the change in my tone and then softened his.

"Just business, Freddy," he managed a slight smile. "I'm his barrister . . ." he chuckled at his use of the word," . . . and I need to know these things."

I allowed his flip-flop to encourage me. "You know, when we were in London—and I mean you and me this past week—we never got around to seeing any plays. Do you think we could drive in one evening? An actress I know through friends—Pamela Abraham—is playing in *Mame*. I saw her do it in the States, and she's fabulous. She's British, maybe you know of her."

Sherwood looked away and at the fire. "I don't believe I've heard the name but then I don't take in shows much."

"Pamela's amazing. She can sing, dance, and do serious drama or comedy equally well. I also saw her in . . ."

"If the weather lifts," Sherwood's voice became almost harsh once again. "We'll definitely try and nip over for the show. Right now traffic's a slog out there."

He returned his gaze to the fire and so did I. We sat for quite awhile like that. I'd like to call it sitting-together-in-comfortable-silence, but it didn't exactly feel that way. Maybe Sherwood was just tired from his London business meetings and the drive to Rawleigh House.

If only to break the monotony, I got up and carried my wineglass over to one of the floor-to-ceiling windows. The drapes were plain and heavy and in a lighter blue than the fireplace mantle. I pulled one aside. The earlier graceful flakes had grown into a full-blown storm. I could hear the wind whistling. It didn't bode well for a trip back to London or anywhere.

I turned around to see Sherwood using a little brass shovel to scatter some ashes over the flames.

"We should probably turn in now," he said. "I'm sure you're tired. I know I am. I'm going to clean things up in the kitchen—no, no, I insist—you're the guest."

I walked over to Sherwood, handed him my glass and planted a gentle kiss on his cheek.

Barrister Benjamin smiled at that. "Your bedroom is the first one to the right, the one with the four-poster. I'll see you in the morning. Sleep as late as you like."

He returned to banking the fire and I returned to my hope that I might ignite a fire of a different sort the next evening.

chapter 62

SHERWOOD REGINALD BENJAMIN paced the floor of the spacious, yet sparsely- decorated, bedroom of the mansion. He considered building a fire in the room's ornate relic of a fireplace, then thought better of it, and settled for pulling his overcoat over his pajamas in order to keep warm. He'd brought a fresh bottle of wine to his room and deposited it on the large mahogany night table. He lifted it and took a swig. The damn snowstorm was a nuisance but also a blessing in disguise. Now he had a perfect excuse not to leave the mansion but just get the job done.

Only one flaw—*where the hell was Ryan*?

Ever since Tim Ryan had switched his allegiance from Alex Roma and joined Sherwood's team, as it were, he'd been a bumbling buffoon. First, nearly tossing the Roma girl onto a subway, thinking she was Frédérique, and now he was four days late.

Four days! Unconscionable!

Sherwood had provided airfare and over a thousand dollars for Ryan's trip from New York to London.

Has the bloody little turd finked out on me?

Sherwood should have known if he'd double-cross a man like Frankie Roma, he was capable of anything. Lurking behind the Southampton church and then shooting Winifred's chauffeur instead of Freddy as they'd planned was sheer idiocy. He was essentially a major screw up. Frankie and all his motley crew were like the gang that couldn't shoot straight.

Darker recollections invaded his ruminating—the day he arrived in Brooklyn to meet Sonny Bob at a Brownstone in Park Slope . . . only to find him dead. He had been shocked at the sight of the crumpled body, the pool of blood by the head. Had Bonnaire fallen somehow, hit some object in the room and then stumbled toward the door? He looked around. It didn't seem likely. Then there'd here been foul play. That had to be it . . . but who? It didn't take Sherwood long to recover from an emotional reaction and begin to plot. He thought of Dina, Sonny's wretched stepsister. She'd been aggressive as hell of late and could be counted on to go after her share of the money and then some with a vengeance. Perhaps this situation was an opportunity to implicate her somehow as Sonny's killer. He'd raced down the stairs, out the door to the nearest cross street and hailed a cab.

"Atlantic Avenue." He'd fairly screamed the words, in spite of himself.

His mind wandered. One too many complications had invaded his plans. That wretched housekeeper he'd spoken to from London. He advised he had a key to his client's home and was expected as a guest. She insisted Mrs. Renner had left no such instructions. She became fairly hysterical at his angry insistence and threatened to call the authorities. He pretended to renege, allowing perhaps he had his dates wrong. Any hour now, the bitch would call Renner in Italy. There was no help for it but for Sherwood to make an advance trip to the mansion, deal with her, and then swiftly return to the city.

Now, too many strange things were happening. Well, maybe just one. Earlier he'd left Freddy and ducked into a first floor loo to call Kimberly on his cell. Her conversation had been hurried, disjointed. More puzzling, she'd mentioned "Mr. Roma." Sherwood had long forgotten that connection but now it appeared she had not. When he called, she was somewhere enveloped in loud noise—obviously not at their flat where she belonged—and she'd cut the conversation short. Something she never did. What the bloody hell was going on?

He continued to pace, returning his thoughts to the present, to Ryan and Frédérique. He paced and thought, pausing only to chug wine. Finally, after about fifteen minutes, he gave it up. He returned the nearly empty bottle to the night table with a thud, shrugged out of the overcoat, fell unto the bed and was snoring in no time.

chapter 63

Lucas Jefferson, Jr. burrowed under the two quilts in the narrow bed. He'd flown to England in the same plane as Freddy and the English clown, according to Buck's plan. Freddy had not noticed him on board and, of course, Benjamin did not know him. He'd tailed Freddy on foot all over London, then rented a car and followed them to this god-forsaken house in the middle of nowhere.

He'd had to park a mile away behind a heavy cluster of pine trees and after midnight go by foot through the storm to the mansion. There he managed to jimmy the lock on a back door and slip in. Off the large kitchen and down a narrow hallway was what appeared to be a maid's small bedroom. He'd already determined the house was empty, except for Freddy and the guy, so he was sure if it were going to be occupied, it would have been by this time. It was locked but he broke that down too and made it his headquarters. For the trip to the mansion, he'd filled a backpack with some food and a .475 magnum an Army buddy had given him and kept a Glock 17 in the rented jeep.

The bed was a twin with a plain iron frame. The only other furniture was a rickety night table with one drawer and a tiny lamp and a somewhat larger, but equally humble, table in one corner on which rested a small television set. The once white walls looked stained and the yellow and blue-checkered cotton curtains on the small window were faded. A metal footlocker was full of women's cotton dresses and underwear. There were three or four cotton sachets scattered here and there among the clothes. They emitted a heavily sweet aroma that reminded Luke of his grandmother's talcum powder. The maid, wherever she'd gone, would not be away for long.

It all worked according to Luke's plan. He knew, in a house that large, there'd be some way to gain entrance by stealth in the back of the mansion and some place, be it a small room or a closet, to use as a hiding place.

But from here on in, he had no plan. His plan was whatever this Sherwood dude's plan was. Whatever it involved, he doubted anything would happen tonight so it was safe to catch some shuteye. He'd gotten into bed fully dressed, not only as a device to keep warm in this damn meatlocker of a house but also to be prepared for any action. He unzipped a side pocket of his pack, removed the gun and laid it on the night table.

Luke had left his hidden car with time to spare before it was late enough to seek entry to the house. First, he bided his time crouching beneath the mansion's various windows, sneaking a peek inside now and then. It had been a painful enterprise, with the cold wind whipping around him and his feet sinking into snowdrifts. Now, the dreariness of his little room was the least of his problems. He rested and thought about his mission.

He'd met former cop Buck Lemoyne in a bar in California, never suspecting hooking up with this white dude would lead to friendship and supplementing his job of big rig hauling around the country with minor private eye assignments for Lemoyne. He certainly didn't envision a job that would involve hotfooting around New York City in order to keep an eye on their mutual friend Freddy Bonnaire. If you'd asked him a year ago, if he'd virtually give up trucking to settle in Manhattan and then fly to London, England for a gig, he would have said you were crazy but one thing he did know:

he considered Freddy a soul sister and nothing was going to happen to her while he was around.

Suddenly Luke tossed off the quilts and sat up. It occurred to him that readiness also meant wearing his heavy construction work shoes. He retrieved them from under the bed and laced them up. Another urge hit him. He was prepared to pee in the corner of this miserable room, if need be, but he looked at his watch. It was almost two in the morning and there was a small bathroom down the hall next to the kitchen. At this hour, it was safe to use it.

Why suffer any more than was necessary?

He opened the small bedroom's door. Quickly he took several lopping strides down the hallway and into the kitchen area. Then he heard a noise. It might be nothing, but Luke wasn't taking chances. He was closer to the kitchen's back door than to the maid's room so it appeared to be the quickest route to a hiding place. He quietly opened the narrow door and heard the crunch as his right foot and then his left hit the packed snow. Luke turned slowly and started to close the door behind him but as he did so, there was another sound.

He heard the gunshot before he felt it.

chapter 64

PRIOR TO ITS current state, St. Sebastian Roman Catholic Church was the former location of a Lowe's Woodside Theatre, a movie theatre that opened in 1926. It had the capacity to seat 2,000 people. Later in 1952, it was sold to the St. Sebastian Roman Catholic parish in order to found a chapel, which was transformed into a church building. The construction of the church began with the demolition of the entrance and lobby of the theatre, where a Romanesque bell tower was erected.

St. Sebastian's and its Sunday eight a.m. mass, was the destination of Maria Sanchez as she locked the door of her small apartment in Queens, rushed down the stairs, out onto the street, and swiftly made her way to the subway station three blocks away. Last Saturday, she and her working partner, her cousin Theresa, had had to clean a house on Manhattan's Upper East Side or she would not have missed confession at the church. And on this blustery, cold day, the confession of her soul was uppermost on her mind.

As she hurried along, she thought, *Missing confession is not my worse sin. Lacking respect for the dead is!*

Maria slid her subway card through the turnstile and raced to the nearest edge of the platform as her car had just arrived. She squeezed through the doors with a tall, gray-haired woman and two teenagers and saw that she had her choice of seats. It was Sunday, no packed-like-sardines rush-hour crowds. She made her way toward an empty two-seater near the connecting-car door, took the place next to the window and leaned her head against the pane.

Maria licked one forefinger and used it to clean up a smudge of dirt on her left leather boot.

I shouldn't worry about the dirt on my boot, she thought, I should worry about the soil on my soul.

With that, she felt tears gather and she pulled her wool cap off her head and used it to dab her eyes, knowing her purse was fresh out of tissue. She had played over and over in her mind the events and details of that awful day—so many times in so many days since that she'd finally learned to suppress the memory and had become adept at switching to different subjects.

But today was different. Today she had an appointment with a priest after mass, and she would have to revisit that bizarre day and confess all. It was her luck that the church office assigned this meeting to Father Vincent, her least favorite priest. He would undoubtedly condemn her to hell and back again and who knew what penance he would prescribe? If only she could have gotten Father Michael. He often talked about the beauty of that sacrament, of reconciliation, about confession being ultimately about forgiveness and God's love. Father Vincent, she wasn't so sure. He seemed to be perpetually scowling. Perhaps she should rehearse exactly what she would say. She pulled off her gloves, laid them and her wool cap neatly in her lap, and sat up straighter.

Father Vincent, this is what happened . . . should I first say, bless me, Father, for I have sinned . . .? No, probably not, she decided. Get right to it.

Theresa and I, we was hired by Mrs. de Foucauld . . . we work for her on Thursdays . . . to clean the Brooklyn house her niece Freddy owns. It gonna be a surprise for Miss Freddy. We cleaned all the downstairs real good. It spotless. Then we go upstairs to clean. We walk down the hall because we gonna start with the back bedroom first. Actually, Theresa, she go before me. I come upstairs after her. I hear Theresa scream! She see a man's body on floor. We call to him. We push him. Then we look at his eyes. He's dead! What can we do? We can't call the policia. We no got our papers, we're illegal. Oh, Father, holy Mary mother of God, we just go on cleaning. Like he not there. God for-give us, we cleaned the floor all around him, we waxed all the furniture, we vacuumed the rug . . . like the poor soul, he not there. And we go home. We tell no one. Till now.

chapter 65

I REMEMBER WHEN my family moved from New Orleans to New York City. My dad had just received a partnership offer from a very prestigious Manhattan law firm. This was to be a step up for us financially, and my seventeen-year-old imagination had a vision of what our new home—and specifically my new bedroom— would look like. Our house in New Orleans had been a spacious two story with rooms larger than they needed to be and wide windows that overlooked a flower-filled back yard that was lush and green. Thus it was a culture shock to discover that our new dwelling—a condo on Park Avenue—boasted a living room the size of our previous den, bedrooms barely large enough to con- tain our furniture and the smallest kitchen I'd seen anywhere.

As I opened my eyes on this first morning in Rawleigh House, I felt a similar sense of disappointment. I squinted against the brightness that glowed from a floor-to-ceil- ing window. The sky outside was still overcast but a pale enough gray to provide contrast to the gloom of my room. In its glare, the drapes that had appeared passable last night looked worn, the furniture's wood scarred, the large Oriental rug faded and even torn in some places. The walls boasted some peeling paint.

It was when I threw back the bedcovers and sat up that I decided the decor was the least of my problems. The chilly temperature was. I grabbed a bra and panties from my suitcase and padded quickly to the bathroom and a hot shower. I brushed teeth and hair, put on lipstick and shivered as I slipped on jeans and a long-sleeved black turtleneck. I was about to shrug into a jersey hoodie when I spied something Winnie had packed. She'd thoughtfully added a sweater of hers, a heavy brown number with large square pockets on the breasts and at the hem. Hardly a fashion statement but it looked extra warm and that certainly filled the current bill. I put tissue and a few essentials in the roomy pockets and headed down the stairs to find Sherwood.

The downstairs was no warmer than the upstairs but the first thing I heard was the whistle of a kettle and its promise of hot tea was reassuring. In the kitchen, Sherwood's back was to me and he was scrambling eggs. The window to his side revealed that snow had begun falling once again and I envisioned a nice walk over the grounds once it stopped and the sun came out. Another heartening factor greeted me: Sherwood was actually humming. I decided this, too, bode well for a wonderful day—an improvement over his seemingly dour mood of the night before.

"Good morning," I said brightly.

Sherwood spun abruptly around to look at me, a sharp knife suddenly in his hand.

"Good morning, Frédérique, I trust you slept well and . . ."

"Slept great actually," I smiled. "I wonder if after breakfast we could . . ."

"I was going to say," he interrupted, "that I hope today will be more productive."

Productive? There was that word again.

The lopsided grin I'd always been fond of appeared. Only now it looked to be more of a sneer.

chapter 66

LUKE JEFFERSON WAS the black sheep of the family. His father—a white man— was a lawyer, his mother, an accountant. His one and only sibling, a brother, had become a dentist. None of these professions appealed to him. Their lack of appeal was in direct proportion to the pressure he'd received from his family to embrace one of those careers—or at least something similarly prestigious. Instead, Luke decided to become what would most shock and dismay his family—a truck driver. He got his CDL—commercial drivers license—after quitting his sophomore year at the University of California in Riverside. He hooked up with another college dropout and almost immediately began considering becoming a trucker dropout because he couldn't stand the TM—the terminal manager. But the straw that broke the proverbial camel's back was once when he drove solo with a gig starting in Lake Tahoe, California. He was hauling a single city trailer on I-80 east. Luke fell asleep at the wheel and 40 miles later woke up, noticed he was in Reno, Nevada, and couldn't remember what he did. Body shaking, he headed back to the yard and his TM and quit on the spot. He bummed around for the next four months, living off a loan from the dentist brother.

And then he met Ringo. At a bar frequented by other truckers. Ringo matched Luke's height of six, four and at two hundred eighty-five pounds, exceeded Luke's weight. He had the kind of look that made women describe him as a grizzly bear of a man. He had a beard and gray, thinning hair he pulled back into a long ponytail. Ringo had a boom-ing baritone voice he used to regale other bar flies with tales of the road, real and imagined. Luke became an immedi-ate fan when they met and in two weeks' time became his partner and was on the road again.

A favorite Ringo story was when he'd been held up at gunpoint and in trying to escape suffered a flesh wound to his thigh. The anecdote included a detailed account of how Ringo devised a tourniquet for his injury. Luke remem-bered this as he pulled down his jeans to his ankle, wincing at the pain. Then sat in the cold snow and pulled off his jacket, shirt and undershirt, using the latter as tourniquet. He found a piece of twig, placed it on the overhand knot and tied a square over it. He then twisted the stick to tighten the knot.

He put his clothes back on and pondered his dilemma. The wind kicked up and Luke felt as if he'd been hit by an onslaught of razor blades. He decided to get out of the night air and do some more productive pondering—like what his next move was going to be. It was predictable that Benja-min would not return to the scene of the crime, feeling he'd mortally wounded his victim. This was probable because Luke had had the presence of mind to fall to the ground and play dead to avoid a second, badly aimed shot.

Once he was satisfied enough time had elapsed. he'd crawled to the cover of a fir tree to perform his tourniquet ministrations. Now he limped back to the kitchen door. It was still unlocked. He went in, grabbed a bottle of water from the fridge and a loaf of bread and decided to hide out in the maid's room until morning. If it was only a flesh wound as he guessed and he survived the night, he had a feeling Freddy would need him in the morning. He sat on the bed but before he could drink the water or eat the bread, he passed out.

chapter 67

THE DAY PASSED fairly pleasantly, if a little too quietly. Outside, the snowfall continued unabated so there was no question of going anywhere. Sherwood retreated to a chair near the fireplace with the book I'd seen him reading back in Brooklyn, *Austerity Britain*. I tried aiming wistful looks at the fireplace now and then, meant to convey my hope he'd actually build a fire. Without success, so I kept Winnie's large brown sweater wrapped around me. It also helped that I'd slipped on my fleece-lined Ugg boots—not glamorous, but utterly necessary in the current chill.

I'd initially brought Maya Angelou's *I Know Why the Caged Bird Sings* for the flight to London. As I sat huddled on the couch reading, I hoped I'd receive some of Angelou's great sense of serenity via osmosis. The sense I was actually feeling was one of fear and foreboding. Without knowing why. Sherwood was being less than romantic, distant even. His preoccupation with Sonny Bob's money was more than somewhat off putting. Maybe the law business was faltering as of late. Certainly the general economy was currently in a slump, so perhaps I shouldn't judge.

Finally my oh-so-silent companion opened his mouth and spoke his first words since breakfast.

"I'm going to skip lunch, Frédérique, but do make yourself a sandwich if you like. There's a chicken in the fridge. Please take out the ham that's in the freezer. We'll have it for dinner."

"Aye, aye sir," I grinned. But the smile was wasted. Sherwood had quickly averted his eyes back to his book.

I put *Caged* down, went to the kitchen and made myself a chicken sandwich and hot tea. Removed the ham, as instructed. Thought about all the calories consumed with the bread and wondered how I'd fit exercise in if we were to stay cooped up like this for several days. I sat alone at the kitchen table, eating my lunch.

The only sounds were the ticking of a large clock in the dining room and dogs barking in the distance. They must belong to a neighbor as no bowls for food or water were in evidence anywhere. But what neighbors? The other thing not visible was other houses. There seemed to be two cupboards in the kitchen, judging by the side-by-side doors to my left. Maybe at least one contained dog food, providing a clue. Better yet, maybe one contained cookies. I got up and tried the door nearest the outside door. It was locked. I tried the door next to it. It was unlocked and merely contained a small grouping of cans of peas and beans on one shelf. The other shelves were empty.

Discouraged at the paucity in this house of everything that supported human comfort, I sat down and finished my tea. I was also discouraged at my yearning for cookies, so I averted my focus back to possible exercise. I washed and dried my dishes and put them away.

As I re-entered the living room, I looked around. Furniture covered almost every inch of space. Together with the numerous chairs and couches were a large coffee table, a few occasional tables, four floor lamps and several heavy footstools, each covered in a faded animal print. Two large ceramic lions bordered one archway and appeared to be the only items that looked reasonably new and unmarred by age and neglect.

"Sherwood . . .," I began.

He looked up immediately with an expression that for some reason I read as *here it comes*.

"Is there a room with some space in it around here? I'd like to do some floor exercises."

"Floor exercises," he repeated.

His tone was flat. He turned his face away and seemed to snicker.

This was amusing?

Sherwood looked back at me. "Bloody good. I know just the place. Was going to show it to you anyway."

He smiled and I smiled back.

I mused on his words, *I was going to show it to you anyway.* Was there actually some area in this damp, cold, war-torn place that qualified as a showroom?

Then I mused on my own use of the term *war-torn.* Rawleigh House had undoubtedly been standing during Wars I and II but those events were years behind us. What made me think of the word *war?* I was soon to find out.

We took the stairs to the second floor. Then we headed to a corner of the hallway to mount a small, narrow set of stairs I'd never noticed until now. They led to a hallway, also quite narrow. Sherwood led me away from the stairs to a room at the opposite corner. The door to it was closed and he drew a key from his pocket and unlocked it.

We stepped inside and I found myself in a small office. A slanted wall on one side contributed to its claustrophobia. A slim, elegant desk stood at one corner. Undoubtedly beautiful in its prime, it was now marred by peeling paint and was fronted by a scarred Louis XVI-style chair. It matched the dining room chairs. They appeared to be copies, inspired by French 18th century designs.

The only evidence that the current year was 2011 was a laptop and a modern Eames lamp on the desk. The rest of the room was dominated by bookshelves, their tomes and woodwork even dustier than the rest of the house. Three more of the dining room chairs had been placed here and there in a random arrangement. Sherwood pulled one forward to the center of the room.

"Sit down," he commanded. "I know a chair exercise that's thoroughly beneficial." He gave me a kindly smile.

Seeing no reason not to comply, I sat down.

Sherwood stepped behind me. "First, stretch your legs way out in front of you, feet together."

I did.

"Now, stretch your arms backward as far as they'll go."

I did so.

"And close your eyes," he added.

Was this a Zen side of Sherwood?

Seconds later Sherwood was in anything but Zen mode. I felt something wrapping around my wrists—swiftly and tightly.

"Sherwood, what in God's name . . .?"

"Now's not the time to invoke the deity, my dear. Just hold still."

With that, he stepped around in front of me and knelt down. I saw the roll of duct tape and began struggling but he had the advantage of strength and dexterity. I managed to kick vehemently and protest loudly. The kicking part merely succeeded in upending my chair and Sherwood succeeded in his mission of duct taping my ankles, despite my now prone position. He stood for a moment, catching his breath, and then pulled my chair and me upright.

"Have you lost your mind?" I was breathless myself but managed to be loud and to convey my anger.

My host, on the other hand, was now calm and composed. "My dear, mere conversation doesn't seem to work with you. I decided a bit of persuasion was in order."

"Persuade me to do what?"

"Well, to stop screaming at me for one thing. Most unbecoming, Frédérique. And then to tell me just where your beloved ex-husband has stashed his cash and then . . ."

"I got that message forty miles back, Sherwood. But you don't get the message that I . . ."

"Have no idea where it is!" Now *he* was yelling. "Yes, I got that message! Rubbish! Here's my retort—I think you're a bloody liar! Sonny Bob went on two tours of England. I know for a fact you were with him on one of them so stop being so freaking shrill and this will all go quite easily."

I noticed Sherwood's hands were shaking. He seemed to be more nervous under the circumstances than I was.

"Be glad I didn't tape your mouth." His voice became calm—so much so he was mumbling. "No one would hear you for miles around anyway."

He bent down to pick up the roll of duct tape, which had fallen to the floor . . ., and then it happened. In all the commotion, neither of us heard what would have been footsteps. Suddenly, in front of the now open door and behind Sherwood was a surprising and very welcome sight.

A bloody and disheveled Luke Jefferson holding a gun.

chapter 68

BOB MARLEY WAS crooning over the room's private sound system as Buck sat gazing out an open window at the garden's banyan and mango trees. His friend and client, Martha Fleming, had scored a bit part in a movie—as the proprietress of the real-life, cliff-top retreat Goldeneye. She'd accepted, as part of her wages, a complimentary six-day stay at the luxurious hotel, an 18-acre retreat nestled among tropical forests and lush gardens on a seaside bluff in the quiet little village of Orcabessa. Buck had wondered what the actual monetary portion of her compensation had been since she'd been given no less than the three-bedroom villa once occupied by author Ian Fleming. The desk clerk advised that Fleming had written his James Bond novels here. It featured the writer's own desk carved out of red bulletwood and boasted louvered windows with a spacious view of the sea.

Martha had completed her brief appearances in three scenes in two days. She stayed over half a day to tour Firefly, home of the late playwright Noel Coward, and had then flown back to New York, lonesome for her current beau. She'd insisted "my favorite private eye" remain and occupy the suite the remaining three gratis days, scolding that he deserved and badly needed some down time.

Buck wasn't so sure he needed down time—that only suggested more hours to ruminate over Freddy, her trip to England and whether he'd been right to send Luke off to

London or was merely being paranoid, with a healthy dose of envy added to the mix. Luke had been out of touch for the last two days and he worried what this portended. Problems . . . or simply nothing to report?

If I'm so damn jealous, I should have gone myself.

He lit a cigar and mused as to how lame that would have been.

How big a jerk am I that I sit here alone in this romantic setting while the woman I love runs off with this question-able moron of a Brit?

Buck tamped out his cigar and went to take a shower. It would be five o'clock soon and he was scheduled to meet one of the film's actors in the bar. The guy had some work for Buck back in the states. He was planning a divorce and wanted to get the goods on his wife's infidelity—never Buck's favorite type of gig but it would help pay his newly acquired mortgage.

He decided he really didn't need a shower and instead lit another Cobina and walked outside to the cottage's deck at the water's edge. It had begun to rain.

chapter 69

LUKE'S GUN WAS a .475 Magnum—I know this because Buck is continually giving me a course on weaponry. This pistol is a semi-automatic and was purposefully designed to be a hunting firearm. The one Luke held in his hand had an eight-inch barrel. How Luke came upon this particular revolver is anybody's guess. Buck always carries a Glock and any gun Luke has I would think had to have come from Buck. On the other hand, Luke is a big movie buff and I remember Buck telling me that the .475 was featured a lot in the film *Death Wish 3*. As for my tall, dark and rescuing friend, I guess he was channeling actor Charles Bronson. Whatever the reason, I was just glad he was here and had a gun—any gun.

I was about to speak to Luke when I noticed he looked fragile. He held his gun in a hand that seemed to quiver. Sherwood moved one hand for a moment to rub his chin and his hand also trembled.

Here we are in this weird, very possibly dangerous, situation and it's the girly fashion model that's calm.

Luke had a fierce look on his face. He stood stock still, legs placed wide apart as if to maintain balance, his shiny bald head gleaming with sweat despite the chilly temperature of the room. He was wide-eyed and looked almost confused.

He finally spoke. "I don't know what kinda evil scheme you think you're hatching here, Brit boy, but, man, I'm taking Freddy outta here."

His voice softened as his chest heaved from the recent exertion, and he added, "And now."

Buoyed by Luke's seeming weakening of determination—and more likely by the fact he was about to share—Sherwood stood up straighter. His voice resumed the harsh, authoritative tone he'd taken earlier.

"Good luck, bloke. I don't know where you went but while you were wherever you disappeared to, I shot off the tires of that broken down jeep that apparently got you here."

Sherwood stuck his hands in his pockets. *Did he possibly have a small revolver of his own in one of those pockets?*

I couldn't detect one and I'm no expert on the psychology of the criminal mind—which I'd by now decided was Sherwood's DNA—but that was a mighty brave tone of voice for one facing a huge dude with a formidable weapon in his hand.

Now Sherwood even smiled. "Sorry about the tires, old chap, but I thought you were dead. And the little chippy here also isn't going anywhere."

I continued to level a meant-to-be-intimidating glare toward Benjamin. I'd begun to refer to him in my mind by his last name and couldn't remember when I'd hated anyone more.

I didn't hear a response from Luke. In my frustration, I attempted to wiggle my arms, straining vainly against the taped wrists.

Sherwood looked my way, still smiling but still shouting. "Don't be so impatient, my little minge. In a while, I'll bring you some dinner. Then I'll undo your hands so you can eat. I'm certainly not going to feed you myself. I've had quite enough super model attitude for a great while. You're no longer a guest in this house. Not that I ever regarded you as such, Miss Frédérique. From now on, you're a . . ."

The sound of a muffled thud interrupted Benjamin's diatribe and distracted me from the intense scowl I kept directing toward him.

The mighty Luke Jefferson had fallen to the floor.

—

Joseph Hurley puttered forward in his Ford S-Max, the vehicle the Hampshire Constabulary used for investigating collisions. The bloody snowfall was not letting up and the car's heater was not keeping up. Under his black fleece jacket, he'd put on two of the black wicking tee shirts his unit wore as a uniform but they weren't keeping him warm right now. Neither was the bloody peaked cap on his head. When not on mobile patrol, the Hampshire Constabulary wore the largest-sized helmets out of all the forces in England and Wales. They were a bloody nuisance but Hurley wished he had one now as he was about to get out of his vehicle and look into this accident.

Some car had apparently hit a woman and then taken off. A neighbor waking his dog—*who'd walk a dog in this bloody blizzard? Just send the little bugger out to pee*—had discovered the body and reported it looked like the housekeeper from the old Rawleigh place.

—

Benjamin had the temerity to say, "Help me . . ."

He then looked me over in my bound and taped condition and realized, with a sneer, that I was hardly in any condition to be of assistance in his mission of lifting Luke, positioning him upright onto one of the straight-back chairs and binding him with duct tape.

Luke remained unconscious during this procedure—at least, I hoped that's all he was. His coffee-and-cream complexion looked paler still, one leg of his pants and his sock soaked with blood.

"Don't look so worried, luv." Sherwood's voice dripped with artificial concern. "He'll come to in a bit."

He turned and headed for the door, then turned back and looked me over once more. "Don't feel quite so posh right now, do we, luv?"

I desperately wanted to snarl a pithy comeback ending with the word *luv*, but nothing came to mind. Sherwood left, closing the door slowly and gently as if deliberately opting for some contrast from the anger he'd just displayed and perhaps the violence that was to come.

I sat and resumed normal breathing, alternately looking at Luke for signs of life and looking over my surroundings. The desk in the room was bare but for a tall brass lamp with a faded blue shade and a copy of a book entitled *An Act of Treachery* by Ann Widdecombe.

I know just how you feel, Ann.

The drapes of the room's one window were only partially open, but night was falling in any case. The lamp was not lit. If Sherwood didn't come back soon, we'd be sitting here in complete darkness. Not that it mattered, but I didn't need any extra drama attached to this current scenario.

I looked at Luke. I could see a faint movement in his chest area. He was breathing . . . thank God! I continued to study my injured friend. Luke was a former long-haul truck driver. He'd met our mutual friend, Buck, in a bar in California. They'd hit it off and more and more Buck gave him assignments attached to his private investigation cases and more and more Luke abandoned the trucking business. As far as I knew, Luke still lived in California and only worked on the cases Buck had there. Yet here he was, big as life, all six foot four of him, shaven head, designer glasses and tummy paunch. His presence here could only be attributed to Buck—my cigar chomping, muscle-bound, Hawaiian-shirt-addict buddy had not abandoned me after all.

Suddenly I heard Luke groaning. It was a welcome sound.

"Luke, are you okay?"

Never say I don't come up with sharp, insightful questions under any and all circumstances.

"Sorry . . . sorry, Freddy. Sorry to fink out on you."

"It's me who's sorry. For getting you into this. But how did you know I was here? What are you doing in England? Buck sent you, didn't he? Where is he?"

He turned to me, looking very weary. And maybe annoyed at my barrage of questions but too kind to say so.

"I'm sorry," I said. "You've lost blood and here I am blathering away and . . ."

"Not so much the blood, babe. Took a lotta effort gettin' here, stairs and all. Got just enough of a wound that I . . ."

"Don't talk. Take it easy. We'll get food soon. I hope, that is. Then we can think more clearly."

It was Luke's turn to look me up and down. "What's that bulge in your sweater?"

"I'm glad to see you?" I grinned.

"Funny girl. Glad you ain't lost your sense of humor." He stopped to take a few breaths. "Seriously . . ."

"I'm sorry." *I keep saying that.* "I'm not feeling witty, Luke, just scared. I wish I could do something for you. I don't know what I . . ."

"Babe, that bulge in your pocket. I'm askin' you. Is it a gun?"

My first reaction was to feel sad that I had to tell him no, I have no gun. Then I focused on what Luke was saying . . . and what he was seeing.

"Luke! In my pocket! *I've got my cell!*"

chapter 70

I COULD TELL Luke was glaring at me. I shook my head and turned toward the window. Night had arrived and we were enveloped in darkness. I knew what he was thinking and what he wanted to say. *You could have called for help hours ago, Bonnaire. Have you lost your mind?* I decided to answer before he spoke.

"Look, Luke, I didn't know this guy was going to go postal before he all of a sudden trapped me in this chair. He was obsessive about wanting to know where Sonny Bob had stashed some cash but I thought he was mostly being a meticulous lawyer type. Now it looks like he's crazed to get his hands on any money that might be lying around and he's convinced I know exactly where it is."

"Do you?"

"I haven't a clue."

"Well, hell, Freddy, make something up so we can get outta here."

"Brilliant, Sherlock. And what happens when some fictitious place I name turns up bogus?"

"Buy us time?"

"Time to do *what*? He'll keep us here till he gets his hands on the money, which won't happen, and then what?"

Luke exhaled, then coughed. "Sorry, I ain't thinking straight. Gotta get me some food and water. Get the blood coursing thru my veins, instead of out of 'em, so I can deal with that pansy."

"Don't be sorry . . . you're in bad shape. We've got to . . ." I paused. "Deal with the pansy? Just how?"

I was making demands of poor Luke again. *Change the subject.* "Speaking of name calling, Sherwood called me a minge. What in the world is that? Something to do with money?"

Luke sighed. "Noooooo. Listen, I been following you and your girlfriend and Sherwood all over London. When I got done for the day, I headed for the nearest pub. Heard a lotta guy talk. Seems *minge* is Brit slang for vagina . . . but it's used like asshole or bitch. Sorry, but you asked."

"Lovely," was all I could say.

I shifted as much as I could in my chair in an effort to get more comfortable. My shoulders had started to ache from the unnatural position of my arms and I was beginning to feel chilled, despite my heavy sweater.

My sweater. The cell. I turned my attention back to the more pressing problem at hand.

"Luke, you need food. I need food. According to the creep downstairs, he's coming back with food and something else good will happen at that time."

"Yeah, what? He gonna give us his best bottle of Chateau Lafite?"

"Nope." I managed a slight smile in spite of my current state of fear. *"He'll untie our hands."*

chapter 71

WINNIE SAT AT her kitchen table, trying to enjoy a hot cup of coffee topped with whipped cream—a treat she indulged in when no one was around. It harked back to her days in a trailer park outside of New Orleans when she couldn't afford both milk and whipped cream in any given week and had to choose between the two. *Any given week.* She repeated the phrase in her mind. This particular week had been horrendous. First, in yesterday's *New York Post*, her name had been spelled incorrectly—some idiot writer had added an extra 'L' to de Foucauld. As if that were not enough, the same reporter had leaked her recent purchase of a Florida home in West Palm Beach. She'd planned a special party at the Yacht Club's Commodore's Room to announce this. Now the surprise element was destroyed.

On top of all of that, her house cleaner of the past two years had to be fired. She'd grown increasing lazy and neglectful over the past several months—failing to dust certain places, vacuuming only the center of each room, rarely cleaning the stove and often forgetting completely to change the sheets. She'd hired a new girl, Rosa, who was young and energetic but needed instructions for the slightest task.

Then, too, she missed "her kids" as she'd come to call them—Freddy, who'd gone off to London with her beau Sherwood, Jeannette who'd moved into Freddy's house in Brooklyn and was apparently working too steadily to drop by for a visit and then there was Buck. He'd gone off on a job with his elderly actress client to some exotic movie set and decided to stay, finally calling in and identifying his location and his plans this morning.

Her melancholy mood led Winnie to pick up her coffee cup and head for the tall French windows on the west side of her apartment to take in the magnificent view of the New York skyline. As she entered the living room, she was greeted by the incessant roar of the vacuum cleaner as Rosa pushed it around with great vigor.

"Rosa, dear, why don't you do this room last," Winnie shouted. "Go do the guest rooms right now. Clean the blue one first. *C'est du billard.*"

The blue room had not been used for quite a while. It wouldn't require much effort but telling Rosa *it's a piece of cake* in French probably had no impact. Winnie didn't care. She'd picked up that phrase from Freddy and loved to use it.

Rosa switched off the vacuum, left it standing where it was and headed for the hallway. Winnie walked over to the windows and surveyed the scene. She had loved this city ever since her Grandpa Pete had come up from Baton Rouge when she was eleven to treat her to a trip to New York. Grandpa was almost six foot four and everyone called him Long Pete. He was retired from the Southern Pacific Railroad and had a lifetime pass to travel wherever he wanted. As the oldest of five children, Winnie was chosen for this honor and Long Pete whisked her away from a near-poverty existence in Louisiana to this place of enchantment.

From the moment she'd set foot in the massive Grand Central Station, surrounded by its hollow, unfamiliar noises and the blaring announcements of train departures, she'd felt not only thrilled but somehow at home. Little did she know that decades later, after a lifetime of waitress jobs, failed marriages, heartbreaking miscarriages and a flirtation with alcoholism, a dashing, prince of a man named

Charles de Foucauld would fall in love with her, marry her when she was at the overripe age of sixty and transport her once again to the land of her dreams.

Now she was sixty-eight and her beloved Charles had been gone for three years. Winnie shivered as she thought of this loss even though the thick walls and windows of her large condo isolated her from the gray cold outside.

"Mrs. de Foucauld."

The sound of the maid's voice interrupted her reverie. Rosa had entered the living room quietly and was standing just behind Winnie, wringing her hands nervously.

"I hate to bother you, but the mattress. I can't lift it. You can help, no?"

Winnie had never really forgotten her roots, despite occasional airs and the pretentious efforts at French, and helping the maid was not beneath her even though she was a little disappointed in Rosa.

"My dear, ah'm not a kid . . . that is, I didn't sleep well last night. Are you trying to tell me you're going to flip the mattress—and, you're right, it's probably due—but you're not strong enough to do it by yourself? Ah really believed you were . . . "

Rosa's face puckered as if she was about to cry. "No, no, no. I pick up Mrs. Matthews' mattresses and Mrs. Taylor's and Mr. Spencer's too. I strong . . . I not need help. I do all those and . . ."

"Now, now, don't get so upset." Winnie placed one hand on the girl's arm and gave her back a quick pat. "Ah'll go with you. You'll see, it's very easy."

C'est du billard had almost sprung from Winnie's lips again, but she resisted.

They made their way down the long hallway together, then entered the guest room. Winnie was still carrying her coffee cup and she placed it on the magazines stacked on one mahogany end table.

"You take that end," she commanded Rosa, slipping her own hands under the opposite corner. She'd actually performed this and many other housekeeping chores herself from time to time when a maid was on vacation or out sick. She knew she still had the muscular strength honed from a lifetime of hard work.

Rosa grunted. Winnie groaned. The mattress didn't budge. From her side, Winnie gingerly felt a few inches across the top of the box spring. Nothing on it that would cause a problem. The mattress itself seemed to weigh a ton.

"You see?" Rosa said in an almost pleading voice. "Something, she is wrong. This too heavy. Not right. I pick up plenty mattress. I know. Like I say, I pick up for Mr. Spencer, his easy. And Mrs. Taylor too and I have no trouble. This too heavy. Something wrong and . . ."

"Rosa, dear," Winnie said, her own breath heaving from the effort. "Do stop. Talking, that is. Just one minute."

Winnie stepped over to the end table, retrieved her coffee and took a long swallow.

Lordy, this maid could be such a chatterbox. She took another big gulp.

But Rosa was right abut one thing . . . *something was very wrong.*

chapter 72

THE AROMA OF warmed-over lamb stew filled the air as the door to the tiny office creaked forward. Sherwood opened it, then stooped to pick up a tray he'd placed on the hallway floor. I noticed he hadn't needed to *unlock* the door. His tray contained two steaming bowls, spoons, a half loaf of bread, a cup of butter and two cans of Pepsi. He was obviously generous enough to offer more than a Spartan diet, but his brow still held a frown. He set the heavy tray down on the desk. His words came out in the now-familiar snarl.

"Where's that devoted private eye chap who fancies you now, Frédérique?"

An hour ago, I would have thought *where indeed*? But Luke had filled me in on his assignments from Buck to follow me all over Manhattan, including the temporary stint as Winnie's chauffeur in order to drive me to the airport and board my flight. Then his daily tail of me and Sherwood or me and Kendrick.

"Closer than you think," I lied.

Sherwood merely smirked and proceeded to step behind me, then Luke, to free up our wrists. He removed the duct tape slowly, obviously enjoying protests of the pain via high-pitched squeals from me and angry curses in Luke's deep, gravelly voice. That accomplished, he slid the desk in front of us and left, again leaving the door unlocked. We popped open the soda cans, and hastily spooned the stew, stuffed bits of bread into our mouths and gulped our drinks.

We made such quick work of this process that we were astounded when Sherwood burst through the door just as I'd retrieved my cell phone from my pocket and moved a finger to press Buck's number. Our host was faster. He immediately leaned over the table to grab the phone from my hand. I just as quickly stiffened my hand and chopped his forearm. This only resulted in the cell flying from his grasp. All this took mere seconds. The cell was in speaker mode and we could hear a voice on the other end—*but it was not Buck's.*

"Freddy? Is that you? are you still out in the . . ."

Country would have undoubtedly been the next word but Sherwood began yelling and swearing at my temerity in attempting to make a call. The cell had landed near the window with a muted thud as it hit the carpet.

"Freddy? Frédérique? Where are you? We should get together and . . ."

Sherwood yelled at me again, then at Luke, reciting the hopelessness of any attempt to escape. He paused as the phone emitted another "Freddy?"

He smiled, then laughed out loud. I knew why—the voice was that of a female. Harmless, of no consequence, of no danger to Sherwood Benjamin and whatever designs he entertained. He stepped over to the fallen cell and snapped it shut just before a final "Freddy?" sounded forth—*from Kendrick.*

Buck's last name is Lemoyne. Kendrick was listed right after him on my speed dial. In my haste, I'd pressed her last name of Levine instead.

Sherwood pocketed the phone and, for the second time, said, "Don't be so thick. You fools are going out into the ice and snow."

He'd made this threat during his screaming tirade but now he announced it with calm and quiet satisfaction in his voice.

I looked at Luke but his gaze was focused on our captor. He was standing and breathing heavily, with an expression that was both helpless and venomous if your can imagine that combination on Luke's dark, round face.

I stood up too, in case there was a Plan B in play. To no effect, as Luke merely continued to glare, his chest heaving. Sherwood stood, hands on hips, feet spread apart, smirk in place.

"Sit down, you idiots," he fairly shouted.

We obeyed.

He had segued from a state of composure to his more frequent mode of anger and commenced another tirade. His voice rose and fell as he strode back and forth to the window, looking out, and then returning to face us. Sherwood appeared more nervous in his role as villain than we were as his victims.

"I'll be back." Now he fairly whispered.

He opened the door, stepped out, and began to push it closed. Then with a vaudevillian-like move, stuck his head back in.

"With a gun," he added.

chapter 73

KENDRICK CLAUDIA LEVINE clicked off her cell phone, stunned and perplexed. She opened her wallet and pulled the slip of paper containing Freddy's cell number from a plastic cardholder, wondering if she should call back. As she did so, she looked at the photo that had been covered by the note—a shot of she and her sister Rachael, arms around each other's shoulders, taken five years ago.

Kendrick had been sitting at the small, round kitchen table in her boyfriend's London flat, eating a solitary dinner as he was working. She had been considering whether to top off her sensible meal of fish, broccoli and sliced tomatoes with a glass from one of the wine bottles resting on a nearby butcher block. Deciding in the affirmative, she chose the Tishbi Estate chardonnay, a white wine from Israel Percy had purchased especially for her. She plucked a wine glass from a cabinet and poured. Once again seated, she pulled the photo from its plastic holder and gazed at it as she sipped her drink.

She'd been preoccupied with numerous concerns this past week—her British boyfriend Percy and whether he'd ever commit, would she move to London if he *did* pop the question, would she continue to visit England if he didn't. Not to mention how jobs would go if she did relocate. Her

career was finally achieving a foothold in Manhattan—
would she give all that up for Percy?

Kendrick mused over the *all that* phrase. More than
her professional life was at stake. She loved her walk-up
apartment on Cornelia Street in New York's West Village.
She adored all the young and not-so-young musicians and
actors who were her neighbors.

Living in London, she'd miss the free pastries bestowed
on her at the neighborhood bakery to celebrate each new
gig she landed, the diner next door boasting the greasiest
food around but also friendly, familiar clientele, the smell of
New York when it rained that was unlike any other place,
the stuffy warmth of subways that was almost welcome on
cold winter days.

The curly-haired fashion stylist contemplated all this
while looking out the kitchen window at the falling snow, still
relentless but lighter now. She turned her attention again to
the black and white photo of she and Rachael, in their uni-
forms, guns slung over their shoulders. The weapons were
Tavor assault rifles and they maintained them and continu-
ously practiced with them during their entire two-year stint
with the Israeli army. The truth was, gun or no gun, they were
rarely in harm's way, but violence and bloodshed were an
ever-present part of that existence.

Something among these random thoughts catapulted
her back to the present—today—this hour—the disjointed
phone call from Freddy—the strange background noise—
the word's she'd heard.

Kendrick gulped the last two ounces of wine and
picked up her cell. She'd better call Percy. Of all people,
he'd know what to do.

chapter 74

IN THE MIDDLE of Sherwood's anxious pacing, Luke had turned toward me, a fierce look in his eyes. Sensing this, I turned and met his gaze. He jerked his head slightly backward. I saw what he was indicating and followed suit. Our less-than-gracious host was contemplating the window view of darkness and grounds thick with ice and snow while this bit of action was going on. What we accomplished was an obvious act of subterfuge but thankfully not so transparent to Sherwood. Luke had wrapped his arms around the back of his chair as if his wrists were bound together a la Sherwood's original duct taping. I did the same and in his adrenalin-fueled rage, Master Benjamin had given no notice but merely proceeded to execute his theatrical exit.

"Let's give him ten minutes," Luke said.

"Let's give him closer to fifteen," I countered.

"Sold," Luke answered, and smiled.

"So glad we agree on that," I said. "Now what are we going to do when the fifteen minutes are up?"

"Beat it outta here."

"Gotcha. That's brilliant. We sneak out of this godforsaken hell house and we escape."

"That be the plan."

"No, that be craziness. And then what? We get outside, stroll casually to the road acres away from here and hail the first passing cab?"

Luke adopted a Sherwood-like frown and sneer.

"You gotta better idea, missy? I got a Glock in my car. We'll need that whatever we do."

I matched his glare and raised him one sneer. "Great. The car that's a mile from here and buried in snow. Never mind . . . are you by any chance carrying a cell phone of your own, bro?"

Luke shook his head in the negative and looked away. He waited several beats before speaking.

"At the end of the day back in London when I knew you were in for the night, I'd hit the pubs."

He looked at me sadly. Several more beats as I waited for further commentary.

"Oka-a-a-y," I strung out the word. "The minute we get back on New York soil, we'll cab over to the nearest AA meeting. That the issue here?"

"No-o-o-o," Luke mimicked my drawl. "The issue here ain't that. The issue is some dude pinched my cell in one of those fine establishments. So it be gone."

"And we be screwed," I said.

"No we be more positive," Luke said softly, then added with sternness, "I repeat, you gotta better plan?"

It was my turn to look away and think—or pretend to. Fear was gripping my intestines and I felt the lamb stew catch in my throat.

"You're right, Luke, there's no alternative. I saw no phones around the mansion and . . .."

"Be dangerous to go hunting for them."

"That too. Job one is to get the duct tape off our ankles, "I said.

As we did this, I looked around for something—any-thing—that could provide some sort of insulation against the cold. Luke was dressed for the outdoors but I wasn't. A long red shawl lay across the bottom shelf of the desk. I removed the ceramic knick-knacks resting on it, wrapped it around my head and tied a knot under my chin. Even in my current state of fright, I managed to muse that my outfit looked like something Kendrick might wear.

Kendrick! What must she think of the crazy phone call she'd received? Probably that Sherwood and I were in the throes of passion and pressed the cell by accident.

Luke stared at me but, understandably, was too filled with anxiety over the hopelessness of our situation to render a quip about my attire.

I squeezed his arm and managed a smile.

"I know I look like hell . . . but soon we're gonna *run* like hell."

He smiled and nodded agreement, then looked down and pointed to his feet in another silent bid for action. We both removed our shoes and crept down the staircase. Just as quietly, we made our way through the rooms to the kitchen.

Luke pointed to the maid's room and made the one-minute finger sign. I stood stock-still and in seconds, he emerged with a heavy jacket for me from his backpack. I shrugged it on as he leaned against a wall and put his shoes back on. I sat on a chair to get into my boots, then pointed to a knife holder on a nearby counter. We each grabbed the two longest knives in the collection and moved on tiptoe to the back door. Luke turned the knob, it opened soundlessly.

Outside!

chapter 75

Selah Harmon Benjamin stood at the counter of her small, all-white kitchen and poured her third glass of merlot of the evening. She was doing a lot of that lately.

I must remember to report this to Richards on Monday, she thought.

Dr. Richards was her psychiatrist and Monday was the regular weekly appointment she'd maintained for the past ten years.

She'd spent this particular evening dwelling on regrets and she had many. As she took her glass into the living room, her gaze fell upon the day's newspaper. A long column of a New York crime story was featured on the left side of the first page buttressed against world news headlines regarding the Middle East and a volcanic eruption in Japan. The subject of crime reminded her of one fortunate aspect of her immediate past—the selective memory of one Lindsey Muldoon, that ridiculous little sales person who worked at Dina Hutton's dusty and vastly uninspiring antique shop. That, or the inadequate reporting of an Officer Ray Holmes.

The police hadn't called Selah in for questioning so it would seem that the fact that she had been there at the same time on the same day as Sherwood had gone unreported by the good Officer Holmes. The shop's owner—that white trash Dina Hutton—was also not interrogated. Selah had called Bella and wormed that out of her. The shop girl and the cop had not remembered her apparently. That must be it. But *why?* She was more attractive than that little Lindsey—well, in a more mature way at least—and she'd certainly been more charming than Dina.

I must tell Dr. Richards about this phenomenon also.

Selah looked at the television set, wondering if she should seek that distraction. She regarded her now-empty wine glass and decided instead to return to the kitchen. There she picked up the bottle of wine and carried it into her bedroom. Taking a healthy swig, she then placed the wine on the nightstand. Pulling the comforter around her, she sat upright on the bed, her back against the head-board. She picked up the bottle once more and cradled it in her hands. Thoughts of regrets stung her consciousness once again.

The times I cheated on Sherwood, she lamented. *The golf pro when we lived on Long Island and, last year, that loser of a tennis player.*

And Sonny Bob Bonnaire.

Especially Sonny.

She had thought at the time of the affair that Sonny was the love of her life. He seemed to understand her in a way Sherwood never had.

A sensitive, creative musician type is exactly what I need.

Her monogrammed note pads had begun to fill up with doodles of *Mrs. Selah Bonnaire.* She had a dream.

And then he ruined everything.

Sonny had said he had an errand to run. She had insisted on accompanying him. He protested, but Selah was adamant.

He'd taken her via two subways to a brownstone in Brooklyn. They walked a few blocks, arrived at the destination, he used a key to enter. Selah looked around at the warm, homey atmosphere. He led her up the stairs and through an open door to a bedroom. Sonny remained silent and looked around, seemingly searching for something.

He's feeling romantic but more than that he's ready to really settle down, put down roots. And he brought me here. This is to be our home.

She then looked up at him lovingly and spoke the words aloud.

"This is to be our home?"

Selah was confident of what Sonny would say. She'd experienced rejection many times in the past several years. God knows, her therapist had heard story after story of romantic failures and talked her through the long period afterward of pain and self-doubt.

But that won't happen with Sonny Bob. He loves me.

Sonny just looked at her for several beats. Then he spoke.

With one cruel answer, he destroyed her hopes and fantasies. He virtually visited violence upon her soul.

Violence begets violence.

What could she do? She swiftly returned to the open door, picked up the heavy cast-iron doorstop. . .

She killed him.

chapter 76

WE WERE OUTSIDE but the so-called freedom we'd attained was one realized in a forbidding, frigid night. The snow was piled higher than it appeared the last time I'd viewed the grounds from a window. The brightest signs of light were fading beams emitting from lights in the mansion. The snow on its roof was piled high and thick. A full moon hung low in the sky and via the slight illumination it afforded, we could see Luke's car in the distance, its tires resembling melted licorice. Columns of snow had separated on its hood and trunk and slowly moved downward toward the frozen earth, giving the jeep an acutely forlorn appearance. *I knew how it felt.*

The snow was frozen so solid the earth looked like an undulating ice rink. Sequestered as we'd been, we hadn't heard the muted roar of the wind but now we felt the blowing ice on our skin like dozens of tiny pinpricks.

I looked over at Luke. He was not faring well. His gate was slow and hesitant. Snow swirled around him and fresh blood seemed to ebb from the cuff of his jacket. Cold air rushed in under my own sweater and my nose, ears and feet felt numb. We briefly heard the howl of a dog. It erupted from a distance we could not determine and just as suddenly ended in a whimper. Where did it come from?

Luke pointed toward the trees and pantomimed driving—another wordless communication of his which I understood to mean we should head for the car—the jeep that was now immobile but which contained his Glock. Our movements were a combination of jogging and walking. The cold air burned in our throats, making a steady run impossible. The still-falling flakes blurred our vision and occasionally we stumbled and fell when the hard snow turned deep and crusty.

We were a mere twenty yards from our destination on the other side of a small hill when we heard the sound of a dog once again. This time closer. Another whimper. His tiny head suddenly appeared at the rim of the mound but it was the blinding light that preceded him that drew our attention.

Then a form appeared behind the flare of light—*Sherwood!*

The overwhelming brightness cast a wide illumination, taking in the area in front of us and behind and beyond us. My first impression was that of a subway train heading straight for us. Luke and I shielded our eyes in a vain attempt to dispel the glare. The entire space resembled a conjured scene from *Star Wars* with Sherwood cast as Darth Vader. His face looked even more sinister in the shadowy light.

"Man, cut that thing off," Luke said in a voice that sounded far less than the shouted command he intended and more like the fractured plea of a desperate man.

I struggled over the ice to his side, fearful he would pass out again. Luke threw one welcoming arm around my shoulders, clearly grateful for both the physical and moral support.

Thus buoyed, he managed to yell. "Benjamin, cut the crap and let's talk."

Sherwood's laugh began deep throated and rose to a high-pitched cackle.

"Such a trite phrase, old chap." More cackling. "It sounds like a line from an American movie . . ." He waved the light back and forth now, his shoulders shaking seemingly from uncontrollable giggling.

"That's a military hand-held searchlight, probably Pro-filer II," Luke whispered to me. "How the hell he get his hands on that?"

"Who cares, Luke? The question is what the hell do we do now? Do you think you can run? Should we make a dash for the house?"

Luke looked at me incredulously. As he slowly opened his mouth to answer, we heard a shot.

We looked back at Sherwood who now held the light steady and waved a small revolver above his head.

"Stop mumbling, you idiots." He fired again in the air, looking increasingly like a frenzied mad man. He was warmly garbed in a large quilted jacket and heavy rubber boots but without a hat, his hair was blowing wildly in the fierce wind.

The cackling began once more.

"The phrase is it's past time for talking," Sherwood bel-lowed. "Understand that? Maybe John Wayne said it once. Before your time, Frédérique? Well, never mind, you had your chance. Now you're nothing but a liability to me."

He used the back of his gun hand to wipe his lips. Even a harangue as determined as Benjamin's was hampered by the falling snow blowing into his mouth and, if he were at all human, his throat must sting from the freezing air.

"Luke," I said softly, gently rubbing his back as I spoke. "If you can move at all, let's head back to the house. Buck once told me in a case like this you run away in a zigzag fashion Makes you less of a target."

My words came in sporadic gasps. Luke appeared to be only half listening, his gaze focused intently on Sher-wood, eyes narrowed and upper body thrust forward, as if by sheer force of will he could somehow overcome our miserable circumstances.

Fear made me impatient. "Luke! Last I looked, neither of us have a gun right now and we don't have . . ."

"That damn sure be a Golight Profiler," Luke interrupted. "It can run steady for an hour . . . used for night time special ops . . . got those babies worldwide now . . . used 'em in Iraq for sure and . . ."

We all deal with anxiety in different ways and Luke's method was clearly to decide the devil's in the details.

"Luke!" I said again, "I don't care . . . who cares if its military . . . we gotta . . . "

But the next sound we heard suggested that something like the military was indeed a factor here.

chapter 77

PERCY JAMES WALKER'S first love was photography. He'd tried free-lancing in this field for a while but, despite a spread in the United States publication *Time* and a few assignments for the U.K.'s *Hello* magazine, his career never really took off. At least not to a degree approved by his father, a Special Constable with London's Met-ropolitan Police Service—better known as Scotland Yard.

It was on a *Hello* shoot that he'd met Kendrick Levine whose artistic inclinations, friendly nature and dark, glossy curls had won his heart. Kendrick then and to this day was supportive of his creative abilities but pressure from his father had won the day and Percy had gone into police training, ending up in the ASU—Scotland Yard's Air Support Unit.

Despite his original misgivings, Percy was learning to love his current vocation. ASU was gradually replacing the Bell 222 helicopter with the newer Eurocopter, introduced in 2002 with each unit costing over five million to manufacture. Scotland Yard currently had three EC 145's, a twin-engine light utility aircraft, capable of carrying up to nine passen-gers along with two crewmembers.

For ASU purposes, each aircraft was typically staffed by a pilot and two officers acting as Observers. The 'copters were particularly useful in aiding searches for missing per-sons, car pursuits and large public events such as football matches.

Adding to his job satisfaction was the fact that the lively and multi-talented Kendrick could relate to this endeavor as enthusiastically as she did to his now-largely-dormant photographic profession. She herself had entered the army when she was eighteen and still carried a copy of her pledge in her wallet—"I solemnly swear . . . to devote all of my strength and to sacrifice my life to protect the land and the liberty of Israel."

During her service, Kendrick was employed in the Spot and Search program. She'd described it to Percy once when they first began dating.

"On the screen it may look like a video game but the figures you see are very real people—Palestinians in Gaza—who can be killed with the press of a button on the joystick."

"I thought women in the Israeli army worked far away from the battlefield and the more dangerous areas," Percy had commented.

"That's pretty much true," Kendrick had said. "They use female companies to patrol the quiet desert borders with Jordan and Egypt."

Percy raised his eyebrows. "Looking for?"

"Drug smugglers and the rare terrorist infiltrator," she'd answered.

"Look," Kendrick patiently continued, "in Spot and Shoot we're far away from any real action in an operations room. We're responsible for aiming and firing remote-controlled machine guns mounted on watch towers located every few hundred meters along an electronic fence that surrounds Gaza."

"So you're basically a button pusher," Percy had said, grinning widely.

"You could say that, you smart aleck Brit." Kendrick had playfully punched his arm at that retort. "But I also toted around an M-16 rifle and I knew how to use it."

More laughter from Percy. "Wow . . . a rifle!"

"And some small arms too as well as the Uzi submarine gun."

"I *am* impressed," Percy had teased. "I wouldn't have guessed you knew what a Uzi *was* let alone . . ."

"Hey, my friend, the Uzi was invented in Israel," Kendrick interrupted him.

They were both stimulated by this mutual meeting of the minds and all the military talk had blissfully dissolved into a romantic interlude.

Now just when Percy had put in his hours and was looking forward to the warmth and quiet of his small flat in Shepherd's Bush, Kendrick was demonstrating a bit too much interest in his ASU duties.

She'd called and announced she had a late-night mission for him.

chapter 78

AT FIRST, THE noise resembled the mother of all sewing machines. Then the whump, whump, whump sounds were more recognizable. They seemed like one more unreal element in this most unreal atmosphere. But it took me just seconds to determine their location—*the sky*.

"What the hell?" Luke rasped.

In the distance, I could vaguely hear Sherwood speak in what sounded like a similar exclamation.

Whereas Luke stood silent and motionless, with his head cocked backward and his eyes transfixed high above into the seemingly interminable darkness, Sherwood gazed upward only briefly and was then prompted to action.

In the form of more gunshots.

That, thankfully, missed.

"Time to do that zigzag thing," Luke said.

"You're right."

We turned and ran and began to achieve a decent speed, despite feeling cold, hungry and scared out of our minds. I dashed and darted and via my peripheral vision saw Luke executing the same movements with almost equal speed.

It only vaguely registered with me that the strange sight in the sky was a helicopter and that it undoubtedly represented our ultimate rescue. The continuous gunshots from Sherwood diluted any complete sense of relief.

I heard a loud voice and risked a book backward. A figure sat at a side opening of the copter, half hanging out. The person was holding a bullhorn.

"Drop your weapon!"

A shot whizzed by me, so close that I could feel my hair, matted from the moist air against my face, suddenly blow backward on my right side. I dropped to the icy ground, then heard a cry of pain. I realized it was not my own nor was it Luke's, who'd not zigged or zagged very far from my own route.

I turned my head again in time to see Sherwood grasp his right hand, which was covered with blood. It was his gun hand.

"Leave your weapon," the bullhorn announced and the voice sounded oddly familiar.

Sherwood bent downward. His searchlight had dropped to his side and he used its illumination to run his good hand frantically over the frozen earth.

I averted my eyes toward the aircraft. There was some-one still sitting at the opening, this time holding what looked like a rifle. The figure looked to be female. The voice had sounded familiar, now this person also looked familiar. I rose up on my elbows and brushed some flakes from my eyes.

Kendrick Levine!

My feelings of surprise were quickly distracted by another gunshot—this time emanating from Sherwood's left hand and aimed at the lowering aircraft.

No!

The distant figure that was Kendrick appeared to flinch. She seemed to withdraw backward into the helicopter—at least one leg did. Was she wounded?

In my momentary fascination with the events in front of me, I had not heard the crunch of Luke's footsteps. Now I saw him, somehow achieving breakneck speed, and head-ing—not away from our tormentor—but *toward* Benjamin.

I yelled, "No!" again, this time out loud.

Sherwood stood still aiming his gun skyward. He seemed not to notice Luke, even though he was almost upon him.

What was Luke thinking?

I heard another shot, as Luke appeared to fall to the ground.

"Luke!"

In another instant, I saw that he'd deliberately dived forward as he grabbed the fallen searchlight, rose, raised the light and hit Sherwood square on the forehead. A solid contact. Luke, clearly functioning on an adrenaline rush, spun to one side and kicked our attacker's legs out from under him. Sherwood crashed down, his face half buried in the snow, blood seeping from his head and arm.

Luke placed one foot on Benjamin's back like a con-quering hero, and waved a thumbs-up gesture toward the helicopter.

chapter 79

"HEY, BABE, I'M lookin' at *New York Post* headlines as we speak. Here's what it say—more than one hundred U.S. mobsters arrested, largest Mafia round up in history. Carried a photo and if one of them dudes ain't Beppe, I miss my guess. Not only that, but they rounded up two dirty cops. One of them be that Brennan dude. How's that grab you?"

"I saw the article. Picked up guys in New York and New Jersey."

"How 'bout New Orleans? There ain't nothing in the *Times Pic*?"

"Nada. Our friend Alex DeCicco is probably sitting at Cafe du Monde nursing an espresso and a beignet, living to extort, deal and whack another day."

I was walking along Fifth Avenue as a mild breeze—portending the start of an unusually warm November—gently tugged at my hair and coat. I had my cell phone firmly pressed against my ear, the better to hear Luke above the noise of traffic and chattering pedestrians. My tall, dark and handsome friend was giving me a shorthand version of recent events, most of which I already knew but they were all positive so I was savoring every last word.

"That Benjamin broad got convicted. Don't remember if she got life or not but leastways we know who whacked . . . er . . . killed poor ole Sonny Bob. Saw it in the *New York Post* two days ago, on the front page. Said, 'Society Matron is Murderer,' something like that . . ."

"Selah would love the *society* part," I injected.

"'Deed she would, girl, but nobody know all you went through 'fore this justice got done."

"All *we* went through. Speaking of which, how are you feeling?"

"I'm good. Got me a chauffeur gig from one of Winnie's friends. Ain't heard from your friend and mine Buckley Joseph Lemoyne, but that's cool. He'll check in sooner or later."

"He's bound to resurface. He always does."

"Right on. We still on for dinner tonight with Kendrick at Il Cantinori? It's on Tenth Street, correct?"

"You got it. I made the reservations for seven. See you then, Luke, and thanks for the call."

"Okay, babe, over and out."

"Over and out," I smiled.

I snapped the phone shut. I could see the Grand Army Plaza just ahead of me and facing its southern portion was my destination—The Plaza Hotel. Gram wouldn't appreciate that the Grand Army Plaza commemorated the Union Army in the Civil War nor the nearby bronze statue of none other than that Union General, William Tecumseh Sherman. Maybe she would have been appeased by the fact that the good General married a devout Catholic and one of his granddaughters married the grandson of a Confederate general. She would definitely have enjoyed the fact that the Plaza Hotel itself was designed in the French Renaissance chateau style.

Earlier in the day, I'd declined Winnie's suggestions of a week at her favorite spa, hiding out at her home in Southampton or flying out for a stay at her new home in Florida and hobnobbing with the West Palm Beach crowd. Therefore she had insisted a more immediate and local remedy to soothe my soul after my harrowing adventure in England would be to join her every-Friday lunch "with the girls." I reluctantly agreed, fearing abject boredom, but Winnie filled me in on the backgrounds of "the girls" who turned out to be an interesting bunch.

So it was that I made my way up the steps of the famous and imposing hotel. I'd heard Donald Trump no longer owned it but it had been designated a national historic landmark and well it deserved to be. I walked through the lobby to the magnificent Palm Court with its luminous stained-glass ceiling and immediately spied Winnie seated at a round, white table clothed table with seven of her regular companions for Friday lunch—or, in this case high tea. They waved at me effusively as I made my way between the other tables and yellow-caned chairs. I was seated only a matter of minutes when the Earl Grey tea, sandwiches, pastries and scones with jam arrived. We all dug in—*maybe that's a too pedestrian term for such an elegant event*—and the girls began catching each other up on their latest travels, shopping acquisitions and random society gossip.

They were each talking over one another but soon Winnie had the floor. I wasn't too thrilled about this particular dissertation as my darling aunt was going on and on about what was essentially personal family business but there's no stopping Win once she's on a roll.

". . . and, my dears," she was saying, "you coulda knocked us over with a feather when we discovered that all that money in the mattress was what Sonny Bob had left. Well, we're givin' it all to charity I might add and . . ."

"I thought you said Sonny had a will, Winnie. Don't tell me Freddy here wasn't in it?"

This from interior decorator Rusty, a tall redhead, looking elegant in a black wool picture hat.

"For heaven's sake, Winifred, you must have been in the Will yourself. Don't try to tell us . . ."

"Shush, Molly. Ah'm donatin' my share to the opera. And as for Sherwood Benjamin's share, well, he's in jail, courtesy of Scotland Yard. Gonna do him no good there."

"What about Sonny Bob's stepsisters?" a petite lady with short blonde hair asked. Her name was Geraldine and earlier Win had told me she was an accomplished pilot—a skill I greatly admired, especially since my recent rescue.

Winnie chuckled, "Seems Sonny left his furniture to them. Ah remember he said once they made no secret of coveting it and all, but then he forgot he did that and shortly before his death went and sold every last bit of it to cover some sorta gamblin' debt."

"Serves the greedy little bitches right," Margot said. She had lovely white hair, black rimmed glasses and a killer smile that she flashed as she made her comment about Dina and Bella.

A very chic woman, who I recognized from a brochure promoting her sculptures, piped up, "That older sister especially thinks the world owes her. Such a self-centered piece of work."

"Oh, Rhoda, you've never even met her," said Esta, patting her coiffed hair.

"We've heard every last morsel of gossip about them and so have you, Esta," Geraldine said, casting a meaningful glance my way.

Obviously Winnie had been spilling the beans about Sonny Bob and me for some time.

Rusty followed suit and looked right at me as she said, "Enough of all that. I want to hear about this wonderful Buck Lemoyne. You said he's quite the man, Winnie."

She addressed Win but aimed a knowing glance in my direction. Again, dear auntie had apparently not spared them scintillating tidbits about her version of the Freddy-Buck relationship.

A waiter arrived with menus. "I'm not just having pastries, I'm getting a salad," Judy announced. "You should too, Winnie. You've been looking a little peaked lately. Order something for a change with leafy greens, tomatoes, celery. You'll like it."

"Honey," Winnie replied. "The only way I'd like celery is if there's a Bloody Mary wrapped around it."

"Very funny, Winifred," Rusty said. "Judy, dear, order your damn greens and don't change the subject. I want to hear more about the hunky private investigator and, Win, if you don't tell us, I'm sure Frédérique will."

I had a perfect solution to this interrogation.

"Excuse me, ladies," I said. "Gotta go to the little girls' room."

I stood up and cast my own meaningful look at Winnie intended to convey, *you opened up this can of worms, toots, you handle it.*

As I stepped away, Win was saying, "Buckley's such a dear, sweet man really. Completely devoted to Frédérique. He's in the Caribbean right now. He had to go over there to . . ."

I didn't hear the rest as I swiftly made my way to the restroom, anxious to get away and be with my own thoughts. I pushed through the ladies room door. It was empty of other guests. I was grateful to be alone. I didn't need to pee. Instead, I stood in front of the large gilt mirrors and stared at my image while at the same time remaining oblivious to it.

"Completely devoted to Frédérique." Winnie's words. *and completely true.*

I thought some more. Brushed my hair. Thought. Freshened my lipstick. Thought. Then returned to the table and Win and her entourage.

My darling aunt was saying, "And she and Buck, they . . ."

Then Winnie looked up, startled to see me, and seemed to change the subject. That is, her topic was still Buck but, for some reason, she lapsed into a physical description.

"Buckley's got the bluest eyes . . .," she rhapsodized and looked at me, then looked away. "And such a masculine build. Well, just altogether a very macho man." Eyes back toward me. "Wouldn't you say so, Frédérique?"

I become Frédérique, instead of Freddy, when Auntie's with her society clan.

I opened my mouth to ask a question, but Rhoda beat me to it.

"Exactly where in the Caribbean did Buckley go, Winifred?"

"Jamaica," was the answer. "He emailed me that he loves it there and . . ."

"I went there one December with my previous husband," Rusty interrupted.

"I may go to Jamaica in June," Molly offered.

"Whatever happened to the ex-wife of that Brit you dated?" This from Geraldine.

"She's in jail, just like hubby," Winnie supplied.

"All so depressing," Margot correctly observed, "let's get back to the subject of the Caribbean."

With that, the girls were off and running on the topics of clothes to pack, tales of baggage mishaps, the state of airlines today, where to get the best luggage . . . and on and on.

They were by no means boring me but, on the other hand, I found I couldn't fully concentrate on the conversation. I could hardly plea another bathroom break but I didn't need to. I now had a decided purpose in doing so—to catch a plane.

Winnie had shifted the talk back to Buck and where he'd possibly be staying. I waited until she finished and then I stood up.

"Frédérique, honey, are you leaving us?" said Rusty.

"'Afraid so," I said, hitching the straps of my purse over my shoulder. "Have to catch a plane."

"Well, hell fire," Winnie said, "Where on earth to?"

I smiled and called out my answer after I'd turned and begun walking away.

"Jamaica!"

FEB 7 – 2023

Made in the USA
Las Vegas, NV
18 November 2022

59748360R00236